STEPHANIE FAZIO

HEX KITCHEN SERIES BOOK 2

CUTTHROAT CUISINE

Syafant Press

To Noah, Sydney, Avery, and Miller

CHAPTER 1

KENZIE

Kenzie's eyes stubbornly resisted her attempts to open them. Her lashes felt like they'd been fused together with molasses. Her mouth was as dry as if she'd swallowed raw flour. She smelled damp earth, and something sour and unpleasant.

Where am I?

How long have I been here?

Oh God. Who was taking care of Kiwi?!

Kenzie's chameleon had very specific dietary needs. He wouldn't touch his mealworms unless they were fresh, and he only liked greens that were cut into tiny ribbons. He needed his vitamin powder and fresh water and—

Calm down, she ordered herself.

Finally victorious in the epic *Kenzie vs. her own eyelashes* battle, she opened her eyes. The surrounding darkness transformed to actual shapes.

Unfortunately, her sight didn't provide any additional clarity into the all-important question of where the hell she was.

She ignored the jelly-like quiver to her legs and got to her feet. She was in some kind of narrow tunnel that was mostly dirt, except for the metal doors on either end. A single, naked lightbulb illuminated the space.

It was hot as an oven, but her teeth were chattering. The goosebumps on her skin made her tattoos look shriveled and misshapen.

"Help!" she rasped, slapping her palm against one of the metal doors. Aside from a harsh sting that went through her hand, nothing happened.

Not that she'd really expected it to.

Before Kenzie's panic reached hyperventilation territory, she heard an electric whine. The door in front of her began to rise vertically, letting in a flood of light from the other side.

Kenzie stumbled forward. In her impatience, she smacked her forehead against the rising door hard enough to see stars. She blinked the unwelcome constellation away and shimmied under the door.

What in the….

By this point, Kenzie's vision was working just fine. It was just that her brain couldn't process what she was seeing.

She was standing at the edge of a dirt-floor arena. It looked to be about the same size as her high school's running track that the evil gym teachers had forced everyone to jog around. The circular space was enclosed by slanting, ten-foot cement walls.

Had she somehow been transported back in time and ended up in a gladiator ring?

No, dummy. Gladiators didn't have electric doors.

They also didn't have full kitchens in the middle of their arenas the way Kenzie's did. There were two adjoining cooktops, a stainless-steel fridge, a free-standing freezer, and two sinks.

On the opposite end of the arena, another door identical to the one Kenzie had just come through was opening. A hulking male figure ducked beneath the rising door…without hitting his head. Some people had all the luck.

A raucous shout came from above.

Kenzie tipped her head back to look up. About ten feet up, the cement turned into black glass that encircled the arena.

It was probably one of those one-way glass situations, where people could see her but she couldn't see them. Normally, that would freak her out. Fortunately, she had so much else to be panicking about that she barely registered that particular creepiness.

Because the whole situation wasn't insulting enough, people on the other side of the glass were shouting at her. Kenzie couldn't make out their specific words, but she was willing to bet they weren't complimenting her. Something sailed over the wall of black glass and hurtled toward her.

In a rare moment of physical coordination, Kenzie side-stepped the object. A tomato splattered against the ground two inches to her left. The sickly-sweet aroma of rot filled the air.

"Seriously?!" she demanded.

The jeers from behind the glass grew louder.

"This is a mistake," she began.

The rest of her plea died in her throat as laughter bounced off the high ceiling and filled the arena. She flinched again as a digital scoreboard flashed to life overhead, like this was a hockey game or something. There was a timer that was paused at 60. The neon orange beneath the timer read *Brute* on one side, and *The Champ* on the other.

The man on the opposite end of the arena was striding toward the kitchen. He seemed to know what he was doing, so Kenzie took her cues from him…despite the fact that he had a skull and crossbones tattoo on his forehead.

Kenzie was in no position to judge someone else's ink, but seriously…who did that?

They met at the kitchen in the center.

"Um, hey," Kenzie began. "Do you have any idea—"

"We ain't here to make friends," the man said. His voice was so low and ominous it made the back of Kenzie's neck prickle.

He was wearing a sleeveless shirt that showed off his obscene biceps. Veins bulged out from his thick neck and ran down his arms. Even his fingers had veins. The guy had to be close to three-hundred pounds of solid muscle.

"Just out of curiosity," Kenzie ventured, "is that tattoo to tell me you're a badass or is it to remind yourself when you look in the mirror?"

The man bared his snaggle teeth. "You're already dead, fresh meat. You just don't know it, yet."

Alrighty, then.

"Ladies and gentlemen," a familiar voice boomed. "Welcome to Cutthroat Cuisine!"

One of the black-glass panels flickered and turned clear, revealing an enclosed area that looked like one of those skyboxes in sports arenas.

Hex Kitchen's emcee and judge—and the woman Kenzie would most like to smack upside her fluffy-haired head—stepped to the front of the clear glass box.

Polly Berrywhite's blue-streaked cotton candy hair bobbed along with her every movement. Light bounced off her silver ball gown, practically blinding Kenzie. The woman looked like a freaking disco ball.

"We have a treat for all of you tonight," Polly announced in a breathless voice. "This decade's Hex Kitchen champ will be competing in her first-ever Cutthroat Cuisine match. Today, she's up against the ruthless Brute."

Kenzie crossed her arms in the universal *screw you, bitch* pose and glared up at Polly.

"You don't get to kidnap me and then expect me to cook for you," Kenzie called out.

Maybe the spectators behind the one-way glass didn't realize she'd been brought here against her will and would help put an end to this.

And maybe a spotted unicorn would fly down from the ceiling and carry her off to Neverland.

"I'm afraid you don't have much choice," Polly said. Her gleeful expression didn't match her apologetic words.

That two-faced granny!

"Invitations aren't optional," Polly continued. "But you should be grateful. You're one of only twelve culinary magicians with the opportunity to become the next leader of the Gourmands."

Hysterical laughter bubbled out of Kenzie's throat. She wanted nothing to do with the group that had kidnapped her…the same people who had murdered Loretta and Max and stuffed their bodies into *Good Ol' Apple Pie's* walk-in freezer.

"I'll take a hard pass on that one," Kenzie said.

Polly had the gall to wink, like they were both in on this least funny of jokes.

"Now," Polly chirped. "I'm sure we're all dying to find out what today's mystery ingredient is, aren't we?"

Shouts of agreement came from behind the black glass. The man standing across from Kenzie—*Brute*—tensed. All of his attention was on two wicker baskets resting on top of the counter. His hands hovered over the basket on his side of the counter.

"Competitors, let's see what you're cooking with!" Polly shouted.

Kenzie stayed where she was. Brute tore the top right off his basket and reached inside.

"Shit, yeah," he muttered, holding up a tiny jar of green peppercorns.

"Magical peppercorns!" Polly gushed. "This variety is called *pepped peppercorns*. They're tricky little buggers when it comes to harvesting. You'll all get to see why." She offered up another wink and flashed her pearly whites, which were probably as fake as her personality.

"Magic peppercorns?" Kenzie asked no one in particular. She eyed the jar in Brute's hand.

It made sense that the wish truffle wasn't the only magical ingredient in existence, but Kenzie hadn't heard of any others before. She had no idea how cooking with these peppercorns—sorry…*pepped* peppercorns— differed from the variety she was familiar with. Judging from the audience's excited murmurs, this new development didn't bode well for her.

"What a treat, folks," Polly jabbered. "I can't wait to see what Brute and The Champ will do with them."

"You'll be waiting a long time," Kenzie muttered, still making no move to open her basket.

Brute let out a raspy chuckle. "You're gonna make this easy on me, ain't ya?"

"What's your real name?" Kenzie asked her…opponent.

Instead of answering like a normal person, Brute gave the collar of his shirt a vicious tug. A loud ripping sound filled the air as the fabric tore down the center.

Cheers erupted from the invisible crowd as Brute balled up his shirt and threw it high into the air. A hand shot up above the black glass and caught it.

Gross.

"Competitors, don your aprons!"

Brute took a red apron that was draped over his side of the counter and put it on.

There was another apron on Kenzie's side. She chewed on her lip, considering. Maybe if she played their little game and won, they'd let her out of here.

The last thing Kenzie wanted to do right then was cook, but she could think of worse tasks. At least a cooking competition was in her wheelhouse. And if she could out-cook Rick and Crazy Aralia, she could beat this man.

Alright, buddy, she thought as she watched Brute unscrew his jar of pepped peppercorns. *Let's see what you've got.*

Kenzie took the starched apron and pulled it over her head. She swept her tangled hair into a high ponytail and secured it with the hair tie that was still on her wrist.

Small miracles were not to be undervalued.

"I hope you don't mind if I keep my shirt on," she told Brute as she knotted her apron.

Her opponent didn't crack a grin.

Tough crowd.

"Cook like your lives depend on it, chefs," Polly said, playing to the audience hidden behind the black glass. "Because they do."

I'm sorry…what?

Kenzie thought she'd just heard—

"The winner of this round will be whichever chef is still alive at the end of sixty minutes," Polly said.

Kenzie turned to Brute, but he was busy crushing his peppercorns with a mortar and pestle. Small bursts of lime-green fire spurted up from them.

"Umm," Kenzie stammered. "I'm a little new to this whole magic ingredient thing…." She trailed off, hoping Brute would take a little pity on her and clue her in.

No such luck, apparently.

Brute just said something that sounded like …*whole lotta fun.*

"Come on, Kenzie!" Polly shouted. "You've only got fifty-five minutes to cook some magic!"

Kenzie looked around.

"They don't seriously expect us to…cook to the death…do they?" she asked Brute.

In answer, Brute pointed to the tattoo on his forehead before mixing his crushed peppercorns into a bowl full of tempura batter. An acrid scent wafted into the air as the whole concoction glowed emerald.

Kenzie glanced around, looking for some way out of this. She'd used her cooking to kill once, before she'd even heard the words *culinary magic*. She'd never use her ability to do that again.

"Listen," Kenzie told Brute. "I don't want to hurt you. Hell, I don't even want to be here."

"That ain't my problem," Brute replied. "Me? I'd be rottin' in jail for killin' my cheatin' whore of a girlfriend if the Gourmands hadn't scooped me. As long as I'm in here, I ain't back there."

There was no arguing with that logic.

Since she was fresh out of ideas, Kenzie went to her side of the counter and opened the waiting basket. An identical jar of green pepped peppercorns rested on the bottom. Kenzie unscrewed the lid and pinched one of the peppercorns between her fingers.

There was a small *pop*, and then the peppercorn disappeared in a puff of green smoke. Pain lanced through Kenzie's fingers. She looked down to find a neat little hole had been burned into the pads of her thumb and forefinger.

"Son of a—"

"Forty minutes, chefs!" Polly called.

Kenzie looked around for a towel to wrap around her hand. Little drops of blood fell from her fingers onto the counter, and she didn't even care. Her dad would be horrified.

Speaking of her dad….

Kenzie had an idea.

She found all the necessary ingredients for her dad's famous deep-dish pizza recipe. He'd always claimed it was the cure-all to a bad day. Maybe, if she combined her dad's recipe with the magic that was formulating in her mind, she could put an end to this violence before it began. Gently placing her pepped peppercorns back in their basket, she went to the large fridge and helped herself to a shiny red bell pepper and ground sausage. She grabbed a bunch of sweet Vidalia onions from the open pantry on her way back to her cook station. She looked around.

"Where are the knives?" she asked. There were blunt butter knives, but nothing for cutting meat or veggies.

Surprisingly, Brute deigned to answer.

"It ain't Cutthroat Cuisine if we could just kill each other with knives."

The *duh* wasn't said explicitly, but it was there all the same.

Brute turned back to his dish. He tore open a brown paper package of squid and began ripping the head from the tentacles with his hands. He dropped the heads onto the arena floor before turning all his attention on the tentacles, which he was dredging in his peppercorn tempura.

Cheers arose from behind the one-way glass as Brute dropped the tentacles into the deep-fryer. He got out of the way as hot oil and green sparks splattered up.

Kenzie's hands continued to work on her deep-dish pizza as she watched Brute pull the fried tentacles out of the oil. Where normal tempura was fried to a beautiful golden color, Brute's were almost black.

She didn't think she needed to inform the shirtless chef that his oil was way too hot.

Instead of throwing the charred concoction away, Brute was rolling the blackened tempura squid in more ground peppercorns. At the rate he was going, there'd be more pepper than squid.

He couldn't possibly be expecting anyone to eat those….

Kenzie was just sliding her sausage, pepper, and sweet onion pizza into the oven when she felt it.

Magic.

Translucent threads hovered over Brute's tempura squid. He placed one tentacle on the palm of each hand and squeezed his eyes shut.

Brute's face reddened as rivulets of sweat snaked down his thick neck. The temperature in the arena began to rise.

The squid tentacles started to grow.

"This is fabulous, folks," Polly crooned into her mike. "As we all know, it's only possible for a culinary magician to control a single aspect of magic at a time. But our homemade magical ingredients contain their own power. That means our chefs have *two* types of magic at their fingertips. Isn't that grand?"

Hah, big deal, Kenzie thought.

During Hex Kitchen, she'd astonished everyone by her ability to control multiple magical properties at once. No one knew why the rules of magic didn't apply to her, and right now, she didn't much care. All that mattered was that the man standing opposite from her was using every ounce of his mental strength to infuse a little bit of magic into his fried tentacles. Kenzie could do what he was doing…and so much more…without batting an eye. Not that she'd want to.

Within seconds, the few-inches-long tentacles were each over a foot. And they were still growing.

Kenzie watched in morbid fascination as the tentacles grew until they were almost as long and thick as Brute's enormous arms. Gripping a tentacle in each hand, his fierce gaze locked on Kenzie. He bared his teeth at her.

Kenzie realized what was happening a moment too late. Brute flicked his wrists, and then both tentacles were lashing down on her.

Burning hot tempura raked over her body. Kenzie screamed as the hardened tempura coating tore right through her shirt. There was a green flash, and then heat was searing her ribcage.

Kenzie yanked up her shirt.

Steam was rising from slivers of peppercorn embedded in her skin. Blood oozed from the green flecks, which were pulsing with an unnatural light.

Kenzie clawed at her skin, doing whatever she could to get the peppercorns out. She was dimly aware of Brute laughing and Polly saying, "Oh, dear. The Champ will need to be quicker if she wants to survive!"

Kenzie was digging out the last of the peppercorns when movement caught the corner of her vision. She dove to the ground, skinning her knee as Brute flung the tentacles at her again.

"Are you insane?!" she shouted at him. "Stop this!"

"No chance," he snarled.

He snapped his giant tentacle whips at her. She dodged one, but the other scraped across her stomach.

Kenzie doubled over. All the air whooshed out of her lungs as green sparks erupted from her abdomen.

Her body was on fire.

Kenzie threw herself onto the ground and rolled. Whimpers of pain slipped from her pursed lips as she probed her charred flesh for slivers of still-smoking peppercorns.

Kenzie was in hell.

Her apron had been sheared in half and was dangling off her. She balled up the remains of the shredded fabric and pressed it to her stomach as she limped back to the kitchen. If she could get the counter between them—

Her fingertips grazed the edge of the metal counter as Brute attacked again. One of the tentacles whipped around both of her ankles. A vicious tug unbalanced her, and Kenzie fell hard on the unforgiving dirt floor.

That was when the reality of her situation finally sank in.

She saw the truth in Brute's unrepentant gaze.

"We don't have to do this," she gasped. "I don't want to fight you."

"Only one of us walks out of here," he said in his rumbling voice. "And it's gonna be me."

Whoops and booing trickled down from their invisible audience above.

Kenzie forgot all about the tentacle wrapped around her ankles when the second one encircled her neck.

Kenzie tried to breathe. Failed.

Green sparks sizzled across her throat as the tentacle wound tighter. Tears squeezed out of her eyes as she wrestled with her body's overpowering need for oxygen.

"Haven't had this much fun in years," Brute grunted. "Love hearing you squeal."

Kenzie flailed on the ground, kicking up dirt as her feet scrabbled for purchase. Her arms shook as she tried to yank the tentacle from around her neck.

Brute moved around her, pulling his magic tighter.

"So damn easy," Brute crowed. "Like takin' candy from a motherfuckin' baby."

Kenzie was going to die here on this dirt floor. A freaking squid tentacle was going to kill her.

Here lies Kenzie Ashner. She lost her brave fight against a magic tentacle....

Hell. No.

Kenzie stopped trying to draw air into her starved lungs. She stopped trying to rid herself of the tentacle. Using the ground beneath her as leverage, she rocked back and kicked out with her bound ankles.

She got Brute right in the groin.

He went down, and both tentacles slackened.

"Come on, Champ!" Polly shouted into her microphone. "You can do it, dearest!"

Kenzie wrenched off the tentacle that was strangling her. She didn't pause before thrusting away the one around her ankles. Spluttering and wheezing, she scrambled to her feet.

The pepped peppercorns stuck in her flesh were still smoldering, but they'd lost their potency. Green welts were rising on every part of her skin the peppercorns had touched. The pain was bearable, though.

Cursing, Brute stood. He tipped back his head and bellowed up at the ceiling. His bulging arm muscles flexed. The temperature in the arena spiked, which meant her opponent was regaining his hold over the magic tentacles.

Move it or lose it, Kenzie.

"Come on, Champ," Polly called down. "The Gourmands want to see what you're made of. Let's cook some magic!"

Kenzie grabbed two towels on the counter and pulled her pizza out of the oven. She jerked to avoid a flying tentacle, biting back a yelp as a drop of boiling sauce spurted out of her deep-dish pizza and onto her forearm.

Brute pulled back his tentacle whips. She could sense his magic writhing within them. Between his magic and her clumsiness, there was no way she'd be able to dodge them again. So, she acted before he could.

Kenzie didn't bother with magic. She hurled the ceramic dish and its molten contents at Brute.

His scream was horrible. Brute clawed at his face as boiling-hot cheese and tomato sauce oozed down his cheeks.

Kenzie could see blisters already forming on his skin.

He yelled obscenities as he came for her, his fingers curled into claws.

She didn't wait for him to reach her. Kenzie snatched one of the abandoned tentacles off the ground.

"Cook!" voices chanted from behind the one-way glass. "Cook!"

More rotten tomatoes sailed over the black glass and pelted the ground beside Kenzie. She ignored them.

With Brute's focus severed, the tentacles were starting to shrink. Kenzie forced herself to block out Brute's cries and the spectators' shouts. She ignored the way every peppercorn fragment still embedded in her skin was beginning to feel like live coals.

She focused on the tentacle's rough texture and the heavy weight of it in her hands. As the briny smell filled her nostrils, she let her own magic out.

She thought about how it had felt when the tentacle was wrapped around her neck. She let herself recall that hopelessness. Her eyes watered in remembrance of the way her vision had started to blur as her lungs begged for air.

"Bitch!" Brute growled. "That's my dish!"

He made a grab for the tentacle, but Kenzie darted out of reach.

Pearly threads of magic hovered in the air. The tentacle twitched in her unmoving hands. Kenzie gritted her teeth as she added another layer of magic to the one Brute had already created. She firmed up the fading power of the pepped peppercorns and added a little something of her own.

"Gimme my dish!" Brute roared.

Now or never, Kenzie thought.

As soon as she uncurled her fingers, the tentacle sprang forward. It sailed through the air like it had a mind of its own. Kenzie just stood there, allowing the magic to work for her.

"—impossible," Polly was saying. "—two magical properties at once!"

Rotten tomatoes stopped splattering the dirt around Kenzie's feet. The jeers cut off. Kenzie could almost feel her invisible audience suck in a collective breath.

The onlookers' silence only made Brute's pained cries more deafening. He stopped clawing at the molten cheese stuck to his skin and whimpered. The tentacle was flying right for him.

Brute tripped and fell. He tried to crawl away on his hands and knees.

The tentacle halted mid-air and changed course. It shot over to Brute and looped around his neck.

Kenzie squeezed her hand into a fist. The tentacle wrapped tighter.

Brute fought, but big as his muscles were, they were no match for her magic. The harder he tugged, the more tightly the tentacle wound around his neck. Green sparks danced across his skin everywhere the peppercorn crust touched.

His eyes bulged. His lips parted, but no sound came out.

Brute's skin—the parts that weren't red from boiling sauce or green from fire—turned blue.

The pepped peppercorns still in Kenzie's skin scorched her insides. Her vision began to warble. She gritted her teeth as she tightened her hold on the magic. She pulled on those invisible threads.

Just until Brute passes out, she told herself. She was doing everything she could to stay conscious herself.

Kenzie was going to let go of the magic. Just as soon as—

Even with all the shouting that was coming from the audience above, Kenzie heard a sickening *crack*.

Brute's head lolled back against the coiled tentacle. His arms went slack. His body slumped to the arena floor. His open, unseeing eyes remained fixed on Kenzie.

The onlookers erupted.

CHAPTER 2

BRAXTON

Braxton paced across the room. He glanced out the floor-to-ceiling windows at the lake surrounded by pine trees. The sun was setting, and the weak rays threw a golden light over everything. It was serene and beautiful and—

Frustrating as fuck.

Braxton was in this remote hideout, safe and comfortable. Meanwhile, Kenzie was missing.

Why hadn't he been more specific with his wish?

When he'd eaten the truffle, he'd been consumed with the knowledge that Kenzie was dying of poison. The possibility of her being kidnapped by the goddamn Gourmands—the culinary magic authorities who were supposed to protect all of them—hadn't crossed his mind.

Braxton raked his fingers through his hair. He started for the stairs, breaking his own resolve not to interrupt his sister. He didn't want to do anything that would distract or annoy Sofia while she was trying to help him track down Kenzie.

Before he reached the first step, Aralia careened into him. She was wearing a deer-hide dress. The panels of fabric crisscrossed and showed off far more skin than he wanted to see on her…ever. Braxton kept his gaze fixed on the wooden beads she'd braided into her platinum-blonde hair, which seemed like the safest place to look.

"And people call me crazy," Aralia said with a little smirk.

"What are you talking about?" Braxton frowned at her.

Aralia swirled her finger around in front of his face. "You have crazy eyes, stud. Like you're a little bit rabid."

Braxton scowled. "Is it possible to be a *little* rabid?"

Aralia shrugged, which made her flimsy sleeves fall off her shoulders and bare even more skin. "There was a bat that got in here last New Year's. I think it was a little rabid."

"How do you figure?" Braxton glanced up the stairs at the closed bedroom door.

Was Sofia making any headway? Did she have any leads on where the Gourmands might have taken Kenzie? Of what they were doing to her?

"Well, the little beast tried to bite me, but it followed Graham out of the house calm as anything. Hence, a little bit rabid."

Braxton snorted. "Got it." He started to move past Aralia, but she snaked out a hand and latched onto his arm. Her nails dug into his biceps.

"I know you've been all *Kenzie, Kenzie, Kenzie* for the last three days," Aralia said. "But I hope you haven't forgotten our deal."

Braxton's stomach flipped. A cold feeling spread through his limbs.

In a moment of desperation, Braxton had promised to do whatever Aralia asked in exchange for helping him and Sofia escape Hex Kitchen. Aralia had kept up her end of the bargain and brought them to her off-the-grid upstate cabin.

Then, she'd told Braxton exactly what she expected of him.

"I need some time," he told Aralia, hearing the tightness in his own voice.

"I'll let you rescue Number Eight." Aralia gave him a little smile. "Then, you're going to do what you promised."

Braxton cleared his throat. "I'll do it. Just let me find Kenzie and—"

Say goodbye to my family.

"Good." She reached up to pat his cheek in a condescending way. "Now, you can help me get dinner ready. Watching a man hunt gets me all hot and bothered."

"Which is a very compelling reason *not* to help you," Braxton grumbled.

Besides, he had no appetite. The last thing he wanted right now was one of Aralia's venison steaks that were so raw they were practically mooing…or whatever the deer sound equivalent was.

"You need to start leading a more sustainable lifestyle," Aralia informed Braxton. She pulled an arrow from the quiver on her back and wagged the tip in front of his face. "The collapse of our civilization is inevitable. When that happens, you'll thank me for teaching you to live off the land."

"Get off your soap box, Aralia," he said tiredly. "It's not like you've exactly been roughing it out here like you made all of us believe."

Not that Braxton was complaining. From everything he knew about Aralia, he'd been expecting her home to be little more than a tent made out of biodegradable canvas. While they were certainly in the middle of the wilderness, the building that Aralia referred to as *the cabin* was more of a luxury lodge. When they'd arrived, Sofia had taken one look at the high ceilings, exposed beams, and stone fireplaces and said, "I can work with this."

That was Sofia-speak for *This place is beautiful.*

It was a far cry from his family's penthouse in the middle of bustling Sydney. The quiet unnerved Braxton, but all that mattered was that no one would think to look for them here. Aralia had the culinary magic community believing she lived somewhere in Canada. Besides, everyone knew Braxton and Aralia weren't friends. They were safe here.

"It's not my fault," Aralia complained. "If you ask me, electricity and running water are superfluous. But Graham has a taste for extravagance."

As though the mention of her foster-brother summoned him, Graham appeared in the doorway to the kitchen. For someone so big, he moved almost silently. He was always lurking in the shadows and randomly appearing. It creeped Braxton out.

Not least because that polite, soft-spoken routine was a sham. Braxton knew about the monster that lay beneath.

It was a true testament to their situation that Braxton was allowing Sofia to get within throwing distance of that bastard. Especially since Braxton hadn't missed the way his sister had spent the last three days eyeing Graham like a lion stalking its prey. Or its mate.

With Sofia, it could really go either way.

Sofia wouldn't fall for a dangerous criminal, Braxton consoled himself. Even if Braxton had sworn to Aralia that he'd never reveal Graham's secret, Sofia was smart. She'd see right through Graham.

Besides, it wasn't like Graham was even Sofia's type, unspeakable crimes aside. Sofia liked her men in bespoke suits with hundred-dollar haircuts. She'd never go for this lumberjack.

Seriously. Who was that muscular? It wasn't advisable.

"Where are you off to?" Aralia asked Graham.

"Setting more traps," he replied in his low voice. "We're going through supplies faster than I expected."

Ah. There was the shame Braxton had been feeling incessantly since he'd arrived at the cabin. As much as he distrusted his temporary hosts, he loathed being at their mercy.

"I'm sorry to be a burden," Braxton said stiffly. "Sofia and I will do whatever we can to help out while we're here."

"Oh, this isn't charity." Aralia reached up and undid one of the buttons on Braxton's flannel shirt, which he'd needed to borrow from Graham. "Enjoy it while you've got it."

Braxton was trying not to think about what he'd promised Aralia, which wasn't easy when she made a point of reminding him every five seconds.

"What are you talking about?" Graham asked Aralia, frowning a little.

"Nothing," Aralia said.

She flicked open another of Braxton's buttons.

Braxton swatted her hand away and re-buttoned his shirt. "Might want to stop undressing me," he told her. "Otherwise you'll have to deal with Kenzie."

Once I find her.

Aralia giggled and did something suggestive with her hands. Braxton wasn't sure what, exactly—he'd gone back to staring at the beads in her hair.

"Lay off, Aralia," Graham told her in a quiet voice.

She jutted out her lower lip, pouting. Graham wrapped a thick arm around her shoulders and gave her a quick squeeze.

The two of them shared a look that tugged at an empty space inside Braxton, because it was the kind of look he used to exchange with Aidan. It was the language of two people who knew each other so well that whole conversations could be had without uttering a word.

I miss you, Aid. I miss you so fucking much.

Braxton's pocket began to buzz. He pulled out his phone and glanced at the screen. He bit back a curse and tucked it away before Aralia could get a good look at the number.

"I need to take this," Braxton said, trying to keep his voice even.

He hurried to the door before his nosy host could ask any questions. As soon as he was out on the porch, Braxton answered the call.

"How did you get my number?" he snarled.

"Hello to you too, McKaid."

Rick Santiori, son of the powerful mobster who now owned the McKaids' eight-million-dollar debt, chuckled.

"You missed your first payment," Rick needlessly reminded him.

Braxton hated that haughty American accent more than any other sound on Earth.

"I'm aware," Braxton grated out. "But I have six months to get you the money. I'm—"

"—a little short on cash, given that you didn't win Hex Kitchen. My family's concerned, McKaid."

Rick's smugness oozed into Braxton's ear.

"I just need some more time," Braxton said.

Christ. He felt like a broken record. First his promise to Aralia, and now this. Everything was unravelling, and there was nothing he could do to stop it.

"Sorry," Rick said. He sounded like the exact opposite of sorry. "No can do. We've got a strict policy on when it comes to this sort of thing. Pay up or…." Rick trailed off. "Actually, there is no *or*. You made a deal, McKaid."

A deal that stipulated that if Braxton couldn't pay the money he owed, his family belonged to Rick's.

"I'm not telling you where my mum and sister are," he said, his heart thumping against his ribcage. "I'll do whatever else—"

"You're not in a position to bargain," Rick interrupted. "I own you and the rest of your family now." He paused to let that horrible truth sink in.

Braxton promised himself that he'd die a thousand deaths before he let Rick anywhere near Mum and Sofia.

"Listen," Braxton began, but Rick cut him off.

"Don't get your panties in a wad, McKaid. As it happens, there's something I need more than your sister's fine ass. For now, at least."

Braxton gripped the porch handrail hard enough to make the wood groan.

He's all talk, Braxton told himself as he tried to get control of his rapid breathing. *Sofia's safe here. Rick can't find her.*

And, once his mum got here, she'd be safe too. Braxton just needed to make sure the Santioris didn't have a reason to come looking for them.

"What do you need from me?" Braxton asked in a flat voice.

"How fast can you get to Manhattan?" Rick replied.

Braxton hesitated, not wanting to give Rick even the slightest clue about where he was staying.

"I can get there by tomorrow," he said.

If I grovel and beg to borrow Aralia's truck…and lie to Sofia about where I'm going….

"Not good enough," Rick said. "I'll text you an address. Be there by midnight." He made an obnoxious gurgling sound as he sipped a drink that was probably a Reserve label. "My old man wants to talk to you. We're in Manhattan on some business, and then we're flying back to Chicago on the *family plane*." He emphasized the words in case they somehow slipped past Braxton's notice.

"What do you want—"

"Midnight, McKaid."

The call ended.

Braxton resisted the urge to hurl his phone across the yard and into the still lake.

"Brax?"

He spun around. Sofia was standing in the open doorway, her brow creased in concern.

"Everything's fine," he muttered, shoving his phone back into his pocket. "Did you find out anything about Kenzie?"

Sofia's expression tightened even more.

"I thought you were going to ask me…never mind." She shook her head. "I honestly don't know why I'm surprised anymore."

Braxton sighed in exasperation. "I was just—"

"Putting Kenzie first," Sofia said. "I get it."

Her green eyes bored into his. Her glare spoke volumes, even though she didn't say a word.

Mum and I did everything for the restaurants while you screwed around with our brother's murderer, that look accused. *You're the reason why we're on the run. Why our lives are in danger.*

And Braxton couldn't defend himself, because everything Sofia was thinking was true.

"Sofe," he began, not even knowing where to start. His sister didn't want apologies. She wanted him to fix what he'd broken.

"Most of my contacts won't even take my calls," Sofia said in the crisp and efficient voice she used when her armor was fully in place. "The ones who did have no idea where Kenzie is."

"Did you tell them she was going by the name Brookerton?"

"I told them, Brax."

"How about the names of people involved with the Gourmands? I just need one."

Knowing the Gourmands were involved in Kenzie's capture didn't do him any good on its own. The Gourmands were a notoriously secret society that worked behind the scenes. Their names weren't publicly available. They didn't even have a headquarters.

"Braxton!" She gave him a little push. "Stop being so…*you.*"

Braxton took a few calming breaths.

"I know you can't understand," he said quietly. "But I have to find her. I have to know she's okay."

Hurt flashed across Sofia's face so quickly that Braxton wasn't sure whether he'd imagined it.

Sofia was wearing one of Aralia's fur capes. It swamped her, making Sofia look almost…delicate. It was the last word Braxton would ever associate with his kickass sister, and yet when he really looked at her, he didn't see the same person who had almost single-handedly kept their family's restaurants afloat for the last five years.

Sofia's eyes were bloodshot. It would be an understatement to say neither of them had slept well since they fled the tournament, but this went beyond simple exhaustion. Now that he was really paying attention, Braxton noticed the hollows in Sofia's cheeks and the way her collarbone protruded.

"Let's get you some dinner," he said, trying not to be obvious about his worry.

Sofia opened her mouth, probably to tell him to shove off, but she didn't have a chance. They both whipped around at the sound of a car crunching up the driveway.

A beat-up silver sedan with Florida license plates came into view.

"Get Aralia," Braxton told his sister. "Tell her—"

The sedan rolled to a stop. The driver's door opened.

"Mum?!"

Braxton's feet were moving before his brain caught up. Sofia squealed and raced past him. A few seconds later, he was colliding in a happy tangle with his mum and sister.

"Thank goodness you're both alright," Mum said as she wrapped an arm around each of them. "I missed you so much."

She kissed them both on the cheek, laughing and sniffling as she wiped her nose on her sleeve so she wouldn't have to let go of them.

Her relieved laughter was contagious. Braxton found himself holding onto his mum with one arm and Sofia with the other. The three of them leaned in close as they took in the enormity of this moment. They were all alive and together.

All of Braxton's problems felt more manageable. With his mum and sister on his side, there was nothing he couldn't do.

"Have you both been eating?" their mum asked, reaching up to brush Braxton's overgrown hair off his forehead. "Sleeping?"

"We're fine," Sofia assured her. "Don't worry about us. I'm just—" Her voice hitched. "I'm just glad you're here."

"Me too, loves."

Their mum looked tired. Her hair, which she always meticulously straightened and curled…something Braxton had never understood…hung limply. There were bags under her eyes. Like the rest of them, she was wearing borrowed clothes.

But they were together now.

"Let's get you inside," Sofia said, wrapping an arm around their mum's waist and leading her toward the porch. "What do you want first, dinner or shower?"

Aralia, her bow slung over her back and a knife in her hand, filled the doorway.

"There's more of you?" Aralia asked, even though Braxton had already told her that his mum was coming.

Before Braxton or Sofia could say something that would piss off their armed host, their mum took charge. She offered Aralia one of her smiles that had won over even the prissiest of their restaurant customers.

"Thank you for taking care of my babies," Mum said, holding out her hand. "And your home is absolutely lovely. It reminds me of the time my husband took me camping for our honeymoon. It was the best week of my life." She squeezed Braxton's arm. "That was the week you and your brother were conceived."

"*Mum.*" Braxton gaped at her.

"Um…*eww,*" Sofia groaned, covering her face with her hands.

"TMI. Seriously," Braxton added, even though he couldn't stop smiling. For the first time since he'd gotten to the cabin, Braxton felt like he could breathe again.

Finally, something was going right.

Sofia led their mum into the cabin, while Braxton went to the car to unload her luggage.

Aralia waited until she and Braxton were the only ones outside.

"Enjoy this little reunion while you can, stud." She sauntered over and pinched his arse. "I'm giving you more time out of pure generosity, but my patience has a deadline."

Just like that, Braxton's lightness started to fade.

Because the universe was conspiring against him, his phone buzzed with an incoming text. From Rick.

There was an address to a private airfield outside Manhattan, along with a reminder not to be late. *Or else.*

Braxton pulled up his maps app and clocked out the distance. It would take him almost six hours to get to the meeting spot. That meant he had to leave…now.

Braxton peered through the window into the cabin, where his mum was settling in. He glanced back at the rental car, and the keys that were resting on the driver's seat.

If he went back inside and then tried to leave again, his mum and sister would ask questions he wasn't ready to answer.

"Here." Braxton rolled the suitcase over to Aralia. "Tell my family—"

That I'm trying to keep the Santioris happy so they don't come after us. That my choices put both of their lives at risk. That, unless I can find a way to fix this, they'll never be safe.

"—something came up. Tell them not to worry, and that I'll be back in the morning."

Braxton didn't wait for Aralia to start peppering him with questions. He got into the car and started it up. He caught a glimpse of Sofia's startled face in the window.

Before his sister could come outside and demand answers, Braxton hit the gas. The wheels squealed in protest as he flew down the gravel drive.

He didn't look back.

CHAPTER 3

BRAXTON

Braxton barely made it before his midnight deadline, since he hadn't accounted for getting a flat tire an hour into the drive. The spare tire he'd put on the car himself—courtesy of some YouTube video tutorials—had been making a strange sound for the last fifty miles.

A man in a black suit and with a suspicious bulge in his jacket pocket waved Braxton through a security gate and onto the tarmac. A stretch limo was idling next to a small jet that was all lit up and ready to fly. Rick got out of the limo and started toward Braxton. His smirk was visible even from this distance.

"Nice ride, McKaid," Rick called out. "Did that hunk of junk wipe out your life savings?"

Rick's brown hair was slicked back with enough gel that not even the wind could coax it out of place. His dark pinstripe suit and polished dress shoes said more *upscale dinner meeting* than *bloody shakedown*, but Braxton knew better than to be fooled by his civilized appearance.

"You have bird shit on your jacket," Braxton informed him.

In spite of his situation, Braxton couldn't stop his snicker as Rick tore off his jacket and started inspecting the flawless and shit-free fabric.

"Asshole," Rick said, tossing what was probably a thousand-dollar jacket onto the ground.

A small group of men hovered around them. The goons were armed and made no effort to hide the fact that they were watching Braxton's every move. There was an ominous click of safeties being switched off as the men pointed their guns at the ground and waited.

And here Braxton had been thinking this would be a friendly visit….

The limo's back door opened, and Veneziano Santiori stepped onto the tarmac. He looked as immaculate as his son in his usual three-piece suit. He had one hand tucked into his trousers pocket. The other held an unlit cigar.

"Mr. Santiori," Braxton began, wanting to head off the conversation he knew was coming.

"Shut up, McKaid," Rick snarled. "You're not the one in charge here."

"Neither are you, Ricardo," Veneziano said in a silky voice. "Be silent."

Rick's face contorted in rage and humiliation, but he didn't dare utter a sound of protest.

"You know what really irks me?" Veneziano asked, turning away from his son and toward Braxton. He twisted the cigar between his fingers, inspecting it. He didn't wait for Braxton to hazard a guess. "Chasing down my money. It's so time consuming. And tiresome."

"I have every intention of getting your money, Mr. Santiori," Braxton began. "I just need—"

Veneziano held up a hand. "You missed your first payment, and we both know winning that wish truffle was the only way you'd ever have a chance of repaying your debt."

From behind his father, Rick laughed. "Look on the bright side, McKaid. You threw away your chance at winning, but you got the girl. For eight million dollars, I sure hope she puts out."

Veneziano glanced over his shoulder. Just that small motion was enough to make Rick wince and take a few steps back from his father.

"You didn't win either, jackass," Braxton couldn't stop himself from reminding Rick. To Veneziano, he said, "Once my family liquidates our assets, I'll be able to start paying you. I won't be able to get it to you all at once, but I'll make sure you have the full amount by our deadline." *Somehow*.

"Mm."

Veneziano switched on an expensive-looking lighter and held it up to the end of his cigar. He blew a cloud of smoke into the air.

"My people tell me I'm not the only one standing in line for McKaid money," he said. "I wonder how much will be left after you pay the banks and other lenders."

Christ. Was there anything Veneziano Santiori didn't know about Braxton's life?

Braxton's shirt clung to his clammy skin. He balled his hands into fists as the sheer impossibility of his situation stared him in the face.

"Mr. Santiori—"

"I have a problem that I think you might be able to help me with. In exchange, I might be willing to reconsider the amount of your debt."

"What kind of problem?" Braxton asked warily. He knew better than to think this new arrangement would benefit him.

Veneziano took an idle puff on his cigar. "In a word, the Gourmands."

Braxton straightened at the mention of the Gourmands.

Veneziano whipped his head around to his son. "Show him," he ordered.

Rick looked like he was about to protest, but then one of the thugs put a hand on Rick's shoulder.

Rick flinched a little before moving away from the thug and pulling up his pantleg. A pink-and-yellow candy anklet rested above his black dress sock.

"Fuckin' Gourmands," Rick muttered.

Braxton swallowed down a laugh. He'd seen these anklets before. When he'd been at university, one of his friends had gotten obscenely drunk at a culinary magic night club and decided to try his hand at bartending. His jungle juice had turned everyone who drank it sky-blue for a full week.

Braxton's mate had come back from holiday wearing one of these candy anklets, which allowed the Gourmands to track every magical recipe he cooked.

"This is what happens when you cheat, Ricardo," Veneziano told his son. "You bring shame on your family and the Gourmands' scrutiny on our business."

"I didn't—" Rick began.

Moving lightning-fast, one of the thugs smacked the back of Rick's head hard enough to make Braxton's own skull ached in sympathy. Rick staggered back against the limo.

"Papà," Rick whined.

"Get in the car," Veneziano ordered his son.

Rick's lip trembled. For a second, it seemed like he was going to argue. Then, he did as he was told. Braxton glimpsed Rick's sour expression before the door slammed between them.

"My son is a fool," Veneziano said. "But of all the culinary magicians in my employ, he was the only one powerful enough to help me expand my business. Now, he is useless."

"What does this have to do with me?" Braxton asked as his unease spiked. He quickly added, "I'm not going to become a hitman for you, or anything."

Veneziano's eyebrows rose in what could have been either amusement or scorn.

"As it happens, I have no need of an additional hitman," Veneziano said. "What I need is a chef who is talented, discreet, and motivated."

There was no denying Braxton was all of those things, so he didn't try to object.

"I came to Chicago with a few hundred dollars to my name and created a bakery empire that spans the globe," Veneziano said.

Braxton's chest squeezed, because the Santioris had succeeded where his own family had failed. Of course, the McKaids' business had been entirely legal and without a side order of violence.

"I have more money than even my idiot son will be able to spend in his lifetime."

Must be nice, Santiori….

"And yet," Veneziano continued, "I find myself hungry to conquer new horizons." He dropped his cigar on the ground and stomped it out. "It has come to my attention that the Gourmands have begun producing magical ingredients. Powerful ones."

Braxton, who had been staring at the crushed bits of cigar on the ground, snapped his head up.

"What?"

There was a decent number of magical ingredient cultivators, but most couldn't do anything more impressive than grow extra-large vegetables or fruits that were slow to rot. Only a Reaper had all the knowledge passed down from generations past, and had magic that was infinitely more powerful than normal cultivators.

There was only one Reaper alive at a time. And they were all famously anti-establishment and never shared any of their ingredients, with the exception of the wish truffle.

"How?" Braxton asked. "Who's doing the growing? And what are the Gourmands planning to do with the ingredients?"

"Valid questions." Veneziano nodded. "But the how and why are of little interest to me." A little smile curved his thin lips. "I wish to acquire these ingredients and sell them to the highest bidder."

Braxton managed a hoarse laugh. "You're going to steal from the Gourmands?"

Good luck, mate.

"For starters, yes," Veneziano said, as calm as if he were discussing stealing a candy bar from a gas station.

Veneziano Santiori might be a powerful mobster and rich as fuck, but he was nothing compared to the Gourmands. The Gourmands were judge and jury when it came to culinary magic crimes. They had a finger in every government and military in the world. Anyone with even a shred of self-preservation stayed as far from the Gourmands' ire as they could.

"I need to find out more about where the ingredients are kept," Veneziano said. "Unfortunately, my men's methods of extracting information aren't always enough. Which is why I need a powerful culinary magician to help me conduct the interrogation."

"Oh, no." Braxton held up his hands and took a step back. He would have retreated farther, but he felt something cold and metallic dig into his lower back. He froze.

"I could make you," Veneziano said softly. "But I always prefer to use honey rather than vinegar." He rocked back on his heels. "Word is that your girlfriend left Hex Kitchen against her will…in a Gourmand vehicle."

Braxton ears started to ring. "What do you know about it?" he demanded.

"Nothing more than that." Veneziano gave him an inscrutable look. "But the man I need to question about the magical ingredients is very close with the Gourmands. If you help me get the information I need, I wouldn't begrudge you a few pointed questions about your girlfriend's whereabouts."

"I'll do it," Braxton said.

Consequences be damned. He'd go down to hell and interrogate the Devil himself if it would get him closer to Kenzie.

"I have business to attend to back in Chicago," Veneziano said. "You will go visit my contact with Ricardo. You will do precisely what he says. Then, he will report to me. Do you understand?"

Yeah, Braxton understood.

Veneziano rapped on the limo's tinted window. A few seconds later, the window slid down and Rick's head poked out.

To Rick, Veneziano said, "Show me you can handle this responsibility, and perhaps I will give you more. Do not disappoint me again, Ricardo."

"Don't worry, Papà," Rick said, grinning like he just discovered he'd won the lottery. He rubbed his hands together and looked at Braxton expectantly. "You ready, McKaid?"

"I'm ready," Braxton said, feeling the heaviness of those words settle onto him like a physical weight.

"Mr. Santiori," Rick said.

"What?" Braxton stared at him.

"I'm ready, *Mr. Santiori*," Rick said.

"I'm ready, Mr. Santiori," Braxton repeated. He felt something inside him shrivel up and die. Definitely his pride. Probably his integrity, too.

"Hop in," Rick said, scooting over and patting the seat beside him. "Your night's about to get a whole lot more interesting."

CHAPTER 4

KENZIE

*C*rack.

Like a snapping twig. Or a merry fire.

Or a man's neck breaking.

Oh God. She'd killed Brute. She'd killed another person. Again.

Kenzie was in a state of shock. She barely registered what was happening as she was lifted onto a stretcher and carried out of the arena. She was brought into a white room that smelled like antiseptic. A woman wearing green scrubs and the world's whitest sneakers cleaned her, stitched up her wounds, and bandaged her with brutal efficiency. Kenzie would have known just from the shoes that this woman was up to no good…even without the added clues of kidnapping and cooking-to-the-death. No one could wear white shoes to work and keep them that pristine.

The nurse offered Kenzie a turkey sandwich and a paper cup of milky tea.

Kenzie tried to refuse the food, even though she hadn't eaten in what felt like forever. She could sense that the meal was laced with magic.

"Either eat," the nurse said, "or I'll force a feeding tube down your throat."

Kenzie glared at the woman. "I'm going to go out on a limb here and guess you're not a registered nurse, are you?"

Clinging to her sarcasm helped prevent Kenzie from succumbing to terror.

"Eat," the nurse ordered without answering the question. Typical.

Kenzie picked up the sandwich and began to eat. Before she'd even swallowed her first bite, a warm feeling overtook her. Her limbs grew heavy. When she tried to move her arms, they felt like thousand-pound weights had been attached.

The bitch drugged her.

"You'll be thorry," Kenzie slurred. Her tongue felt like a fat sausage in her mouth.

Kenzie's eyelids fell closed without her permission. Everything went quiet. Even her own thoughts began to fade. She embraced the darkness.

* * *

Kenzie stared at the red apron draped over her counter as she experienced an unpleasant sense of déjà vu. Muffled jeers came from behind the one-way glass above the arena.

Now that this whole scenario was a little less new, Kenzie was able to appreciate just how disturbing it was to have an audience she couldn't see. Especially when that audience was trying to pelt her with rotten tomatoes.

Somehow, not knowing who was behind that window put Kenzie even more on edge than she already was.

The flashing scoreboard overhead noted that her opponent today went by the name Scarlet.

Kenzie was still *The Champ*.

When the metal door at the other end of the arena opened, Kenzie got her first glimpse of her opponent.

She felt her jaw go slack.

"Are you kidding me?!" she demanded, directing her question upward, to where Polly had just stepped into her clear glass skybox.

Polly, of course, was too busy welcoming the invisible audience to pay any attention to the poor schmucks down in the arena.

Scarlet was a girl who couldn't have been older than seventeen. From the way she squinted into the lights and tipped her head back to take everything in, it was obvious this was her first time in Cutthroat Cuisine.

Scarlet…or whatever her real name was…was a little gangly and wearing an orange prison jumpsuit that clashed with her badly dyed, flame-red hair.

The sight of that jumpsuit sent a pang through Kenzie that was so fierce she had to clutch the metal counter for support. Kenzie wasn't supposed to be here. She was supposed to be figuring out a way to rescue her father from jail.

Scarlet caught a rotten tomato out of the air and pitched it right back into the crowd.

Nice.

Scarlet held both her middle fingers up at the one-way glass as she prowled over to the kitchen, where Kenzie was already waiting. The girl had a thick metal hoop in the center of her nose that looked like a bull's nose ring.

"Your ink's sick," Scarlet said, admiring Kenzie's tattoos.

"Thanks," Kenzie replied. *I think.* "Sweet…piercing."

Scarlet gave her a withering look. "I don't know what the fuck is happening, but I know that if you fuck with me, I'll fuckin' tear you apart."

"Um, right," Kenzie said. "Good to know."

Scarlet took a step forward and raised her fists, like she was a boxer rather than a chef. Kenzie had to resist the urge to duck behind her counter. Every motion tugged at the stitches across her stomach, and her body ached from the various cuts and bruises she'd gotten during her match with Brute. The last thing she needed right now was to anger her opponent before the cooking even began. There was no doubt which one of them would come out on top in an all-out brawl. It wouldn't be Kenzie.

"Hey, I know you," Scarlet said in a way that wasn't at all friendly. "You're the bitch who won Hex Kitchen."

Um…thanks?

"Yeah, I am," Kenzie managed.

"Let's see what kind of big shot you are without your pretty boy toy to keep you safe."

Kenzie swallowed. She tried not to let herself think about Braxton, and what he'd sacrificed for her at the end of the tournament. Thinking about him would only make her even more worried and paranoid than she already was.

Something told her that she couldn't afford to be distracted for even a second during this match.

"Remember chefs," Polly said into the microphone she was clutching in her manicured hands. "You will each get a magical ingredient to incorporate into your dish. You may use that ingredient in addition to your own magic."

It was hard to tell from this distance, but it seemed to Kenzie like Polly's pensive gaze turned on her, like she was trying to figure Kenzie out.

Welcome to the club.

"We get to use magic ingredients?" Scarlet asked. "Hell, yeah!"

"It is quite special, isn't it?" Polly said, seeming delighted that someone in the arena appreciated this whole experience.

Kenzie gripped the edge of the counter as she stewed quietly.

"The Gourmands are proud to have the greatest stockpile of magical ingredients in the world," Polly boasted. "We produce them in-house, and—" She cut off abruptly and cocked her head to the side, listening to voices coming from behind the one-way glass.

"Oh." Polly tittered, sounding embarrassed. "Right. Of course. The point is, we have these incredible ingredients, and we're sharing just a few during this tournament to spice things up a little." She gave an exaggerated wink.

"Shiiiit," Scarlet said, drawing out the word. "No wonder the Gourmands rule the world." She let out a raspy laugh. "Always wanted to see a magic ingredient up close."

"Go on, chefs," Polly encouraged. "Let's see what you're working with, today."

Scarlet needed no persuading to dive into her basket. Kenzie just watched and waited as her apprehension mounted.

Scarlet's hand emerged from the basket with a small packet of yeast.

"Razor yeast!" Polly declared. "I can't wait to see what these chefs come up with. There's going to be blood, folks!"

Scarlet was cackling like an evil maniac. Kenzie was sweating profusely.

"The winner of this match will go on to compete for the most coveted prize of becoming the next head of the Gourmands," Polly said.

Pass, Kenzie thought.

"As the leader, you will have the honor of choosing a new flock of Gourmands to aid in protecting our secrets from the rest of the world. You will become a protector, enforcer, peace-keeper—"

Kenzie couldn't help a snort at that. She might be a culinary magic newbie, but it didn't take a genius to spot corruption when it came in the form of kidnapping and cooking to the death.

The Gourmands were as pure as driven snow. In Manhattan. During rush hour.

"In order to protect the Gourmands' identities and ensure there are no threats to our new leader, this match will be to the death." Polly smiled, like this detail was a cause for celebration.

Psycho maniac granny.

"Wait," Scarlet said. "Is she sayin' what I think she's sayin'?"

Kenzie swallowed against the sudden tightness in her throat. "Yeah, that's the rules they came up with, but—"

"You mean we get to cook to the death?" Scarlet interrupted. "Without gettin' in trouble?"

"Uh, yeah," Kenzie replied, not appreciating the spark of excitement in the other girl's eyes. And here she'd been thinking they were almost getting along.

"*Sick*," Scarlet said, grinning demonically.

How the hell was this teenager in the running to become the next Gourmand leader? Scarlet was a lot more *I'll knife you in a dark alley* than *let's sing Kumbaya while I plot the future of culinary magic.*

"Are you ready, chefs?" Polly called gleefully. "Let's cook some magic!"

Scarlet didn't hesitate. In seconds, flour and sugar were spraying up around her like a dust storm. Kenzie, feeling the sense of urgency that hung over the arena, went to her own station.

The last time she'd cooked something in this kitchen, Brute was her opponent. Kenzie could almost smell the acrid tang of the burnt tempura batter on his squid tentacles.

Crack.

Kenzie looked down at her palms, which still bore red marks from where the pepped peppercorn crust had dug into her flesh. She could hear Brute's labored gasps as the tentacles wound tighter around his neck.

Crack.

After Hex Kitchen, she'd promised herself she would make amends. She wanted Braxton to use the wish truffle to save his family. She'd wanted to find a way to save her father from spending the rest of his life paying for her crime.

Instead, she was trapped in here and being forced to use her cooking skills to kill again. Why? Because Polly Berrywhite and some degenerate culinary magic gods told her to?

Screw. That.

Kenzie glanced over at Scarlet, who was busy heating what appeared to be pig's blood in a saucepan. She molded a loaf of dough into the shape of a dagger and was sliding her tray into the oven.

It would seem a truce probably wasn't going to happen.

"Come on, Champ!" Polly called from her little stage. From behind the one-way glass, a more muffled voice called out, "Cook, bitch!"

"No mercy!" Scarlet shrieked, feeding off the invisible crowd's bloodlust.

Well, that wouldn't do. Kenzie might not be willing to kill again, but she wasn't going to lay down and die, either.

She surveyed the ingredients on her counter. Whatever she was going to make, she'd need to be quick about it. And it definitely wasn't going to involve yeast. There was no way Kenzie was getting involved with any ingredient that started with the word *razor.*

Her eye caught on some ramekins. That gave her an idea.

Kenzie got to work. She roughly-chopped a bar of dark chocolate and placed it in a double-boiler. After the chocolate melted down into a glossy liquid, she whisked in egg yolks and sugar.

Within a few minutes, her chocolate mousse was smooth and giving off a heady aroma. Kenzie added the mixture to her ramekins and put them in the blast chiller.

An uncomfortable fifteen minutes passed while she waited for her mousse to set, and for Scarlet's dagger-shaped bread to rise.

Kenzie took the mousse out as soon as it was semi-solid. It could use another half-hour to set, but it was good enough. She placed the chilled ramekins on her counter and got to work on her magic. She had never done anything like what she was about to attempt, but she was confident it would work. She could sense the dish's willingness to perform the magic she was weaving through its every molecule.

The gelatinous mousse began to take on a life of its own. It burbled out of the ramekins and formed in a single chocolate lump on the counter. Kenzie stood back as the chocolate blob began to take shape.

She could hear Polly narrating in the background, but all of Kenzie's attention was on the four-legged mousse creature that was coming to life on her counter.

As soon as the miniature animal was standing on wobbly legs unassisted, Kenzie adjusted her magic.

The animal began to grow.

Kenzie's creation was still growing and solidifying when an unpleasant aroma from Scarlet's side of the kitchen drew her notice. Scarlet was drizzling her pig's blood reduction over the dagger-shaped pastry. As Kenzie watched, the blunt edges of the blade turned sharp. It might look like bread, but Kenzie had the distinct impression it would cut like an actual dagger…no doubt thanks to the razor yeast.

Note to self: don't get killed by the bread dagger.

Kenzie gave her magic a tug. The mousse animal rose up and let out a wall-shuddering bellow.

"Oh, how clever, Champ!" Polly called into her microphone. "Never, in the history of Cutthroat Cuisine, have we seen anything so magically complex. The Champ has made a chocolate mousse *moose*. That's moose with two O's, folks!"

"Glad to be so amusing," Kenzie grumbled.

Scarlet prowled forward. She tossed the bread knife high into the air and caught it one-handed behind her back.

Okay, so, this wasn't Scarlet's first go-around with a deadly weapon. Good to know.

Kenzie adjusted her magic. The full-sized mousse moose positioned itself between Kenzie and Scarlet. The creature let out another rumbly bellow that would have scared any normal person into submission.

Scarlet wasn't normal. She jabbed out with her bread knife.

The audience behind the one-way glass went wild as the knife plunged into the moose's flank.

Kenzie's moose might look like a real animal, but its innards were still just chocolate and cream. There was no blood to be spilled, no bones to break. The moose's soft interior absorbed the blow. The animal held its position.

Hah. She'd beat the Gourmands at their own game.

The moose, seeming to take on a will of its own amid Kenzie's magic, turned its head and regarded Scarlet. The expression in its chocolate eyes said, *Really? Is that all you've got?*

Scarlet hissed out a string of profanity. She wrenched out her chocolate-drenched dagger and tried to bypass the moose to get directly to Kenzie.

"Sorry, not happening," Kenzie told the girl.

The moose kept itself positioned between Kenzie and Scarlet. Whenever Scarlet got close, the moose used its antlers and hooves to push her back.

The moose wasn't solid enough to hurt Scarlet, but it was big and bulky enough to edge the other girl back any time she tried to come at Kenzie.

"I can keep this up all day," Kenzie announced, feeling calmer and more in control than she had since she'd first woken up in this place.

It was obvious Scarlet was getting tired and had reached the end of her magical stamina. The girl was swaying on her feet. Meanwhile, the chocolate moose would keep Kenzie from getting knifed before Scarlet's energy ran out.

Win-win.

Kenzie looked up into the audience and locked gazes with Polly.

How's it feel to be beaten at your own game, you old witch?

Polly cocked her head, like she was listening to someone standing out of view.

Kenzie's pulse began to speed up as she waited for whatever was going to happen next.

"Cutthroat Cuisine's rules clearly state the match isn't over until one of you is dead," Polly announced.

"Then I think you'd better start re-writing the rules," Kenzie called back. "I'm not killing anyone else, and I'm sure as shit not getting killed."

Kenzie stepped out of the way as rotten tomatoes came pelting down at her from the onlookers. Kenzie's moose caught one in its mouth and spat it back up into the air. It splattered across the one-way glass.

"Speak for yourself," Scarlet said, tossing her bread knife all the way up to the rafters and deftly catching it as it hurtled back down.

Kenzie slid behind her mousse moose as Scarlet waved her weapon in the air.

"We don't have to do this," Kenzie said.

"Sure we do." Scarlet twirled the dagger around in her hand. "'Cause I'm gonna win this shit. Then, the Gourmands will belong to me."

That thought was almost as terrifying as the bread knife Scarlet was wielding. Then again, it didn't seem like the current Gourmand leader— whoever he or she was—was playing with a full deck. In Kenzie's experience, well-adjusted people didn't engage in kidnapping or culinary murder. They just didn't.

The chocolate moose moved, catching Scarlet's blade in its gooey shoulder. The moose let out an enraged roar before grasping the handle with its chocolatey teeth and flicking it away.

Scarlet shrieked and dove for the weapon. Kenzie gave her moose a little pat of gratitude.

The next time Scarlet came at the moose, she wasn't holding back her punches…er, stabs. She plunged her knife into the moose again and again, until semi-liquid chocolate innards began to pour out.

The overhead lights weren't helping, and Kenzie's fearless steed was starting to look more like the Blob than a moose.

Not. Good.

Scarlet kept hacking through the moose until Kenzie could see the tip of the bread knife. It looked even sharper than an actual dagger. Brutally sharp. Magically sharp.

The moose gave a loud groan and pitched to the side as its midsection caved in. Kenzie had to roll to avoid being smushed under a chocolate avalanche. She tried to run, but her stitches gave a fierce tug, reminding her that she was injured.

Scarlet didn't share Kenzie's hesitance. The girl gave a victorious whoop and threw herself at Kenzie.

They both went down in a tangle of flailing limbs. The bread dagger flashed. Kenzie jerked away just before the blade impaled the ground where her head had been seconds before.

"Stop this," Kenzie begged, ignoring the throbbing ache in her stomach as she tried to grasp Scarlet's arms.

"Nah, bitch," Scarlet panted. "Gonna cut you apart."

They rolled onto their sides, scrambling for the weapon. Somewhere in the background, Kenzie heard Polly shouting into her mike.

Scarlet's elbow caught Kenzie's ribs, right in the place where Brute's magic tentacles had raked over her skin. For a second, Kenzie's vision went white. When her surroundings came back into focus, she was on her back. Scarlet was straddling her.

"Please," Kenzie whimpered.

Scarlet just laughed and raised the dagger up high.

There was no way Kenzie was going to survive this. Heat seared across her belly. Her muscles quivered. She was trapped beneath Scarlet, and the tip of the bread dagger was descending toward her chest.

She felt the point scrape against her sternum.

Kenzie didn't think. She reached for the translucent cords of magic wrapped around the dagger.

Come on. Come on….

Scarlet screamed and drew back. Blood seeped between the girl's fingers. She was clutching the dagger's handle…which was no longer a handle. Instead, it had transformed into a blade. Kenzie had reversed the magic, so the sharp edge was cutting through Scarlet's hands instead of impaling Kenzie.

Kenzie bucked her hips off the ground, trying to get Scarlet the hell off her.

"You bitch!" Scarlet hollered. "I'm gonna make you die slow. I'm gonna make it hurt. I'm—"

Kenzie grabbed the dagger's handle and yanked the weapon out of Scarlet's bleeding hands. Then, she drove the blade straight up and into Scarlet's heart.

CHAPTER 5

BRAXTON

How do you know they're not going to come home before I'm done cooking?" Braxton asked.

He slid a sheet pan into the pre-heated oven before turning to a smirking Rick.

"Because." Rick crossed his arms and leaned back against the granite counter. "He takes his wife and daughter out for Mexican food every Friday night." He held up his wrist and tapped his Rolex watch. "They're never back before eight."

That left more than enough time for Braxton's granola to bake.

Soon, the rooster-themed kitchen filled with the scents of warm honey, cinnamon, and burnished macadamia nuts.

The granola medley was a recipe he'd learned from Aralia. She'd made it for him after he promised never to endanger Graham by revealing his secret. Aralia had called it *promise granola,* and true to its name, it prevented Braxton from going back on his word.

This magical recipe was one of a few that lasted, even if the chef cooked something new. As long as it was consumed by another culinary magician, the granola bound to a small fragment of the eater's magic and laid dormant…unless that person reneged on their bargain.

It was up to the specific culinary magician who cooked the dish to determine what precisely would happen to a person who failed to uphold their promise after eating it. Knowing Aralia, it would be an excruciating death by poison if Braxton recanted on his promise.

Braxton was using a variation of the recipe now. Except, instead of forcing the ones who ate it to uphold a promise or risk a brutal punishment, it would make them speak the truth. So…*truth granola.*

"Did you put enough magic in?" Rick asked, flipping on the oven light and giving Braxton's work a critical glance.

"Don't you want to wait in the car?" Braxton retorted.

Rick had been second-guessing Braxton's work every step of the way. The only time Rick had stopped criticizing was when he was busy complaining about his anklet.

Braxton kept his cool by fantasizing about putting Rick's head through the nearest wall. If it wasn't for the two goons who stood menacingly behind Braxton while he cooked, he might actually do it.

"No need," Rick replied. "The anklet only alerts the Gourmands if I touch magical food. That's why you're here."

Rick's phone chimed.

"They're home," Rick said.

The two goons slipped into the adjoining dining room, which was dark. Braxton went motionless behind the counter, fighting an almost-overpowering urge to call out and warn the family.

This bloke might know where Kenzie is, Braxton reminded himself.

Not to mention, he was fairly certain that if he pissed off Rick right now, he'd never see his mum and sister again.

A door slammed.

"Whew," a male voice said from the hallway. "I'm stuffed. Those enchiladas are really something, I'll tell ya."

"Daddy? Can we watch a movie?" a little girl's voice asked.

Cold sweat slithered down Braxton's spine.

Heels clicked against the marble floor.

"Ohmygawd!" A woman coming into the kitchen halted in her tracks. She clutched at her triple-strand pearl necklace. Her eyes widened in terror as she caught sight of Braxton behind the kitchen island.

Braxton raised his hands. "I'm not going to hurt you."

"Jacob, get in here!" the woman shouted.

"In a minute," he called back. "Hold your horses!"

The woman looked at Braxton. "I know you." Her terrified expression turned hopeful. "My husband proposed to me at one of your family's restaurants when we were visiting Sydney. We were rooting for you during Hex Kitchen."

Braxton swallowed past the gravel in his throat. "I appreciate it."

The woman tilted her head. "Why are you in my house?"

Braxton couldn't stop his gaze from darting to Rick, who was standing behind the pantry door. "I need to talk to your husband, and then I'll get out of your hair."

There was a slight rustle from the dining room as the two thugs adjusted their stances.

"Jacob!" the man's wife shouted again. "Move your bum!"

Footsteps that were much too light to belong to a grown man padded across the floor. A little girl, maybe five or six, came to a skidding stop when she caught sight of Braxton. She peeked at him through blonde bangs. A few seconds passed, and then she offered him a shy smile.

"You're handsome," the little girl informed him, ducking behind her mother. "I like your eyes."

From behind the pantry door, Rick snorted.

Braxton offered the little girl a grin. He suspected random children didn't often stop Rick to tell him they liked his eyes.

"Jacob!" the woman shouted.

The unstrung tenor of her voice finally got through to her husband. A man with a beer belly and bad comb-over huffed into the kitchen. He was in the process of loosening his tie when he caught sight of Braxton. His mouth fell open.

Jacob took a few steps to the side, his gaze straying toward the knife block on the counter.

"Nah," one of Rick's bodyguards said as he emerged from the shadows. He pressed his gun into Jacob's lower back and pushed him away from the knives.

"Let me put our daughter to bed," the woman said, her lower lip trembling as she bent down to scoop up the little girl.

"Don't move," the second goon said, his massive frame filling the kitchen doorway. He gestured with his gun for the woman to join her husband.

The little girl, who had started sucking her thumb, looked at Braxton. He gave her a smile that he hoped was more reassuring than he felt. He didn't like anything about this.

The woman also turned to Braxton, as though he were the one in charge. Betrayal swam over her face.

"You seemed like such a nice young man," she said, her voice quavering. "You and your brother both." Her eyes slitted. "Unless every interview I've ever read was a lie, then your angel of a twin never would have done this." She swept her hand around the room, indicating the goons.

Braxton's whole body went rigid. He had no response.

"Let's not be melodramatic," Rick drawled, stepping out from behind the pantry door.

Jacob's expression went from alarmed to terrified.

"Y-you," he stammered.

"Me," Rick agreed. He threw a careless look over his shoulder at the man's wife. "And don't believe everything you read."

The woman's face reddened. "Jacob, I want these people out of my house. Do you hear me? I want them out!"

Jacob's expression was fearful, but not surprised. Any question Braxton had about whether this man knew anything important was answered in that moment.

"I'm not telling you sh—anything," Jacob quickly corrected himself, his eyes darting to his daughter. "My loyalty is to the Gourmands."

"I'm confident you're going to tell us everything," Rick said with his characteristic haughtiness. He picked at his thumbnail to emphasize his boredom.

Both thugs simultaneously clicked off their weapons' safeties.

"I can't," Jacob choked. "I'm just their distributor. If I betray them, the Gourmands will torture and then kill my whole family. I'd rather die than tell you anything."

His words were brave, but Jacob's sour sweat was overpowering the honeyed aroma of the granola.

"I'd oblige you," Rick told Jacob. "But you're no use to me dead. Not yet, anyway." Without taking his attention off Jacob, Rick snapped his fingers at Braxton. "McKaid, you're up."

Braxton pulled the granola out of the oven and let the pan clatter onto the counter. Jacob's wife startled at the noise. Braxton hated himself a little in that moment.

"Eat some," Braxton told Jacob.

Jacob gave the granola a wary look. The thug standing next to him did something with his gun that made Jacob scramble forward and grab a fistful of the granola. Wincing at the heat, Jacob shoved the handful into his mouth.

Braxton knew the magic had caught hold when Jacob inhaled sharply.

"Tell us about the Gourmands' magical ingredients," Braxton ordered.

The sooner they finished with this part of the conversation, the sooner he'd find out what Jacob knew about Kenzie.

Jacob sputtered and spit as he tried to form his mouth around a lie. Braxton felt the magic wrap taut around the man's throat, preventing him from speaking anything but the truth.

"The Gourmands found a way to make their own magical ingredients," Jacob said, panting and sweating as each word was drawn out of him. "I don't know how, but they've got a lot, and they're making more."

Braxton turned to Rick and raised an eyebrow.

The whole concept of Gourmands producing their own magical ingredients was very strange. Magical ingredients were notoriously difficult to cultivate. If the Gourmands really had a stockpile of them, there would be no limit to the price they could command for them.

"They're artificial," Jacob continued, "but high quality." He took a step toward the fridge but stopped when Rick's guards moved in.

"I have some," Jacob said, his pleading look going from Rick to Braxton. "I can show you."

Rick nodded. The two goons stepped back enough to let Jacob get to the fridge.

Braxton's guilt and reluctance at being here gave way to intrigue.

Jacob produced a small burlap sack. He untied the drawstring and overturned the sack. A dozen golden zucchini flowers tumbled onto the counter.

Braxton had worked with this ingredient—the non-magical variety—plenty of times. Aidan used to make fried zucchini blossoms with herbed goat cheese that made Braxton's mouth water at just the memory.

"These were a gift for my assistance with transporting the ingredients," Jacob said miserably.

"So kind of you to share," Rick said. He lifted one of the zucchini flowers off the counter but froze before he put it into his mouth.

"You trying to pull a fast one on me?" Rick asked Jacob.

"No. I swear." Jacob put out plaintive hands.

"Hmm." Rick tossed the zucchini flower to Braxton. "You eat it. Just in case."

Since it would be pointless to argue, Braxton did as he was told.

The delicate petals gave way between his teeth, releasing a flavor that was mild and faintly sweet.

"Well?" Rick prompted. "Are you dying?"

"Not yet," Braxton replied dryly.

He was about to level a glare on his nemesis, when he realized the room looked different.

"Wow," he muttered.

"What?" Rick demanded as he stuffed a zucchini flower into his mouth.

Braxton stopped paying attention to anyone else in the room and just let himself absorb the magic. He was standing in an enclosed kitchen, and yet, he was looking straight through the wall and into the adjoining room. The darkness didn't hamper his vision, and he could see even tiny details like the textured wallpaper and a dead fruit fly on the carpet.

He adjusted his stance, and his vision shifted. He was looking straight through the house's front wall and onto the street outside the house.

"This is useful," Rick said. "Damn."

Braxton could see through Jacob's house and into neighboring houses. He was just starting to grasp how disturbing this magic was, when it began to fade. Dizziness swept through him as his vision narrowed until walls became impenetrable, and he could see nothing more than the enclosed kitchen where he was standing.

"The magic works with the zucchini flowers' natural Vitamin A content," Jacob explained. He licked a droplet of sweat off his upper lip. "I think that's why they enhance eyesight."

"Wish they lasted longer," Rick said, "but I'm sure I can find a good use for these babies."

"No!" Jacob lunged for the zucchini blossoms, sweeping them into the sink.

"Stop him!" Rick ordered, just as Jacob hit the switch for the garbage disposal.

Jacob's wife and daughter screamed as the goons yanked Jacob back. Rick shouted obscenities at anyone and everyone.

Braxton glanced down at the floor, where a single zucchini blossom had fallen and escaped the massacre. While everyone else's attention was elsewhere, Braxton picked up the flower and stuffed it in his pocket.

Jacob made a strangled sound as Rick's men pinned him against the wall. He cried out when one of them cuffed him across the face. Blood gushed from his split lip.

"Where are the Gourmands taking these ingredients?" Rick demanded.

Jacob's swollen lip quivered. His head whipped back as the other goon hit him.

"Talk," Rick ordered.

"All I know is that I pick them up from one warehouse and bring them to another one. I swear it."

"Addresses," Rick said, snapping his fingers at Jacob the same way he had to Braxton earlier. "I want to know where, when, how, and everything in between."

One of thugs picked up a notepad from the counter and slid it over to Jacob.

The man's hand shook so violently that his writing was barely legible. Rick snatched the paper as soon as he'd finished.

"That wasn't so hard, was it?" Rick asked Jacob. He patted the trembling man on his cheek.

Rick tore off the top page and folded it. He jutted his chin at his men. "Let's blow this popsicle stand."

"No." Braxton whirled on Rick. "Your dad said I could ask about Kenzie."

For a second, it seemed like Rick was going to refuse. Then, he shrugged. "What the hell?" He leaned back against the fridge. "I don't have anywhere else to be right now."

Braxton turned back to Jacob.

"Leave my daddy alone!"

The little girl, who had been keeping quiet, flung herself out of her mother's arms and positioned herself in front of her father.

In that moment, the girl reminded Braxton so much of Sofia that he almost obeyed. If he'd been there for any other reason than finding Kenzie, he would have.

"I won't hurt your dad," Braxton told the kid. "Promise."

She gave him a skeptical look.

"Pinky promise?" she asked, holding out her tiny digit.

Braxton nodded, solemnly hooking his finger around hers and giving their joined hands a careful shake. Then, he turned all of his attention on Jacob.

"What do you know about Kenzie Ashner—I mean, Brookerton—disappearing after Hex Kitchen?" Braxton demanded.

Jacob blinked. "Who?"

Braxton ground his molars. "Kenzie. My tournament partner. The Gourmands took her somewhere after Hex Kitchen. I need to know where."

Jacob's tongue darted out to lick at the blood congealing on his lip. "I'm not a Gourmand. I don't even talk to them directly. You know how careful they are to keep their identities secret. That way, folks like you can't do to them what you're doing to me."

Rick laughed coldly. "Please. The Gourmands are so protective of their identities because they're up to shadier shit than any of us."

Braxton wasn't about to argue with that.

"Please," Braxton said, unable to keep the emotion from his voice. "You must know something that can get me closer to them."

"I know they need powerful culinary magicians to make their ingredients," Jacob admitted.

The words came reluctantly, and only because the truth granola forced them out. Braxton could feel Jacob straining against the magic.

"What do you mean?" Braxton demanded.

Jacob gave him a helpless shrug. "There's a guy I know who's like me." His gaze darted to his wife before coming back to Braxton. "He helps the Gourmands out with some…stuff…from time to time."

Braxton drummed his fingers on the counter as he waited impatiently.

"There have been…bodies," Jacob said. "My acquaintance helps the Gourmands dispose of them."

Braxton's world tilted. Rick said something, but the meaning didn't penetrate the fog of panic that had settled over his mind.

Jacob lowered his voice. "The guy—he calls himself the Bonecruncher, on account of what he does for the Gourmands—said there's something shady about the bodies, aside from them being dead." He gave another little shrug. "Don't know anything else."

Someone's harsh breathing filled the kitchen. It took Braxton several seconds to realize the sound was coming from him.

Kenzie. His Kenzie.

He could see her smile and feel her silky hair between his fingers. He knew the soft sounds she made when she slept and that tart apple smell that trailed in her wake.

He could see her darting around the kitchen, humming to herself as she defied every law of magic. His memory supplied him with images of her flushed cheeks and tattoos standing out against her pale skin as she rocked his world.

The one vision his brain couldn't conjure was all that vitality and beauty extinguished.

She isn't dead, his panicking brain insisted. She couldn't be. He would know if she was. He'd feel it.

"Tell me—" Braxton had to pause while he got a hold of himself. He gripped the counter, letting the cold granite ground him. "Tell me where to find this man."

"Jersey," Jacob said. He scrawled an address on another piece of paper and shoved it over to Braxton. "If you wanna know more, you'll have to go talk to him."

Braxton took the paper and made sure to memorize the address before stuffing it into his pocket with the zucchini flower.

"Are we finished here?" Rick asked, checking his watch and yawning. "It's past my bedtime."

Braxton gave him a jerky nod. Between all the magic he'd expended and what he'd learned from Jacob, he felt stretched thin.

"No traces," Rick told his goons before striding toward the door.

The meaning of Rick's words permeated Braxton's distracted mind at the same time he heard the click of a safety.

"No, please!" Jacob cried. "I told you what you wanted to know. Don't do this!"

One of the goons pressed his gun to Jacob's temple.

"Rick," Braxton said, his pulse raging. "What the fuck are you doing?"

"You heard him," Rick drawled. "His loyalty is to the Gourmands. This fat idiot will call them the second we leave."

"I won't," Jacob gasped. "I promise. You don't—"

A blast tore through the kitchen. Jacob thudded against the island before sliding down to the floor. Blood began to pool beneath him.

His wife screamed. The little girl was crying and clinging to her mother.

The second thug raised his gun.

Braxton's paralysis lifted. He leapt in front of the man. Braxton grabbed his gun arm and thrust up, just as another deafening shot rang through the air. Dust and plaster rained down from a hole in the ceiling.

Braxton backed up, wedging the woman and girl between him and the wall.

"Stop wasting time, McKaid," Rick said. "Haven't you heard chivalry's dead?"

Braxton didn't move. "I can make sure they don't talk," he said, gesturing to the truth granola. He could sense that both mother and daughter had enough culinary magic that the recipe would work for them.

Rick turned to his men. One of them shrugged, looking mildly disappointed. The other said, "Would make cleanup easier, Boss."

"Fine." Rick sighed, like this whole thing was a great big inconvenience.

Braxton reached for the pan of granola, trying to keep his body in front of the mother and daughter.

Braxton took two handfuls and knelt down next to Jacob's cowering wife and daughter.

"Eat this," he said. "Please."

The little girl raised her tearstained face from her mother's shirt and blinked at Braxton.

"You said you wouldn't hurt Daddy." A little hiccup escaped her parted lips. "You pinky promised."

I'm sorry. I'm so, so sorry.

"I know," he whispered. "That was an accident. But I'm not going to let anything happen to you."

He opened his palm, offering her the crushed granola.

Jacob's wife picked up a few crumbs and put them in her mouth. She nodded to her daughter to do the same.

In a voice loud enough for Rick and his thugs to hear, Braxton said, "You aren't going to tell anyone that we came here tonight, are you?"

"No," the woman whispered.

"No," her daughter echoed. Her lower lip was trembling.

"You won't tell anyone what happened to your husband. You'll say it was an accident. If anyone asks if you've ever seen any of us before, you'll say no. Okay?"

"Okay," mother and daughter agreed.

Braxton turned to Rick. "Satisfied?"

The recipe would prevent either of them from ever going back on a truth they'd spoken after ingesting the granola.

"Sure." Rick thumped Braxton on the back. "Your savior complex is fully intact."

Hardly.

Braxton followed Rick out of the house, staggering a little as the cool night air struck his fevered skin. He moved to the side as the thugs carried out a rolled-up carpet with Jacob's dress shoes peeking out of the bottom.

Braxton collapsed against the porch railing. He leaned over and retched.

"Buck up, McKaid," Rick said. "That could have been your beautiful sister instead of that lardo. Besides, now you're one step closer to finding your precious girlfriend." He gave Braxton's back a hard thump. "Turns out, you're a natural at the gangster life."

Rick laughed as another bout of nausea had Braxton heaving into the bushes.

"Now what?" Braxton asked dully, when there was nothing left in his stomach to throw up.

"Now?" Rick let out a satisfied chuckle. "You're gonna crawl back to whatever rat hole you've been hiding in and get some sleep. Then, tomorrow night, we're going to steal those ingredients."

CHAPTER 6

SOFIA

There was a statistically significant chance Sofia was going to punch someone. Namely, her brother.

Since Braxton wasn't within reach, she turned back to the sack of flour she'd been pummeling. Her knuckles were cracked and her hair was sticking to her sweaty face, but she didn't care. The physical release was keeping her sanity in check. For the moment, anyway.

It was freezing in this storage shed, but it was blessedly quiet aside from the rhythmic thwapping sounds she made every time she hit the flour sack.

Maybe if she kept this up long enough, she'd be fit for company again.

Punch. Flour puffed into the air.

Goddamn Braxton, disappearing within seconds of Mum arriving. Without so much as a courtesy text.

Punch.

Goddamn Kenzie Ashner. It wasn't enough for that tattooed murderess to take Aidan away. She'd gone and stolen the Hex Kitchen win that should have belonged to Braxton. The wish truffle had been wasted on her sorry excuse for a life.

Punch.

Now, the restaurant empire Sofia had given most of her teenage years to rescue was in shambles.

And all Braxton could talk about was finding Kenzie.

Punch. Punch. Punch.

"You're overextending your elbow," a voice said from the doorway.

Sofia whipped around. Graham, Aralia's slightly creepy and extremely attractive boyfriend, filled the narrow opening to the storage room. At least, Sofia thought he was Aralia's boyfriend. She'd never seen any evidence of romance between them—which seemed weird since Aralia seemed touchy with everyone else—but they clearly weren't related. Aralia was white as a sheet and obviously of Nordic descent. Graham was dark-skinned and dark-haired. There wasn't a shred of physical resemblance between them. And friends didn't shack up with each other in the middle of the wilderness….

Sofia had never asked for clarification either way. First, because Braxton had a coronary every time she so much as looked in Graham's direction, and second, because she didn't want to give the impression that she cared.

"And you're the expert?" Sofia asked coolly.

Uninvited, Graham entered the cramped room. For as big as he was, he had a way of making himself seem smaller. He kept his back pressed against the wall and rounded his shoulders, as though that would be enough to hide the expanse of muscles that filled out his clothes.

"Try it again," Graham replied without answering her question.

The dusty lightbulb hanging overhead created a golden halo around his dark skin. The stupid flannel shirt and ripped jeans he wore did nothing to hide muscles that could have been cut from stone. His eyes were rimmed in the color of good whiskey, which made it that much more intense whenever he looked at her.

"Why are you awake right now?" Sofia asked.

It was late…sometime after midnight.

"Never been a good sleeper." Graham shrugged. For the first time since this bizarre conversation had begun, he didn't meet her eye. Sofia's inner shark told her to push him for the explanation he was clearly hiding.

"Stop stalling," Graham said, maybe because he could tell she was gearing up for an interrogation. "Try that again."

Sofia didn't make a habit of doing what she was told. But she'd been planning to do that anyway, so….

She hit the flour sack, mindful of her elbow.

Huh. That could very well have been the strongest punch of her life.

"You're relying too much on your upper body strength," Graham said. His voice was low and a little smoky. It did things to Sofia's insides that would be better left unexplored.

She hit the flour again, splitting the bag right in the center.

Take that, mental angst.

Graham shook his head. "If you really want to learn how to hit, you need to practice on something better than a sack of flour."

That comment grated. Sofia had three years of self-defense and kickboxing classes under her belt. Who did this sexy mountain man think he was?

"Any suggestions?" She raised an eyebrow and gave him the stare that made most people either fall madly in love with her or want to piss their pants out of fear.

Graham's only reaction was to come all the way into the cramped storage room.

"Hit me," he said.

Sofia scoffed. "Then you'll have a bruised ego and chest."

In Sofia's experience, the former took much longer to heal than the latter.

"I don't have an ego," Graham said.

Sofia would have laughed, but he looked so serious.

"Come on," he gestured at her with one big hand. "I'm ready."

Sofia gave him a little shrug. "You asked for it, big guy."

She readjusted her elbow and struck.

Sofia barely saw Graham move. One second, his arms were dangling at his sides. The next, he'd caught her fist in a gentle grip.

Well, hell.

"Try again," he said. He nudged her toe with his foot, widening her stance.

Her next effort had more power but no greater success. Sofia somehow managed to hold back a frustrated roar. Two more blocked punches had her ready to go back to her bag of flour. At least it didn't talk. Or smell annoyingly good. Like pine and wood smoke.

"The motion starts in your hips." A pair of warm, firm hands came to rest on the aforementioned hips. "Use your core to put more force behind your throw."

Sofia let out a steadying breath. She might guard her independence and pride the way a dragon coveted treasure, but she recognized when she was in the presence of someone who knew more than she did. This was one of those times.

She followed Graham's instructions and struck.

"Oof!" Graham stumbled back.

There was the sound of splintering wood as his back smacked against the wall.

"Oh, God. Sorry!"

Graham righted himself and inspected the hole in the wall. When he turned back to her, he was rubbing his chest and…smiling.

"Good arm," he wheezed. "Once I can breathe again, I'll get out my old punching bag before you break my sternum."

Sofia felt her lips twitch into a genuine smile. People so rarely surprised her, and almost never for the better.

"So." Graham winced as he rubbed his hand over his chest again. "You want to tell me why you were in here beating up dry goods in the first place?"

"Do you think I give up my secrets for every stranger who butts into my business?" Sofia said, a little more harshly than she'd intended.

She knew nothing about Graham…unless she could count the fact that Braxton hated him. Not that her brother had bothered to explain why.

"Alright," Graham said, still studying her with unnerving intensity. "But if you need someone to talk to, I'm a good listener."

Sofia snorted a little. "You'd be way out of your depth on this one, mountain man."

The ghost of a smile fluttered across Graham's full lips. "Try me."

"Alright." Sofia crossed her arms and glared at this sorry sod who had no idea what he was getting himself into. "Let's start with how my brother gave up the Hex Kitchen win to save our other brother's murderer. And now, we owe eight million to one of the most dangerous men in the culinary magic world."

God. How had it come to this?

Before this decade's Hex Kitchen, the most illegal thing a McKaid had ever done was buy fake IDs. Sofia had commissioned them for herself and her brothers as soon as Aidan and Braxton got their driver's permits. The three of them had snuck out to magical bars every chance they got. Braxton would charm the bartender into giving them half-price drinks, and Aidan—

"Anyway." She cleared her throat. "Things are…complicated."

Graham gave her a solemn nod.

"If there's anything I can do to help." He made a vague gesture with his hand. "I'd like to. Help, that is. If I can."

"This punching thing was helpful," she said. "Cathartic."

Graham gave her a rueful grin and massaged his chest. "Then I better find some padding."

She couldn't help but return his smile.

"Unless you're hungry," he offered. "We could—"

"Oh shit." She grabbed Graham's wrist and held up his watch. "Shit!"

"What's the matter?" Concern washed over Graham's face.

"Gotta go," she said, skirting around him and racing out of the shed.

She couldn't believe she'd forgotten about her meeting with the only investor who had deigned to reply to her email. And now, she was wearing one of Aralia's slutty dresses and dripping in sweat.

Bloody terrific.

* * *

After the world's fastest shower and outfit change, Sofia was settled at her makeshift desk in the room she was sharing with Mum. She waited impatiently for her laptop to boot up.

Sofia smoothed her skirt. It was the only outfit she had here that wasn't borrowed from Aralia. She'd been wearing it during their harried escape from Hex Kitchen, and it had required multiple washings to get rid of the dirt and desperation. It wasn't even one of her designer outfits…just a regular old violet top and matching pleated skirt that brought out the green of her eyes. It was wrinkled and smelled strongly of Aralia's homemade citronella soap, but it was hers. Wearing it offered a tiny slice of rightness amid all this wrong.

She stared into the camera on her laptop and offered it an over-bright smile. She widened her eyes and suppressed a yawn.

The fact that Sydney was fourteen hours ahead of New York was just one of the inconveniences she'd been working with over the last few days. The other was that her family was Enemy Numero Uno of every unsavory character in the world of culinary magic.

The clock at the bottom of her screen shifted to 2:00AM. She tapped the call button.

The video call rang. And rang. And rang some more.

Finally, the call connected. A balding man with thick-framed glasses appeared on her screen.

"Good afternoon, Mr. Dunlow," Sofia said, displaying her practiced smile. "Thank you for taking the time to meet with me."

"Sofia. How are you?"

The question was innocuous enough, but she hadn't been prepared for it.

"I—"

"I was so sorry to hear about your father," Mr. Dunlow continued. "He was a good man. He'll be missed."

A weaker set of tear ducts would have sprang into action. Sofia's knew to stay inert.

"Thank you," she managed. "And we're doing alright." She straightened her spine and folded her hands in her lap. If this man thought she would linger over small talk, then he didn't know the first thing about her.

"I have a proposal I'd like to run by you," Sofia said. "I know you've been eyeing our Darling Harbour location ever since we first bought it."

Even though she'd rehearsed this speech in her head a dozen times, the words came out reluctantly, like honey through a sieve. That property was the first one her family had acquired after Aidan won Hex Kitchen. It had been their father's favorite of all their restaurants. It had been their home.

"I'm offering you an exclusive first opportunity to purchase it," Sofia said.

"I never thought this day would come." Dunlow leaned closer to his screen. "I was under the impression that property would belong to generations of McKaids."

His sympathy irked Sofia beyond the point of reason.

"Yes, well, things change." She tucked her hair behind her ear. "Are you interested? The price is twelve million."

Dunlow smiled ruefully. "I've always admired your ambition, Sofia."

"It's not ambition. It's three stories of the best waterfront space in Sydney." She raised her chin. "You know that's a steal."

"Not for a building with bad juju."

"Bad *juju*?" Sofia gave the camera her infamous stink-eye. "Is that how we evaluate a property's worth these days?" Sofia clicked over to the spreadsheets and complex financial models she'd used to estimate the property's worth.

"It is when buildings collapse for no reason," Dunlow replied, his expression caught somewhere between amusement and sympathy.

"Everything has been repaired," she said, making a Herculean effort to keep her temper in check. "And we've had two independent engineers confirm the building is juju-free."

Dunlow's lips quirked into a smile.

"I like you, Sofia. I always have. Your dad and I were friends for many years, and I can see you've inherited both of your parents' business savvy."

Sofia wasn't going to correct him, but the truth was, neither of her parents had been especially intuitive about the business side of owning restaurants. They were both passionate and tireless, but when it came to crunching numbers and the nitty gritty behind-the-scenes paperwork, they'd both been clueless.

Their shortcomings had provided Sofia, with her questionable people skills, the perfect opportunity to find her niche.

In a family with two of the most talented culinary magicians in the world, finding a way to contribute hadn't been easy. She'd spent years trying to will some spark of magic to appear. The results had been a lot of dirty dishes, an unfortunate incident with a microwave that nearly burned down the house, and well-meaning but merciless teasing from her brothers.

"So, what's the issue?" Sofia asked, realizing that Dunlow had gone quiet. "Aside from juju."

Dunlow pinched the bridge of his nose and shook his head.

"I'm afraid your brother's…performance at Hex Kitchen has made your family…how shall I put it?"

"Bad for business," Sofia supplied flatly. Because it was the truth, and Sofia didn't have time for lies.

Dunlow gave her an apologetic smile.

"Ten million, then," she said.

The number was so low it made her neck itch.

"Sofia—"

"Your company finances culinary magic establishments," she pressed. "Are you seriously going to pass up the opportunity to capture the single best location in all of Sydney because of *juju*?"

"If circumstances were different, I would accept your generous offer in a heartbeat," Dunlow said. "However, things being what they are, I've been told by my superiors to pass on this deal."

Sofia allowed several moments of uncomfortable silence to fill the space between them.

"I see. In that case, have a nice evening, Mr. Dunlow."

"Sofia, wait." Dunlow held up a hand. "I'm going to tell you something, not as my company's property acquisition manager, but because I respect you."

Sofia waited.

Dunlow sighed. "Your family's…issues…with the Santioris haven't gone unnoticed. They are powerful in the world of culinary magic and beyond. Anyone who bought your building would be seen to be…taking sides."

"I see."

And it didn't take a genius to figure out that her family's side was the losing one.

"No one in the culinary magic world will buy from you," Dunlow said bluntly.

"Yes, I got that," she snapped.

Gourmand rules aside, Sofia had wanted to sell the building to a culinary magician. It felt like less of a betrayal of her father's dream that way.

"And you can't sell to a Vanilla," Dunlow continued, referring to members of the non-magical community.

"I took a whole year of culinary magic law at university," she said, her professional façade slipping as her temper rose. "I'm aware of our laws."

Culinary magic restaurants were equipped with secret entrances and hidden dining rooms that weren't on the original blueprints. If and when those inconsistencies were discovered, it would bring unwanted attention. And secrecy was the Gourmands' top priority.

As a member of the culinary magic community who didn't have magic herself, Sofia was in an especially precarious position. The Gourmands' law stated that any person who had at least one culinary magician in their family tree could be in on the secret. They were a little like honorary members of a secret club. Or second-class citizens.

"I can imagine this isn't easy for you to hear." Dunlow took off his glasses and began to polish them with a microfiber cloth. "I just wanted to appraise you of the situation so you're not surprised when everyone else you call refuses your offer."

Sofia sat forward in her chair. "I'm going to tell *you* something, Mr. Dunlow. Our family is going to get our restaurants back with or without financial backing. And then you'll have to go to your superiors with your tail between your legs and tell them you passed on the deal of a lifetime…and that, for some inexplicable reason, no one from your company can get reservations at the best culinary magic restaurants in the world."

Petty? Maybe a little. But it felt bloody good.

Out of the window next to her, Sofia saw a pair of headlights bouncing up the dirt road that led to the house. She glanced at the clock. Braxton had been gone for eleven hours and twenty-six minutes. And thirty seconds. Approximately.

"I believe I've taken up enough of your time," she said. "I know we both have other things on our agenda for today."

Like ripping our idiot brother a new one for disappearing for so long....

"It's such a shame you aren't a culinary magician, Sofia," Dunlow said. "You would have done your family proud."

Sofia's hackles rose. The only person in the world who was allowed to criticize her family was her.

"I'm proud of Braxton's performance at Hex Kitchen," she said. "And I don't need culinary magic because my talents lie elsewhere. Goodnight, Mr. Dunlow."

She closed her laptop before the man on her screen could see her shaking with rage. Ignoring the dozen other calls she needed to make before the end of business hours in Sydney, Sofia stalked downstairs to confront her brother.

She paused at the wood table that had previously been occupied by an array of taxidermized squirrels, and which now held a large reptile habitat. Sofia peered through the mist-covered glass. Kiwi, Kenzie's chameleon, stared back at her from the top of one of his fake branches.

"You see what I have to put up with?" she asked the little creature. "Be grateful you don't have siblings."

She reached into the habitat and adjusted Kiwi's heat lamp. Sofia glanced at his water to make sure it didn't need to be refilled. She saw, to her annoyance, that the fussy little reptile had eaten all of his crickets but left the greens she'd spent a sweaty hour harvesting from Aralia's garden.

As if her hands weren't full enough, Sofia also had to keep Aralia from either setting Kiwi free or turning him into lunch. Better yet, the chameleon was a slow-walking, breathing reminder of the source of all of their troubles: Kenzie Ashner.

Sofia would never hold an animal accountable for its poor luck in owners, and Braxton had been too busy losing his mind over Kenzie's disappearance to worry about her pet. So, Sofia had found herself the reluctant caretaker of a persnickety and ungrateful little chameleon.

He was kind of cute, though.

The cabin door opened. Finally.

"Where the hell have you been?" Sofia demanded before Braxton even shut the door.

Her brother didn't reply. That was when Sofia noticed his shirt. It was covered in dried blood.

CHAPTER 7

SOFIA

It's not my blood," Braxton mumbled. "Just leave it alone, okay?"

"Not okay!" Sofia fumed, resisting the urge to stomp her foot on the floor the way she had when they were kids. "This would all be so much easier if you'd just talk to me."

Braxton let out a humorless laugh. "Nothing about this is easy, Sofe."

Don't you think I know that? she wanted to shout. She'd just tried to sell off the last piece of her father and brother…and no one wanted to buy it.

"Brax—"

She let out a little yelp of surprise and outrage as he lifted her up, moved her to the side, and started up the stairs. Anyone who thought women were the moody ones clearly hadn't grown up with brothers.

"Asshole!" she shouted after him, only belatedly remembering that it was three in the morning and other people might be trying to sleep.

Braxton's hasty retreat was stopped by an immovable force at the top of the stairs. Mum was wearing the same pink flannel bathrobe she'd worn every morning of Sofia's life. Her hair was perfectly curled and her makeup was pristine.

"What is all this yelling about?" she asked, frowning as she looked from Braxton to Sofia. "And, Braxton, where have you been?"

Take that, Mr. Mysterious. No one could hold out against Mum when she was looking as determined as she was right at that moment.

Braxton sighed. "I can't talk about it. Can you both just trust me?"

"We already tried that," Sofia snapped. "You gave up everything for Kenzie Ashner and left your family out to dry."

"Maybe if you hadn't poisoned her, I would have been able to use the wish truffle the way you wanted," Braxton shot back.

"Braxton. Sofia." Mum's voice wasn't loud, but it carried a note of warning they'd learned long ago never to ignore.

"Here's what is going to happen," Mum said. "We're going to sit down and have a conversation. There won't be any yelling or cursing." She took Braxton's arm and led him back down the stairs. "We're going to remember that we're in this together." She looped her free arm through Sofia's and guided all of them into the living room. A fire was crackling in the hearth. It was the picture of coziness…and totally wasted on her. All Sofia wanted was to kick her brother's arse to Sydney and back.

Mum pulled both of them down onto the leather couch, which was lumpy and ugly and comfortable as hell.

In spite of herself, Sofia found her anger ebbing as she tucked herself against Mum's furry bathrobe. The smell of her Chanel perfume was so familiar and comforting.

"We need to remember that family is everything," Mum said, looking from Sofia to Braxton. "As long as we have each other, it'll all work out."

"I'm sorry," Braxton said, his voice cracking. "I never wanted to let either of you down."

"And you haven't." Mum gently combed her fingers through his messy hair. "Your sister and I are so proud of everything you've accomplished."

Sofia felt herself nodding, and not even because it was expected of her. It was true. She might want to kill Braxton half the time, but Mum was right. Their little family was everything.

"I'm so proud of both of you," Mum said.

Sofia wasn't affectionate by nature, but Mum didn't leave room for anyone to pull away. She was like sunshine and good coffee—a force in and of herself.

"Tell us what's going on, son," Mum said to Braxton in a gentle voice. "Let us help you."

Because it was Mum's superpower to get people to do whatever she wanted, Braxton did as he was told.

For the next several minutes, her brother's raspy voice filled the quiet room. Sofia absorbed every word of his violent story.

"The bloke told me the Gourmands are using culinary magicians to make artificial magical ingredients," Braxton explained. "He said…." He swallowed, and Sofia was sure that he wouldn't have continued without Mum's comforting embrace. "He said there are bodies." He whispered the last word.

Sofia hated Kenzie and all the trouble she'd caused their family, but in that moment, her chest ached for her brother. If Kenzie was dead, Sofia wasn't sure Braxton would be able to bear it. He acted tough, but the truth was that Aidan's death had changed him. It had changed all of them, but it had been different for Braxton. They'd had that twin bond that Sofia had always envied. When Aidan died, part of Braxton did too.

For reasons Sofia couldn't comprehend, Braxton was in love with Kenzie Ashner. If she died, Sofia didn't want to think about what would happen to her brother.

"I don't know the specifics," Braxton continued, "but these ingredients are lab-grown, or something. Not as powerful as ones that are grown naturally, but still impressive."

He pulled away from Mum so he could dig something out of his pocket. He held a limp squash blossom on his open palm as he explained how eating one had let him see through walls.

"Veneziano Santiori wants those ingredients," Braxton continued. "I have to help intercept the truck tomorrow night—"

"You most certainly will not," Mum interrupted. "It's illegal and dangerous. I won't have my children mixed up in gang activities!"

"I don't have a choice," Braxton said, hanging his head.

Mum bit her lip, and Sofia could see the internal war raging in her mind. It was the same conflict Sofia was feeling.

They both hated the idea of Braxton being in danger, but the situation was out of their control.

Mum heaved a sigh. "Very well. Then, we'd better discuss how Sofia and I can help you do this as safely as possible."

"I don't want either of you involved," Braxton argued.

Mum used her gentle voice and soothing fingers to relax Braxton while she started to problem solve. Sofia was only half-listening, though. Her attention had snagged on the squash blossom that Braxton had let fall onto the side table. She picked it up and studied it.

The blossom didn't look like anything special. If she'd been a culinary magician, she would have been able to feel power emanating from the ingredient, but to her, it just looked like a regular old squash blossom.

Magical ingredients were virtually impossible to come by. A whole stockpile of them would be worth a literal fortune, which was no doubt why the Gourmands were making artificial ones…and why the Santioris planned to steal them.

If Sofia could get her own stash of magical ingredients, she'd finally have some power over the Santioris.

The only issue was how to acquire some. It wasn't like magical ingredients grew on trees. Well…okay…maybe they did, but they were bloody scarce. There was only one magical ingredient cultivator who could do anything truly impressive. The Reaper.

The problem was that no one seemed to be able to find him. And rumor had it that even if he could be found, the Reaper would never agree to part with any of his ingredients.

But maybe Sofia could do something other starry-eyed business people had undoubtedly already attempted. She was going to find the reclusive Reaper and persuade him to sell her some ingredients.

Sofia already had a head start. She happened to know the Reaper's name—Qiang Lee. And she had a contact who likely knew his whereabouts.

"You're not going to help the Santioris steal anything," Sofia decided, startling Mum and Braxton out of their quiet conversation.

"I'm not?" Braxton raised a brow.

"Nope." Her pulse began to race with sheer possibility. "Let the Santioris waste their time stealing from the Gourmands. We're going to get our own stash. Then, while the Gourmands are busy chasing down those mobsters, we're going to become the sole distributor for legitimate magical ingredients."

It might be a long shot, but Sofia had been managing a restaurant conglomerate since she was sixteen. She had the McKaid stubbornness running through her marrow. How hard would it be to find one old man and convince him to share his ingredients?

Mr. Dunlow and every other person in the culinary magic world would come to rue the day they bet against the McKaids. Sofia would make damn sure of it.

CHAPTER 8

KENZIE

The next time she opened her eyes, Kenzie was lying on a cot that squeaked at her every movement. The waffle blanket pulled over her didn't offer much in terms of warmth, and goosebumps puckered the tattoos along her arms. Kenzie turned her head to the side, taking in her surroundings.

There wasn't much to see. She was in a windowless room. Another cot was pushed against the opposite wall. Aside from a pile of blankets and a sad little excuse for a pillow, it was empty. Two folding chairs propped against the wall made up the only other furniture in the room.

Cozy.

Kenzie looked down at herself. Her bloody, food-stained, and shredded clothes had been replaced with a pair of scrubs that could easily fit two more of her.

She had to think. Maybe she could find a spoon or something to dig her way out…*Shawshank Redemption* style.

No, dummy. Who would leave a spoon in a windowless cell?!

Kenzie needed a cup of coffee. Preferably a vat. She forced herself to her feet, feeling groggy but otherwise in full possession of her body.

Of course, the room's metal door was locked. She pounded on it with both fists.

"Let me out, you shitheads!" Kenzie shouted.

When that didn't achieve the desired result, she started kicking at the door with her socked feet.

"I have a pet chameleon who won't survive without me," Kenzie called, trying a different tack. "You'll have to live with his death on your conscience!"

Nothing.

"Where do I pee?" she shouted. "If you don't let me out of here, it's going to get messy. I'm serious, you know!"

The door handle turned.

Hah.

"Kenzie, I need you to go sit on your bed for us, alright?" Polly Berrywhite called. "I don't want you to get hurt, dearest."

Kenzie started to laugh. It made her stitched-up stomach and sore throat ache, but she couldn't stop.

"You…don't…want me…to get…hurt?!"

Her laughter abruptly cut off when the door opened a crack. Kenzie tensed, readying herself to bulldoze Polly on her way to freedom.

But the sliver of light on the other side of the door revealed a masculine profile rather than Polly. He seemed vaguely familiar, although Kenzie couldn't see enough of him to place him.

"Try anything," he said in a smooth voice that reeked of confidence and entitlement, and I'll send you right back into Cutthroat Cuisine. Not to mention, there are five guards behind me who will stop you before you even make it down the hall." He stepped to the side, revealing that there were, in fact, five men wearing red uniforms at his back.

"Peachy," Kenzie mumbled. With no other choice, she retreated to her cot and sat down.

The door swung fully open, revealing the man who matched the arrogant voice. He was dressed in a black suit and was leaning on a cane. The intricate handle looked like it was made out of ivory.

Wasn't that illegal?

You were kidnapped and forced to cook to the death! You think these people care about a few dead elephants?

The man had thick, gray hair that was cut short. His gray goatee was meticulously shaped and probably made him feel incredibly dignified. If it wasn't for his limp, Kenzie might have thought the cane was just part of his image.

"You," Kenzie said, finally remembering where she'd seen the man before.

He'd been one of the men who came into that room at Hex Kitchen, after Polly had tricked her into thinking she was going to be interviewed. He hadn't had the cane then, though. Or the limp. At least, Kenzie didn't think he had. It had been a little hard to concentrate on anything besides Polly screaming at her to give up the truffle.

"You're one of the Gourmands, aren't you?" Kenzie asked, her mind racing as she tried to remember everything Polly had told her before she blacked out and ended up here.

"I am in charge of the Gourmands," the man corrected. His cane clicked across the floor as he fully entered the room. He seemed to be dragging his left leg.

Kenzie filed that information away for later. Maybe she could kick him in that leg, or whack him with his own cane—

Every muscle in her body seized up as a thought occurred to her.

"Are you the one who killed Loretta and Max?"

The man's cool stare flickered in confusion.

"My coworkers at *Good Ol' Apple Pie*," Kenzie clarified. Images of their mangled bodies flashed through her memory, along with Polly's explanation that the Gourmands were willing to do whatever it took to make sure the general population didn't find out about culinary magic.

"I gave the order," the man replied shortly. He waved his hand, as though Loretta and Max's deaths were of no consequence to him. Like Kenzie didn't still have nightmares about walking into the freezer and finding their bodies stuffed inside….

"Oh good, you're looking so much better-rested!" Polly Berrywhite bustled into the room with a broad smile that displayed a trace of fuchsia lipstick on her front tooth. Kenzie didn't point it out to the woman out of pure spite.

Polly had changed out of her silver ball gown and was wearing a tweed skirt and jacket that had giant lemons printed on the fabric. She hurriedly unfolded the chairs so they were facing Kenzie's cot and settled her sizeable rump in one of them. The Gourmand man, who hadn't stopped staring at Kenzie since he'd entered the room, sat down and leaned his cane against the other chair. Through the open door, Kenzie could see the guards standing on either side of the narrow hallway.

"Would you like something sweet, dearest?" Polly asked. "You're looking a little peaked." She held out a plastic bag full of salted caramels.

Kenzie stared at the woman in disbelief. "What I would like," she said, "is for you to tell me what the hell I'm doing here, and then for you to let me go!"

Polly's expression sagged, like Kenzie had hurt her feelings. She put the bag of candies on her lap and popped one in her mouth.

"You're here for two reasons," the man told Kenzie. "The first is because you're competing for the chance to take over my job when I retire."

"Benedict is the single most important person in the world of culinary magic, dearest," Polly added, speaking around the caramel in her mouth. "Being able to compete in Cutthroat Cuisine is such an honor."

Yeah, you mentioned that. Right before you made me break a man's neck with a magically-enhanced squid tentacle.

"Fine, I'll bite," Kenzie said. "If this is such an honor, then why choose me?"

Kenzie wasn't exactly a pillar of the culinary magic community. She hadn't even known it existed before Polly showed up at the diner.

"All twelve of Cutthroat Cuisine's participants were selected based on a variety of criteria," the man—Benedict—said. His voice carried the hint of an English accent, and Kenzie wondered whether it was real or just part of the dignified old man persona he was rocking. "It was important that all of our competitors were solitary enough that no one would question it when they disappeared."

That stung. For the last five years, she'd worn her aloneness like a badge of honor. It wasn't until she met Braxton and learned about her dad's sacrifice that she realized how wrong she'd been.

"Particularly if your absence becomes permanent," Benedict continued.

Permanent. Like with Brute and Scarlet.

"And, of course," Benedict said, "all of our contestants are powerful culinary magicians who also happen to be murders. You have all proven that if you do become the next Gourmand leader, you won't hesitate when the need arises to sacrifice a few for the greater good."

Kenzie's jaw dropped. "But before you forced me, I never—" She faltered, her mouth going dry when she realized who Benedict was referring to.

Aidan McKaid.

Kenzie could still see the horror in Braxton's expression when he learned she was his twin's murderer.

"I don't want to be here," she pressed on. "And I don't want to be a Gourmand."

Polly gave her an affronted look. "Of course you do, dearest. Everyone wants to be a Gourmand."

"Are you deranged?" Kenzie asked. It was a serious question. These people were not right in the head.

Polly stuffed another caramel into her mouth. Benedict studied Kenzie with equal parts curiosity and disdain, like she was an unclassified specimen under a microscope.

"Tell me how is it that you can control multiple magical properties in a single dish simultaneously," Benedict said.

"I have no clue." Kenzie crossed her arms, ignoring the shooting pain that went through her midsection.

"She said neither of her parents are culinary magicians," Polly interjected. "Our people verified she was telling the truth on that front."

"I'm telling the truth on *every* front," Kenzie snarled.

Polly winked at her, like they were in cahoots.

"Her mother's dead," Polly continued. "And her father doesn't know anything."

"You stay away from my father!" Kenzie shouted, startling Polly enough that the bag of caramels fell off her lap. Several of the candies spilled onto the floor.

Polly made a distressed sound.

"Stay away from my dad," Kenzie said again, her voice unsteady. "He has nothing to do with any of this."

Benedict tapped a finger on his lips as he studied her.

"Secrets will do you no favors now," he said. "What aren't you telling us?"

"Nothing," Kenzie grated out. "I don't know why my magic is different."

"You may as well cooperate," Polly said coldly. All of her goodwill seemed to have spilled onto the tile floor with her candies. "No one's going to come save you. No one except for the Gourmands even knows you're here. You're all alone."

Those words rattled Kenzie as much as Polly had clearly intended them to. She felt a fierce prickle at the back of her eyelids.

You're all alone.

But that wasn't true anymore. She had her dad. And Braxton.

Her dad was in jail, though. And Braxton? Kenzie had no idea what had happened to him after he used the wish truffle to save her life.

Polly was right. No one was coming for her.

Benedict got to his feet. It was only because Kenzie was watching him intently that she noticed his slight wince as he extended his left leg.

"What happened to your leg?" Kenzie asked, mostly because she figured it would annoy a man like him to have any weakness exposed.

He peered down at her, his gaze inscrutable. "Your friend shot me with an arrow."

Kenzie tried not to let her confusion show. The only person she knew who could shoot arrows was Crazy Aralia, and that girl was definitely *not* Kenzie's friend. She'd threatened Kenzie's life on more than one occasion, and the threats hadn't seemed idle.

Polly threw another heartbroken glance at the caramels on the floor before stiffening her upper lip and letting herself out of the room.

"What's the second?" Kenzie asked, suddenly desperate for any excuse not to be left in this claustrophobic room all alone.

Oh crap. If she was craving company even when it came in the form of her captors, did that mean she was developing early stages of Stockholm syndrome?

"I beg your pardon?" Benedict said.

"You said I was here for two reasons," she said, trying to tamp down her frantic emotions. "The first is to compete for your job. What's the other reason?"

Benedict traced the outline of his goatee with his thumb and index finger as he regarded her.

"You will be of use to the Gourmands, one way or the other," he said. "Either you will inherit the most powerful organization in the world of culinary magic, or you will die, and we'll harvest your magic." His pale lips gave a little twitch of satisfaction.

"What does that even mean?" she asked as Benedict limped to the door.

He glanced back. "If you survive your next opponent, we'll talk again."

He let himself out of the room and slammed the door shut. Kenzie was left alone.

CHAPTER 9

BRAXTON

Braxton glanced down at his phone. There was a text from Rick with an address and a reminder to *hurry the fuck up*.

"You'll be waiting a while," Braxton muttered as he shoved his phone back into his pocket.

He'd left the cabin six hours ago and was now in New Jersey…nowhere near the Manhattan address Rick had summoned him to. Since Mum's rental car had barely gotten him back to the cabin last time, he was reliant on Aralia for transportation.

"Hm?" Aralia asked. She was sitting in the driver's seat and peering at the unassuming brick house across the street.

"Nothing."

As Braxton watched shadows move behind the gauzy curtain, he couldn't help but remember what Jacob's wife had said to him.

Your angel of a twin never would have done this.

The woman had been right. Aidan never would have broken into someone's house and threatened them. He never would have stood by while one of them was killed.

I'm sorry, Aid, he thought. *For letting you down and making a mess of everything.*

On the heels of that weighty silence came a revelation that sent a shockwave through his entire body.

It should have been me instead of Aidan.

"Are we going in?" Aralia whined. "If not, you may as well fuck me before I die of boredom."

"I'm not fucking you, Aralia," Braxton said, still breathless in the wake of his disturbing revelation.

"This baby has seen some good lovin'," Aralia said, stroking the upholstered seat next to her.

"Remind me to put down plastic before I sit in here again," Braxton grumbled.

"You may as well have some fun while you still can," Aralia said, unperturbed. "Once you find out what happened to Number Eight, you're holding up your end of our bargain."

Braxton gave her a sharp nod. The deal he'd made with Aralia hung over him like a storm cloud, following him everywhere and tinting everything the same murky haze.

Braxton slung the small cooler bag he'd brought over his shoulder and got out of Aralia's mut-spattered pickup truck. He skulked up the driveway, ignoring Aralia's, "Where's the fire, stud?" as she hurried to catch up.

Braxton hadn't wanted backup, but he wasn't about to start taking unnecessary risks now. If anything happened to him, there would be no one to help Kenzie.

"Just don't shoot anyone unless you have to," Braxton said in a low voice.

"No promises," Aralia retorted, whipping an arrow out of her quiver and fitting it to her bow. "Long drives make me cranky."

Braxton pressed the doorbell and moved to the side where he wouldn't be seen.

The door opened.

"Hello?" a voice called.

Braxton exchanged a look with Aralia. Then, he stepped forward.

The emaciated man standing in the doorway faltered back a step. He grabbed for the door, trying to slam it shut. Braxton wedged his foot in the open space and barged in.

"Are you the Bonecruncher?" Braxton asked.

Just the sound of those words made Braxton's insides clench.

The man's eyes, already protruding from his skull, widened in recognition. He reached into his jacket pocket.

"I'll take that as a yes," Aralia said. She tucked her bow under her arm. Handling her arrow like a ruler, she smacked the metal tip against the man's skeletal hand, making him curse and drop the knife he'd been holding. Aralia knelt and picked it up.

Braxton's stomach soured at the rotten cabbage smell that filled the entryway.

"You alone?" Aralia asked. She flicked her arrow so the tip rested against the man's Adam's apple.

"Y-yes," the man stammered.

It was strange that a man called *the Bonecruncher* would turn out to be such a wimp. Not that Braxton was complaining.

Aralia backed the Bonecruncher into the dimly-lit foyer. Braxton shut the door and locked it.

"Don't hurt me," the man begged. "I was bettin' on you to win Hex Kitchen."

Braxton didn't answer. He led the way into the kitchen and started flipping on lights.

"I would say that wasn't a very smart choice," Aralia said. "But seeing as you're trying to butter him up while I'm the one holding this arrow, I'd say you're not the sharpest knife in the drawer."

The kitchen was spacious and high-end, but that pervasive cabbage smell made it difficult to appreciate the design. Fortunately, Braxton didn't need to go near the refrigerator, which seemed to be the source of the horrendous stink. He unzipped his cooler bag and pulled out the single cookie he'd baked back at the cabin.

The smell of confectioners' sugar and butter rose into the air as Braxton carefully pulled the wax paper away from the half-moon cookie. The golden cookie was covered with vanilla icing on one side and chocolate on the other. It was brimming with magic.

Aralia hopped up on the counter, swinging her legs while she tossed the Bonecruncher's knife from hand to hand.

"Why are you's in my house?" the man asked. His New Jersey accent was an affront to Braxton's ears.

"I heard a rumor," Braxton said, "that the Gourmands are imprisoning culinary magicians. And that you're the one who—" He couldn't finish the thought.

Aralia made a sound of disgust. "Listen, loser," she told the Bonecruncher, since Braxton's tongue refused to form around the words. "We know you dispose of bodies for the Gourmands. Why don't you start talking about that?"

"I don't know what you's talkin' about," the man hedged.

He sucked in his hollow cheeks, which made his milky eyes bulge. He picked at a scab on his shaved head.

"Figured you'd say that," Braxton said. He broke the cookie in half and offered the white part to the Bonecruncher. "Eat it."

"Nah," the Bonecruncher said, eyeing the cookie warily. "Not hungry."

"Eat it, arsehole," Braxton ordered.

The Bonecruncher pulled in his lips and shook his head.

Aralia hopped off the counter. In two quick strides, she was in front of the Bonecruncher.

Braxton heard the Bonecruncher scream before his eyes could follow Aralia' quick movement.

A fresh, bloody X was slashed across the Bonecruncher's right cheek.

The next time Braxton held out the vanilla cookie, the Bonecruncher took it. He ate a small bite.

"The whole thing," Aralia said. "The calories will do you good."

Blood dripped onto the dusty wood floor as the Bonecruncher choked down his half of the cookie. Having little more appetite, Braxton ate the other half.

As chocolate frosting and golden crumbs melted on his tongue, Braxton closed his eyes.

An electric buzz went through him, and he felt a surge of heat through the air as he took hold of the magic. He could see the spiderweb-like threads as they twisted and writhed. A tingling sensation began at the back of his skull.

As soon as he felt the magic settle and congeal, Braxton opened his eyes.

The Bonecruncher was standing a few steps from him. The man was breathing hard as blood continued to dribble down his cheek.

"Here's what we need," Aralia told the Bonecruncher, her voice sounding far away as Braxton concentrated on the magic. "You need to think hard about this business you're mixed up in for the Gourmands. We want to know about every corpse you've disposed of for them."

"This recipe is illegal," the Bonecruncher protested, catching on to what Braxton was doing.

"So is murder," Braxton growled.

The Bonecruncher yelped. A new X appeared on his other cheek. This one looked deeper than the first.

"Okay," the Bonecruncher panted. "Okay!"

The room began to spin, and Braxton had to cling onto the counter to keep his balance. Fragments of conversation and strange smells zipped in and out of his consciousness. Then, all at once, the sounds and smells disappeared.

Braxton was no longer standing in the Bonecruncher's kitchen. He was staring down into a truck bed. The image was slightly blurry, and when Braxton looked at himself, he couldn't see his own body. That was how he knew his recipe was working. He was inside the Bonecruncher's memory.

"Easy now," the Bonecruncher was saying as he grasped one end of an enormous wooden crate. He grunted and heaved against the crate, finally managing to drag it to the edge of the truck bed. The crate hit the ground with a dull thud.

Braxton watched with impatience as the Bonecruncher dragged the crate across a cement floor to a steaming bathtub. The astringent smell rising up made it clear the tub was filled with more than water.

Even in his disembodied state, Braxton felt himself holding his breath as the Bonecruncher used a pry bar to open the top of the crate. He kicked the lid off.

Since Braxton was only inside a memory, not present in the moment, he couldn't make a sound as he stared down into the crate. He could only manage to let out a silent scream into the void of his own mind.

Two bodies were stretched out over the wooden slats. Braxton had little experience with corpses, but it didn't take a medical examiner to know there was something very wrong with these bodies…aside from the obvious fact of them being dead.

The two bodies were shriveled. It was like everything inside of them had been sucked out, and all that remained was the husk. Braxton couldn't even begin to guess at their ages or what they'd looked like before they became…this.

Their naked bodies were gray. They made a crinkling sound like old paper when the Bonecruncher reached in and clutched one of the corpses. He handled the body like it was close to weightless. It was a man—that much was clear from his anatomy. The only other notable feature was a skull-and-crossbones tattoo on his forehead.

There was an acidic sputter as the Bonecruncher unceremoniously dumped the corpse into the bathtub. If the magic had allowed it, Braxton probably would have looked away rather than watch as the toxic liquid ate right through the corpse.

The frothing liquid turned a dark shade of purple. It made a belching sound as it sucked the corpse down into its murky depths. What appeared to be a femur bone popped to the surface. It sizzled and hissed, and then burst apart into porous chunks of bone.

Less than a minute passed before the churning liquid quieted. All evidence of the corpse was gone.

The Bonecruncher muttered to himself as he went back to the crate for the second corpse. This one was female. Her skin was as gray and raisin-like as the first, except for her shock of orange hair. The color was clearly unnatural; the woman's hair roots were as gray as her skin.

The image dissolved, and Braxton was plunged back into a dizzying swirl of shapes and sounds.

"I've got you, stud." Aralia gripped his shoulders and leaned in to nibble his ear.

Braxton gasped and blinked as his surroundings came back into focus. The cabbage smell made his already-turbulent stomach roil. The Bonecruncher was slumped against the wall, looking as sick as Braxton felt.

"What the fuck?" Braxton croaked, when he finally found his voice. "What happened to those bodies?"

The Bonecruncher gave a weary shrug. "I don't ask questions. I just get rid of the bodies."

"Didn't it ever occur to you to wonder what the Gourmands were doing to those people to turn them into those…those…things?!"

Braxton was shouting, but he was too strung out to control himself. The image of those dried-out corpses would haunt him to his dying day.

"The Gourmands pay me not to wonder," the Bonecruncher said. "And besides, they're the Gourmands. If they're doin' it, then it's gotta be okay."

There wasn't enough time in the world to set this man on the path to morality, so Braxton wasn't going to try. Instead, he asked the only question that mattered.

"Have you—" He had to stop and swallow the bile that surged through him. "Have you seen a…body…with tattoos all over her arms?"

In the two seconds it took for the Bonecruncher to shake his head, Braxton lost a decade off his life.

"Are you sure?" he demanded. "She has a dragon tattoo here." Braxton traced the spot across his collarbone and over his shoulder.

"Haven't seen one like that yet," the Bonecruncher said.

Yet.

"Where do you go to pick up these bodies?" Braxton asked.

"I don't," the Bonecruncher replied. "They're brought to me in an unmarked truck. They open the back and I unload 'em myself. Then, the truck leaves. I've never seen their faces."

"Who's your contact, then?" Aralia asked. "And before you think about lying, just remember that I will happily separate your skin from your bones." She smiled.

The Bonecruncher lifted his hands up. "Restricted number. I don't even know his name. He calls me, and then twenty minutes later, the truck shows up."

Fucking useless.

"What else can you tell us?" Aralia asked. "And don't bore me by saying *nothing*. Since I had to waste gas and expand my carbon footprint to come here, you'd better make it worth my time."

The Bonecruncher's tongue darted out to moisten his chapped lips. "I did overhear somethin' the last time the bodies were dropped off. The guys were saying somethin' about how the bodies looked like that on account of the magical ingredients the Gourmands are cookin' up."

Braxton swore to himself. Maybe he'd have been better off going with Rick to steal those magical ingredients. That way, he would have had a chance at interrogating someone who actually had a clue. All he had now was a reminder that every second that passed could make him too late to save Kenzie.

Unless....

Rick had gone to Manhattan to steal those ingredients. Maybe Braxton could still make it in time.

He pulled out his phone. That was when he saw he had four missed calls from Rick and as many texts. The earliest text was from two hours ago. It read, *The job is going down. Where the hell are you?* The text was followed by, *Not funny, McKaid. Get your ass over here.* Then, *Hope you're happy. They fuckin got away.*

As Braxton read over the most recent text, his blood ran cold.

I warned you what would happen if you crossed me.

"What's the matter, stud?" Aralia asked.

Braxton didn't answer. He was already running back to the truck.

CHAPTER 10

SOFIA

Mum smiled at Sofia over the rim of her teacup. They were sitting in a charming little tea house, with crocheted window dressings and hand-painted china. She and Mum had driven to this ritzy Manhattan suburb in the hopes of getting an introduction to the Reaper.

Luis, the tea house's owner, had a connection to the Reaper. Sofia knew this because Luis had worked for a McKaid restaurant years back, and he'd once let slip that his aunt was friends with Qiang Lee, the Reaper.

Once Sofia remembered that little detail, all it had taken was a phone call and a reminder that Luis owed his success to Sofia's family. Sort of.

After Luis's family left Australia, Mum had called in some favors to get him a pastry chef job in an up-and-coming New York restaurant. And that job set him on the path to opening his own tea house.

Luis had been more than a little hesitant to make the introduction, since apparently his aunt was almost as reclusive as Qiang Lee. Fortunately, Sofia wasn't above reminding Luis that he wouldn't be where he was today without her family.

Most halfway-decent people preferred to reciprocate generosity than feel indebted.

So, here they were. It was after hours, and Luis was supplying Sofia and Mum with a steady stream of treats while they waited for his aunt.

"I have to say," Mum said, sipping from her delicate tea cup, "this is the best afternoon I've had in ages." She squeezed Sofia's knee under the table.

"Me too," Sofia agreed.

"Have you heard from your brother?" Mum asked.

"Mhm." Sofia swallowed a bite of scone. "He's still with the Bonecruncher. I told him to meet us here when he's finished."

Sofia wrinkled her nose and put her scone back on its plate. It was difficult to maintain an appetite when saying words like *Bonecruncher*.

Mum must have shared the sentiment, because she said, "Let's talk about something more pleasant."

"Like?"

Mum gave her a knowing smirk. "Like how cute Graham is."

"*Mum*," Sofia groaned.

"Don't tell me you haven't noticed." Mum tried to hide her smile behind her teacup. "I've seen the way he looks at you." One of her eyebrows rose. "And the way you look at him, for that matter."

Was it hot in here? Luis should get the air conditioner checked out….

"Come on, admit it," Mum nudged. "You like him."

"I don't even know him." Sofia stuffed the rest of her scone into her mouth.

"He seems sweet," Mum insisted. "Not like those stuffy, boring blokes you usually go for."

"They aren't boring," Sofia muttered.

They totally were. It was why their faces and names blurred together until they were more or less indistinguishable.

"You deserve someone who can see past how gorgeous you are," Mum continued.

"Can we not talk about this?" Sofia pleaded.

"And someone who doesn't have his head up his own arse."

"*Mum!*"

"What?" Mum spooned sugar in her tea. "Darling, if you aren't embarrassed to be in public with me, then I haven't done my full duty as a parent."

Sofia, who had been mid-sip of tea, laughed. Which turned into a snuffling snort. Which made Mum start to giggle.

In seconds, the two of them had devolved into unrestrained guffaws. It was fortunate they were the only ones in the place, because otherwise their behavior would get them kicked to the curb.

"I can't bring you anywhere," Sofia managed, wiping away hysterical tears.

Luis appeared at that moment with fresh pots of tea and a worried expression on his face. No doubt, that was thanks to the walrus-like sounds she and Mum were making.

"Don't mind us," Mum said. She swept her hand at the table. "I can't tell you how much we needed this. Thank you."

Something like guilt flashed across Luis's face, but it was gone so quickly Sofia thought she'd imagined it.

"Your aunt isn't standing us up, is she?" Sofia asked.

"What? No. Of course, not." Luis was already retreating toward the kitchen.

"Luis," Sofia prompted, but he had disappeared from view.

"It's okay," Mum said, frowning a little as she tidied their plates on the table. "Even if Luis's aunt can't help, I have an idea about where we can find the Reaper."

"Seriously? Why didn't you say anything earlier?"

"I'm not certain," Mum hedged. "But I was doing some research on my laptop earlier, and I found some obscure reference in a wildlife magazine that made me think—"

A phone at the host stand began to ring. Luis came flying out of the kitchen. He didn't look in their direction as he raced over to answer it.

Sofia massaged her chest as the beginnings of indigestion burned through her esophagus.

Luis didn't say a word as he listened to whoever was on the other line. As Sofia watched him, she saw his face drain of color. A few seconds later, he carefully placed the phone back in its cradle.

"Everything alright?" Sofia prodded.

He still wouldn't look at them. He was busy winding the phone cord around and around his index finger.

"I—" Luis began, and then stopped.

"What's wrong?" Mum asked, her tone far more inviting than Sofia's had been. "Is there anything we can do to help?"

"I'm sorry," Luis blurted.

Sofia wasn't sure if he was apologizing to them, or the phone cord that he was in the process of strangling. She couldn't find her voice to ask Luis what his poor phone had ever done to deserve such treatment. Her creeping sense of wrongness was getting stronger.

"I'm sorry," Luis said again. "I had to. I didn't have a choice. You don't understand how things work. He could shut my business down, and—"

Luis continued to babble, but Sofia's brain got stuck on a single word. *He.*

There was only one man Sofia could think of who had the power—and the inclination—to destroy someone's business just because they helped a McKaid.

Veneziano Santiori.

"We need to go." Sofia leapt up from her chair. Her elbow knocked into a pot of tea, which wobbled precariously before falling onto its side. Maroon liquid flooded out of the spout and soaked into the white lace tablecloth.

"Sofia," Mum gasped, hurrying to right the pot before there was any further damage.

"Leave it," Sofia ordered, her voice unsteady.

Luis was still just standing at the host stand. He was staring at the phone, mouthing *I'm sorry.*

As Sofia grabbed her phone off the table, she saw a dozen missed calls and texts from Braxton.

"Shit," she whispered, not even needing to read them to know what the messages would say.

"Mum, come on," she urged, taking her mother's arm and dragging her to the front of the tea house.

Sofia didn't bother with threats or recrimination. She'd deliver those to Luis after, when she and Mum were back at the cabin. For now, they just had to get out of here.

Sofia shoved open the door, and the two of them burst into the late-afternoon sun.

Their truck was the only one in the lot. If they could just get to it—

A car horn blared. Aralia's muddy, oversized truck appeared at the other end of the block. Sofia could see Aralia behind the wheel. Braxton sat next to her with his head out the window. He shouted something, but the truck was too far away and the wind stole his words.

Mum fumbled in her pocket for the car keys.

"Go back inside!"

Aralia's truck was close enough now that her and Braxton's combined shouting was audible.

Sofia turned, but movement at the other end of the street caught her attention. A black SUV was hurtling down the middle of the road.

There was no shoulder, which left Aralia with nowhere to go. The SUV sped up. It was coming straight for Aralia's truck.

"Braxton!" Sofia screamed.

Aralia jerked the wheel an instant before the two vehicles collided.

Her truck hopped the curb and bounced over someone's lawn. They were heading straight for a towering oak tree.

Mum was gripping Sofia's arm hard enough to cut off her circulation, but Sofia barely noticed. Her heart was in her throat.

Grass and dirt sprayed up around Aralia's truck as it stopped centimeters from the tree.

Adrenaline surged through Sofia. Her legs were quivering.

The SUV halted in the middle of the street, directly opposite from the tea house. One of the passenger windows lowered. The long barrel of a gun appeared.

"Get down!" someone shouted.

There was a deafening *bang*. Wetness sprayed across Sofia's face.

Her ears were ringing. She was distantly aware of the SUV turning around and speeding away.

Dazed, Sofia looked down at herself.

She was covered in blood.

Strange. She didn't feel any pain. Maybe she was in shock….

Mum released Sofia's arm.

No. "No!"

A howl tore from Sofia. She grabbed her mother's shirt before Mum fell and cracked her skull on the pavement. Clumsily, both of them sank onto the ground.

There was so much blood. It gushed out of Mum's chest and coated Sofia's hands.

"Come on," she begged. Mum had to be okay. Sofia wouldn't let her *not* be okay.

"Mum. Come on!"

Sofia pressed one hand against the wound, trying to slow the blood that was slipping between her fingers. The other fumbled at Mum's wrist, frantically searching for a pulse.

She wasn't dead. She couldn't be.

"I won't let you!" Sofia cried, the words tearing out of her. "Do you hear me?"

Braxton and Aralia appeared beside her. Sofia had no memory of them arriving.

Braxton was kneeling on Mum's other side. His mouth was moving…his lips saying the same word over and over. *Mum.*

"Are you hit?" Aralia asked, giving Sofia a little shake when she didn't answer.

It was only when Braxton's wild, grief-stricken eyes met hers, that she forced herself to shake her head.

"Braxton," Aralia said. "Your phone."

For several seconds, he and Sofia just stared at each other. Mum lay between them. A trickle of blood was still oozing from her chest.

Sofia couldn't breathe. She didn't think she'd ever breathe again.

Aralia shoved Braxton's phone in his face so he had no choice but to look at it.

Sofia couldn't imagine anything terrible enough to put that look on his face when they were kneeling before Mum's lifeless body. So, she snatched the phone from his unresisting grip. She stared at the screen.

There was an open text from Rick.

Disobey me again, the message said, *and Sofia is next.*

CHAPTER 11

KENZIE

When the door to Kenzie's little cell opened, she braced herself. She was expecting the evil nurse who came in periodically to change her bandages. It wasn't. A heavyset Latina woman who looked to be about Kenzie's age was shoved into the room hard enough that she went sprawling onto the empty cot opposite Kenzie's.

"Yeah, yeah," the woman muttered under her breath. "Keep tossin' me around. See what happens when the tables are turned."

There was a heavy click as the door was locked from the outside. Kenzie sat up in her cot and waited to see whether this woman was going to be trouble. Kenzie held out her arms so her tattoos were on full display as she tried to give off tough-girl vibes.

Rawr.

The woman wasn't paying attention to Kenzie, though. She was busy unloading various food items she'd hidden under her scrubs. A packet of salted peanuts, an apple, two chocolate bars, and an entire thermos tumbled onto the cot.

"Good haul, good haul," the woman muttered to herself.

Her black hair was cut in a short bob that framed her round face. Her eyebrows were caterpillar-thick and flirted dangerously into unibrow territory. Puckered scars stood out against the bronze skin on her arms and neck. From the careful way she was moving, it was obvious there were more injuries under her clothes. She wore the bullshit one-size-fits-all scrubs Kenzie and the rest of the competitors wore outside the arena.

The cot creaked beneath the woman as she got to her feet and raised the mattress, revealing a treasure trove of hidden food.

"Holy shit," Kenzie said.

"*Shii-iit!*" the woman exclaimed. "You scared the livin' daylights outta me, girl."

"Sorry." Kenzie scooted back on her own cot. "I didn't mean to scare you. I just—that's a lot of food."

The woman huffed. "If you tell Nurse Ratched or anyone else, I'll have to kill you." She grinned and waggled her thick eyebrows.

"I uh, won't. Of course," Kenzie babbled. "Wait. Did you say Nurse Ratched?"

The woman's grin went all the way to her warm brown eyes. "Yeah. You know, like from *One Flew Over the Cuckoo's Nest.*"

"Is that really the nurse's name?" Kenzie asked. What were the odds?

"Nah. I think it's Lynn. But we've gotta take our thrills where we can get 'em. Ya know?"

"True that," Kenzie said with a little laugh. She got up and held out her hand. "I'm Kenzie."

"Kenzie Brookerton," the woman said. "From Hex Kitchen."

Ashner, Kenzie internally corrected, but she didn't say anything. There was no point, and she didn't want to get off on the wrong foot with the first friendly face she'd encountered in this place.

"I'm Cookie." The woman shook Kenzie's hand. Her grip was so firm, Kenzie had to hold back a wince.

Cookie nabbed a bag of chips that had popped under the weight of her mattress. She dumped a handful of crumbs onto her palm and shoved them in her mouth. She passed Kenzie the bag.

"How did you manage this?" Kenzie asked, swallowing a mouthful of salt and vinegar chip crumbles.

It was the first non-magic-laced food she'd eaten in this place. Kenzie didn't think she'd ever tasted anything more delicious.

"Sticky fingers," Cookie replied, wiggling her digits before reaching back under her mattress. Her hand emerged with two pears that looked a little worse for wear and the thermos. Cookie tossed one of the pears to Kenzie, which Kenzie fumbled and barely managed to rescue before it hit the floor. Cookie unscrewed the thermos cap, filling the room with a glorious scent.

"Coffee?" Cookie offered up the thermos.

"Marry me," Kenzie said.

Cookie laughed.

For a few minutes, they ate Cookie's pilfered snacks and drank her coffee in comfortable silence.

Kenzie *ahemed*. There wasn't a delicate way to broach the subject, so she just asked, "Were you kidnapped and forced to come here, too?"

Cookie licked her fingers and dabbed them into the bottom of an empty pretzel bag. "That's how it is for all of us, honey. If it got out that there was gonna be a change in leadership, it would make the Gourmands look weak." She gave Kenzie a wry look. "I think you and me are the only competitors who don't want to be here. It's an honor, dears." She parroted those last words in a perfect imitation of Polly Berrywhite.

Kenzie couldn't help but laugh. Her light mood faded as images of Brute and Scarlet filled her vision.

"I killed two people," she said. "And I don't even want anything to do with the Gourmands."

Cookie leaned back against the wall. "When I first came here, I thought maybe I'd win, and then I could make the Gourmands less—"

"—corrupt?" Kenzie supplied. "Murderous?"

Cookie chuckled. "Yeah. That."

"What changed?" Kenzie asked.

"I saw what I was up against." Cookie licked more salt off her fingers. "Besides, I'm guessin' they already worked out who's gonna win."

"You think it's fixed?" Kenzie squeaked.

She had no idea why that possibility should shock her. It wasn't like the Gourmands had shown themselves to be the most ethical organization on the planet.

"The Gourmands got their own agenda," Cookie said. "And they don't care whether their next leader is good or bad. They only care about keepin' power and makin' sure culinary magic stays secret."

"I don't give a shit about any of that," Kenzie said. "I just want to get out of here."

"Hmm." Cookie crossed her legs, wincing from whatever injuries she'd received from being forced to cook to the death. "You know where *here* is?"

"Not a clue," Kenzie admitted. "You?"

"I think we're underground." Cookie shrugged. "Just a feelin', though. And since most of the contestants are American, we're probably somewhere in the US. Aside from that? Your guess is as good as mine."

Kenzie blew out a breath, making her bangs flutter across her forehead. That was it, then. She was either going to kill her way to the top of an organization she didn't want to touch with a ten-mile pole, or she was going to die in the arena. She'd never see Braxton or her dad again.

"Cheer up, girl." Cookie offered Kenzie the rest of the coffee.

It was lukewarm and grainy, but Kenzie had never passed up coffee in her life. She wasn't about to start now.

"I can't go back in that arena," Kenzie said.

The words were out before her brain had even processed them, but she felt their truth in her bones.

"'Course you're not," Cookie said.

Kenzie let out a humorless laugh. "Right. I'll just tell Nurse Ratched that I need a few days off. I'm sure she'll understand."

"Don't you fret," Cookie said. "You've only got to hang on a little longer, 'cause I've got a plan. You and me? We're escapin'."

Kenzie's pulse went into overdrive. "Escaping?"

Cookie's almost-unibrow did a little dance on her forehead. "Girl, stick with me. I've got a plan."

"Does it involve kicking Nurse Ratched's ass?" Kenzie asked.

"*Hell* yeah."

CHAPTER 12

SOFIA

Aralia had cooked something that preserved Mum's body so they could get her back to the cabin. Later that night, Sofia and Braxton buried Mum on a little hill overlooking the lake. Sofia didn't have any illusions about spirits or souls or any of that nonsense, but it had felt right.

Who was she kidding? Nothing about this was right.

At least she was alone now, which meant there was no one to hear the awful little whimpers she couldn't contain.

Sofia hadn't cried when she watched Braxton dig the grave. She'd swallowed down her tears when Braxton lifted Mum's body and carefully laid her to rest. She hadn't made so much as a peep as the two of them sat next to the grave and watched the sun sink behind the horizon.

Now, curled up on the couch by the fire, Sofia couldn't contain the salty drops that insisted on blurring her vision.

"Sofia?"

She jumped. Graham, his features creased with concern, hunched his shoulders and took a step back.

"I didn't mean to startle you."

Sofia wiped her sleeve across her eyes, which turned out to be a terrible idea. The shirt was Aralia's and made out of some animal hide that Sofia was pretty sure she was allergic to, because her eyes began to simultaneously burn and itch.

"I'm fine," Sofia said.

If the tears hadn't been enough of a clue, the brokenness in her voice would have told Graham everything he needed to know. She was the furthest thing from fine.

"Can I—" Graham began.

He came into the room, moving slowly enough that she could tell him to leave. Maybe if she was less exhausted and heartsick, she would have.

Graham carefully sat on the couch beside her. He wrapped a tentative arm around her shoulders. He held her loosely, giving her a chance to pull away.

Sofia meant to do just that, but his touch felt good. He was sturdy and warm and everything she wasn't in that moment. Almost without her permission, her body moved so she was pressed closer to him. He smelled like laundry soap and fresh pine.

Graham pulled her tighter against him. Sofia went willingly, tucking herself against his side as the tears she was powerless to stop leaked down her cheeks.

"I'm sorry," Graham said in his smoky rumble of a voice. "I wish I'd been there. Maybe, then—"

"It's not your responsibility to be my bodyguard," Sofia whispered.

Graham reached over to brush the tears from her cheeks. For some reason, his kindness only made her cry harder.

Graham didn't push her to say anything more. He just held her against his beating heart and murmured soft words against her hair.

Sofia had no idea how long they stayed like that. All she knew was that Graham's shirt was soaked through from her tears, and her whole body felt empty and raw.

She sat up, murmuring something about a shower. Instead of letting her go, Graham smoothed her hair back from her tearstained face. He regarded her with his steady, whiskey-rimmed gaze. She must look like hell.

"This isn't your fault," he said. "You know that, right?"

Logically, she did. She'd never shared Braxton's hero complex. And yet, she couldn't ignore the inescapable fact that Mum was dead because Sofia hadn't been able to save her. She'd been powerless to stop Santiori's men.

Such a shame you're not a culinary magician.

Maybe if she was, Sofia would have been able to do something.

"It's not your fault, Sofia," Graham said again.

Sofia hated the sympathy in Graham's voice and the gentle way he held her, like he was afraid she might break.

"I'm not usually like this," she said, feeling the need to explain herself.

Graham brushed more tears from her cheeks.

"Wait here," he told her.

He gently untangled their limbs. He said nothing about his shirt, which was covered in wet splotches from her tears. He went over to Kiwi's cage, carefully plucked the sleeping chameleon from his branch, and brought him over to Sofia.

"He'll keep you company for a few minutes," Graham said.

Like if she was left alone for two seconds, she'd fall apart again. Maybe she would.

Kiwi, seeming thoroughly unimpressed at being awakened from his nap, hooked his tiny claws into her sleeve. He transformed to the tan-and-white color of Sofia's shirt as he clung to her.

Sofia was oddly comforted by the little creature. He was rough and aloof and completely consumed with his own agenda. A little like her.

Graham returned a few minutes later, holding a plate in one hand and a glass jug full of clear liquid in the other.

"What's this?" Sofia asked.

He passed her the jug, which was heavy enough that she had to grip it with both hands to keep from dropping it.

"Moonshine."

Sofia snorted. "Yeah, I'll pass." The last thing she needed to add to her already-unstable emotions was alcohol.

"It's magical," Graham said, taking it from her and swigging right from the jug. He licked his lips and hummed in approval. The sound was a low rumble that sent an inexplicable shiver down Sofia's spine.

He gave her a sheepish shrug. "It's the only thing I can make with culinary magic."

"I didn't realize you were a culinary magician," Sofia said.

In all her time at the cabin, she hadn't once seen Graham cook anything. In Sofia's extensive experience, culinary magicians couldn't help but spend hour upon hour creating new recipes.

"I'm not," Graham replied. "Well, I mean, I am. Just a very, very weak one."

There was something…bitterness, maybe?…in the way he said that.

"I prefer growing and harvesting the food to cooking it," Graham explained. "I've always felt more at home in the garden than in a kitchen."

Probably to ward off any follow-up questions, he held out the jug to her. "Try some. Seriously. It's fire."

Sofia managed a little laugh. "And here I was thinking you were humble."

Graham ducked his head. He might have been blushing, but with his dark skin and the weak firelight, it was difficult to tell. Sofia felt her lips quiver into something like a smile. "What does it do?" she asked.

"It alters dreams. Whenever Aralia drinks it, she dreams about the whole world going back to caveman living." Graham chuckled and shook his head.

Sofia noticed he had a smattering of freckles across the bridge of his nose and apples of his cheeks. She had to resist a bizarre impulse to reach up and trace them with her fingertips.

"And you?" Sofia asked, taking the jug from Graham's outstretched hand. "What does the moonshine do to your dreams?"

"It keeps me from dreaming at all," he replied.

Something in the way he said that made it clear he preferred it that way. "Why?" she asked.

Graham turned the full weight of his attention on her. Sofia squirmed, hating the way he seemed to see past her every defense without saying a single word.

"You don't have to tell me," she said quickly. This conversation was already too personal.

Kiwi gave Sofia a grumpy look as she adjusted him. She lifted the jug of moonshine and took a sip.

She'd been prepared for a scent like turpentine and a harsh burn as the liquid curdled her insides. Instead, it had the exact opposite effect.

The smokiness, combined with a hint of earthy peat, was familiar. She didn't know how it was possible, but the moonshine tasted exactly like the single-malt scotch her father had kept locked away and served during special occasions. The moonshine even left the same refreshing aftertaste…or *finish*, as her father would have said.

On her fifteenth birthday, Aidan and Braxton had filched a bottle using the key their father thought he'd so cleverly stowed *underneath the liquor cabinet*. The three of them had climbed onto the roof to drink the pilfered liquor together.

As she sipped the moonshine, Sofia could almost hear Aidan's voice. She remembered how she'd felt that night. The three of them had been balanced precariously on the pitched roof, but with her brothers sitting on either side of her, Sofia had felt safe. She'd felt like she belonged.

She took another sip before passing the jug back to Graham.

"What does this taste like to you?" she asked.

He took a swig, swirled it around his mouth, and swallowed.

"Mango wheat beer," he said. A small smile made his eyes crinkle at the edges. It made the light dusting of freckles on his cheeks stand out, which in turn made Sofia's stomach flip-flop.

"I went through a brief brewing phase the first year we lived here," Graham said. "Every kind of beer I made was undrinkable…except for the mango wheat. Aralia got so wasted she went streaking through the woods." He chuckled softly. "I found her the next morning curled up in a tree with some squirrels trying to nest in her hair."

Sofia laughed.

She held her hand out for the jug, but instead of passing it to her, Graham reached for the plate he'd brought in earlier and set on the table. There were two thick slabs of bread, slathered in butter and drizzled with honey. Translucent salt crystals were sprinkled over the top and gleamed in the firelight.

"Thanks, but I'm not hungry," Sofia said.

She'd buried her mother today. Sofia might never have an appetite again.

"You haven't eaten all day," Graham pointed out.

Sofia realized, with no small amount of irritation, that he was right. She returned Kiwi to his habitat with his own snack of mealworms and a couple of crickets before settling back on the couch.

"It's not poison," Graham said, nudging the plate closer to her.

What a loaded word, Sofia thought.

Because she really didn't want to think about Kenzie or Aidan, Sofia picked up a slice of bread and took a bite.

"Ohmygod," she moaned, and then hurriedly covered her mouth to keep from showing off the chewed-up food within. She laughed a little at herself before taking another big bite.

Sofia was about to wash the bread down with a sip of moonshine, but Graham shook his head.

"Finish the bread, and then you can drink more," he told her.

"You're starting to sound like my brother," Sofia groused.

Graham's expression darkened. "I'd rather you not put me in the same category as your brother."

Speaking of....

"Braxton doesn't like you," she informed Graham.

She'd never been one to mince words.

Graham lifted a shoulder. "Maybe he's judging me based on an incomplete story."

Sofia raised an eyebrow at him. "And what story would that be?"

Graham took another long swig from the jug. "It isn't mine to tell," he said quietly.

Sofia swallowed another bite of her bread, this time savoring the creamy butter that she'd watched Aralia hand-churn the day before. The salt crystals added a pleasant crunch to all the soft honeyed sweetness. Everything was warm and oozy and comforting.

After a lifetime of being surrounded by gourmets, Sofia was used to five-course meals and exotic ingredients. In comparison, this food was simple and inelegant and...perfect. She continued to gobble up the bread, even once Graham passed back the moonshine.

After Aidan died, Sofia had lost all interest in food. Mum had started whispering the word *anorexia*, and then eating disorder summer camp brochures had shown up in the mail.

As if Sofia would have ever sat around a campfire and talked about her feelings. *As. If.*

Sofia hadn't been able to bring herself to tell her parents the truth: that every time she put a bite of food in her mouth, she heard the sound of Aidan choking. She saw his face turn from red to purple to blue as foam spilled out from his lips. She felt him jerking and convulsing in her arms as she failed to save him.

Food had taken her brother away from her.

Well, that wasn't precisely true. Kenzie Ashner had taken her brother away. And that was a whole separate issue.

"I admire you," Graham said, breaking into her morose thoughts.

"Because?" Sofia couldn't think of a single thing she'd done recently that was admirable.

He sipped his moonshine, considering his words. "I can imagine that other people in your position—being related to one of the most talented culinary magicians in the world, I mean—"

Two of the most talented culinary magicians in the world, she thought, but didn't say out loud. She was still too fresh off burying her mother to mention Aidan's name.

"—and yet, you aren't resentful like…some people might be in your position. You've found your own way in the world of culinary magic without trying to be something you're not."

Such a shame you're not a culinary magician.

Mr. Dunlow had uttered those words so thoughtlessly, but Sofia couldn't get them out of her mind. Especially now.

She picked some crumbs off her now-empty plate. "Sometimes I think all the work I put into our restaurants was more about trying to prove I belonged than helping my family."

Sofia froze, realizing what she'd just said.

She'd never admitted that to anyone before. She wasn't even sure she'd acknowledged it herself.

"From everything I've seen," Graham said, "I imagine those restaurants succeeded *because* of you."

That was more generous than she deserved. Sofia was about to tell him that, but then Graham smiled at her. There was a tenderness in his expression that sent her off-kilter. He leaned closer.

Sofia thought he was going to kiss her, but instead, he touched her lower lip. A golden drop of honey balanced on the tip of his finger.

Oddly breathless, Sofia held his gaze as he sucked the drop into his mouth.

Graham made a contented *Mmm* sound that sent Sofia right to the edge…of desire or madness…she wasn't entirely sure.

Graham shifted, and something balanced on the arm of the couch clattered to the floor.

Mum's laptop. Sofia had taken it out of the truck and brought it into the house, but she hadn't been able to look at it since.

The screen blinked, waking up and displaying the last web page Mum had been viewing before they went into the tea shop.

Sofia found herself looking at a map of Acadia National Park.

"Sofia?" Graham asked. "What is it?"

"A solution," she murmured.

She'd thought Luis's betrayal had been the end of her fateful search for Qiang Lee. But Mum had left her with one final gift.

Sofia was going to find the Reaper. And while she was at it, she was going to take everything from the Santioris.

"Sofia?" Graham prompted.

"Tomorrow, I'm going to take a drive up to Maine," Sofia said. "I need to see a man about some magic ingredients."

CHAPTER 13

BRAXTON

Burying their mother had been a nightmare come to life. Braxton had stayed beside his mum's grave for hours, reliving all the pain and helplessness of Aidan's death.

He waited until an ungodly hour to slink back into the cabin. He'd found Sofia asleep on the couch, so he'd carried her up to her bedroom. He was ashamed of how much relief he felt that she hadn't woken.

He wasn't ready to face her.

Braxton should have been there to protect his mum and sister. Instead, he'd painted a target on their backs.

Mum was dead because Braxton had blown off Rick's heist. And all Braxton had learned from the Bonecruncher was that it was impossible to track down the Gourmands. The only way to encounter them was if they came for you.

That was why he was in the kitchen at four in the morning, making paella.

"Christ, Aid," Braxton groaned. "I've made such a goddamn mess of everything."

It should have been me instead of Aidan.

Braxton added a pinch of saffron threads to his paella. He couldn't help but smile a little as he recollected his and Kenzie's first disastrous round during Hex Kitchen. Saffron had been their mystery ingredient, but because

Kenzie had still been shaky with her magic, they'd barely gotten anything on the plate.

Braxton stirred another heaping spoonful of smoked paprika into the golden rice and tasted. The spiciness of the chorizo blended into the fragrant rice. There was nothing subtle about the flavors in this dish.

It would pair perfectly with the magic he was envisioning.

Kiwi, who was perched on a rock in his habitat, was observing Braxton's motions with mild boredom. His bulbous eyes rolled around in his head as he took everything in.

Where is your owner? Braxton thought. *What are they doing to her?*

Braxton added the spring-green peas he'd blanched and shocked in a bowl of ice water. He was tucking shrimp into the skillet when he heard footsteps.

Aralia, her bow slung over her back and her face smeared with dirt, sauntered into the kitchen. She bumped her hip against his.

"Whatcha cookin', stud?"

Aralia fiddled with her mini-dress, which was made out of strips of leather that had been sewn together. For some inexplicable reason, there seemed to be a squirrel tail dangling from her braided rope belt.

"Making paella," Braxton replied.

Aralia bent down until her face was centimeters away from his pan.

"If it were up to me," she said, picking up a coral-pink shrimp from the dish and inspecting it, "the only ingredients we'd have here would be ones we hunted or foraged ourselves. Graham's the one who insists we get all this other stuff." She gave the shrimp a scornful look before tossing it back into the pan, but her voice was fond.

"I'll try to remember to thank him later then," Braxton said stiffly.

"You can thank him by getting a move on with our bargain," Aralia replied, crossing her arms and giving him an arch look.

I can't, he wanted to say. *Because then Sofia will truly be alone.*

He couldn't say that, though. He'd made a deal with Aralia, and he would see it through. As soon as he found Kenzie.

Braxton finished off his dish and set the flame to simmer. He cleared his throat and waited for Aralia to take the hint that he wanted privacy.

It didn't work.

"Go on, then," she said, giving his arse a patronizing smack. "Don't let me interrupt."

Braxton grumbled under his breath. He tried to block out Aralia's looming presence. He didn't let himself think about what was going to happen to him after he served this dish. He forced himself to concentrate only on the magic.

Braxton felt the tingle of hot and smoky spices on his tongue. He saw the vibrant colors of the dish: pink shrimp, golden rice, green peas.

As Braxton wove threads of magic through the dish, he realized it wasn't enough. If his plan to get the Gourmands' attention was going to work, then he needed more. More drama, more sensation…just *more*.

His mind conjured images of the night he'd spent with Kenzie. He felt her soft skin beneath his fingertips. Heard her moans and sighs.

The magic coiled and thickened. Still, Braxton pushed for more. If this didn't attract the Gourmands' notice, then nothing would.

"Enough."

Aralia's voice penetrated his magic fog.

"Braxton, stop! You're pushing your magic too hard."

He gripped the counter as the room spun. He felt Aralia holding him up, but his vision was wavering too much for him to see more than her blurry shape.

"Dumbass," she muttered as she helped him into a chair. "Were you trying to kill yourself?"

"No." Braxton mopped his sweaty brow with his sleeve. "I just needed to make the recipe powerful." His voice was thin, and his mouth felt like it was stuffed full of cotton.

Aralia's boots clicked across the wood floor. A few seconds later, she was back and pressing a wet towel to his face. The damp cloth felt amazing against his fevered skin.

"Well," Aralia said. "Might as well taste what the famous Braxton McKaid was about to kill himself making." She sounded a little too chipper at the mention of Braxton's potential death.

"Don't eat that," he warned her.

"Why?" Aralia sniffed the air over the pan. "If it was poison, I'd be able to tell." She snatched the mixing spoon and shoveled a huge bite of paella into her mouth.

"Damnit, Aralia," Braxton growled. "Spit that out before you get any of the magic."

"This is really good," Aralia said, displaying a mouthful of half-chewed paella. She swallowed and licked her lips. She was about to dip the spoon into the pan a second time when her pupils dilated.

Braxton caught the spoon as it fell from her hand. Aralia staggered back against the wall.

"Oh." Her eyes rolled back in her head. "*Oh*. God. Yes!"

Braxton rubbed his aching neck and kept his gaze fixedly pinned on Kiwi. The chameleon turned himself the same sandy-brown color of his rock. Except for his eyes, the chameleon was barely visible.

Braxton wished he had the ability to disappear right about now.

Aralia was writhing against the wall and moaning. She arched her back and slid her hands down her breasts. When her hand moved between her legs, Braxton cursed.

The recipe was working as intended…but he hadn't considered how uncomfortable it would be to watch someone he had no romantic interest in have a spontaneous orgasm from his food.

"So good!" Aralia moaned. "Braxton! Braxton!"

Aw, hell.

"Keep your voice down," he hissed. "You'll wake Sofia."

Aralia didn't even seem to hear him.

Braxton closed his eyes and tried to block out the sound of Aralia's moans.

"Please," Aralia whimpered. "Too good. Can't…take it…anymore."

"Un-fucking-believable," Braxton muttered as he hurriedly tried to at least reduce the magic's potency.

Aralia continued to moan and call out his name. Braxton kept the table between them, lest she try to touch him.

The last traces of magic slipped away. Aralia collapsed on the floor.

Braxton sighed up at the ceiling. "I told you not to eat it."

Aralia, still breathing heavily, blinked at him through glassy eyes.

"Holy shit," she panted. "Talk about a food-gasm. Was this supposed to be some kind of welcome home present for your girlfriend?"

In spite of his annoyance and the gravity of the situation, Braxton couldn't help a small chuckle. "I don't need culinary magic to do that to Kenzie."

Aralia let out a wheezy laugh. "Let me get this straight. Your plan is to pleasure the Gourmands until they give Number Eight back to you?"

Braxton shook his head. "I'm going to go somewhere crowded and keep serving this up until the Gourmands take notice and come for me."

Some focus returned to Aralia's gaze at that. "They'll kill you for such a public display."

"Not if I can help it," he said. "I just need to figure out where they're keeping Kenzie."

"You're no good to me dead, stud," Aralia informed him.

"I'm not going to die," he said.

Probably. Maybe.

Aralia *hmmed.* She sauntered over to Kiwi's habitat and opened it. She reached in, allowing the chameleon to slowly climb up her arm.

"Aralia," he said, forcing himself up from the table.

"Oh, relax," she said, rolling her eyes. "His skin is too tough. It would take hours of slow cooking to make him even halfway edible."

For several seconds, they watched Kiwi make his leisurely way up to the top of Aralia's head. The chameleon crouched down in her blonde braids and fell asleep.

"I have to find her," Braxton said quietly.

"You sure your whole martyrdom plan is about Number Eight, and not just you punishing yourself because you fucked over your family?" Aralia asked.

He gave her a scathing look. "Thanks for the reminder."

Aralia shrugged. "I just call it like I see it." She tapped the skin beneath Braxton's eyes, which were probably shadowed. "Seems to me like you're giving up."

"I'm not giving up!" Braxton ran his fingers through his sweat-tangled hair. "I'm just trying not to fail everyone who's depending on me."

And I refuse to be Rick's puppet anymore.

Aralia opened her mouth, but before she could speak, a tremendous pounding came at the cabin's front door.

Braxton's first thought was *Rick.* Somehow, he'd tracked them down.

Braxton seized a rolling pin off the counter and gripped it like a baseball bat. Aralia yanked up her dress and pulled two knives out of sheaths strapped to her upper thigh.

Well, then.

Aralia signaled to him so they approached the door without putting themselves in view of the window.

"Braxton McKaid!" an authoritative female voice called from the other side of the door. It was familiar, but Braxton couldn't immediately place it. "Open up. I know you're in there!"

Aralia cocked her head at him.

"Who are you?" Braxton called, figuring there was no point in pretending no one was home.

"Did you leave your brain behind when you ran away from Hex Kitchen, or did you never have one to start with?"

Braxton's mouth fell open, just as the sound of fiddling came at the deadbolt.

"If you idiots can't figure out how to move your feet, I'll just let myself in," the woman muttered.

Aralia reached for the lock. Before she could unbolt it, the door flew open. Chef Elyannah Levy, the Hex Kitchen judge who had repeatedly berated Braxton's cooking, strode into the cabin like she owned the place.

CHAPTER 14

KENZIE

I have demands!" Kenzie shouted, banging on her room's metal door for emphasis. "I want my roommate to be my next opponent in the arena. Her feet smell, and she snores. If I win, I get my room back to myself!" She thumped on the door again.

"And this skinny little bi-atch talks to much!" Cookie yelled, clearly not wanting Kenzie to feel left out in the insult department.

Kenzie stuck her tongue out at her roommate. Cookie pinched her butt. They both grinned.

"What is all this racket?" Nurse Ratched's muffled voice demanded from the other side of the door.

The nurse's sneakers squeaked on the tiled floor. Kenzie clutched the sandwich Cookie had made and she'd magicked. She bounced on the balls of her socked feet while she waited for the door to open.

As soon as Nurse Ratched unlocked the door, they sprang into action.

Cookie kicked the door out so it struck Nurse Ratched right in her ample bosom. Before the nurse could recover, Kenzie stuffed the PB&J sandwich she was holding into the nurse's mouth.

"Whathemrrrr," Nurse Ratched demanded, trying to spit out the sandwich.

Too late.

The nurse's lips were glued shut with magically-enhanced peanut butter. Sticky-fied to utter perfection, if Kenzie did say so herself.

Nurse Ratched, with all her flailing and eye-bugging, couldn't manage more than a weak grunt. It certainly wasn't loud enough to alert anyone else that two of the competitors were on the loose.

Phase 1 of Plan *Get the Fuck Outta Here* was complete. Sweet.

Taking full advantage of her whacky magic, Kenzie closed her eyes and initiated the second piece of magic she'd added to the sandwich.

Nurse Ratched raised her fingertips to her face and grazed them over the new addition. Her muted squawk of dismay was music to Kenzie's ears.

"Mrrwrrbrrr!" Nurse Ratched cried through her glued lips as she tugged at her brand new, Pinocchio-style nose. Actually, it looked more like a plum-colored sausage that had been stuck on her face…complete with a hairy mole on the tip.

Because being petty was fun.

Cookie wrenched Nurse Ratched's ring of keys off her wrist and gave the woman a hard shove into their room.

"Stay," Cookie commanded as she found the right key and fitted it into the lock.

Nurse Ratched's eyes crossed as she tried to stare down her nose at the two of them.

Kenzie snickered. Cookie's laugh ended on a snort.

Adrenaline and victory pumped through them. They weren't out of the woods yet, though. Not hardly.

As soon as Nurse Ratched was locked away, the two of them sprinted down the empty hall, their socked feet almost soundless on the tiled floors.

"Follow me," Cookie hissed.

Somewhere nearby, a door slammed. Voices floated toward them.

"Here," Kenzie whispered, pulling open the nearest door and dragging Cookie inside.

They were in a kitchen that smelled strongly of bleach. The scent was so potent it burned Kenzie's nose.

All self-respecting chefs abided by a certain standard for cleanliness, but this went beyond any of that. This room was sterile. It gave her the creeps.

"—ready for the Bonecruncher," Polly Berrywhite's voice said from somewhere nearby. Kenzie froze.

This time, Cookie was the one who grabbed Kenzie's arm and dragged her through the nearest door. A whoosh of frigid air hit Kenzie's face as she followed Cookie into the walk-in freezer. A whole side of beef was hanging from a hook by the entrance.

They moved deeper into the freezer, past enormous bags of produce and—

"Oh my gawd!" Cookie cried out.

Kenzie couldn't make a sound. A man, his eyes wide open and full of terror, was wrapped in plastic and propped against the wall. A thin layer of frost clung to his hair.

"He was my last opponent," Cookie stammered, her teeth chattering from some combination of shock and cold. "I—I killed him days ago. What the fuck they keepin' him on ice for?"

"That's none of your business, dearest," a voice said from behind them.

Cookie shrieked loud enough that Kenzie thought her hearing loss might be permanent.

They both whipped around. Polly filled the freezer's doorway. One of the red-uniformed Cutthroat Cuisine guards was right behind her. He stuck his hand into his waistband and pulled out a Taser.

Kenzie snagged the nearest item—a wheel of brie—and held it out in front of her like a shield.

"Give that back, you little brat," Polly snarled.

"If you say so." Kenzie pulled back her arm, squinted at her target, and threw the cheese.

She missed. Of course, she missed. Kenzie was probably the only person in the history of Bright Futures Elementary School to receive a *Doesn't Meet Expectations* for gym class—sorry, *physical education*—on her report card.

The wheel of cheese hit the wall two feet to the right and bounced off.

"Get her," Polly ordered the guard.

The Taser made a clicking sound as electricity buzzed through the weapon.

"Girl, lemme show you how it's done," Cookie said, plunging her hand into a bag of lemons. She started pummeling the guard with citrusy missiles one after the other.

"You deal with the granny," Cookie told Kenzie. "I've got this."

With that, Cookie chucked a purple onion at the guard, catching him in the throat. She let out a snorting laugh as the man lost his hold on the Taser. Cookie launched herself at him. In a blink, Cookie had the guard in a one-armed headlock and was bashing him over the head with a frozen lambchop.

Cookie might be enjoying herself a little too much. Then again, this was the most fun Kenzie had had in what felt like forever.

Something to consider when she was alone, maybe….

"Come back here!" Polly shrieked.

"Only if you can catch me," Kenzie taunted.

She almost added a *Nah nah, nah-nah-nah* but thought that might be overkill.

Kenzie grabbed a pint of tutti-fruitti ice cream—*and, yuck! Have some standards, people…*—and hurled it at Polly.

This time, her projectile found its mark.

The carton struck Polly right on top of her poofy-haired head. The woman's eyes swiveled back in her head. She thudded to the tile floor.

"Sorry, not sorry," Kenzie called. She trotted over and made sure the woman was out cold. As an added safety measure, Kenzie unwrapped Polly's wool sweater from around her waist and used it to create a makeshift straightjacket.

For just a second, Kenzie considered killing the woman and stuffing her in the freezer.

Just like the Gourmands had done to Loretta and Max.

"You're so lucky my dad raised me right," Kenzie grumbled at the unconscious woman.

"Girl, whatchya waitin' for?" Cookie demanded.

One of Cookie's sleeves was torn, and there was a smear of something down the front of her scrubs. Other than that, she seemed unscathed.

They made it out of the freezer and into the sterile kitchen, but that was as far as they got.

Four chefs in red aprons—two men and two women—blocked their escape. Each of the chefs was holding a bowl or plate full of food. Benedict, dressed in a black suit and leaning on his cane, stood off to the side. Six red-uniformed guards flanked him, awaiting his command like good little soldiers.

"Put The Champ back in her room. Kill the other one."

Magic was heavy on the air.

"No," Kenzie began.

The guard that Cookie had taken down in the freezer hobbled over. He had an egg-shaped bump on his forehead. He scowled at Cookie before locking his arms around Kenzie.

When Kenzie tried to wrench out of his grasp, the guard kicked out her legs and wrestled her to the floor.

Kenzie could only watch as a skinny chef with an unkempt beard stepped forward. He balanced his bowl in one hand and then threw it at Cookie. Red liquid splashed across her face and down the front of her shirt.

For a few seconds, nothing happened. Then, Cookie started to scream.

CHAPTER 15

BRAXTON

Braxton looked at Chef Elyannah Levy. Her spiky hair was a little wind-tousled. She wore a puffy jacket that made her appear even shorter and thinner, albeit no less terrifying.

"What are you doing here, Chef?" Braxton asked.

She raised an eyebrow. In that simple motion, she managed to insult Braxton's intelligence and dent any self-worth he had remaining.

Thanks, Chef. Just what I needed….

"Looking for you. Obviously." Chef Levy pulled off her jacket and threw it at Braxton, like he was a walking, talking coat rack. She unwound her scarf.

"How did you find us?" Aralia asked. She'd lowered her bow, but she didn't put the arrow back in her quiver.

Chef Levy leveled her disdainful gaze on Aralia. "I might not be in the Mossad anymore, but I still have resources. You should be pleased." She glanced around at the cabin. "It took me longer to find you than the time I sniffed out a Syrian rebel group that had the entire western world chasing its tail."

Aralia's features softened in relief, and maybe pride. "You never would have found us at all, if it weren't for *someone's* penchant for electricity and running water." She pointed upstairs in the general direction of where Graham and Sofia were sleeping. Not together.

Christ. Were they together?

No, he'd checked on Sofia a little while ago. She'd been asleep in her bed. Alone.

"People have always been soft," Chef Levy grumbled.

"Tell me about it," Aralia agreed.

"Can we get back on track?" Braxton asked, making every effort to keep his voice low and soothing. With these two, it was better not to make any sudden moves.

Chef Levy turned to Braxton. From the expression on her face, Braxton figured she was about to tell him to fuck off. Instead, she said the last thing he'd ever expected to hear.

"I believe I can help you find your girlfriend."

"Kenzie?" Braxton choked. "You know where she is?"

Chef Levy rolled her eyes. "Have you gone hard of hearing, McKaid? I said I think I can help you find her." She rolled her eyes again, in case her opinion of him hadn't been made clear enough.

"What do you know?" Braxton asked Chef Levy.

He tried to make it sound more like a request than a demand. If the frown marring Chef Levy's face was any indication, he hadn't quite succeeded.

"I don't *know* anything for certain," Chef Levy said. "I assume Polly Berrywhite was the one who abducted her. I'm also assuming that corrupt marshmallow delivered Kenzie straight to the Gourmands."

"Polly…*what?*"

"Has ties to the Gourmands," Chef Levy said, like it was old news. "I've been trying to get proof of her involvement in illegal activities for twenty years, but she's got the Gourmands on her side. And they're slipperier than eels on a water slide."

"Okayyy," Braxton said, even though he couldn't imagine sweet, old Polly moonlighting as a kidnapper. "So, we just find Polly and make her bring us to Kenzie?"

"If it was as easy as that, I'd have dealt with everything myself and wouldn't be wasting my time with you," Chef Levy said. "However…." She sighed deeply, making it clear how vexing it was to subject herself to Braxton's company. "Polly Berrywhite has not returned to her Manhattan apartment since Hex Kitchen. That's why I think that, wherever the Gourmands took your girlfriend, Polly Berrywhite is there, too."

"If you don't know where they are, then how do we find them?" Braxton asked, feeling his optimism begin to slide into defeat.

"There's a recipe," Chef Levy began.

Ah. That was why she needed Braxton. Chef Levy might be the harshest critic of magical food on the planet, but she wasn't a powerful culinary magician herself.

"It's risky," Chef Levy continued. "There's only been a handful of culinary magicians who have ever cooked it without burning themselves out."

Braxton knew about those types of recipes. They were unstable and generally ended in tragedy.

"No way," Aralia cut in. "Stud's already about to burn out from magic overload, and I have plans for him that don't involve him dying."

Braxton glared at Aralia. "I'm fine." To Chef Levy, he asked, "How's it going to help me find Kenzie?"

"If you manage to make it without killing yourself?" Chef Levy crossed her arms and glared at him. "It'll form a telepathic link between the two of you."

A jolt went through Braxton. "Is that even possible?"

"Do you think I'd be here if it wasn't?" Chef Levy countered. Her harsh expression softened just a little. "Even if you do everything correctly, I'm told the magic will be very painful for you."

"I can handle it."

Chef Levy studied him. "I suppose you won't care that this particular recipe is among those banned by the Gourmands?"

"Not even a little," Braxton replied.

He'd already been planning to break the cardinal law of culinary magic in order to get the Gourmands' attention. Cooking a banned recipe would be child's play in comparison.

"I always knew there was a spine hiding somewhere in that soft body of yours," Chef Levy said.

Aralia chuckled.

"Thank you?" *I think.*

"Alright, McKaid." Chef Levy knocked her fist against the table. "Enough chit-chat. Time to cook."

"Just a second," Braxton said. "What's in it for you?"

He really didn't care what Elyannah Levy stood to gain from all of this. But he heard Sofia's voice in his head chiding him, *No one ever does something for nothing, Brax.* It was a reminder that he couldn't afford to make any more stupid, desperate decisions. He had to go into this with his eyes wide open.

"The Gourmands murdered my girlfriend twenty years ago," Chef Levy said. "At least, I believe they did. I've never been able to find certifiable proof one way or the other."

"You had a girlfriend?" Aralia asked.

Chef Levy's icy sneer fell on Aralia. "You have a problem with that?"

"Not at all," Aralia replied. "Just didn't see you as the relationship type."

"I'm not," Chef Levy grunted. "But…." Her voice softened. "Hanna was different."

"Shit. I'm sorry," Braxton said.

Twenty years. Braxton had been looking for Kenzie for little more than a week, and already, he felt like his sanity was hanging on by a thread. No wonder Chef Levy was so peevish.

"Sorry won't bring her back," Chef Levy snapped. "Hanna was careless, drawing attention to her magic and cooking for friends who weren't like us. But I loved her, and the Gourmands took her." She traced a groove in the wooden table with the pad of her thumb. "I need to find out exactly what happened, and I think finding your girl will help me do that."

Braxton tried to process everything Chef Levy was telling him.

"And you really think Polly Berrywhite is involved?" Braxton asked.

It seemed so preposterous. Polly was like the grandmother of the entire culinary magic world.

"I've suspected her involvement for some time," Chef Levy said. "I confirmed it during this decade's Hex Kitchen."

"How?" Aralia asked.

"White wine spritzers," the chef replied. The corner of her lips gave a little twitch.

"Come again?" Braxton asked.

"Polly Berrywhite has a fondness for white wine spritzers," Chef Levy explained. "I had to endure an hour in her company and choke down her horrid butterscotch cookies, but it was worth it. That woman cannot hold her liquor. After her third spritzer, she started boasting about how she works for the Gourmands. She also gave me reason to think the Gourmands have plans for Kenzie."

Braxton clenched his fists. He knew the Gourmands occasionally took lives when someone posed a threat to their world. It was a necessary evil when it came to keeping culinary magic a secret from the general population. But this was different. Kenzie wasn't a threat. She hadn't done anything wrong.

What the fuck were they doing to her?

"Make no mistake," Chef Levy said. "I'm not here out of charity. I want answers, and I think the ones who can tell me what happened to my Hanna are the same people holding your girl hostage."

Braxton nodded. "Tell me about this recipe."

CHAPTER 16

SOFIA

Sofia was surprisingly un-hungover from the night before. She'd only slept a few hours, but they had been restful. She'd dreamed about quiet gardens and calm lakes, and for a little while, her subconscious had been mercifully free from reality.

Braxton had been gone by the time she woke up. He left her a note saying he'd gone with Aralia and Chef Levy to get ingredients, and that she shouldn't worry.

Braxton hadn't mentioned exactly what he needed ingredients for or why Elyannah Levy was now part of their merry band of outlaws, but Sofia didn't need her pristine university GPA to figure out it had something to do with Kenzie.

Braxton ended his note by begging her not to leave the cabin until he got back.

Sofia sent her brother a quick text telling him that she was catching up on sleep and didn't want to be bothered. As strained as things were between them, she didn't want to add to Braxton's list of worries.

Sofia dressed in one of the more modest and less furry outfits Aralia had leant her. She carefully wrapped up the zucchini blossom Braxton had given her the night before and pocketed it. After a brief deliberation, she crossed the hall and raised her fist to knock on Graham's door. She hesitated.

It was early, and she didn't want to face him after she'd broken down in his arms the previous night. But she needed his truck.

Before she could reach a decision, the door opened.

"Oh, um—" she stuttered.

Graham was standing there, a foot away, wearing nothing except a pair of jeans that were slung so low she didn't know why he even bothered. The V of muscle at his pelvis looked like it had been chiseled from stone.

Damnit. She was staring. Definitely staring.

"Good morning," Graham said, his voice a little scratchy. He was sleep-mussed, with a shadow along his jaw.

Sofia couldn't keep a telltale heat from rising to her cheeks. How could those two simple words sound so sexy?

Argh.

One of Sofia's ex-boyfriends had once dubbed her the Robot, saying that the only emotions she ever displayed were calculated. He'd meant it as an insult. She'd taken it as a compliment.

She needed some of that cool control now.

Be the Robot.

"I need to borrow your truck," she said.

When Graham didn't immediately respond, she tacked on a "Please." Because she wasn't a complete barbarian.

Graham's mouth turned down. "You said you were going to Maine, right? That's a long drive."

Sofia bristled. "I don't know what you've heard about my driving abilities, but I assure you I'm perfectly capable of not wrecking your truck."

One time, and her reputation was forever tarnished. Also, because her brothers had big mouths.

"I wasn't worried about that before, but now…." Graham trailed off. He didn't smile, but his whiskey eyes brightened in a way that made it clear he was teasing her.

"Are you going to let me borrow it or not?" Sofia asked, knowing she sounded petulant.

But could she really be blamed for being unsettled when he was standing in front of her, looking like *that?*

Down girl, she ordered herself. She wasn't going to lust after Aralia's…whatever he was.

Just because she didn't see any evidence of anything beyond platonic affection between them, it didn't mean it wasn't there.

But then, why do they sleep in separate bedrooms? her traitorous subconscious asked.

Shut up, subconscious. I'm trying to be practical….

"You can borrow anything you want," Graham said, serious again. "But after…everything that's happened, I don't think you should go alone."

Sofia hardened herself against the tidal wave of pain that threatened to knock her down. Mum wouldn't want her to fall apart right now. She'd want Sofia to do whatever it took to protect Braxton and herself. So, that was what she'd do.

"I'll be fine," she said. "Keys?" She held out her hand.

Graham shook his head before disappearing into his room. He returned a few beats later wearing a hoodie and holding a set of keys.

"I'll go with you," he said.

Sofia would have argued with more fervor, but there was a small part of her that was grateful for the company. She didn't want to be alone with her thoughts right then. Besides, Americans really were terrors on the road.

"Why are we going to Maine, by the way?" Graham asked.

"I'm meeting with the Reaper," she replied.

Not that Qiang Lee was aware of their meeting, but that was how it worked when you didn't have an email or phone number or fax or—

"The wish truffle maker?" Graham's brows furrowed. "Why?"

"Because he's going to sell me his magic ingredients," Sofia replied. *He just doesn't know it, yet.*

* * *

For the first part of their drive, Sofia and Graham were quiet. In spite of her best efforts to focus on the trees zooming past, Sofia couldn't keep her attention from drifting to the man in the driver's seat.

One of his hands loosely gripped the steering wheel, while the other rested on top of the gear shift between them.

He had nice hands.

Who are you, really? Sofia thought.

When she'd first arrived at the cabin, Sofia had done her due diligence and investigated Aralia and Graham. At least, she'd tried.

Sofia hadn't discovered much about Aralia, except that she was an orphan and had been in the foster system for most of her young life. As little dirt as Sofia had found on Aralia, there had been even less about Graham.

Guilt had stopped her from probing any deeper, since Aralia and Graham had been kind enough to open up their home to her and Braxton. Sofia didn't think they would appreciate finding out that she was digging into their pasts.

They were about an hour into Massachusetts when Sofia noticed a shift in the air between them. Graham, who had been humming along to some jazzy Blues playlist, went stock still. He was gripping the steering wheel with both hands, and Sofia could see a muscle ticking along his jaw.

"Are you alright?" Sofia asked.

Graham didn't answer. He scrunched down in his seat and tugged on his hood, which Sofia only just realized he'd kept up for their entire drive. She'd thought his sunglasses were for headlight glare, but now she was starting to wonder if he'd worn them for a different reason.

What…or who…was Graham hiding from?

For the first time, Sofia thought maybe she should have listened to Braxton about staying away from this man.

A shudder rolled through Graham as a police car, its siren wailing, flew past them.

Graham sucked in an unsteady breath.

"Um, what?" Sofia began, feeling shaken herself and not knowing why.

"It's nothing," Graham said in a hoarse voice.

Sofia crossed her arms. "You're an even worse liar than my brother, and that's saying something." She waited a beat. "Are you about to tell me you're a fugitive from the law?"

Graham didn't answer. His whole body was trembling.

That was when Sofia heard more sirens.

She glanced in the side mirror and saw two state troopers, their lights flashing, coming up behind them.

"Graham?"

He didn't respond. Sofia didn't think he could. She could see his chest rising and falling with his rapid, shallow breaths.

The sirens grew louder.

Graham's eyes rolled back in his head.

"Graham!" She grabbed the wheel before they went off the road.

"Can't breathe," he gasped, clutching at his chest.

The state troopers flew past. In seconds, the sirens had faded.

"Pull over," she ordered.

By some miracle, Graham managed to obey.

Between the two of them, they got the truck onto the shoulder without killing themselves or anyone else. As soon as they came to a stop, Graham sagged against her.

Bloody hell, he was heavy.

His breathing was raspy and shallow. At a loss for what else to do, Sofia took one of his big hands in hers and squeezed.

His fingers were freezing.

"You didn't faint on me, did you?" she asked, trying not to let her rising panic show in her voice.

Should she call 9-1-1? Considering the way Graham had responded to some sirens that had nothing to do with them, the answer to that was a strong negative.

"I didn't faint," Graham scowled.

Sofia was gratified to see that her goading had brought some life back into him.

For a few minutes, they just sat there, hand-in-hand, while Graham got himself under control.

"I'm good now," he said, turning the key in the ignition and checking his mirrors.

Sofia waited until they were back on the road before she spoke again.

"Who the hell are you?"

Graham offered her a grim smile. "Trust me, Sofia. You don't want to know."

* * *

They arrived in Acadia National Park without further incident.

If Sofia had thought Aralia and Graham's cabin was remote, it was nothing compared to this wilderness hideout. They turned onto a dirt road that was completely hidden by overgrown bushes and bowing trees. Sofia had to get out of the truck and move aside branches so Graham could drive through.

If it hadn't been for the coordinates Mum had left on her laptop, they never would have found their way.

They drove up a slight hill lined by white pine and fir trees.

"Are you sure this is right?" Graham asked. "I don't see anything."

"If we don't find it in the next minute, we'll turn around." Frustrated, Sofia checked her phone again. It should be here.

The ground sloped down, and then a log cabin came into view. Sofia heaved a sigh of relief.

Unlike Graham and Aralia's house, this cabin was actually a cabin. It honestly looked closer to a shack.

There was no reason why the only person who knew how to make a wish truffle should be hurting for money. So, Sofia could only surmise that this sad little abode was a lifestyle choice rather than a necessity.

"Let me do the talking," Sofia said as they got out of the car.

"Um." Graham slouched down in his seat and glanced at the tiny hut. "I'd better stay here."

Sofia felt her eyebrows lift. "I see. And I don't suppose you're going to tell me why?"

Graham licked his lips and managed to sink even lower in his seat. "I'll keep a lookout," he said, dodging her question. "If you're in trouble, I'll be there."

A dozen questions rose to the tip of her tongue, but Sofia held them back. Right now, Sofia had other things to worry about.

"Suit yourself," she said before getting out of the truck.

Sofia strode purposefully up to the shack. She refused to give in to her urge to turn back and make sure Graham was, in fact, keeping an eye on her. She didn't want to admit to herself that everything she'd been through had shaken her confidence. And her courage.

Sofia climbed the lilting front porch.

Here goes nothing, she thought. Sofia relaxed her shoulders, took a deep breath, and knocked on the door.

CHAPTER 17

KENZIE

The Thief is coming out strong today, folks!" Polly strode across the width of her skybox, narrating to whoever was watching through the one-way glass.

Kenzie slammed her roll of dough onto the cutting board. It didn't really require kneading, but it felt good to punish something. She stretched the dough with enough force that a gaping hole opened up in the center, and she had to shape it again.

Kenzie's name on the scoreboard no longer read *The Champ*. After her two "victories," Polly had changed her show name to *The Thief*. You know, because Kenzie stole her opponents' magical dishes…and killed them with said dishes.

Her opponent was called *Toxic*.

The hidden audience was shouting for her to start cooking. They were calling her all sorts of lovely names and pelting rotten tomatoes at her head.

Kenzie didn't give a flying fig about any of them. All she cared about was the fact that Cookie, her only friend in this hellhole, was dead. And the man standing on the other side of this kitchen had been the one to kill her.

Toxic's magicked wine had burned through Cookie's skin and bones. Now, all Kenzie had to remind her of her friend was an empty cot and some food wrappers. And an unquenchable thirst for revenge.

She was going to make this skinny chef, with his ratty beard and sullen expression, scream in agony the way Cookie had.

Kenzie removed the bag of magical cherries from her wicker basket. Toxic, her opponent, was already busy with his.

If Polly's jabbering was anything to go by, Cookie wasn't the first person Toxic had killed with his magic wine. But she'd sure as shit be the last.

Kenzie dumped her bag of cherries onto the counter with enough force that half of them bounced off and dropped to the ground. Kenzie left them there. When she accidentally stepped on one and felt the fruity flesh give way beneath her foot, the invisible crowd gasped. After that, Kenzie made a point of squishing every single cherry she didn't need, just for the perverse pleasure of ruining something the Gourmands had created.

"Tart zap cherries, folks," Polly narrated. "This is a feisty little ingredient, although it's not much good for eating, I'm afraid." Her voice actually broke at that tragic observation.

While Polly babbled on, Kenzie pitted her zap cherries. Every time she touched one with her bare hand, a small zing of electricity sizzled through her body.

Kenzie collected the pits into a bowl, and then tossed the cherries on the ground behind her. Above her, Polly was needlessly blathering about how chefs usually keep the cherries and dispose of the pits, and *what in the world is The Thief up to today?!*

Toxic was letting his cherries blend in a food processor while he emptied out the pantry's vinegar supply into a saucepan.

Whatever.

Kenzie pulled her pastry out of the oven. For once, the scent of cinnamon did nothing to comfort her.

Without waiting for it to cool, Kenzie picked up the pie crust that was molded into the shape of a gun. She loaded in the cherry pits.

"Ooh, it looks like The Thief has a sweet treat in store for her opponent," Polly narrated from above.

Kenzie focused on stuffing the cherry bullets into the chamber. A few flakes of buttery crust fluttered down onto the arena floor.

"I didn't want to kill her, you know," Toxic said out of the corner of his mouth. His shoulders slumped as he continued to stir his liquified cherries.

"Then why did you?" Kenzie snarled.

Toxic stopped stirring. He studied his fingernails, which were bloody and ragged. "It wasn't like I had a choice," he mumbled.

"You freaking melted my friend!" Kenzie roared.

Toxic glared at her across the counter. "You going to pretend you're better than me?" he demanded. "You're in here now, which means you killed the same number of people as me."

Images of Brute and Scarlet's lifeless bodies filled Kenzie's vision. She thought about Aidan McKaid.

Just like that, her anger wilted like old lettuce.

Unable to respond, Kenzie went back to transforming her pastry and cherry pits into an actual weapon. Her heart wasn't in it anymore, though, and the magic refused to cooperate. Every time she pulled the pastry trigger, the cherry pit "bullet" popped out with a sad little *plink*. Harmless.

"Oh no," Polly called gleefully. "Looks like Plan A didn't work out. Time for The Thief to strike again!"

"Steal the magic!" a few muffled voices called from behind the one-way glass. "Steal. The. Magic!"

I'm not here to entertain you! Kenzie wanted to shout. She knew from experience, however, that goading her audience would only earn her more rotten tomatoes to the head.

Toxic seemed to be having as much trouble with his magic as she was. His hands were shaking, and thick smoke was wafting up from his cook station. If Polly's narration was to be believed, the magic cherries weren't meshing with his usual wine recipe.

All that mattered to Kenzie was that her opponent had his hands too full to come after her. For the moment, anyway.

She tossed her lousy pastry gun in the sink and ran the water until the weapon began to dissolve. She didn't want to take the risk that Toxic would succeed where she had failed and use the weapon against her.

Toxic let out a little whoop of triumph and pulled his saucepan off the stove.

Steam carrying the overpowering smells of cherry syrup and white vinegar wafted toward Kenzie.

"Toxic is going for it, folks," Polly said into her microphone as Kenzie's opponent added lime juice to his mixture. "If The Thief doesn't want to melt like the Wicked Witch of the West, then she better get thieving!"

Hard pass on that one. Thanks anyway.

Kenzie stood there, trying to decide what to do. She wasn't going to let someone melt her, and after the disturbing revelation that Toxic was as powerless as she was, Kenzie didn't want to melt him, either. She needed to figure something else out.

Not that inspiration was especially easy to come by when she got mildly electrocuted every time she touched her cherry juice-stained countertop.

Crap, crap, crap on a cracker.

Kenzie took stock of the ingredients strewn across her prep area. Her attention caught on a small container of activated charcoal powder.

Hmm....

Toxic was pouring his scalding liquid into a glass bottle. He was almost ready, which meant Kenzie needed to act fast.

She dumped all of the activated charcoal into a pitcher before adding filtered water, fresh lemon juice, and a pinch of sugar. She finished mixing her...*lemonade*...just as her opponent fitted a spray nozzle over his glass bottle.

Kenzie kept one eye on Toxic as she coaxed and cajoled her magic to work.

"Come on," she gritted out. Sweat rolled down her face, making her neck itch. The back of her skull prickled.

Toxic prowled toward her, the spray bottle gripped in his outstretched hand.

Shit.

Since shouting *Not ready* probably wasn't going to get her anywhere, Kenzie grabbed her pitcher of lemonade and ran to the other side of the arena. She needed to buy herself a few more seconds—just long enough for the magic to kick in. She tripped over a crumpled soda can on the ground, but she managed to keep the pitcher from overturning.

Come on, she begged the magic. *Work, damnit!*

Footsteps pounded the dirt behind her.

Kenzie felt the magic in her lemonade snap into place. She spun around, only to find that Toxic was right in front of her. He raised his bottle.

Kenzie tossed the entire pitcher of lemonade at her opponent.

At the same moment, she felt a wine-scented mist spray across her face.

CHAPTER 18

KENZIE

Kenzie threw her lemonade at the same time Toxic doused her with his acid mixture.

Was her face about to melt off or….

"What the hell?" Toxic demanded.

He spritzed more of his magic wine all over Kenzie. She let the mist wash over her, because if his magic had been working properly, she'd already be dead.

That meant her lemonade was stronger.

Kenzie had lived up to her moniker of *The Thief* with this dish more than any other, she supposed. Because she'd stolen his magic.

Well, that wasn't completely right. She hadn't taken his magic for herself. Instead, she'd neutralized his power.

Rotten tomatoes stopped pelting the ground. Even Polly seemed struck dumb…which Kenzie counted as a victory in and of itself.

"What did you do to me?" Toxic demanded.

"If you stop squirting me with that stuff," she said, annoyed, "I'll tell you."

Kenzie's voice echoed in the cavernous arena that had gone disconcertingly quiet.

"I temporarily took away your culinary magic," she told him. She'd seen the activated charcoal and gotten the idea to remove his ability, the same way someone might try to remove an infection from their body.

Not that culinary magic was an infection….

"Good grief," Polly said. "It…isn't possible."

"What's happening?" Toxic asked nervously, as Kenzie's least favorite nurse on the planet appeared in the arena. Nurse Ratched's nose was almost completely back to normal.

Pity.

Nurse Ratched gestured for Kenzie to follow her. Kenzie went, because she'd learned firsthand what happened when she didn't do what that evil woman commanded.

"Where are you taking me?" Kenzie asked.

As usual, Nurse Ratched didn't respond. She just grabbed Kenzie's elbow and gave her a hard tug as she led her back to her windowless—and roommate-less—cell.

Apprehension knotted in Kenzie's stomach when she found Benedict and Polly already waiting for her. Perhaps most alarming of all, Polly was neither eating nor smiling.

Something was definitely up.

Benedict and Polly were looking at her in a way that was deeply unsettling…like, even more than usual. All at once, she got a distinct impression of what Kiwi must feel like every time people put their noses up to his habitat and stared at him.

Kenzie made a mental note to apologize profusely to her chameleon in the form of extra crunchy crickets…if she ever got out of here and got to see him again.

"That explains why neither of her parents is a culinary magician," Polly whispered. "I never—"

"Quiet," Benedict ordered.

He didn't say the word loudly, but it was laden with threat. There was real emotion on his face. He looked…shaken.

"What explains why my parents aren't culinary magicians?" Kenzie asked.

Because, clearly, her self-preservation instincts weren't as up to snuff as Polly's.

"How long have you known?" Benedict asked Kenzie.

The ferocity in his voice made goosebumps rise on her arms in warning. "Known what?"

When Benedict didn't answer, Kenzie turned to Polly. The woman's mouth was hanging slightly agape. The skin underneath her chin wobbled, and Kenzie realized it was because Polly was trembling.

"Don't lie to us, Kenzie," Polly said in a shrill voice. "Answer the question!"

"How long have I known what?" Kenzie grated out. She was growing less afraid by the second. Now, she was just ticked off. These two knew something about her that they weren't sharing.

"Your culinary magic," Benedict said. "Have you known all along what you are?"

What. Not *who.*

"And what am I?" Kenzie said carefully, sensing she was balanced on the edge.

On the edge of what, she didn't know.

Polly tilted her head, like it would allow her to somehow see inside Kenzie. "I believe she truly doesn't know."

No shit, Sherlock! Someone give this brainiac an award….

Benedict didn't say anything.

"I had no idea any of them still existed," Polly said, sounding awed and a little reverent.

"Quiet!" Benedict thumped his cane on the floor. Both Polly and Kenzie jumped.

"You're a very special girl, Kenzie," Benedict said.

The way he said it made Kenzie feel like the exact opposite of special.

"Get some rest," Benedict told her. "The tournament will need to be completed, but I am confident I'm staring at my next successor."

Benedict's cane clicked against the tiled floor as he headed for the door. Polly hurried after him, whispering excitedly. Kenzie strained to hear what they were saying, but all she caught was something that sounded like *super food.*

"Hey!" Kenzie snapped out of her stupor a moment after the door clicked shut. She banged her palm against it. "Come back here. What do you mean, I'm special? Why is my magic different?"

What am I?

Her only answer was a deafening silence.

CHAPTER 19

BRAXTON

Braxton carefully pulled his pan of sea bream out of the oven. They'd had to drive two hours to a specialty fish market, and then another hour to a specialty mushroom farm. And that hadn't even included the fact that Aralia had insisted on coming with them, and then proceeded to get into lengthy discussions with each of the farmers about their growing methods and whether their farms were sustainable.

As soon as they'd gotten back to the cabin, Aralia hurried off to get started on her new hallucinogenic mushroom garden.

"Be gentle," Chef Levy snapped. "Do you manhandle all delicate fish this way?"

"I know how to cook sea bream," Braxton replied, trying to keep his temper in check. "Just let me do my thing."

"I would if you were halfway to competent!" Chef Levy retorted.

Braxton ground his teeth until his jaw ached. If Chef Levy were anyone else, Braxton would have ordered her out of the kitchen. But aside from the fact that the petite woman could kick his arse across the state without batting an eye, he wanted this dish to be perfect.

No, he *needed* it to be perfect.

The dish was barely half-finished, and already, Braxton felt stretched thin. He'd been adding and adjusting magic at every step of the recipe. It was sucking the life out of him.

"In ancient Rome, people ate sea bream to have hallucinogenic dreams," Chef Levy said. "The fish eat algae and plankton that are full of indole, which is made by bacteria. Hence the hallucinations."

"Fascinating," Braxton grumbled.

"Don't be a smart-ass," Chef Levy retorted. "You need to know these things if you're going to make the magic right."

Braxton didn't reply, because Chef Levy was right. There was nothing intuitive about this recipe. He needed all the help he could get.

Recipes as complicated as this one required specific ingredients that would properly harmonize with the magic. If Braxton tried to use store-bought mushrooms, for instance, the contamination from their packaging would upset the magic's delicate balance. Either the recipe would fall flat, or it would produce a magical concoction that would kill him. With these sorts of volatile recipes, it could really go either way.

Braxton put the steamed fish on a platter. He spooned over the chunky puree he'd made from unripe miracle berries, which were so tangy and sour that the mere thought of them made Braxton's mouth pucker.

He'd cooked with the ripe variety of the plant before, which had the unique property of making other foods taste sweeter by binding to a person's taste buds.

"No, you idiot." Elyannah slapped his hand as he reached for the nutmeg. "Mushrooms first."

"Yes, Chef," Braxton said, infusing the words with as much rancor as he thought he could get away with.

Braxton sprinkled the dried and chopped mushrooms—which definitely weren't of the legal variety—on top of his dish. Then, he shaved a liberal amount of fresh nutmeg on top.

Braxton's *Spectacular Spices* course in culinary school had taught him that nutmeg contained myristicin, which affected the brain if eaten in large doses. The French chef who had been a guest lecturer for the class had been a fantastic cook but woefully underprepared for a kitchen full of teenagers. She'd made the mistake of telling them that eating large quantities of nutmeg would alter their minds similarly to if they took LSD. The result had been a total obliteration of the school's nutmeg stock.

Aidan had sworn the nutmeg let him recall the day of their birth. Braxton had gotten a monster headache and spent the night puking.

To this day, he didn't willingly eat anything that contained the spice.

For you, Kenz.

Some blokes bought flowers to show their affection…. Braxton ate nutmeg.

"What are you smiling about?" Chef Levy barked. "Are the fumes getting to you, or are you just simple-minded?"

"I assume that's rhetorical," Braxton muttered.

Chef Levy tilted her head up to the ceiling, like she was addressing a higher being. "You give me the one chef talented enough to make this dish, and he's a simpleton."

If Braxton hadn't used all of his energy on this dish, he might have come up with a worthy retort. Instead, he put what little focus he had left into harmonizing the magic that ran through each ingredient.

"The next part's up to you," Chef Levy said. "And God help us all."

Braxton ignored the jab. "Any tips?"

He could put up with Chef Levy's insults if they would help him find Kenzie. He could suffer through anything if it would get him to her.

"Think of the clearest memory you have of her," Chef Levy said. She had her arms clasped behind her back and recited the words like she was reading them off a page.

Clearest memory….

"In that case, can I get a little privacy?" Braxton asked. He couldn't very well relive his favorite Kenzie memories while Chef Levy was breathing down his neck.

"You most certainly cannot," Chef Levy barked. "And stop stalling. We don't have all day!"

Braxton scowled. Chef Levy backed up a couple of steps and did her searing one eyebrow-raise, making it clear that was as much of a concession as he was going to get.

So, Braxton closed his eyes and blocked out everything except the food and his magic. He inhaled the briny scent of the fish and earthy mushrooms. He tasted the berries on his tongue. He felt his stomach curdle at the memory of his last experience with nutmeg.

Then, he turned his thoughts to Kenzie. In his mind, he felt the soft warmth of her skin as he licked a path across her dragon tattoo. He saw the gleam of her slate-gray eyes, with their flecks of silver and charcoal. He shivered at the memory of her lips trailing gentle kisses along his jaw.

The smell of her hair, the feel of her in his arms, the sound of her voice….

Braxton stabbed a forkful of the food, making sure to get an equal part of each component. He forced himself to taste it, choking back a gag at the overwhelming nutmeg flavor.

Come on, Kenz, he thought as he pulled the threads of magic taut. *Where are you? Talk to me.*

He swallowed another bite. And another.

His insides compressed as the harsh ingredients and harsher magic took hold, but he ignored the discomfort.

Come on. Please. Please.

The threads of magic snapped into place. Braxton's surroundings dissolved. His vision plunged into darkness.

CHAPTER 20

SOFIA

Sofia didn't have to wait long before she heard uneven footsteps coming from inside the shack. The door cracked open to reveal a hunched elderly man wearing a tattered poncho. His wispy beard hung down to his sunken chest. His skin was wrinkled and covered with age spots. Several large moles on his cheeks were sprouting white hairs. An unlit pipe hung out of the corner of his mouth.

"Who are you?" the man demanded in a warbly voice. He took his pipe out of his mouth and waved it at her like it was a weapon.

"Are you Qiang Lee?" Sofia asked instead of answering him. It seemed less dire than asking *Are you the Reaper?*

"Yes," the man said. "And if you don't get off my property, you'll regret it."

Before everything with the Santioris, Sofia wouldn't have taken that kind of threat seriously. Now….

"Reaper Lee, be nice," a soft female voice chided. "We never have guests."

A girl, maybe a year or two younger than Sofia, appeared beside Qiang. She offered Sofia a wide smile and thrust the door all the way open.

The girl was beautiful. Petite and delicate, she looked more doll-like than human. With her jet-black hair, pouty lips, and flawless skin, she reminded Sofia a little of Kenzie.

Sofia hated the girl on sight.

"I'm Clementine, Reaper Lee's apprentice," the girl said in a breathless voice.

"Assistant," Qiang corrected. "Your magic has proven too weak for you to be anything more than a common cultivator. You will never become a Reaper."

"Not everyone was born to enjoy digging around in the dirt," Clementine pouted. "And not everyone needs to be the next Reaper to be useful. Besides, don't you like spending time with your grandniece?" Then, she let out a tinkling laugh that sounded to Sofia like glass breaking. She held out one tiny, fine-boned hand to Sofia. "Reaper Lee never lets people come visit us."

"He still doesn't!" Qiang thundered, waving his pipe threateningly in their direction.

Ignoring him, Clementine gestured for Sofia to come inside.

"My name's Sofia McKaid," she said, stepping into the hut.

Qiang grunted and hobbled over to a rough-hewn wooden table with two splintered chairs. There was a potbelly stove in the corner, giving off a dry heat that made the room feel like a sauna.

A strange, herbal smell permeated the air. When Sofia looked up, she saw that the ceiling was covered in a lattice, where dozens of dried herbs were hanging from strings.

Sofia absently stretched out a hand to touch a nest of dried flowers dangling from a hook on the wall. Qiang batted her hand away before her fingertips could make contact.

"Don't touch that unless you want to divine the future," he told her irritably.

"Seriously?" Sofia yanked her fingers back. She had no desire to see into the future; the present was complicated enough.

The chair creaked and Qiang groaned as he settled himself. "Let me guess." He gave Sofia a sour look. "You are here for wish truffles, yes?"

Well, she wasn't, but if they were being offered….

"That is all anyone wants from me," Qiang grumbled without waiting for her reply.

"I thought you could only make one each decade," Sofia said carefully.

She knew this dance…the one where a single wrong word could get her ejected from the negotiation table. The stakes were too high for missteps.

"That is true," Qiang grudgingly acknowledged. "The nectar I use in the truffle comes from a rare flower that takes a decade to distill." He scowled. "Besides, my wish truffles are promised to the Gourmands. If you want one, I suggest you win next decade's Hex Kitchen."

"My timeline is a bit tighter than that," Sofia said. She couldn't quite keep the acerbic bite from her response. "And I can't compete in Hex Kitchen, because I'm not a culinary magician."

Speaking those words out loud had never made her feel so powerless.

An awkward silence followed, during which Qiang nibbled on the stem of his pipe and stared at her. Clementine scampered over and set chipped mugs down in front of Sofia and Qiang. Steam curled up from the dark liquid that looked like tea but smelled strange and earthy.

Qiang put his pipe down on the table so he could raise his mug with both hands. He took a long sip.

"I'd like to know how magical ingredients are made," Sofia said, directing the conversation away from wish truffles and her lack of magic. "I read everything I could find, but there wasn't much—"

"That is because I am the only living Reaper," Qiang said with surprising voracity. "The other cultivators are impostors."

There were probably better questions she needed to ask, but the one that came out of Sofia's mouth was, "Why is your position called the Reaper? It sounds so…grim."

He sat up a little straighter. "Because my magic creates ingredients that have the power to bring both life and death."

"Oh," Sofia said. "I see."

She didn't really, but Qiang seemed like someone who explained things in his own way in his own time.

"It takes more than magic to become one of us," Qiang said. He pressed an arthritic palm to his chest. "The training is arduous, and there is only a single Reaper living at a time."

"Their magic is the rarest type and different from normal culinary magicians," Clementine burst in. "Don't forget that part, Reaper Lee."

Qiang humphed and pointed his pipe at Sofia. "You could spend a thousand lifetimes studying my magic and never be able to replicate it."

Sofia shook her head, trying to process everything she was hearing.

"I don't understand," she said. "If you have this much power, then why is your wish truffle the only product anyone knows about?"

"I give the Gourmands my wish truffle to satisfy their avarice," Qiang grumbled. "The rest are meant to be created but never used."

"Come again?" Sofia asked, trying to keep her voice even.

"My ingredients are too powerful," Qiang said. "Humans cannot quench their thirst for more, and my ingredients have the ability to topple entire civilizations." He pointed his pipe at her. "*That* is why I am called the Reaper. Because of how many deaths our ingredients have caused."

"Like with the Mayan Empire," Clementine jumped in. "One of Reaper Lee's predecessors gave them magical ingredients, and it led to the collapse of their entire civilization. You'd be amazed at how many times in history that's happened. That's why Reaper Lee can't share his ingredients."

"You're telling me that magic ingredients are the reason for the fall of the Maya?" Sofia asked dubiously.

Qiang and Clementine both nodded with utter certainty.

"If your ingredients can't be shared," Sofia said, deciding not to press any harder on that particular point, "then what do you do with them?"

Clementine made a choked sound and covered her face in her hands.

"I destroy them," Qiang said, raising his chin in defiance.

"*What?*"

This man was either insane or…. Nope, there was no *or*. Insanity was the only option. Qiang Lee was certifiably insane.

"It is a Reaper's sacred duty to ensure his ingredients are not misused," Qiang said. "After seeing the devastation so much magic can bring, my ancestors determined that, save for the wish truffle, our knowledge should remain a secret."

"And the Gourmands let you get away with this?" Sofia didn't have the time or inclination to sugarcoat her words.

"They don't *let* me do anything," Qiang grumbled. "Reapers are too powerful to destroy." He pointed an arthritic finger at his own chest. "And my ancestors began the tradition of providing the Gourmands with a single wish truffle every decade to appease them. It is all they will ever receive from us."

"And if they kill Reaper Lee," Clementine added, "the Gourmands will get nothing at all."

"So, you make the ingredients only to destroy them?" Sofia asked. Her voice went a little high-pitched at the end.

"Wait," Sofia said. "Is this like those sand art things the Tibetan monks make?"

"Sand mandalas," Clementine chirped.

"It is precisely like that," Qiang said. His lined face softened into something that might be approval. Or maybe Sofia was just reading into things.

"The monks create the mandala to enlighten their minds," Qiang said. "It is similar with my ingredients. I am compelled to create them, but they are not meant to endure. They are nothing but a brief flash of perfection and harmony." He paused, frowning at the rim of his chipped cup. "And when I destroy the ingredients, that ritual reminds me that everything is temporary. It is humbling."

Sofia absently picked up the mug in front of her and took a small sip. Instead of the bitter taste she'd been expecting to go along with the dark color, a robust and fruity flavor slid across her palate. Even with her years of experience in her family's restaurants, she couldn't identify these exotic flavors. Almost as soon as she'd swallowed, a feeling of calm stole over her. Since *calm* wasn't an emotion Sofia felt…ever…she knew it was a result of the tea.

"This is incredible," she said, stopping herself before she drained the entire mug.

"It's Reaper Lee's special brew," Clementine jumped in. "It restores vitality and tranquility."

Sofia looked at the herbs hanging from the ceiling.

What a waste.

"Are you aware that the Gourmands are making their own magic ingredients?" she blurted out.

Qiang, who had his mug halfway to his lips, dropped it.

The mug hit the wood floor and shattered.

Clementine let out a little squeal and hurried off—presumably to get something to mop up the mess. Sofia didn't spare her a glance. All of her attention was glued to Qiang.

"That is…. No. It cannot be," Qiang whispered.

"They're artificial," Sofia said, parroting what Braxton had told her. She had no idea whether her brother's source had been telling the truth, but at the moment, it didn't matter. She had Qiang's attention.

"My understanding is that the Gourmands are kidnapping culinary magicians in order to produce these ingredients," Sofia continued.

Qiang's eye twitched. Sofia reached into her pocket and pulled out the zucchini blossom she had carefully wrapped in cheesecloth. She unwrapped the flower and offered it to Qiang.

Qiang plucked the zucchini blossom off the cloth and brought it inches from his face.

Sofia watched Qiang's expression as he inhaled the flower, rolled it between his fingers, and touched its petals with his tongue. With each second that passed, his frown deepened.

"What do you think, Reaper Lee?" Clementine asked in a breathless voice. She was holding a dripping towel and the shards of broken pottery.

"This is wrong," Qiang said. He let the zucchini flower fall onto the table. "The magic is wrong. It is evil."

That seemed like overkill to Sofia, but if it helped her get what she wanted….

"What are the Gourmands doing with these ingredients?" Qiang asked.

His voice had lowered in pitch. He no longer looked like a grumpy old man. He seemed dangerous.

"I don't know," Sofia answered. She flinched when Qiang picked up the flower and threw it across the room.

"This breaks every accord between the Gourmands and my predecessors," Qiang fumed. "This is an outrage!"

"I think so, too." Sofia took a deep breath. Then, she faltered.

Every argument she'd thought up on the way here, about why Qiang should let her distribute his ingredients, was going to fall flat.

Qiang expected people to be greedy. If Sofia wanted him to agree to anything she proposed, she'd need to convince him that she was nothing like the corrupt Gourmands.

Her pulse picked up in the way it always used to when she was in the heat of a negotiation and about to close the deal. There was a sense of victory, coupled with a fear of everything falling apart.

"The Gourmands are doing the very thing your ancestors wanted to prevent," Sofia said, choosing her words carefully. "If left unchallenged, the Gourmands will use their artificial ingredients to further their own selfish goals." She nodded in the direction of the zucchini blossom, which lay on the floor.

Sofia pushed on, emboldened by Qiang's silence. "You've told me all the ways magical ingredients can be abused, but you're missing the other half of that scale. There is so much good your ingredients could do for the world, and all of that potential is being wasted."

Because she could sense that Qiang was preparing to unleash a verbal storm, Sofia hurried on.

"You keep telling me about balance," she told Qiang. "Well, if you want to combat all the harm the Gourmands are doing with their artificial ingredients, then we need to use your real ingredients to help others." She pointed at the dried bundles hanging from the ceiling.

"Reaper Lee can't share his ingredients with the world," Clementine said with a giggle. "He doesn't even have a driver's license." She sobered almost immediately at the glares both Sofia and Qiang shot her way.

"You don't need one," Sofia told Qiang. "I'll do it for you. And I'll make sure the people who receive your ingredients won't abuse them." She was about to mention the profit-sharing models she'd put together on the drive up, but she stopped herself just in time.

"Why do you want to help me?" Qiang asked, peering at her.

A test.

Sofia took another sip of her tea for courage. A dozen different responses sped through her mind, but she disregarded all of them. Instead, she took the biggest risk since walking through this door. She told the truth.

"I grew up in a family of culinary magicians without having any power myself," she said. "It never mattered—" *much* "—until recently." Sofia tried to keep her voice steady, but even the tea's calming effects couldn't stop her chin from trembling. "My mother was murdered by some mobsters. I might have been able to stop them if I had magic."

"Oh, no," Clementine gasped, covering her mouth with her hand. "How tragic."

Sofia ignored her. She didn't need anyone's pity.

"If you let me distribute your ingredients to people who truly need them," Sofia told Qiang, "I'll make sure they don't simply go to the highest bidder. We can come up with a vetting process to make sure no one can hoard the ingredients or use them to do evil."

She deliberately used Qiang's own language.

"Your ingredients will help restore the balance that the Gourmands have upset," Sofia added. She realized she was laying it on a little thick, so she made herself shut up.

As she waited for a response, her brain was already ten steps ahead. There was so much to consider. She'd need to come up with a fair pricing system, identify buyers, establish an infrastructure for getting the ingredients to their new owners….

The whole thing was a puzzle Sofia couldn't wait to solve.

"I will think about it," Qiang said, rising from his chair.

Clementine hurried forward to help him.

Sofia tried to swallow her disappointment. She'd been hoping for an unequivocal *yes*.

"Give Clementine your telephone number," Qiang said, making it clear this meeting was over. "If I decide to proceed with this plan of yours, she will contact you." He limped across the room. He bent down and picked up the zucchini flower. Pinching the blossom between his thumb and forefinger like its touch burned him, Qiang carried it over to the potbelly stove.

Don't.

The word was on the tip of Sofia's tongue, but she kept her mouth sealed shut as Qiang opened the hatch and stuffed the flower into the fire.

A burst of yellow sparks belched out of the stove before the fire quieted down again. Qiang waited until the flower had disintegrated before turning to Sofia.

"It is time for you to leave," he said. "Do not come here uninvited again."

Sofia's shoulders wanted to droop in defeat.

"Thanks for the tea," she murmured.

She allowed Clementine to show her to the door.

CHAPTER 21

KENZIE

Kenzie could feel the effects of the sedatives wearing off. She kept her eyes shut, trying to will herself back to sleep. She'd been having the strangest and most wonderful dream. She wanted to hold onto it for as long as she could.

She'd been dreaming about Braxton.

"Kenz. Baby. Can you hear me?"

"Mmm." Kenzie loved the sound of his sexy Aussie accent. She rolled onto her back, keeping her eyes squeezed shut. "I hear you. Stay with me a while?"

"Holy shit. Kenzie?!"

She sat bolt upright.

"Braxton?"

Kenzie looked around dumbly, like he might actually be in the room with her. He wasn't, but damn, he sounded so close.

"Can you seriously hear me?" His incredulous laugh was like a balm for her aching heart.

"Yes!" Kenzie did another visual sweep of the empty room. "Please tell me I haven't started hallucinating."

Although, honestly, it wouldn't be surprising. Or entirely unwelcome.

"You're not hallucinating," Braxton's voice said in her mind. The sound was rich and deep. And way too real for it to be her mind playing tricks on her.

"Elyannah Levy came to see me," Braxton's voice said in her mind. *"She gave me a recipe for telepathically connecting with you."*

Kenzie's heart was thudding so hard she could practically see her chest vibrating.

"That's amazing," Kenzie babbled. "I can't believe it's working. I can't believe Chef Levy is helping you."

She didn't know whether Braxton would be able to "hear" her if she just thought the words rather than speaking them aloud. Since this seemed to be working, she wasn't about to mess with it.

"Are you okay?" Braxton asked. *"Where are you? What are they doing to you?"*

Kenzie faltered. How could she possibly explain this horrible place to him? How could she admit what she'd done to survive?

"I'm okay," she said, wondering whether Braxton would be able to hear the slight stammer in her voice. She cleared her throat. "The Gourmands have me. Polly Berrywhite, who by the way is a total bitch, is here too."

"What do they want from you?" Braxton growled in her mind.

Kenzie shrugged helplessly. She'd thought this tournament was just about competing for Benedict's job, but it was starting to become clear that there was more going on. "They know something about me…about why my magic is different." She massaged her aching skull. "Braxton, they're making me compete to be the next Gourmand leader."

Kenzie felt Braxton's surprise.

"It doesn't matter what they want. We're going to get you out of there."

"You have no idea—" She broke off as a wave of emotion welled up inside her. "I've been losing my mind in here."

Unbidden, the faces of her Cutthroat Cuisine victims flashed through her mind. She heard the crack of Brute's neck.

"I've been trying to find you," Braxton said.

Kenzie's breathing hitched. "You have?"

"What the hell else would I be doing?"

Kenzie chewed on her bottom lip. She didn't want to start sniffling or make any other sounds that would keep her from hearing every syllable Braxton uttered.

"Where are you, baby?" Braxton asked.

"I have no idea." Kenzie scanned the sparse room, like it would offer her some clue that she'd missed before. "I'm in a room. No windows. Sometimes they take me out into a big…arena. They call it Cutthroat Cuisine. Does that ring any bells?"

"Never heard of it. Underground, you think?"

"Maybe?"

Kenzie wanted to scream. She had the opportunity to lead Braxton right to her, and she had nothing useful to tell him.

"Really helpful, I know," she huffed.

"I'm not going to stop looking. Trust me."

The certainty in Braxton's voice bolstered her. She wasn't alone.

"All I know is that we're all competing to take over when Benedict— he's the guy who runs the Gourmands—retires. There's also something about the Gourmands needing us to make their own magical ingredients, but that part was super vague."

"Do you know Benedict's surname?"

Kenzie wracked her brain, trying to remember if she'd ever heard him mention his last name.

"No," she lamented. She hurriedly described his appearance, emphasizing his limp, ivory-handled cane, goatee, and English accent.

When she'd finished, it occurred to Kenzie that she'd probably narrowed the pool of suspects from millions to thousands. Not super helpful.

Kenzie huffed out a frustrated breath. "I'll try and get more answers." *Somehow.* "Can you do this again later?"

The thought of Braxton needing to sever this connection made her want to bash her head into the nearest wall.

"I will," Braxton promised. *"As many times as it takes."*

Kenzie swallowed down her tears. "Thank you."

"In the meantime, how about some telepathy sex?"

Kenzie snorted. "Only you would think of something like that at a time like this."

She reclined against her metal headboard. If she could just forget about where she was, it would almost seem like she was lounging in bed and talking to the guy she was head over heels for.

Almost.

"So," she said, trying for a sexy purr. "What are you wearing right now?"

The connection between them stuttered.

"Er, right," Braxton's voice said in her head. It was faint, though.

"Braxton?" she asked, the slight panic in her voice reverberating through the small room. "You still there?"

"Still here, Kenz."

She almost wept with relief.

"Chef Levy wants to know what kind of dirt is in that arena. What accents do the people have? Did you get any sense about the weather or temperature outside?"

Kenzie squeezed her eyes shut and tried to picture it. "Um, regular dirt? Just brown and packed."

God, she was useless.

"As for accents, everyone except Benedict is American. Definitely."

Good one, Kenzie. That *really* narrowed things down.

"I haven't been outside so I have no clue about the weather, but the temperature down here is kinda cool but not cold."

Again, Kenzie felt the murmur of Braxton's voice in her mind more faintly than she had before. She realized he must be relaying her worthless responses to Chef Levy.

Kenzie grimaced. She could almost hear the judge's voice proclaiming the details useless and more useless. Not that she'd be wrong.

"Wait, there was one thing," Kenzie said, as she mentally flipped back through all of her recent conversations. "I asked Benedict how he got injured, and he said my friend shot him with an arrow. You don't think Aralia…?"

"Aralia said she shot one of the people who took you. That was the Gourmand leader?"

Aralia shot Benedict? For Kenzie? That was almost as shocking as the fact that she was talking to Braxton inside her own mind.

"I'll talk to Chef Levy and Aralia," Braxton said. *"See if we can't put together some of these clues."*

"I'll try and find out more before we do this again," Kenzie promised.

"Okay. And Kenz?"

At that moment, the door to her cell swung open. Kenzie let out a little squawk of surprise as Benedict and Nurse Ratched entered the room.

"Come," Benedict said.

"Can't," Kenzie replied. "I have plans today. I need to clip my toenails, learn how to do yoga, bake a pie…."

Hatch an escape plot with Braxton….

"Want me to sedate her?" Nurse Ratched asked. "I can make sure she's conscious but too lethargic to open her big mouth."

"Beats having a big nose," Kenzie retorted.

She was feeling all kinds of bold now that she had Braxton in her head.

"You still there?" she silently thought, knowing that saying the words aloud would arouse too many suspicions.

Braxton's voice didn't reply.

"Can you hear me?" She asked out loud, her growing panic overwhelming her short burst of courage.

No answer. He wasn't in her head anymore.

"Fuck!" Kenzie yelled. She punctuated the word with a smack to her metal cot, which bent the flimsy headboard and made her knuckles throb.

Benedict leaned on his cane and watched her.

"What did I tell you?" Nurse Ratched asked him. "Anyone who has that many tattoos is deranged. Pure and simple."

"I'm deranged?! You're freaking kidnappers!" Kenzie was about to unleash a torrent of profanity, but then she remembered she had a job to do. Braxton would never find her unless she could tell him where to look.

She forced herself to calm down and think.

"I'm going stir-crazy in here without any sunlight," she informed her captors. "If you let me go for a walk outside, I'll stop trying to fight you on everything."

There. That was nice and subtle. Right?

"I don't think so," Benedict replied.

Damn.

"If you plan to keep me here forever, then at least tell me where *here* is," she pleaded. "I deserve to know that much."

Benedict and Nurse Ratched shared an evil chuckle. Kenzie thought about stealing Benedict's cane and bashing it over both their heads.

"Think you're going to escape?" Nurse Ratched asked. She stalked right up to Kenzie until their faces were inches apart. "Think again."

"If I'd wanted you to know where you are," Benedict said, "I wouldn't have asked my guards to blindfold you and drive you around for hours to disorient you."

"And I was starting to think this whole situation wasn't screwed up enough," Kenzie grumbled. "Thank you for clearing up just how wacko you really are."

"Shut your mouth," Nurse Ratched commanded.

"Enough," Benedict said.

It wasn't clear if he was talking to Kenzie or Nurse Ratched.

"Kenzie, if it's a change of scenery you're after, then you're in luck," Benedict said. "There's someone I'd like you to meet."

Nurse Ratched smirked, which wasn't at all encouraging.

Kenzie crossed her arms. "What's in it for me?"

Benedict shrugged. "If you come with us, you'll get a respite from the Cutthroat Cuisine arena."

Kenzie didn't have a smart-aleck response for that. She had no illusions that wherever she was going would be enjoyable, but maybe this was her chance to gather some useful intel for the next time Braxton contacted her.

And…bonus…she wouldn't have to kill anyone else in Cutthroat Cuisine.

Kenzie swept her hand at the door. "In that case, lead the way."

CHAPTER 22

SOFIA

Sofia stood on the uneven porch and blinked into the unfamiliar landscape. Dusk had fallen while she was inside, and the sky was bruised blue-black. It suited her mood.

With no other options, Sofia trudged back to the truck. When she got to the vehicle, she found the doors were locked and Graham was nowhere in sight.

"Really?!" she demanded. She stomped her foot on the ground and then kicked the tire.

Amazingly, her little fit didn't produce either Graham or an unlocked door.

Muttering to herself, she scanned the darkening yard as she looked for any sign of Mr. *I'll stay in the car and watch to make sure you're alright.*

She caught sight of some twinkling lights behind the shack. Cursing Graham to New York and back, she headed for the lights. The whole thing made her feel like some kind of pissed-off moth.

A narrow footpath led through a dense tangle of trees and toward the lights.

"If I get murdered looking for you," she said into the dark shadows. "I'm going to come back and haunt the hell out of you."

She rounded the corner of the splintered shack and stopped short. Sofia's breath caught.

When she'd seen those dried herbs in Qiang Lee's hut, Sofia hadn't really considered what they might look like when they were alive. Now, she knew.

The garden was like nothing she'd ever experienced before. It felt like she'd stepped into another dimension.

The garden was everything Qiang's hut wasn't. It was bright, with clusters of luminescent flowers that didn't resemble any plant Sofia had ever seen. A fire-red carpet of moss lit the path ahead of Sofia. When her foot pressed down, the moss deepened to a vibrant magenta.

Streams had been carved into the loamy soil, and the water bubbled merrily as it trickled through the garden. Blackberry bushes laden down with fruit lined her walkway. The berries emitted a smell that was so mouthwatering Sofia had to clasp her hands behind her back so she didn't pick all of them. A few of the berries were opal-colored, and they shone as though they were lit from within. A tomato plant was heavy with unripe tomatoes that were the size of her head. In certain areas, the soil had somehow become transparent. Sofia could see green roots snaking underground.

The entire garden was surrounded by tall, night-black trees that sprouted leafy boughs from the ground all the way up to the highest branches. The branches interlocked and created a nearly-solid wall, completely enclosing the garden.

Sofia didn't possess so much as an ounce of culinary magic, but even she could sense the power in this place. Every seedling was bursting with magical energy. She'd never seen any place that looked—and felt—so *alive*.

Sofia was so overwhelmed by the garden's beauty and strangeness, she forgot about everything else. She was quickly reminded of her reason for being here when she recognized Graham's silhouette. He was kneeling on the ground in a corner of the garden that was noticeably absent of light.

Sofia hurried over.

"What's wrong with you?" She demanded. "Are you okay?"

When Graham didn't answer, fear seized hold of Sofia.

Was he hurt? Having another panic attack?

"Graham." She crouched down and grabbed his arm. "What happened?"

Graham, who had been staring down at a bare patch of ground, raised his gaze to hers.

"Sofia." He put his palm over her hand, which was still wrapped around his biceps. He blinked a few times. "I'm sorry. I think I lost track of time." He looked around, like he wasn't entirely sure how he'd gotten here.

"Did you eat something in the garden you shouldn't have?" Sofia asked, her worry dissolving into annoyance.

They had an eight-hour drive ahead of them, and Sofia had to get back before Braxton realized she wasn't asleep in her room the way he'd left her.

"The garden…called to me," Graham said, shaking his head. "I couldn't help myself."

Sofia was about to make a snide comment about him needing to help himself back to the truck, but something in Graham's expression stopped her.

He let his hand drop from hers, and Sofia immediately felt the loss of his warmth. The nights were even colder here than in upstate New York.

Graham sank his fingers into the dark soil like he was going to dig something out of it. A pervasive smell of rot was rising up from the thick tangle of weeds. Sofia was no botanist, but even she could tell that this part of the garden was dead.

Still, something about the tension in Graham's back and shoulders stopped her from pointing out this very obvious fact.

Sofia wasn't sure if she was imagining it, but she could feel a kind of energy pulsing in the ground beneath her feet. Tiny pinpricks of light sparked in the soil where Graham's fingers were buried. The smell of decomposition was replaced by something fresh. There was a crackle of dead branches, and out of the bare soil, new green shoots sprang upward.

Holy shit. What was happening?

Graham murmured to the seedlings, his smoky voice making the vines perk up and curl toward him.

Sofia felt her heart swell as she watched Graham work. Her body hummed with awareness and…awe.

In what could have been seconds or minutes, the ground beneath them was covered in vines of velvety green leaves. The leaves were densest around Graham, and every time he reached out and brushed one of them, Sofia heard a tiny, contented sigh rise up from the plant.

When she touched the leaves, they didn't react at all.

That just figured.

Then again, Sofia never had much patience for plants. It seemed only fair that the apathy went both ways.

"I…don't understand," Graham said. His skin had taken on a subtle glow. "Why is this happening?"

Qiang Lee's voice filled the garden.

"You are one of us."

Sofia and Graham jumped up and spun around. Qiang stood only a short distance away, but he'd been so silent there was no way of knowing how long he'd been there.

Graham yanked up the hood of his sweatshirt and moved to the side, where an overgrown bush partially hid him from view. If Qiang noticed Graham's…shyness…he gave no indication.

Qiang hobbled down the path toward them. Graham moved farther behind the bush. Qiang wasn't interested in Graham's appearance, though. All he seemed to care about was the patch of garden. The plants were still growing…and they were growing *toward* Graham.

Qiang's pipe slipped out of his hand and thudded softly onto the mossy ground. He didn't even seem to notice.

"Reaper Lee?" Clementine's high voice called. "Where did you run off to? It's time for your tea."

"Later," Qiang barked, using a tone that brooked no arguments. "Go back inside."

Sofia heard Clementine sigh, and then the hut's door squeaked shut.

Qiang, who hadn't taken his attention off Graham, said, "I have been trying to revive this part of my garden for months. I have never seen such raw power." He took a few steps closer, which caused Graham to hunch into his sweatshirt even more, like he was a turtle retreating into its shell. "Who trained you?"

"Uhh," Graham stammered. "No one."

"Impossible," Qiang said.

Graham stared down at the plants, like they might hold all the answers.

"It's true," he said in a rough voice. "The only magical recipe I've ever been able to make is moonshine, and even that isn't very powerful."

"Ack." Qiang threw up his hand. "You are not a chef." He said it like the word was something dirty. "You are a cultivator. A real one. With the power to become a Reaper."

"What does that mean, exactly?" Sofia asked, sensing that Graham wasn't in the right frame of mind for information-gathering. He seemed to be more worried about keeping his face hidden.

"It means you were not born to cook magic," Qiang told Graham. "You were born to bring it forth from the earth."

Um, wow. And Sofia felt like she was under a lot of pressure.

"Do you have any idea how rare your magic is?" Qiang demanded.

"I'm…not sure," Graham replied with an apologetic little shrug.

He seemed to be accepting this revelation about his magic with the same calm composure he approached everything in his life.

Except police sirens.

"Your magic is raw," Qiang said, undeterred by Graham's lack of enthusiasm. "I can teach you how to harness and channel it. Some day, you could replace me."

Sofia felt, rather than saw, Graham withdraw even further into himself.

When he didn't say anything, Qiang continued, "There is so much you need to learn, and I am the only one who can teach you. These jalapeños, for instance." He pointed to the leafy bush that Graham had just brought to life. "This plant can only support a single magical jalapeño. If the nonmagical ones aren't pruned, the magic pepper will be stunted."

"What will the jalapeño be able to do once it's full-grown?" Sofia asked.

She couldn't help herself. This was the sort of knowledge that didn't exist in any culinary magic textbook. It was fascinating stuff.

"If cultivated properly?" Qiang studied the plant. "A single one of its seeds will make whatever food it touches cook to perfection. No heat needed."

"And if…not cultivated properly?" Sofia asked.

"Perhaps it will be a dud and simply behave as a normal jalapeño would," Qiang said. "Or, it might spontaneously combust and raze an entire city to the ground."

Well, then.

"I would like to make you my apprentice," Qiang said to Graham, who was standing stiff and silent beside Sofia.

His words hung in the air.

"No," Graham said gruffly. "Thank you, but…I can't."

"You cannot let this gift fester and rot," Qiang said, aghast. He pressed a gnarled hand to his chest, as though Graham's refusal was causing him physical pain.

Sofia had to bite her tongue to keep from jumping in. If she was the one with this magic, she'd be bursting with questions and a need to see how far she could take it.

But it wasn't her magic.

"Think about what I am offering you," Qiang pressed. "I have never before seen a cultivator with so much raw talent."

"I don't have talent," Graham said. Even though his face was shadowed, the uncertainty in his voice was evident. "I'm just…good with plants."

Qiang let out a long-suffering sigh. He limped over to where he'd abandoned his pipe on the ground.

Sofia moved to help him, but Qiang made a noise that clearly meant *back off*, so she returned to Graham's side.

"I'd appreciate you not saying anything to Aralia about this," Graham told Sofia in a low voice, while Qiang was busy reclaiming his pipe. "Things are…complicated enough already. And I'm sure you've seen how stressed out she gets whenever she thinks I might leave."

Sofia held back an exasperated sigh. With this man, it was secrets on secrets.

"I won't say anything," she said in her most magnanimous tone. "It's not my business to get between you and Aralia."

Graham gave her a silent nod that conveyed deep gratitude.

Qiang made a grunting sound as he grasped his pipe and straightened back up. The whole endeavor seemed to thoroughly exhaust him. Or maybe it was Graham's refusal to become his apprentice. Either way, the old man appeared to wilt and age before Sofia's eyes.

"I have no children," Qiang said quietly. "No heirs. No one to whom I may pass on my expertise. For many years, I have thought my magic would die with me." He studied the long stem of his pipe for several long moments. Then, as though shaking himself out of a private reverie, Qiang's head jerked up. His focus landed on Sofia.

"Are you going to tell the Gourmands about all you've seen here?" he asked. His tone was laced with accusation and mistrust.

"No," Sofia said, startled by the question. "From everything I know about the Gourmands, I don't trust them as far as I could throw them."

Qiang nodded, seeming to relax.

"I have changed my mind about your proposal," he said. "If your friend will heal the rest," he gestured to the small swath of garden that was still dark and dead-looking, "then I will let you distribute some of my ingredients to help restore the balance." Qiang's eyes were like twin pinpricks in the dark. "And I will allow you to keep any profits you earn. I have no need of money."

"Really?" The word came out a little squeaky, so Sofia cleared her throat. "I mean, thank you. I'll make sure the ingredients go to people who won't abuse them, and that the Gourmands won't get anywhere near them."

Breathe, Sofia reminded herself.

"Our deal is only concluded if your friend will heal the rest of my garden," Qiang said. "And I'll start you off with a small batch of my ingredients to see if you are as good as your word." He tapped his pipe against his arm. "Do we have an accord?"

Yes! Sofia wanted to shout, but the question wasn't meant for her.

Graham stepped out from behind the bush that was half-hiding him from view. He leaned close enough that his warm breath tickled Sofia's neck.

"Is this what you want?" he asked in a low voice.

Sofia could only nod. There were no words to describe how much she wanted this. Needed it.

"Alright," Graham said, loud enough for Qiang to hear. "If you give Sofia the ingredients, I'll heal your garden."

"Very well," Qiang replied. To Sofia, he said, "Clementine will prepare some for you to take with you." He pointed his pipe at Sofia. "As a trial only. I will see how you do with this batch before deciding if I will give you more."

Sofia had to hide a giddy smile.

To Graham, Qiang said, "If you change your mind, there is much I could teach you."

"I appreciate the offer," Graham said. "But I can't."

Qiang nodded, his posture hunching a little more.

Sofia should feel sorry for him, but she was too busy being elated over her own shift in fortune.

As soon as Qiang shuffled back into the hut and shut the door, Sofia spun to face Graham.

"Thank you!"

She didn't even realize she'd thrown her arms around him until she felt Graham hug her back. He was so warm and strong and solid—

She pulled back.

Graham kept his arms loosely wrapped around her waist. Both of them were breathing harder than the simple act of standing still required.

"Should you really be touching me?" Sofia asked, trying to sound casual. "I mean, I'm pretty sure Aralia would flay both of us if she knew about this." She gestured to their proximity. "I can take care of myself, but I'm not sure you'd survive."

Graham's thick eyebrows pulled together in confusion, and then his whole face scrunched up like he'd eaten a sour berry.

"It's not like that with Aralia and me," he said quickly. "She's my sister."

"Do I look stupid to you?" Sofia scoffed. There was no way, with their completely opposite appearances, that the two of them were related.

"Foster siblings," Graham amended.

Oh.

"But she's more family to me than my real one ever was," Graham added.

Something jagged and raw flashed across his dark eyes. It disappeared as quickly as it had come. Graham's fingers tightened on her waist, drawing her closer.

"I can't believe you're a true magical ingredient cultivator," Sofia whispered, feeling strangely giddy. "You heard what Qiang said. If you wanted, you could become the next Reaper." She gestured vaguely at the vines that were curling around their ankles. "This is kind of amazing."

"Yeah," Graham said as he leaned closer. "It is."

Somehow, Sofia knew he wasn't talking about his magic or the garden.

"I want to kiss you, Sofia." Graham reached up with a tentative hand and brushed his knuckles over her cheek. "Can I?"

No one had ever explicitly asked permission to kiss her before. It was weird. And kind of charming.

But mostly weird.

"Okay," she whispered.

Graham smiled as he leaned in and pressed his lips to hers. For such a big man, he was so gentle.

Always impatient, Sofia stretched up on her toes and pulled his mouth more firmly against hers. She prodded the seam of his lips with her tongue.

Something like a growl rumbled through Graham as he reacted, lifting her up and gripping her thighs as she wrapped her legs around him. Sofia dug her fingers into his broad shoulders.

"Wow," he panted when they came up for air. "That was…you are…."

Sofia managed a wheezy little laugh.

"Incredible," Graham finished, his chest still heaving.

Sofia wanted to touch the freckles she could only see because their faces were centimeters apart. So, she did just that.

Graham closed his eyes and leaned into her touch.

She felt addicted to the warmth of his body and velvet heat of his tongue. Never before had she been desperate to repeat a kiss as soon as it was over.

It scared her. But not enough to pull away when Graham kissed her again.

This time, it took less than a second for Graham's self-control to crumble. They clutched at each other as the heat between them built to an inferno. Sofia thrust her hands under Graham's shirt, tracing the chiseled planes of his stomach.

"Sofia," he groaned.

Just the sound of her name on his lips sent shivers racing through her.

His big hands came up to frame her face, holding her with the lightest of touches as his mouth ravaged hers.

More, her body commanded.

Graham kissed her neck as his hands squeezed her arse. Sofia felt him everywhere.

"Oy!" a voice that was neither Sofia's nor Graham's called out. They broke apart on a gasp. "Are you going to fix my plants, or are you going to spend the rest of the night defiling my garden?"

Qiang was standing amid an array of brightly-colored flowers, pipe dangling from his mouth and hands fisted on his hips.

For some reason, Sofia found the whole situation absurdly funny. She began to giggle.

Graham, who had flinched at the sound of Qiang's voice, gave her a quizzical look. Then, he started to chuckle, too. The sound of their laughter filled the quiet night as Qiang grumbled to himself and went back to his hut.

It was a long time before Graham got around to healing the magic plants. And even when he did, he kept one hand laced tightly with Sofia's. By the time they made it back to their truck, Sofia's cheeks hurt from a smile that wouldn't fade.

CHAPTER 23

BRAXTON

Braxton finished recounting his telepathic conversation with Kenzie for Chef Levy, who kept interrupting him to ask questions.

Braxton let his head fall back against the couch cushion. His eyelids were heavy and his voice was hoarse. His muscles felt like liquid. If he tried to stand up, he'd probably pass out. It didn't matter, though. He'd talked to Kenzie.

She was alive.

"What else did she tell you about this Benedict person?" Chef Levy demanded.

"Nothing I haven't already told you," Braxton said.

He'd answered Chef Levy's last dozen questions with some variation of this response.

"Maybe if you'd done something useful instead of flirting, we might have something to go on!" Chef Levy shoved back her chair and started to pace. She muttered to herself in Hebrew.

Braxton stayed where he was. His insides felt squeezed, like his body had been drained. An image of those raisin-like corpses in the Bonecruncher's garage came to mind.

A persistent throb at the base of Braxton's skull warned him that he was angling for one hell of a magic hangover. He needed to sleep.

Instead, he started psyching himself up to make the dish again.

An angry shriek came from upstairs. It was followed by a pounding of footsteps.

Aralia stalked into the room and jabbed her finger in Braxton's chest.

"What did your seductress sister do with Graham?" she demanded.

"What?" Braxton swatted her finger away. "I don't know where Graham is, but Sofia's sleeping. So lower your goddamn voice and stop throwing around accusations."

Admittedly, the last time Braxton had seen his sister had been more than twelve hours ago. Then again, Sofia usually stayed in her room when she was working on her laptop so she wouldn't be bothered. And she and Braxton hadn't seen much of each other since everything with Mum. Braxton wasn't avoiding his sister, exactly…he just didn't know what to say to her.

"I thought they were fucking in the barn," Aralia ranted. "But they're not—"

"You thought they were…what?!"

Braxton was going to kill Graham. He wouldn't even bother with culinary magic. He looked around for the biggest knife he could find.

"Graham's truck is gone," Aralia continued. "He shouldn't have left. Wherever your sister made him go—"

Braxton didn't give a shit about Graham. He started hunting around the kitchen for wherever he'd left his phone.

Graham was with Sofia. If that criminal so much as looked at her….

The nutmeg he'd ingested earlier was making his stomach roil.

"You're not going anywhere," Chef Levy informed Braxton. "You're halfway to a magic coma, and if you don't sleep, you'll kill yourself before I get what I came here for."

Thanks for all of your concern about my wellbeing, Chef….

Movement outside the window made Braxton forget about trying to find his phone. Graham's truck was bumping up the driveway toward the cabin.

"I'll kill 'em," Aralia muttered as she ran out the door.

Get in line, Braxton thought. He'd told Sofia to stay away from Graham.

Yeah? And when has Sofia ever listened to anyone?

"Where the hell were you?" Aralia shouted as soon as Sofia and Graham got out of the truck.

Graham winced.

Braxton ignored the argument that was heating up between Aralia and Graham. He turned all of his attention on his sister.

A quick once-over told him she wasn't bleeding or suffering any immediate threat to her life. These days, that seemed like half the battle.

"I told you not to leave the cabin without me, Sofe." He tried to sound calm. He really did. "If you need to go somewhere, I'll go with you. And I told you to stay away from Graham."

Anger lit up Sofia's green eyes. Because it was like looking into a mirror of his own emotions, he knew he'd pushed her too far.

"You'll come with me?" Sofia's laugh was high and cold. "You're never around, Brax. You don't tell me shit about what you're doing. And all you bloody talk about is finding Kenzie!"

Braxton had to stop himself from flinching at her words, because she was right.

Sofia wasn't finished, though. "And you lost the right to give me dating advice after you started sleeping with our brother's murderer!"

The accusation was loud enough that Aralia and Graham stopped bickering. The birds stopped chittering in the trees.

"This is different," Braxton said. The argument sounded weak even to him. "Graham's a—"

He felt the words he wanted to say cut off before they reached his lips. The tang of dried cranberries and slight bitterness of toasted macadamia nuts coated his tongue, as the magic of promise granola forced him to hold back the explanation of what Graham had done. Telling Sofia the truth would endanger Graham's life, which would be a direct violation of the promise Braxton had made to Aralia. He couldn't say more without risking whatever consequence would come from breaking his vow.

"Just trust me," Braxton said lamely when the magic retreated back inside him. "Stay away from Graham."

"I'd be happy to," Sofia said, smiling in a way that meant trouble. It was the expression of a predator that had cornered its prey and was preparing to strike. "If you stay away from Kenzie."

And, there it was.

"Sofe, you know I can't do that. This is different."

Sofia spun on her heel and marched over to Graham. She turned to make sure Braxton was watching. Then, she clutched the front of Graham's shirt and pulled him against her.

Graham's eyes widened a fraction, but he didn't resist when Sofia stretched up and kissed him. Quite the opposite. He dropped the folded-up jacket he'd been holding so he could wrap both his arms around her.

"You've made your point," Braxton growled.

Sofia ignored him. She had her hands on Graham's waist, *under his shirt*, and he was holding her face in his hands.

Braxton wanted to tear the man apart. The problem was that Graham was glued to Sofia.

He needed to get away from here. The image of Graham mauling his sister was already burned into his brain. If Braxton didn't put some distance between them, he might really kill that bloke.

"I need to go for a drive," he choked out, holding out his hand for Aralia's keys. "Please."

The *please* came through teeth ground so tightly together it sounded like *pliz*.

Aralia, who seemed almost as put off by Sofia and Graham's display as he was, handed them over without protest.

A tiny sliver of relief went through Braxton when he started up the engine, and Sofia broke away from a dazed-looking Graham.

"Brax, wait," Sofia called, running over to the truck.

"You're right, Sofe," he said. "You're a big girl, and I can't tell you what to do. Just be careful. He's not…what you think."

"You can't leave now," Sofia said.

She looked and sounded irritated, but Braxton knew his sister well enough to sense the real emotion she was using her anger to cover. It was hurt.

Braxton's fury softened a little. "I'll be back in half an hour," he promised her. "I just need a few minutes to get my shit together."

"I'll do you one better," Sofia said. "Once you see what I've brought, you'll forget you were ever in a bad mood."

Sofia didn't give him a chance to say anything before she hurried over to Graham's truck. She grasped the edge of the tarp covering the truck bed and yanked it back.

Braxton found himself staring at a flower box full of herbs, except there was nothing normal about these herbs. They glowed and pulsed with magical power. It practically wafted off them. Braxton was almost dizzy with it.

"Sofe." He turned to her. "What the hell?"

For the first time in far too long, Sofia offered him a genuine smile.

"We're going to sell these and pay back every cent we owe the Santioris." Her smile turned feral. "Then, we're going to run them and the Gourmands out of their own business."

CHAPTER 24

KENZIE

Two Cutthroat Cuisine guards led Kenzie into a room that was half-kitchen, half-science lab. A few chefs wearing red aprons over their scrubs were chopping, braising, and magicking. The countertops were covered in a rainbow of ingredients.

The whole operation was coldly efficient. There was no shouting or laughter or the usual sounds that Kenzie had always associated with kitchen work. The cheerless atmosphere probably had something to do with Benedict and Nurse Ratched, who were watching the chefs with a vulture-like intensity.

"Why am I here?" Kenzie asked, knowing better than to drop her guard around these people even for a second.

"There are four competitors remaining in Cutthroat Cuisine," Benedict replied. "I believe you will ultimately triumph, and thus, you will become my successor."

Fat. Freaking. Chance.

Kenzie wanted to be in charge of this dysfunctional, corrupt organization the same way she wanted a hole in her head.

"Without strong leadership," Benedict continued, "the art and beauty of culinary magic will be lost."

"That sounds a little fatalist, don't you think?" Kenzie said.

"Stop being an ignorant twit," Nurse Ratched sneered. At a glance from Benedict, she lowered her head and stared at her freakishly-white sneakers.

"It is time for you to learn about the other reason for Cutthroat Cuisine, aside from identifying my successor," Benedict told Kenzie. "Magic extraction."

"That sounds painful," she quipped.

"I haven't heard any complaints," Benedict replied mildly.

Nurse Ratched's laugh sounded unpracticed and wrong.

Benedict led the way around a prep counter to a little alcove where….

Kenzie clutched the side of the counter to keep herself upright. She stared down at the white floor so she wouldn't have to see—

Nurse Ratched's nails dug into the back of Kenzie's neck.

"Look," the evil nurse commanded.

Kenzie did. She couldn't help it.

Cookie's body was strung up on a wooden table contraption that looked like some kind of Medieval torture device. She was naked, and her bronze skin was scorched through in places from the magic wine that had killed her. Kenzie was grateful she hadn't eaten anything recently, because she could see the white gleam of Cookie's ribcage in places where her skin had eroded away.

"You sick fucks!" Kenzie lashed out at Nurse Ratched.

She got in one good kick before the two guards overpowered her. Benedict gave a slight shake of his head, stopping the guards from zapping her with their Tasers. Instead, Benedict hooked the end of his cane around Kenzie's throat and gave it a warning tug. Kenzie choked on lack of air and pure hatred.

"Cutthroat Cuisine is a competition to the death, as you well know," Benedict said. "Part of the reason for that is because our organization is secret, and those who fail to prove their worth in the arena cannot be trusted to keep their knowledge to themselves. You are about to witness the other reason. I hope it will give you comfort to know your friend did not die in vain."

If Kenzie had enough oxygen to spare, she would have laughed. She'd met some delusional people in her life, but this man really took the cake.

Nurse Ratched was busy fiddling with a crank-like arm on the device that was holding Cookie. There was a metallic grinding, and then the table began to fold itself in half.

A pathetic whimpering sound escaped Kenzie. She tried to get out of Benedict's grip, but the cane held her in place.

Cookie might be beyond help, but that didn't stop Kenzie from wanting to save her from this humiliation.

The machine kept going until it had completely sandwiched Cookie. There was a slurping sound, and then a clear, shimmery liquid began to seep between the cracks. It collected in a small metal gutter that trickled downward.

Nurse Ratched was ready to capture the fluid in a measuring cup.

The temperature in the room began to rise. Kenzie got the same tingle at the back of her skull that happened whenever there was strong magic in the making.

"This apparatus harvests a chef's magical essence," Benedict explained, his mouth horrifyingly close to her ear. "When the chef has…expired…a great deal of magic can be harvested. The more powerful a culinary magician, the greater their magical output."

"This is a good one," Nurse Ratched announced, pointing to the ¾ cup marker on the measuring cup. "Scarlet only gave half a cup."

Nurse Ratched released the handle on the machine, allowing it to creak back open.

Kenzie's legs buckled. She didn't even feel it when her knees thudded onto the hard floor. All she could see was Cookie…or what was left of her.

Cookie, who had been as full of life and sass as Kenzie, had been sucked dry. She was the human version of a prune. Her skin, no longer bronze but gray, was shriveled and translucent. It was fused tight to her bones, which looked mottled and brittle.

Cookie's face was the most disturbing part. Her body had lost all its moisture, and so there was a dark gap between her lifeless eyeballs and eye sockets. Her full lips had been sucked dry and peeled back from her teeth to form a ghastly grin.

"I take it back," Kenzie managed, her voice coming out raspy. "You aren't just sick. You're as evil as they come. You're going to get yours. Someday—"

"Shh," Benedict commanded.

He pointed to Nurse Ratched, who was carefully drawing some of the magic liquid from the measuring cup into a syringe. She brought it over to the prep counter, where a bunch of radishes was sitting on a cutting board. Nurse Ratched plucked one of the radishes off its stem and injected a small amount of magical liquid into the vegetable.

Almost at once, the radish began to quiver. It pulsed ruby red before settling back to its original color. Tendrils of magic danced above it like wisps of smoke.

"Eat it," Benedict ordered.

Kenzie was about to refuse but realized the command wasn't for her. Without so much as an eyebrow raise of dissension, Nurse Ratched put the entire radish in her mouth.

The nurse cringed a little. Her tongue was probably on fire from the peppery heat…along with whatever magic was coursing through the vegetable.

"Oh," Nurse Ratched said, startled as she caught sight of her forearms. They were turning red.

It was more than just a flush, and it was creeping over every inch of visible skin on her body.

"Now you look like the devil you are," Kenzie observed. To Benedict, she asked, "Is that what this magic does…show a person for who they really are?" She blinked innocently. Nurse Ratched growled.

Benedict didn't take the bait.

"Touch the girl," Benedict ordered Nurse Ratched.

"The girl has a name," Kenzie said, because it was easier to be petulant than to stare at Cookie's shriveled remains.

Nurse Ratched crossed the kitchen and wrapped her fingers around Kenzie's wrist.

There was a soft hiss, followed by a sizzle. Searing heat shot across Kenzie's skin.

"What the hell?!" she yelped.

Kenzie wrenched her hand away from the nurse. There was a red burn in the exact shape of Nurse Ratched's hand around her wrist. Kenzie's skin felt as raw as if she'd pressed it against a pan just out of the oven.

"This is what you killed Cookie for?!" Kenzie knew she sounded unhinged, but this was all too much.

"It may seem harsh," Benedict said, his English accent sounding even snootier and more forced than usual. "However, I urge you to consider the broader picture. A few deaths are meaningless when compared to the survival of culinary magic."

"I didn't realize it was in jeopardy," Kenzie spat.

Disgust was like a living, breathing thing inside her.

"It's always in jeopardy," Benedict replied. His usually-calm veneer had slipped to reveal hints of venom. His pale cheeks had turned ruddy. "You cannot imagine the devastation the Vanillas would wreak if they got a taste of our magic."

"Vanillas?" Kenzie repeated.

"It's how the Gourmands refer to the non-magic population," Benedict said, his sneer deepening. "I lost both my parents and three siblings because of a single Vanilla who witnessed their magic."

Benedict lowered his head. "You cannot…imagine…." He trailed off. When he looked at Kenzie, his eyes were red-rimmed. "I lost them all," he said, his voice coming out raw and unaccented. "I would do anything to make certain no other culinary magician experiences that kind of loss."

Kenzie was speechless. Under other circumstances, she would offer her condolences. Getting kidnapped and forced to cook to the death had done something irreparable to her sense of empathy, though. At least where the Gourmands were concerned.

"If you win Cutthroat Cuisine and become my successor," Benedict said, "you will see the constant threat our magic world faces every day. You will understand there are no easy choices when it comes to protecting our kind."

Kenzie decided it was better not to think too deeply about what Benedict was saying, lest she actually develop Stockholm syndrome.

"Get the rest of these radishes magicked and deliver half of them to the arena for the next Cutthroat Cuisine match," Benedict told Nurse Ratched. His bossiness and English accent were back in full force. "The rest go into storage."

The two of them strode out of the room. Polly and the two Taser-happy guards less-than-gently escorted Kenzie back to her room. Kenzie was too overwhelmed by everything she'd seen and heard to protest.

"Come along, dearest," Polly jabbered. She was dressed in a floor-length, bubble gum-pink gown. It was studded with pink gems that, knowing Polly, were real. "The next match is starting in half an hour. It's going to be a good one!"

"That so," Kenzie mumbled.

She wasn't really even listening to Polly. Her mind was full of the image of Cookie's dehydrated corpse.

"I know we're not supposed to have favorites," Polly babbled, "but his parents and I go way back. It isn't personal, dear."

"Uh-huh."

"Thomas—oops, I mean *Hammer*—is most definitely your stiffest competition," Polly said. "He was Benedict's choice for the win, up until everything that happened with you and Toxic.

There are still matches to be won, of course, but we all knew from the beginning that it would be you and Hammer at the end."

Kenzie remembered Cookie saying that Cutthroat Cuisine's outcome was fixed. How right she'd been.

"Then why," Kenzie said through gritted teeth, "did you bother bringing ten other people into this hellhole?"

Polly gave her a wounded look.

"Because, dearest. Cutthroat Cuisine wouldn't be very exciting if it was only a single match. Giving the Gourmands an entertaining spectacle has been useful in keeping them fully satisfied."

Kenzie scraped her jaw off the floor. "Are you freaking kidding me?" she demanded.

"Not at all," Polly said in complete earnestness. "Besides, how else would the Gourmands get enough magical essence to make their artificial ingredients?" She gave a tittering little laugh. "We can't just go around killing culinary magicians on the street and squeezing them dry, can we?"

The two guards watching Kenzie's every move were the only reason she didn't sucker-punch Polly. And then stuff her into that body-squeezing machine…see how much she liked being reduced to some liquid in a measuring cup.

"Hammer's mother is a Gourmand, so he's an old hat around here," Polly said, blissfully unaware of the murderous thoughts racing through Kenzie's mind. "In fact, I'm having supper with their family tonight after Hammer's match."

"Uh-huh."

"I don't want you to feel as though he's getting special privileges, dearest," Polly continued. "It's just that when he goes home between his matches, his parents already know where he's been. There's no danger of him revealing sensitive Gourmand information."

"Uh-huh."

"Their family is so classy," Polly carried on, completely oblivious to Kenzie's lack of enthusiasm. "Tina designs stationary during her free time. Look at what she made, just for a simple meal!"

Polly produced a gold cardstock menu with lace and tiny pearls framing the edges. Kenzie was about to point out that the whole thing might be a tad over the top, when she caught sight of the text on the menu.

Kenzie's haze of grief and fury vanished in an instant. Because there, held out in Polly's manicured hand, was exactly what she'd been waiting for.

Shiny black calligraphy covered the gold cardstock:

Please join Tina and Henry Morierty for a magical supper….

There was a menu beneath their names that involved a lot of lobster, and then, at the bottom….

Kenzie used every millisecond of time before Polly pocketed the invitation to memorize the address. The Manhattan address.

Polly was still talking as she locked Kenzie back into her room, but Kenzie didn't answer. She was busy committing the names and address to memory.

The next time Braxton made contact with her, she'd have something useful to tell him.

Thanks, Polly. Thanks very much.

CHAPTER 25

BRAXTON

Stop sulking," Sofia ordered. "We're going out."

Braxton wanted to argue, but there was no point. First, because there was no disagreeing with Sofia when she got in one of her bossy moods…which was pretty much always. And, second, because Braxton couldn't do what he really wanted to do, anyway.

He was itching to make Chef Levy's telepathy recipe again. He was just too magically depleted to manage it.

"Where are we going?" Braxton asked. He caught the set of keys Sofia tossed to him.

"You'll see," she said, leading the way out the door.

Things were still awkward between them, but there was no room left for hostility. All Braxton cared about now was keeping her safe and doing whatever he could to prepare her for when he'd no longer be around.

The closer he got to finding Kenzie, the closer he came to losing the small bit of freedom he still had. Aralia never missed a chance to remind him of their bargain, and the weight of it was like a vise around Braxton's chest.

"Take a left," Sofia instructed when they reached the end of the driveway.

They drove for about twenty minutes without discussing more than directions, until Sofia told him to pull off at an abandoned-looking barn.

"What's this?" Braxton asked, getting out of the truck and looking around.

"It's ours," Sofia replied. "Well, for the day, anyway. I rented it."

"Um…why?"

"It was available, and I figured it was far enough from the cabin that it would be safe."

"Safe for what?" Braxton asked, doing everything in his power to keep his tone even. "And why the hell would you spend money on this?" He gestured at the barn, which looked like it was in danger of collapsing.

"Oh good, they're here," Sofia said, pushing him aside and waving.

A battered minivan was bumping over the grass path that led to where they were already parked.

Sofia reached into the truck cab and lifted out the flower box filled with magical ingredients. Braxton noticed that she had wrapped and labeled each of them individually. Sofia sifted through the individual packets and took one out. She strode over to the minivan.

The man who got out of the driver's seat was probably in his sixties or early seventies. He was dressed in denim overalls, and as he came around to open his wife's door, Braxton saw that the soles of the man's boots were worn almost straight through.

His wife leaned heavily on him as he helped her out of the car.

"Mr. and Mrs. Euroy," Sofia said, her professional smile firmly in place. "I trust you didn't have any trouble finding us?"

"Not at all, ma'am," came the man's polite reply. He wrapped one arm around his wife and extended the other to Sofia. "Thank you for answering our email. We sure are grateful. We've got the money here—"

"Let's make sure it works before we discuss payment," Sofia said in her brisk manner.

Braxton just watched as Sofia opened the packet she was holding and offered a dried banana leaf to Mrs. Euroy.

The woman moved slowly, and her hand shook as she held it out for the leaf.

"It's been a difficult few years," Mr. Euroy told Braxton, as though he needed to apologize for something. "There were layoffs at the lumberyard, and Melly couldn't keep nannying with her chemo schedule. We tried surgery, but it didn't take. And when we lost our insurance—" He broke off as his wife unwrapped the scarf she was wearing around her neck, despite the fact that it was a warm spring day.

Braxton sucked in a breath, but Sofia didn't seem at all surprised by what they were seeing. A lump the size of an orange was protruding from Mrs. Euroy's throat.

"Neck tumor," Mr. Euroy explained. "Very fast-growing. It's…spreading."

Mrs. Euroy rested a hand on her husband's arm. The two of them leaned their heads together. Braxton caught fragments of their whispered conversation.

"…always love you…. No matter what happens…."

Braxton's heart felt like it was pushing up against his ribcage.

"Allow me," Sofia said, clearly undaunted by the couple's intimate moment. She took the banana leaf out of the woman's unsteady hand and pressed it over the tumor.

Braxton felt a surge of magical energy as Sofia removed her hand. Even though no one was touching the banana leaf, it remained fused to the woman's tumor.

Mrs. Euroy let out a little gasp.

"Does it hurt?" her husband asked, his body taut with concern.

"N-no," she replied. "Feels strange, though."

Braxton was a little dizzy from how much magic was wafting off the banana leaf. It pulsed and shimmered, giving the air around it a pearly tint.

There was a flash of light that was so strong Braxton had to look away. Then, as quickly as it had come, the light disappeared. The banana leaf fluttered to the ground, blackened and inert. The magic was gone.

And so was the tumor.

Holy shit. The woman's tumor was gone.

"Oh, Lord," Mrs. Euroy said, raising her hand to feel the place on her neck where the lump had been. Now, there was only smooth skin.

"It's gone," she said, clasping her husband's hands. "Not just that one. I can feel the others are gone, too. And my muscles and bones feel…." She let out a little sob. "I feel so good, Brad."

Mr. Euroy fell to his knees at Sofia's feet. He was crying.

"Thank you," he said between sobs. "Thank you. Thank you. Thank you."

"You're welcome," Sofia said. She'd never been good at receiving gratitude, despite the fact that she was always doing things to deserve it. "Please let me know if the cancer ever returns, although I've been assured that this particular treatment is as close to permanent as they come."

Braxton didn't think Mr. Euroy even heard her. He was on his feet again, and he and his wife were jumping up and down like kids. Both of them were crying tears of joy. Braxton felt a sting at the back of his own throat.

There were more thanks as Mr. Euroy pulled an envelope out of his pocket and handed it to Sofia.

"Wow," Braxton said after the couple had driven away. "That was…something."

Sofia opened the envelope. Inside were five twenties.

Braxton's jaw fell.

"Sofe, you charged that woman a hundred bucks to cure her cancer?"

"I did a thorough investigation of all of our customers' financials before agreeing to sell to them," Sofia said, folding up the bills and putting them back in the envelope. "This was what they could afford to pay."

"Who are you and what have you done with my sister?" Braxton asked.

Sofia was a negotiation shark. Their father used to boast that the only two people he needed to close a deal were his business lawyer and his daughter.

"You do realize you could have sold that leaf for hundreds of thousands, right?" Braxton asked.

"Millions," Sofia replied. "But that wasn't the agreement I made with Qiang. Besides, it felt right."

Braxton shook his head, caught been amusement and a niggling sense that the answer to their financial problems was sitting in that flower box…and they weren't taking advantage.

"Mum and Dad would be so proud of you," he said. "So would Aid."

Sofia's icy exterior cracked ever so slightly. "You think?"

Braxton slung an arm over her shoulders. "I know. And I am too, Sofe. So fucking proud."

"It's the first thing that's felt right in a long time," she said softly.

Braxton tightened his hold on her. "Yeah. I know."

They pulled apart as another car pulled into the lot. This one was a BMW convertible. The BMW came to a screeching halt way too close to the two of them for comfort. Braxton pushed Sofia back a few steps.

The man who got out of the convertible was wearing a suit and designer sunglasses. He also had a sunburn peeking out through his hair plugs and a gut the size of New York State.

"You got the stuff?" he asked…no, demanded. He also only looked at Braxton, completely disregarding Sofia.

"Do you have the money?" Sofia replied.

The man pulled a check out of his pocket and passed it over. Sofia unfolded the check, verified the amount, and then nodded.

"Wait here, please," she said, going back to the truck.

Braxton stayed where he was. He didn't like the way the man stared at Sofia's legs.

"I need a new assistant," the man told Braxton, still fixated on Sofia's legs. "This one available?"

"If anyone's the assistant here, it's me," Braxton said through gritted teeth. "And if you keep staring at my sister like that, I'll break your jaw."

Braxton was gratified when the other man stepped back and studiously pinned his gaze to the ground.

"Here you are," Sofia said, passing the man a lumpy package.

He snatched it out of her hand and tore open the wrapping. He let the paper fall onto the ground without a second glance. Every bit of his attention was focused on the head of broccoli he'd unwrapped.

"Do I have to eat the whole thing?" he asked, giving the broccoli a dubious look.

"Yep," Sofia said. "And it has to be raw. No cooking or added flavors."

Braxton wasn't sure if that was a requirement of the magic, or simply because Sofia took her revenge where she could.

The man began stuffing the broccoli in his mouth. He ate it so quickly he barely chewed. In seconds, he'd demolished the vegetable, stem and all.

"Well?" the man asked impatiently. "How long's it take to work?"

Sofia didn't have a chance to answer. Braxton felt a wave of dizziness as the magic swirled.

The man began to shrink.

Well, that wasn't precisely accurate. The man was still just as tall; only his gut was receding.

His stomach kept going until it was completely flat. Then, other parts of him began to smooth out. His loose jowls tightened up, along with the waddle he was sporting between his double-chin…which was no longer. His flabby cheeks pulled back to show sharp cheekbones. By the time the magic dissipated, the man was unrecognizable. He looked like he'd just stepped off the pages of a magazine.

"Not bad," Sofia said.

The man was busy checking himself out in his car's side mirror. He straightened up and buttoned his jacket, which was now several sizes too large.

"How about I take you out for an early dinner," he said to Sofia.

"Fuck off," Braxton told the man, at the same time Sofia said, "Off you go, now. Shoo."

The man didn't need to be told again. He hopped in his convertible and sped off.

"I really hope you charged that arsehole more than a hundred dollars," Braxton said.

Wordlessly, Sofia passed him the check.

Braxton unfolded it and stared at the amount. He counted the zeroes. Counted them again.

His brain kept fizzing out every time he tried to fully process the number.

"Um." He cleared his throat. "How much of these profits did you say we get to keep?"

"All of them," Sofia replied.

Braxton looked at the amount on the check again. The number was still there.

Eight-million. Fucking. Dollars.

CHAPTER 26

SOFIA

Sofia yawned and rolled her neck. It had been a long day. It had also been the best day she'd had in what felt like ages.

Together, she and Braxton had sold off every magical ingredient Qiang had given her. Clementine had explained what each of the ingredients would do in advance—it was how Sofia had known who to approach for her buyers—but that hadn't diminished the effect of seeing the ingredients do their thing. She hadn't been so thrilled about the tears and inevitable hugs her buyers doled out when the ingredients worked, but it had been worth it.

Sofia, the least magical person in the world of culinary magic, had something no one else did. It was bloody euphoric.

"You did good today, little sis," Braxton said, speaking through a yawn of his own.

"You too, big brother."

She couldn't remember the last time they'd just hung out together. Sure, they'd been working, but still. Kenzie hadn't been mentioned even once. It was glorious.

"You going to get another batch of those ingredients?" Braxton asked as he turned off the truck.

"Already on it," she replied, shooting off a quick text to Clementine.

Sofia might have her doubts about Qiang's ditsy assistant, but there was no denying the two of them made a good team.

"Are you going to wire the Santioris the money?" she asked. Just saying that name out loud made her insides curdle.

When she looked at her brother, she saw her own burning hatred reflected in his eyes.

"Yeah," he said. "It'd raise fewer questions if we paid back our debt in increments instead of all at once, but I just want to be able to wash our hands of that family."

A muscle pulsed in his jaw, and Sofia knew he wasn't any happier about the situation than she was. Rick had ordered his thugs to kill Mum. Instead of taking their revenge, Sofia and Braxton were paying him a small fortune.

"It would cause a world of problems if we tried to go after them," Sofia murmured.

"I know." Braxton gave her a rueful grin. "But I can daydream, can't I?"

"I'll join you in that daydream," Sofia said. "Right after I call the bastard."

Swallowing down the bitter acid coating her throat, she called Rick Santiori.

"Hey, beautiful," Rick said as soon as he picked up. "You wanna face-time?"

Beside her, Braxton made a growling sound. Sofia shot him a warning look.

"What I would like," Sofia said into the phone, "is for you to take your money and then never bother us again. Braxton will be wiring you the full sum of our debt shortly."

"Realllly," Rick said, drawing out the word. "Who'd you have to rob to get it?"

Sofia didn't like the calculating tone in his voice. It made her think they'd made the wrong choice about paying the Santioris off all at once.

"That's not your concern, Santiori," Braxton said into the phone. "Take your money and then fuck off."

"I have a better idea," Rick said. "Sofia can bring a check to me in Chicago. How about it, beautiful? I'll show you around the town…give you a taste of everything you've been missing while you slaved in those sorry little restaurants your parents were so desperate to keep."

"Don't say a goddamn word about our parents," Braxton snarled, before Sofia could pull the phone away from him.

"Mini-mobsters aren't my type," Sofia told Rick. "You can expect the wire transfer by the end of business hours today." Then, she hung up.

For several seconds, she and Braxton stood there, seething.

"Promise me one thing," Sofia said, once they'd both calmed down a little. "If you ever get the chance to take Rick down, I want to be there."

"Deal." Braxton ruffled her hair in the same way he'd done since they were kids. "I'm going to go take care of this money, and then I'll make us some dinner. Any requests?"

"Whatever you want," she replied. "As long as it isn't any of Aralia's weird tree squirrels, or whatever else she catches in those traps of hers."

Braxton chuckled. "I think I can rustle something up. See you inside."

Sofia opened up the list of ingredients Clementine had just emailed her. She mentally went through her list of contacts, already pairing up people and ingredients. She was like a modern fairy grandmother. Except young. And definitely not jolly. Okay, so maybe she wasn't like that at all.

She raised her arms over her head, stretching out her sore back. She turned when she heard the soft tread of footsteps behind her.

"Hey," Graham said, offering her a shy smile. The setting sun was at his back, and the golden light framed his silhouette.

"Hey, yourself," Sofia replied, leaning back against the truck and drinking in her fill of him. "You look hot."

His flannel shirt was unbuttoned, showing off his skin-tight undershirt. She could swear his eight-pack was visible even through the fabric. She wanted to push his shirt up and run her hands along his rock-hard abs. She wanted to trace those grooves with her tongue.

"You always look amazing," Graham said. He was possibly blushing, but he ducked his head before she could tell for sure.

He moved close enough for Sofia to catch a whiff of woodsmoke on his clothes.

"Any interest in going for a moonlight kayak tomorrow night?" he asked.

The request was unexpected. Sofia didn't have the time or inclination to be wooed, which was why she was even more surprised by her answer.

"I'd like that," she said.

Graham beamed at her. "It's going to be a full moon tomorrow and should be a clear night. I'll have the kayaks all ready to go as soon as it gets dark."

With Graham, there was never any artifice or second-guessing his motivations. He was honest in a way that had unnerved Sofia at first, but was quickly starting to add to his charm.

If he's so honest, a little voice whispered in the back of her mind, *then why won't he tell you the reason he can't be seen in public? Why won't he tell you what he's hiding?*

The cabin door creaked open, and Aralia stepped onto the porch. Her gaze zeroed in on the two of them.

It hadn't occurred to Sofia until that moment how close she and Graham were standing.

Foregoing the steps, Aralia leapt over the porch railing and bounded over to them. She wrapped a heavy arm around Sofia's shoulders and gave her a sharp yank that was definitely a few degrees past friendly.

"I think I might like you," Aralia informed Sofia. "But if you hurt Graham, I'll—"

"Aralia," Graham warned.

"—make you squeal like a feral hog," Aralia finished.

Graham gave Sofia an apologetic look.

"That's fair," she told Aralia. "For what it's worth, I think I might like you, too."

Sofia hadn't had time for friends outside of work in years, but she thought there might be potential with this crazy woman.

"In that case, remind me to show you the dress I made that'll do your legs justice," Aralia said. "After dinner, though. I'm famished."

Just like that, the awkwardness was smoothed over.

Aralia traipsed inside. Graham held the door open for Sofia. His whiskey-colored eyes were fixed on her like she was the only person in the world. He didn't even seem to hear Aralia when she asked him a question.

A strange, but not unpleasant, zing went through Sofia's chest. All at once, their moonlit kayak trip seemed much too far away. She didn't want to wait.

The realization scared her. It was bad enough that she was starting to crave this man's touch, but it was even worse that she was growing actual feelings for someone she barely knew.

"I'll be in soon," she told Graham, who was still patiently holding the door open for her. "I just need to make a call."

Even once she was alone on the driveway, she didn't immediately pull up the number she'd been meaning to call.

Sofia didn't know why she should feel strange about what she was about to do. She did background checks on everyone she'd ever hired to work for one of her family's restaurants. Why shouldn't she do the same for someone she wanted to share her body with?

As she pulled up the contact, a feeling of wrongness swept through her. This felt a little like rummaging through someone's belongings while they were out getting groceries. Which she'd never done.

Okay, she'd done it once. But in her defense, her instincts had totally been right. She'd found stacks of cash hidden in his underwear drawer—no points for originality on that one. The cash had also come straight from the till of one of her family's restaurants.

Before she could talk herself out of it, she made the call.

Peter picked up on the second ring.

"Sofia McKaid," he purred. "I miss you, sweetheart."

"Mm. Same. Can you do me a favor?"

"Only if you promise to come out with me the next time you're in the States," he countered.

"Deal."

Sofia rolled her eyes at the darkening sky.

She'd met Peter at a nightclub in Washington, D.C., the summer before university. He'd been lousy in bed, but Sofia had kept in touch when she found out he was a highly sought-after private investigator. For that reason alone, she'd been willing to put up with some D-level pillow talk and pathetic drunk texts.

"I need you to get the scoop on someone for me," Sofia said.

She ignored the sick little feeling in her stomach as she told Peter everything she knew about Graham, which turned out to be infuriatingly little.

"I'll see what I can find," Peter said. "I'll call you as soon as I know anything."

"Thanks," Sofia replied, massaging the cramp that had formed under her ribcage.

"Maybe we can have a phone date," he suggested, far too eagerly. "You know, once work calms down for you."

"You'll be the first one I call," Sofia replied.

Some people would feel bad about using him. Sofia didn't. Her mind was already spinning ahead to tomorrow, and the next batch of magical ingredients Clementine had promised to deliver. That meant Sofia had some calls to make. These ingredients wouldn't find their new owners without her.

CHAPTER 27

BRAXTON

Come on, McKaid," Chef Levy said. "You're not concentrating."

"Trying, Chef," Braxton grated out.

He cursed and let go of the piping-hot pan he'd just touched with his bare hands.

"Are you out of your goddamned mind?!" Chef Levy shouted.

The rest of her insults were drowned out as the pan clattered onto the counter. Braxton managed to keep it from going to ground, getting one hell of a burn for his troubles.

"Idiot!" Chef Levy snarled. "Do you think I have time…."

She was still talking, but her words sounded fuzzy and far away. Braxton mopped his brow, wondering vaguely why he was sweating when he was so cold. His teeth were chattering.

Concentrate, he ordered himself.

The magic that came out of him was sluggish and weak. Too weak to do what he needed.

Kenzie, he thought. *Do it for Kenzie.*

He gave another push, focusing all of his energy on the food in front of him. The taste, smell…. He saw Kenzie's beautiful face shimmering in his mind, like a mirage. And, like a mirage, it vanished as soon as he reached for her.

"Kenz," he mumbled.

The floor warped beneath him. Braxton threw out a hand to catch himself, but he misjudged the distance to the counter.

He heard someone shout his name. Then, he blacked out.

* * *

Braxton blinked. He was lying on something soft, and a heavy blanket was draped over him. Firelight flickered on the wall.

He tried to sit up, but something pushed him back down.

"Easy, Brax," Sofia said, her voice uncharacteristically gentle.

"Sofe?"

"I'm here."

A damp washcloth was pressed to his forehead, which made him realize he had a pounding headache.

"Can you sit up a little?" Sofia asked.

His body felt like it had transformed into a giant boulder. Sofia helped lift him so he was propped against the couch armrest. She held a straw to his lips and ordered him to drink.

"Aralia made it," she explained. "And don't worry. I made her taste it first, just to make sure it wasn't poison. I like her, but I still don't trust her."

Braxton smiled at that.

The juice tasted like fresh oranges and strawberries. There was matcha powder, which had turned everything in the glass a sludgy-green. Color aside, the juice was delicious.

"Easy," Sofia said, before Braxton slurped up the entire glass.

"What happened?" he asked, his brain starting to return as the magic juice hit his system.

He felt like he'd been run over by a truck.

"You pushed your magic too far." Sofia folded over the washcloth so she could press the cool side to his burning forehead. It felt like heaven.

Sofia's brow furrowed. "I need you to start taking better care of yourself, Brax." Her voice grew impossibly soft when she added, "You're all I have left."

The combination of hurt and sympathy in her eyes was a kick to Braxton's gut.

"I'm sorry," he rasped. "You're right. And—" He forced himself to look at her. "I never should have left you and Mum alone that day Rick's people came. If I'd gotten to you sooner—"

"It wasn't your fault," Sofia said.

It was, though.

It should have been me instead of Aidan.

Braxton covered his face with his hands. He didn't cry, but his shoulders shook and he couldn't catch his breath.

He couldn't hear anything Sofia was saying over the drumbeat of regret pulsing through his veins.

Because it was long overdue, Braxton said, "I hate that you and Mum were the ones to pay for the choice I made at Hex Kitchen. I had no right to put either of you in that position. I'm so damn sorry, Sofe."

"It's not so much that," Sofia said, hesitating. She was clearly holding something back.

"Then what is it?" Braxton urged.

He and Sofia didn't have heart-to-hearts, so if she didn't say whatever was on her mind now, she probably never would.

"Honestly? It's that you chose Kenzie over us." Sofia looked away from him.

Braxton felt like he'd taken a punch to the solar plexus.

"I didn't," he began, and then stopped himself.

He kind of had.

He hadn't been thinking about it in those terms when he bit into the truffle and made his wish, but he'd known what the consequences would be. He'd measured up his options, and saving Kenzie's life had come out on top. Even though he'd known that, by saving her, he was condemning his family to this cat-and-mouse fight for their lives.

Sofia helped him drink more of Aralia's magic juice. It worked wonders on his headache. He was feeling almost back to normal.

"What now?" he asked.

Sofia dabbed the washcloth over his heated neck before she spoke.

"If you're up for it, you can come on a little road trip with me," Sofia said. "I'm meeting Clementine in Massachusetts to pick up the next batch of ingredients. And I might have talked Qiang into throwing in some tea leaves that'll get you back to full strength. You'll be able to cook that telepathy dish tomorrow."

"You're the greatest," Braxton told his sister. "You know that, right?"

"I have my moments."

Braxton was surprisingly steady on his feet as he stood and followed Sofia outside. She tossed him the keys to Graham's truck. The world only tilted a little as he climbed inside.

"You sure you're good to drive?" Sofia asked.

"Positive."

Braxton might have one hell of a magic hangover, but that didn't mean he was letting his sister get into the driver's seat. He wasn't that hard up.

"I've got the buyers all sorted out," Sofia said without looking up from her phone. Her thumbs were moving at lightning speed across the screen. "We're going to set up shop at a little cheese farm in southern Massachusetts. They're buying one of our ingredients and offered to let us use their barn for the day." Her fingers were still busy on her phone. "They invited us for dinner, too, before we drive back. Seem like nice people."

Braxton nudged her in the ribs. "Who are you, and what have you done with my sister?"

The old Sofia didn't have the time of day for small farmers or dinners that didn't involve squeezing millions out of prospective investors.

"Well, this whole situation isn't going to turn me into a philanthropist or anything," Sofia grumbled. "But pairing up magical ingredients with the people who need them hasn't been terrible."

Braxton knew enough to hide his smile.

When they got to the farm, an elderly couple was there to greet them. They offered Braxton and Sofia bottles of their homemade cider. The cold tang helped dull Braxton's residual headache even more.

They had just finished introductions when a big U-Haul truck pulled into the driveway.

A petite girl who barely looked old enough to drive hopped out of the truck. She let out a little squeal and raced over to them.

Sofia let out an *oof* of protest as the girl barreled into her, wrapping her skinny arms around Sofia and squeezing her.

"Ohmygosh," the girl gushed. "So good to see you. Missed you so much. This is so exciting. Reaper Lee—"

"Clementine, meet my brother Braxton. Brax, meet Clementine," Sofia said as she peeled herself away from the other girl.

"I saw you at Hex Kitchen," Clementine chattered. "Your sugar glass phoenix was the most gorgeous thing I've ever seen. I cried when it fell apart. For like, the entire day. Maybe, you could…."

Braxton stopped paying attention to Clementine's babble, because Sofia had opened the back of the U-Haul. It was empty save for a small carton that contained two rows of neatly-packaged and labeled ingredients. The container might not be large, but there was so much magic floating in the air that it was almost enough to knock Braxton on his arse.

"I wish you couldda filled that whole truck with magic ingredients," the farmer sighed.

"Oh, so would I, believe me," Clementine said. "But Reaper Lee is a perfectionist and won't let a single one of his ingredients off the vine until they're just right." She covered her mouth to hide a delicate giggle. "Most of our plants only produce one or two magical ingredients in a season, and Reaper Lee has a habit of destroying any plant that isn't perfect. Last year, he burned down a magical apple tree that he'd spent thirty years growing from a sapling. I told him. I said, 'Reaper Lee'—"

"Why are you driving this giant truck?" Sofia interrupted.

"Reaper Lee doesn't have a car," Clementine said cheerfully. "And I have a friend—well, he's not really a friend…more of an acquaintance. But, anyway, we met this one time I had to go to the post office, and—"

"Never mind," Sofia said loudly, drowning out Clementine. "Forget I asked."

Sofia hopped into the U-Haul and picked up the box of ingredients. She cradled it to her chest like it was a baby. Actually, knowing Sofia, she wouldn't treat a baby with half as much care.

Sofia gently placed the ingredients in a patch of shade before dusting her hands on her pants.

"Looks like our first customer is already here," she said, indicating the cloud of dust down the road. She peered down at her phone. "Dr. Gatniss."

"One packet of flaxseed," Clementine recited, locking her arms behind her back and standing straighter. "It'll give him steady hands for the rest of his life."

"He's a surgeon," Sofia told Braxton.

"Useful ingredient for him, then," Braxton said. "How much is he paying for it?"

"Fifty-thousand," Sofia replied.

Braxton whistled.

"He's a plastic surgeon who specializes in butt implants," Sofia said. "Trust me, he can afford it."

The car pulled up right next to the U-Haul, leaving mere inches between their side mirrors. It wasn't the color or make of the car that had the hairs rising on Braxton's arms, although that should have been a clue. It was more of a bone-deep certainty that something wasn't right.

"Get in the truck and lock the doors," Braxton told his sister.

"Brax, what—"

The SUV's back door opened.

"Hello, beautiful. Fancy meeting you here."

Rick Santiori smiled.

CHAPTER 28

KENZIE

Two days had passed since Kenzie's telepathic conversation with Braxton. She'd been locked in her room for all of that time, since her other Cutthroat Cuisine competitors were duking it out to see who would reach the semi-finals. With the exception of Nurse Ratched, who appeared twice a day to dump a trayful of magic-laced food on Cookie's empty cot, Kenzie hadn't seen anyone.

She passed the time by repeating the names and address she'd seen on Polly's dinner invitation. It was the key to helping Braxton figure out where she was being kept. If only she could share that information with him.

When Kenzie's door opened, she was so startled she whacked her head on her cot's metal headboard.

"Son of a bitch." She rubbed her skull.

"Come," Nurse Ratched ordered.

"Woof," Kenzie replied, scrambling off her cot before the door closed again.

She was so desperate for stimulation of any kind that she was willing to go wherever Nurse Ratched led her. Once she got out of here, she was going to need some serious therapy.

Blinking into the harsh hallway lighting like an owl, Kenzie followed the nurse to the kitchen she'd been in a couple of days ago. Cookie's husk of a body was no longer there, although the machine that had squeezed out her magic force was still in the corner. Waiting for its next victim, Kenzie supposed.

She longed for a weapon…or fifteen minutes alone in this kitchen. Then, she'd be able to give Nurse Ratched—pun intended—a taste of her own goddamn medicine.

Nurse Ratched brought Kenzie to a part of the room that was blocked off with plexiglass. A woman was on the other side of the glass. She was sitting in a chair that looked a little like an adult version of a baby's highchair.

Benedict was standing next to the highchair, holding a plate. There was a single red smear alongside a blue gelatin cube. Talk about minimalist plating….

"What am I doing here?" Kenzie asked, all of her nerves prickling in warning.

"Either you or Hammer will be my next successor," Benedict said. "If you are going to lead the Gourmands, then you need to begin to understand what we do."

"You seem to be under the mistaken impression that I'm on board with any of this," Kenzie replied. "The only thing I plan to do with the Gourmands if I win is lock all of you inside the arena and throw away the key. Oh, and I'll invite my friends to come throw rotten tomatoes at you while you cook to the death. Because…fun."

Benedict pressed his fingers into his temple, as though Kenzie's shenanigans were trying his patience.

"If you win Cutthroat Cuisine," he said, "then you may lead the Gourmands in any direction you choose."

How about right off a cliff, Kenzie was about to say, but Benedict kept talking.

"You will be in charge, but as every Gourmand leader has quickly discovered, you won't be free to do whatever you wish."

"Damn. There goes my idea for a sweet Cinco de Mayo party where we use you as the piñata," Kenzie deadpanned. "I'll have to think of something else."

Benedict ignored her. "If you make the wrong decision or rule with too light a touch, it will be a short path to exposing our entire world to the Vanillas." He gave Kenzie his most serious *I'm the savior of all culinary magic-kind* expression. "At which point, you will see precisely how quickly admiration transforms to fear and revulsion."

"That doesn't give you the right to kidnap and kill whoever you damn well please," Kenzie shot back.

If this man was looking for absolution, he'd need to hit up someone who held fewer grudges.

"If you think you've seen too much death in your time here," Benedict said, "then you are not ready for the tasks that await you. I, too, believed leading with a softer touch would be preferable."

"Let me guess," Kenzie drawled. "No one took you seriously, and you had to lop off a few heads to gain respect, and *blah blah blah.*"

"Not exactly." Benedict gave her a wry smile. "In my first week as leader of the Gourmands, a culinary magic family in Idaho held a large anniversary celebration. I was aware that a Vanilla would be in attendance, but I did nothing." He gripped the head of his cane hard enough that Kenzie could hear the ivory handle grinding against the wooden base.

"When the Vanilla witnessed culinary magic, he decided the chefs were possessed by evil spirits." Benedict made a throaty sound of disgust. "By the time we got there, that one Vanilla had shot and killed every single person at the party. He said he did it to exorcise the Devil from their souls."

"That's...insane," Kenzie managed. "But most people aren't like that."

"Aren't they?" The look he gave her was weary rather than the patronizing expression he usually wore. It messed with Kenzie's head as much as the story he'd told her.

Benedict cleared his throat, seeming to shake himself out of his reverie.

"Now that you understand a little more about our organization," he said, his English accent deepening and the self-important edge returning. "I would like to show you the solution to the culinary magic world's greatest obstacle."

"My greatest obstacle is that a bunch of assholes are holding me hostage," Kenzie said, falling back into the safety of sarcasm. "Can this solution help with that?"

Benedict gave her a smile that was as bland as white rice, making it clear her sarcasm was noted and unappreciated.

Everyone's a critic.

"I thought perhaps your performance in Cutthroat Cuisine the other day was a fluke," Benedict said. "I have been carefully monitoring Toxic to see if his magic returned."

"And?" Kenzie pressed.

"It has not," Benedict replied.

Kenzie's stomach flipped. She'd wanted to keep Toxic from burning her alive, but she had no desire to ruin his magic.

"There is only one plausible explanation for how you could manage such a feat," Benedict said, interrupting Kenzie's internal anguish. "Nevertheless, there is a simple experiment I'd like to conduct to confirm that you are truly what you appear to be."

There it was again…*what* she was rather than *who*.

This place was seriously doing wonders for her sense of self-worth.

"This test will not only reveal what you truly are," Benedict continued, "but it will show you what the Gourmands are capable of."

Benedict beckoned for Kenzie to come closer.

"This is Rosemary," Benedict said, indicating the woman in the highchair.

"Rosemary," the woman repeated with a little giggle that made it immediately clear she wasn't mentally all there.

Rosemary was wearing scrubs like the rest of the prisoners. She also wore a charm necklace that had metal fruits and vegetables hanging off the links. Her head was covered in a fine cap of flame-orange hair. She looked like she was in her fifties, but Kenzie guessed she was probably younger than the stress lines embedded in her face suggested.

"Rosemary is special," Benedict said. "She is a vital member of the team of culinary magicians who brought this iteration of the super food recipe into being." He gestured to the plate he was holding.

"There have been iterations?" Kenzie said. "Oh joy."

Benedict leveled his best *This is no joking matter* look.

"This is no joking matter, Kenzie," Benedict said. "All of the prior formulations killed any person who consumed the super food."

Kenzie felt the ironic smile slide right off her face.

"This version of the recipe is much improved," Benedict continued. "However, it interacts with a chef's body in a detrimental way. The brain, in particular, is affected."

As though to prove Benedict's point, Rosemary reached up and stroked her food charm necklace. "Rosemary and thyme and basil and coriander and caraway and dill," she sang. Her voice was so off-key it made Kenzie wince.

"Quiet," Benedict ordered.

Rosemary twitched in her highchair. Her voice cut off, but her lips still made the shape of her little song. Kenzie noticed the woman's fingernails were jagged and the skin beneath had a bluish tinge.

When Benedict positioned the plate on the center of Rosemary's tray table, the woman lunged for it. She swiped her finger through the raspberry-red smear and put it in her mouth.

A flush crept across Rosemary's cheeks. A fevered brightness lit her eyes.

As Kenzie watched, translucent strands of magic stretched between the plate and Rosemary's lips. The threads strengthened and almost seemed to shimmer under the fluorescent lights.

"Yesss," Rosemary hissed.

The threads of magic wound around Rosemary, writhing like pearly snakes. It was beautiful and terrible and…wrong.

This was wrong.

Kenzie didn't know how she knew, but she could sense that the magic was unstable. Unnatural.

The temperature in the kitchen was rising, but Kenzie's head felt like she'd eaten an entire carton of ice cream and gotten a brain freeze for her trouble.

"There's too much magic," Kenzie gasped, finding it difficult to catch her breath despite the fact that she wasn't doing anything.

Why was Benedict standing there as calm as ever? Couldn't he feel this?

"Rosemary, the blue," Benedict said in a sharp tone. He pointed to the blue cube on the plate.

Rosemary, who had her head tipped back and was moaning—in pleasure or pain, Kenzie couldn't quite tell—tried to look at Benedict. Her eyes were unfocused, though. A red rim pulsed around her irises and gave a faint glow to her skin.

Weird.

"No." Rosemary shook her head. "No no no no no!" She pressed her lips together tight enough that they'd gone completely bloodless.

Nurse Ratched, who had been standing quietly in the corner, appeared next to the highchair. She squeezed off a piece of the blue gelatin and brought it to Rosemary's mouth.

Kenzie didn't even have a chance to make a quip about cooties before Nurse Ratched clamped her free hand on the back of Rosemary's neck and shoved the gelatin into the woman's mouth.

As soon as she swallowed, Rosemary started to sweat and convulse in her highchair. The magic, which had been wrapped around her in a shimmery cocoon, began to flash and zing around the room. Kenzie was dizzy with trying to watch as magic threads flew and frayed and ultimately unraveled.

The magic-generated heat in the air dissipated, and the shimmery glow faded from Rosemary's skin.

The woman slumped in her chair, unconscious.

"What the hell was that?" Kenzie demanded.

"My greatest triumph," Benedict said. "But I have taken it as far as I can. The Gourmands require a new leader who will be able to perfect and stabilize the recipe." He studied Kenzie with an inscrutable expression. "I believe you will be the one to bring my dream to fruition."

Kenzie was pretty sure whatever constituted this man's dream would double as her nightmare.

"I will tell you more about the super food once you win Cutthroat Cuisine," Benedict said. "For now, I would like to perform a final test to prove, unequivocally, that you are what I think you are."

Nurse Ratched picked up the plate from Rosemary's tray and held it out to Kenzie.

"You've gotta be kidding." Kenzie looked back and forth between the plate and Rosemary, whose head was lolling back against the chair. If it wasn't for the rise and fall of her chest, Kenzie might have thought the woman was dead.

"If my suspicions are correct," Benedict said, "it won't hurt you."

"And if not?" Kenzie crossed her arms and glared. "I don't want my brain becoming—" *like Rosemary's* "—fried."

"No harm will come to you," Benedict replied. "This," he gestured to Rosemary's limp body, "is the result of too many encounters with the super food and its counter-agent—the anti-super food. A person would need to consume it dozens of times to become like her."

Was that supposed to be some kind of pep talk? If so, this guy had really missed his calling as a motivational coach.

"Eat the red one," Nurse Ratched ordered. "Now."

"Fine," Kenzie relented. "Under one condition."

"You're in no position to refuse," Nurse Ratched sneered.

Benedict gave the evil nurse a stern look before turning to Kenzie. "What's your condition?"

Kenzie had several, in fact. But she knew if she tried for any of the things she actually wanted, she'd just get shut down.

"No more of these allusions and half-assed explanations," she said. "I want to know exactly what you think I am."

"Agreed." Benedict motioned to the plate.

Here goes nothing, Kenzie thought as she dipped her finger in the raspberry smear. The food gave off a strong aroma that somehow carried the essence of winter spices, citrus freshness, bittersweet dark chocolate, and woodsy mushrooms. She brought her finger to her lips.

"Wait!" a voice shouted from the other room.

Polly, her cotton candy hair askew, came rushing into the room. If her lavender gown and chandelier earrings were any indication, she was fresh from the Cutthroat Cuisine arena.

"Did I miss it?" Polly asked Benedict.

Benedict raised his eyebrows and turned to Kenzie, who was frozen with the food on the tip of her finger.

"Oh, thank goodness." Polly clutched her heaving bosom. "I thought I was going to miss it."

And here Kenzie was thinking that Polly was concerned for her welfare. No such luck.

"Go on," Benedict ordered.

Kenzie put her finger in her mouth and sucked off the jam-like substance. It tasted like…actually, Kenzie had no idea what it tasted like. There were notes of fruit, red wine, and maybe a thousand other ingredients. It wasn't exactly bad, but it definitely wasn't something she was rushing off to add to the menu of her nonexistent restaurant.

It tasted like something an amateur chef would make if they were forced to use every ingredient in the kitchen in a single dish without any sense of quantities or moderation.

After a few seconds, Kenzie stopped trying to puzzle out the flavors and moved on to worrying about what she'd just ingested…and what it was going to do to her.

She didn't feel sick. Besides, if Benedict wanted to kill her, he'd had a dozen chances before now that involved a lot less fanfare.

She waited for convulsing and unconsciousness, but nothing happened.

"Well?" Benedict asked. "How do you feel?"

"Um, the same?"

"Eat the blue," Benedict commanded.

"You forgot to say please," Kenzie replied.

When Benedict just stared at her, completely unphased, Kenzie sighed. She couldn't help but sneak a glance at Rosemary, who was still out cold.

Would Kenzie pass out, too?

"Nice knowing all of you," she muttered. "*Not.*"

Kenzie picked up the remainder of the squishy blue cube and put it in her mouth. It tasted like nothing. It was so tasteless it was bizarre. There wasn't even a faint mineral flavor of water or a chalky aftertaste of starch. If the gelatinous particles weren't still swirling around her tongue, she might have thought she'd missed her mouth altogether.

"Well?" Benedict asked after a few tense seconds had passed.

"Well, what?" Kenzie retorted.

Benedict huffed, which was quite possibly the greatest display of emotion Kenzie had ever seen from the man.

"Your culinary magic," he clarified. "Is it different?"

"This is very important, dear," Polly said in a breathless voice.

"No," Kenzie said at once. "It's not different." She didn't even need to cook anything to know it was true. The place in her mind she'd learned to access whenever she needed her magic was there, intact and untouched.

Benedict and Polly exchanged a look.

"There's no question now," Polly said in a low voice, her expression landing somewhere between revenant and afraid. She produced a cling-wrapped brownie from her dress pocket. As soon as she took a bite, she seemed to relax.

Kenzie was beginning to think the woman had a baked goods problem….

"That settles it, then," Benedict said. "You'll have to win Cutthroat Cuisine, but that is just a formality."

"I'm not leading your stupid Gourmands," Kenzie said. She stalked up to Benedict until they were barely a foot apart. "But you are going to tell me what I am. Now, spill."

Kenzie didn't bother to hide her shock when Benedict deigned to answer.

"You're a Culinarian, Kenzie."

"A what, now?"

Benedict sighed. "It is a very long story that will take more than one conversation to explain."

"Give me the TLDR version," Kenzie said dryly, not really expecting Benedict to know the Internet acronym for *Too Long; Didn't Read.*

"This," Benedict pointed to the empty plate on Rosemary's tray table, "is a super food version of you…a Culinarian."

Kenzie just waited, since nothing Benedict was saying made any sense.

"There are three ways to become a culinary magician," Benedict said.

"Don't keep me hanging." Kenzie tapped her foot on the floor, which didn't have the intended effect because she was only wearing socks.

"Most people inherit magic from one or both of their parents. Then, there are Culinarians, who are born with power in spite of their parentage. Your magic is stronger and does not follow any of the normal rules.

"The third method of gaining culinary magic is if a Culinarian bestows it."

"Wait a second," Kenzie said, her mind spinning.

"As a Culinarian, you have the ability to imbue others with culinary magic, as well as take it away," Benedict explained.

Questions and rebuttals churned through Kenzie's mind, but none of them were coherent enough to form actual words.

Benedict rubbed his cane's ivory handle as he said, "A group of Culinarians established the Gourmands several centuries ago, when they realized the necessity of keeping our world a secret. They were very careful about who they imbued with power, so the magic wouldn't become too diluted."

"Are you saying there's a limited amount of culinary magic?" Kenzie asked. "So if we spread the wealth too much or whatever, then all of our magic will get weaker?"

"That's precisely what I'm saying," Benedict agreed. "The early Gourmands realized that if magic was dispersed among too many individuals, it would disappear.

"The Gourmands' most important role is ensuring that culinary magic stays secret and confined to only the most worthy."

That sounded like some serious Hitler/Aryan Race bullshit, but Kenzie didn't say so. Benedict was on a roll.

"Culinarians can do more than give and take away culinary magic," Benedict continued. "As you're well aware."

"Like how I can add multiple magic components to my dishes at a time?" Kenzie asked.

Finally, her non-rule-abiding magic made sense. Because she wasn't a normal culinary magician. She was a *Culinarian*. In her head, she said the word with a snooty English accent. No idea why.

"Correct," Benedict said. "And you've hardly scratched the surface of your abilities. There was a Culinarian who once made an everything bagel, which had more than one-hundred magical properties functioning simultaneously."

"A *hundred?*"

Damn. And Kenzie had thought four was impressive.

Benedict nodded. "Their—or, I suppose I should say *your*—power is without equal."

Kenzie gulped. "How many Culinarians are there?" she asked.

"None," Benedict said. "With each successive generation, fewer Culinarians were born. About two-hundred years ago, the last Culinarian died off, and not a single one has been born since." His frown deepened. "Except you."

CHAPTER 29

SOFIA

Rick and four of his cronies got out of the car. Each of the four henchmen held a gun.

"Get down!" Braxton shouted.

Clementine made a little whimpering sound and crouched next to the U-Haul's rear tire.

Before Sofia could react, Braxton threw her onto the hard ground, using his own body to shield hers.

"Aww, McKaid, let's not be dramatic," Rick tsked. "It doesn't have to be this way."

"Braxton," Sofia wheezed. "Let me up."

It took an elbow to his side to get her stubborn brother to comply. Reluctantly, he let her up, but he still kept his bigger frame between her and Rick.

"How the fuck did you find us?" Braxton growled.

"One of my father's people heard magic ingredients were being sold at this delightful little farmhouse," Rick said. He smirked as he glanced around at the sagging barn and seen-better-days farmhouse. "The name *McKaid* was also mentioned, which got me curious."

"You do seem to have an unnatural preoccupation with me," Braxton said dryly.

"Wrong McKaid," Rick retorted. He made obscene kissy noises in Sofia's direction.

Sofia had to clutch her brother's arm to keep him from going apeshit on Rick, who was flanked by his henchmen.

Rick sauntered over to their truck, where he inspected the dirt flecked along the sides with evident distaste.

"I admit I've been curious about that eight-mil check," Rick said, as his henchmen fluttered into place around him. Sofia thought she saw one of the henchmen bend down to inspect the truck's undercarriage, but he straightened back up before Sofia's suspicion could take hold.

"You know," Rick continued, "since everyone knows the McKaids don't have eight cents to their name."

"Funny," Sofia said. When she was talking to this clown, it was easy to go into full robot-aloofness mode. She'd learned long ago that it was the best defense against people like Rick Santiori. "If this whole mobster thing doesn't work out for you, you should try your own comedy act. You've certainly got the face for it."

The face in question turned lobster-red.

Rick opened his mouth, but closed it when one of his bodyguards whispered something into his ear. Rick's upper lip quivered in an honest-to-God snarl.

"Where are the ingredients?" he commanded.

"Careful, Santiori," Braxton said. "You so much as touch anything magical, and that cute little ankle bracelet you're wearing will bring the Gourmands straight to you."

Rick scowled. "Maybe I'll put in an anonymous tip to the Gourmands that you and your bitch of a sister are trafficking magical ingredients." He gave a pleased little chortle.

"By the time you tell the Gourmands anything," Sofia said lightly, "our ingredients will be gone. Now shoo, little underling." She fluttered her fingers.

"I would have thought, Sofia dear, that you learned your lesson about respect. Don't tell me you've already forgotten." Rick sneered at her. "Mummy. Oh, Mummy, no," He mimicked in a high-pitched voice. "Don't bleed out right in front of me. Mummy—"

A noise that didn't even sound human tore out of Braxton. He lunged at Rick.

"No!" Sofia gasped, just as all four of the henchmen raised their guns.

Braxton and Rick collided. They went down in a tangle of limbs and male shouts.

The bodyguards were yelling and pointing their guns, but they couldn't shoot without the risk of taking down their boss.

In just those few seconds, a lifetime of loss flashed through Sofia's mind. She recalled the sounds Aidan had made as he writhed on the restaurant floor, his wild eyes begging her for help. She remembered walking into her father's bedroom and smelling the sour stink of death. She saw Mum's shirt soaked through with blood.

Braxton got to his knees. He had his forearm looped around Rick's throat and was squeezing hard enough that Rick's pale skin was turning faintly purple.

"Drop your guns," Braxton shouted. "Drop them!"

The mobsters moved in perfect synchronicity. Two of them turned so their guns were trained on Clementine. The other two aimed at Sofia.

"No." Braxton's voice broke. He tightened his grip, causing Rick to make a gurgling sound.

Sofia's mind spun. She had to do something.

"We have two choices here," she heard herself say. "We can either leave behind a whole bunch of bodies for these nice farmers to clean up, or I can show you how we earned eight-million in a few hours of work."

Sofia nodded to her brother. "Let him go."

Braxton hesitated before doing as she'd asked. His expression said *You better know what you're doing here, Sis.*

While Rick collapsed on his hands and knees and tried to remember how to breathe, Sofia backed up toward the carton of ingredients.

Nice and slowly, she told herself. *No sudden moves….*

"I've started up a magical ingredient business," she said. "They're the real deal." She kept her voice calm as her eyes scanned the labeled packages for one that would give her exactly what she needed.

It was a good thing she'd already read and memorized all of them.

There it was: a tiny packet of dried lentils. Sofia had promised them to an impassioned archaeologist who specialized in Bronze Age artifacts. *Oh well.*

"I'll show you an example."

Sofia moved slowly, since there were still two guns trained on her and two on Clementine. She opened the packet and scanned the instructions written on a card inside. She dumped the lentils onto her palm and then dropped them on the ground beside her. Lifting her foot, she gave the lentils one good stomp.

"Ah—"

"What the—"

Rick's four guards stumbled backwards as their guns were wrenched out of their hands. Sofia slid to the side to avoid being struck by the weapons as they raced through the air. All four guns stuck to the ground, right on top of the lentils.

A variety of gold jewelry, a pocket knife, coins, and various other metal objects flew over to join the guns.

One of the thugs let out a bloodcurdling screech as his earring tore right out of his earlobe.

Ouch.

Sofia didn't wait for the men to recover. Her hand dove back into the carton of ingredients.

Sandbox tree seeds left her palm and hurtled through the air with perfect precision. As soon as they made contact with something solid, the seeds exploded. Twin screams filled the air as the two men she'd hit grabbed their arses.

The wounds weren't deadly, but that didn't stop the men from hopping and yelping.

Two down. Three more to go.

Sofia swallowed a packetful of magical flaxseed. As soon as they hit her tongue, her jitteriness faded, leaving behind a focused calm.

The next packet contained a concord grape vine. It left her hand, lengthening in the air as it shot straight for one of the henchmen. It wound around him, binding his hands and feet until he was on the ground and wriggling in place like a worm.

The next packet Sofia ripped open contained a sliver of durian fruit. Sofia tossed it at the remaining bodyguard. There was a loud bang, followed by the most horrendous stink Sofia had ever experienced. The man who was standing in the midst of it started to claw at his nose as he tried to escape the stink.

Only Rick was left.

Sofia didn't have time to find the perfect revenge in the cartonful of ingredients, so she just went for her best option. A single potato that crackled with magical electricity. She threw it.

The potato smacked Rick right in the side of his head.

He yowled. There was no other word to describe the sound that came out of him.

Blue electricity sizzled all along his skin. His slicked-back hair burst out of its confining gel and stuck up in every direction.

Sofia ripped open another packet. The habanero pepper inside set fire to Rick's clothes as soon as it touched him. Sofia caught sight of Rick shimmying out of everything except his boxer briefs while beating a hasty retreat.

Sofia didn't stop there. She tossed honey locust thorns at the men, which went right through their clothes and burrowed under their skin. Shrieking ensued, and the men hopped around like mad hyenas as they raced back to their car.

The next packet contained a single mint leaf. When she tossed it into the air, a tiny snowstorm appeared right over Rick's head and dumped hail the size of golf balls onto his mostly-naked body.

Sofia was breathing hard, even though she was barely moving. The magic pulsed around her. It was heady. Euphoric.

Sofia had never felt so powerful in her life.

Rick's car drove away so quickly that the tires left burn marks on the grass.

Sofia turned back to the carton of ingredients. She wanted to give Rick and his posse a little something to remember her by. When she reached in, her hand met with nothing except for the container's smooth bottom. The ingredients were gone.

Sofia's adrenaline began to fade. Reality came back.

"Shit, Sofe." Braxton ran a hand through his hair. "What do we do now?"

What, indeed?

"Reaper Lee won't be happy," Clementine said. For once, she wasn't smiling.

"I had to," Sofia said, looking around at their small group. She felt strange…bereft, or something.

"Not saying you didn't," Braxton said. "Just—"

They all tensed at the sound of an engine.

It wasn't Rick's black SUV, but that didn't stop nervous sweat from trickling down Sofia's back. Did Rick have reinforcements waiting down the road? She didn't think Santiori employees would drive a station wagon, but anything was possible.

"Get behind me," Braxton said.

Clementine and the farmers quickly complied. Sofia snatched two of the abandoned guns off the ground and handed one to her brother.

Neither of them knew the first thing about guns, but at least they could hold them and look scary.

A single man got out of the station wagon. He was wearing a white lab coat and wire-rimmed glasses. The man did a double-take at the sight of Sofia and Braxton with guns in their hands.

"Ho," he said, stumbling back a few steps and holding up his hands. "I'm not looking for trouble. Sofia McKaid knows to expect me."

"I'm Sofia," she said, lowering her gun. Beside her, Braxton remained tense and ready for a fight.

"I'm Dr. Gatniss. I'm here for my magical flaxseed." He pulled out his wallet. "Do you prefer a check or wire transfer?"

Sofia exchanged a glance with her brother. There was no solution to this particular problem.

They were fucked.

CHAPTER 30

BRAXTON

Braxton took a deep breath and shoved aside the nausea that came with the overpowering scent of nutmeg. It was his first time attempting the telepathy dish since his embarrassing failure the other day, when he'd passed out and given himself a magic hangover.

"What are you waiting for?" Chef Levy, always the bastion of patience, asked.

"Just gathering myself, Chef," Braxton said. "And if you could give me a little breathing room, I'd appreciate it."

Chef Levy made an irritated sound and backed up half a step.

Shaking his head, Braxton tried to block out all distractions and focus on his magic. The healing ingredient Qiang had given Sofia to help revive him had gone to a more important cause. Dr. Gatniss, the plastic surgeon who had driven halfway across the country for his ingredient, had been none-too-pleased to discover it had been used to scare off a bunch of mobsters. So, Sofia had given him the tea leaves as a consolation prize. Afterward, they'd gotten back in their truck and hightailed it out of there before any other buyers showed up.

Thus, Braxton hadn't gotten any help in recovering from his magic hangover. He could feel what little strength he'd regained leaching out of him.

He poured more of himself into the dish. Kenzie's face was all he saw. Her voice was all he heard. He had to find her, and in order to do that, he needed to talk to her….

"Braxton, is that you?"

"Kenz!"

Braxton felt like pumping his fist in the air. He wanted to wrap his arms around her small frame and lift her off her feet. He wanted to kiss the hell out of her.

"Are you alright?" he asked, sensing through the haze of his enthusiasm that there was something not quite right with their connection. It was…sluggish.

Was she hurt? Sick?

"I have so much to tell you," Kenzie's voice said in his head.

Braxton's heart surged. "Do you know where they're keeping you?"

"I'm pretty sure I'm in Manhattan."

Well, that was…something. It narrowed down the haystack, but Manhattan was still a big fucking haystack.

"I don't know how much time I have, so listen. Write this down, 'kay?"

Braxton found himself writing down the names Tina and Henry Morierty, along with a Manhattan address.

"They're holding a dinner to promote Polly's magical food bank on Saturday the sixteenth, Kenzie said. *I don't have much concept of time here, but—"*

Saturday. That was…. Christ. That was tomorrow.

"Polly said that couple's son is competing against me in the Cutthroat Cuisine finale," Kenzie said.

Fury coursed through Braxton. "Polly can say whatever the hell she wants. It's not going to happen."

"I don't want to be part of the Gourmands, Braxton."

"You won't have to be, baby," he promised her. "I'm going to get you out of there, and then we'll sic Chef Levy on those bastards."

That got a little chuckle out of her.

"There's something else," Kenzie said. *"Have you ever heard of Culinarians?"*

"Um, yeah," Braxton said, not sure where she was going with this. "They were the first culinary magicians way back when. I think some of them formed the Gourmands, too, right? What about them?"

"Well, the thing is, I'm—"

He felt Kenzie's attention waver and then heard a quiet curse in his head.

"Freaking Nurse Ratched."

"Kenz? What the hell is happening over there?"

Kenzie let out a cry of pain. Then, their connection winked out.

"Shit!" Braxton slammed his fist down on the counter.

When he opened his eyes, Elyannah Levy's face was centimeters from his own. He jerked back.

"Where?" she demanded.

Braxton gripped his head as he tried to process what Kenzie had just told him. More so what she hadn't told him. What had she been about to say before they were interrupted?

And what were the Gourmands doing to her now?

His mind still spinning, Braxton relayed everything Kenzie had told him to Chef Levy.

"Tina and Henry Morierty," Chef Levy mused as she squinted at the address Braxton had copied down. "I didn't know they had a residence in Manhattan. Their family is big in the Boston culinary magic food scene. I reviewed one of their restaurants once."

"I'm guessing you didn't like the food?" Braxton deadpanned. To his knowledge, Chef Levy had never written a positive review. Ever.

"I should have known they were dirty right then," Chef Levy grumbled. "They un-ironically served me an edible zen garden."

Good to know….

"Kenzie told me she's competing against their son to become the next Gourmand leader," Braxton said. Unable to stand still, he started cleaning up the kitchen.

"There's another culinary magic competition, and I wasn't invited?" Aralia, who was holding a dead rabbit by its ears, strode into the kitchen. She placed the rabbit on the counter and murmured something to the dead animal before pulling her knife out of her belt. She began skinning the rabbit.

"Kenzie wasn't invited, either," Braxton pointed out. "She was kidnapped."

All at once, the shavings of fresh nutmeg scattered across the cutting board hit his nose. He fought against a surge of nausea. When he glanced over at Aralia, who was reaching her bare hand into the rabbit's chest cavity, he lost the battle.

Braxton rushed to the sink before he heaved up everything in his stomach.

"You're going to kill yourself if you keep pushing yourself like this," Aralia informed him. "And—"

"I know," Braxton croaked. "You have plans for me. As soon as I get Kenzie back, I have to pay up. I fucking know, Aralia."

"Someone's touchy." There was a little *pop* as Aralia yanked out the rabbit's breastbone.

"Pull yourself together," Chef Levy told Braxton. She snapped her fingers at him. "This is the break I've been waiting twenty years for."

Working on it, Chef….

As Braxton's nausea began to subside, a myriad of possibilities crowded into his mind.

"Do you think they're holding Kenzie at this address?" Braxton asked, his pulse giving a hopeful stutter.

"How would they manage to hold an illegal culinary magic tournament in a brownstone?" Chef Levy scoffed. "Use your brain, McKaid."

And just like that, Braxton's glimmer of optimism deflated like a chef's first soufflé.

Chef Levy opened Sofia's laptop, which was lying on the kitchen table. Braxton didn't point out that anyone who touched Sofia's computer risked losing a few fingers…or maybe their whole arm.

Braxton waited impatiently as Chef Levy tapped on the keyboard. She *hmmed* and *ahhed* a whole bunch of times, and pointedly ignored Braxton's attempts to get any kind of explanation out of her.

"Gotcha, you son of a bitch," Chef Levy murmured. Her cheeks were flushed and there was a manic, jerky way she was clicking between screens.

"Um, Chef," Braxton began.

"Benedict Vandermeer," Chef Levy said.

Braxton repeated the name to himself. "Benedict," he said slowly, putting together where he'd heard that name before. "Kenzie said the Gourmand leader's name is Benedict."

"Not a very common first name, is it?" Chef Levy asked, her lips curving up into the barest hint of a smile.

She spun the laptop around so Braxton could see a blurred-out image of a row of brownstones. "This one," she tapped the screen, "belongs to the Moriertys. And this one," she tapped the neighboring brownstone, "belongs to a one, Benedict Vandermeer."

"You think—" Braxton began, as the pieces began to fall into place.

"I think it's either one hell of a coincidence," Chef Levy said. "Or we just figured out where the Gourmand leader sleeps at night."

"Holy shit," Braxton whispered. He had an insane urge to give Chef Levy a hug. He wanted to cook the sea bream recipe again so he could tell Kenzie. He wanted to get in the car and drive to Manhattan right that second.

"Have some coffee," Chef Levy said, sounding almost as impatient as he felt. "Then, we're heading out. We've got some Gourmands to interrogate."

Damn right, they did.

CHAPTER 31

KENZIE

Kenzie wanted to kill Benedict for interrupting her conversation with Braxton. Instead, she allowed him to lead her back to the sterile kitchen so she could pepper him with more questions.

The more information she got now, the better-positioned she would be to take her revenge when the time came. Or at least expose these assholes for what they really were.

Two guards fell into step with her, just to make it clear she wouldn't be able to pull a fast one over them. Since her attempted escape with Cookie, these people had been on her like white on rice.

Polly and Nurse Ratched made up the caboose of their little entourage.

"Let me get this straight," Kenzie said to Benedict's back as he led the way. "I'm the only Culinarian alive?"

Just saying those words out loud made her feel like a total narcissist.

"The only one in more than two-hundred years," Benedict affirmed.

"And the Gourmands didn't have you on their radar," Polly added, sounding a little breathless from walking and talking simultaneously, "since you stopped cooking during your formative teenage years. You were a complete surprise!" She winked at Kenzie.

They gathered around the prep table, where all manner of fresh ingredients were spread out. There were charts and special knives and the most intense measuring tools Kenzie had ever seen.

"You will be an asset to the Gourmands," Benedict told her in a way that disturbingly resembled pride. Like Benedict had a claim on her now that he'd solved the mystery of her magic.

"You will be able to protect culinary magic far more effectively and with less effort than the Gourmands have managed for generations," he continued. "You'll iron out the kinks in my super food recipe." He gestured at the jumble of ingredients on the table. "Then, the Gourmands will be able to expand our protection of culinary magicians without any unintended consequences."

Kenzie noticed Rosemary, who had been passed out in her highchair on the other side of the plexiglass wall, was crawling on her hands and knees across the floor. She caught Kenzie's eye and put a finger to her lips.

"I'm not interested in controlling people," Kenzie said quickly, wanting to keep everyone's attention on her rather than on Rosemary. "I told you before that I want nothing to do with the Gourmands."

"And, as I informed you," Benedict said with the air of a teacher chastising an unruly pupil, "culinary magic's survival is tenuous. We are fighting a losing battle to keep our secret from the Vanillas. As the most powerful among us, you will be drawn into the coming battle one way or another."

Rosemary had reached the door that separated her little enclave from the kitchen. There was a soft *snick* as she opened the door, but Kenzie was the only one who noticed. Everyone else's backs were turned to Rosemary, and their attention was focused on Kenzie.

Rosemary stayed on her hands and knees as she crawled out of view. Before Kenzie could even wonder where she'd gone, a tremendous crash came from an adjoining room.

"What the hell?" Nurse Ratched asked, already moving.

"The ingredient room!" Polly wailed.

The guards and Nurse Ratched hurried in the direction of the sound. Benedict followed, his cane clicking against the tiled floor.

That left Kenzie. Alone. In a kitchen.

Snap out of it, Ashner. Now's your chance!

More crashing and shouting came from the adjoining room. Kenzie hooked a chair under the door handle so it would be harder for intruders to open…probably. People on TV did stuff like that, and it always seemed to work.

There wasn't any more time to worry about it. She had this one shot to do what she did best. She wasn't going to blow it.

She saw Rosemary sprint past the other side of the plexiglass window, holding an armful of herbs. Nurse Ratched and the guards were hot on her tail. Benedict and Polly followed slower but with no less enthusiasm. Not a one of them noticed Kenzie.

Alrighty, then. Let's do this.

* * *

Kenzie dipped her spoon into the gravy bubbling merrily in its saucepan and tasted.

It was thick and silky. Perfect.

She tuned out everything else as she added in the magic. Then, she put all of her attention on the pièce de résistance.

Her tarragon and chamomile turkey was a little raw given her time constraints, but if Kenzie gave her captors a little side of Salmonella, then all the better. She sprinkled a little malted milk powder on top of the turkey's rubbery skin.

"We're not going for a Michelin star here," she told the dead bird. "Just a little old Thanksgiving tryptophan."

And magic.

She'd known about turkey making people tired, but she hadn't had a clue about other ingredients to induce sleepiness. So, she'd let the magic guide her.

For a final touch, she drizzled the thick gravy over each slice of turkey.

Even with her dire situation, the gourmet chef in her cringed at the slimy, undercooked meat.

The culinary stars must have been aligned—and about friggin' time—because Nurse Ratched chose that moment to press her face to the glass and wiggle the handle. The door didn't budge.

"Open this door right now!" she hollered.

Kenzie filled her scrubs pockets with turkey slices. Then, she did as she was told.

"What are you doing?" Nurse Ratched barked. "No one gave you permission to touch anything."

"Oops," Kenzie replied, letting the nurse come within grabbing distance.

Then, as Nurse Ratched opened her mouth to speak, Kenzie stuffed a bite of turkey into her wide-open trap.

"Ugh. What—"

Nurse Ratched slumped to the floor, snoring.

Hell. Yeah.

Kenzie hurried past her, slipping and sliding on her socked feet. She followed the sound of commotion around the corner and into the adjoining storage room.

"Nooooo!" Rosemary wailed. She was flat on her stomach with a guard's booted foot digging into her back. Another guard was on the ground, attempting to wrestle away the ingredients Rosemary was cradling beneath her. Benedict was shouting.

Kenzie snuck up behind them like a badass ninja. Reaching up on her toes, she grasped the back of Benedict's collar and gave it a sharp yank.

When Benedict's head dipped backward, Kenzie stuffed a piece of turkey in his mouth.

Donezo.

Polly was so busy shouting at the guards that she didn't notice when Benedict and his cane toppled onto the floor. There was a dull thump as Benedict's head smacked against the wall.

Whoops.

"Give back those ingredients!" Polly yelled at Rosemary.

Rosemary might look frail, but she was wiry and fighting like her life depended on it. Which it kind of did.

Kenzie squatted down. She grabbed hold of Polly's cotton candy hair to hold the woman steady and crammed a tiny piece of turkey into Polly's piehole.

"Mmm," Polly said. "Delish—" Her eyes rolled back in her head, and she keeled over.

The guards soon followed.

"You okay?" Kenzie clutched Rosemary's bony elbow and helped her to her feet.

"Rosemary and thyme and basil and coriander and caraway and dill," Rosemary replied.

"We've gotta get out of here," Kenzie panted. "More guards will be here any minute."

Rosemary clasped Kenzie's hand and started tugging her toward the exit. At least, Kenzie hoped that was where they were headed. Her pulse was crashing in her ears as every fiber of her being told her to run. To escape.

They made it to an elevator without fanfare. They were on the lowest of five levels, so Kenzie punched the button for the top floor.

As soon as the door slid open again, they were on the move. The two of them sprinted up a corkscrew-shaped ramp that led steadily upward. Kenzie kept expecting the red-uniformed guards who always hung around the arena to mob them at any minute, but no one appeared.

Kenzie was feeling downright giddy as they reached a door at the top of the ramp. With a final burst of energy, Kenzie threw it open.

Instead of a rush of fresh air and sunlight, the two of them stepped onto a maroon carpet. The path led to....

No way.

No freaking way.

The Hex Kitchen dome was fifty feet in front of them.

Maniacal laughter bubbled out of Kenzie. She should have known. Cutthroat Cuisine was directly beneath the dome.

The only good news was that Kenzie knew how to get out.

"This way!" she shouted.

She screeched to a halt, dragging Rosemary with her as bullets sprayed into the wall beside them.

"Get 'em!" someone shouted.

Annnd, there were the guards Kenzie had been expecting. There was a dozen of them…maybe more. Rosemary groaned in dismay. She began chanting her food song and clutching at her necklace.

"Fuck you," Kenzie spat as two security guards pried the crumbled turkey remains out of her hands and wrenched her arms behind her back.

Rosemary let out a deafening shriek.

Something hard slammed into Kenzie's head. Then, the floor was racing up to meet her face.

CHAPTER 32

SOFIA

Sofia didn't do nervous. And yet, as she waited for Clementine to put her surly boss on the phone, Sofia's palms sweated and her pulse galloped.

"You used all my ingredients," Qiang Lee seethed into the phone.

At least she didn't have to suffer through small talk….

"I did. I'm not sure if Clementine told you, but—"

"She told me." Qiang made a grumbling sound. "Seems to me like you've bitten off more than you can chew."

Sofia bristled.

"We were caught unawares," she said. "It won't happen again."

She'd make bloody sure of it.

"And what of all the people you promised those ingredients to?" Qiang demanded.

Sofia cringed. Those had quite possibly been the most unpleasant calls of her life. She'd suffered through hours of shouting, tears, and censure. The worst part was, she knew she deserved it.

Sofia hadn't needed to use every single ingredient to dispatch Rick and his cronies. She'd wanted to use them. For the first time, she hadn't just been watching other people's magic from the sidelines. She'd been making her own.

And it had felt good.

"Clementine also told me that you are the only reason she is still alive," Qiang said.

His tone was still aggressive, so it took Sofia a moment to piece together what he was saying.

"Clementine is a fool," Qiang continued. "But she is family. You saved her life, and for that, I am grateful."

"You can thank me by sending another batch of ingredients," Sofia suggested, pouncing on her advantage while she had it.

There was a short pause during which Sofia aged about a decade.

"Clementine is already on her way," Qiang said. His apprehension was obvious in his heavy sigh. "She will arrive at noon, at the farm where you met last time."

Sofia glanced at her phone screen. That was in an hour.

"I'll find good homes for whatever you send me," she promised. Inside her own head, she was doing a happy dance.

"See that you do," Qiang said. "Balance is critical. Make sure you only use them to help others."

With that, the Reaper disconnected the call.

There was a loud thundering as Braxton and Chef Levy came down the stairs. Chef Levy was carrying a duffle bag over her shoulder with a rifle peeking out of the top.

"We're going now," Braxton told Sofia. "You going to be okay here?"

Sofia hated the idea of Braxton going to confront the Gourmands with only Chef Levy as backup, but she knew there was nothing she could say to dissuade him. This Manhattan family was going to help him find Kenzie. It wouldn't matter if Sofia hogtied him and locked him in a cellar. He'd still find a way to go.

"You could wait until I get my shipment from Clementine, and then we could go together," she suggested.

She already knew what Braxton's answer would be before he shook his head.

She sighed. "That's what I thought."

"Look, Sofe," Braxton said. "I know you can't understand this, but it's like I haven't been able to breathe since Kenzie disappeared. I have to get her back."

That stung, because Sofia did understand. It was the exact way she'd felt every day since Aidan died. And again when she'd lost her father. And then Mum. It was the overwhelming sense that no matter how hard she worked, too much was out of her control.

Sofia straightened her spine. "Don't use too much magic," she told her brother. She let him hug her for a solid two seconds before squirming away. "I expect you to come back to me in one piece. Even if you are a dumbass most of the time."

That made Braxton laugh. "Takes one to know one, little sis."

Since it was too early to go meet Clementine, Sofia busied herself with washing the dishes. She was just finishing up when she heard the blast of a car horn.

Sofia frowned. Did Braxton forget his phone or something? He had a habit of doing that.

Sure enough, there his phone was, balanced on the edge of the counter. She rolled her eyes. Her brother really was a dumbass. She grabbed it and headed outside, but Aralia's mud-spattered truck never appeared.

Instead, Rick's goddamn black SUV rolled up the drive. It parked right in front of the cabin.

Sofia's blood turned to ice. *How the hell had Rick found this place?*

Graham appeared beside her. His gaze zeroed in on the SUV.

"Expecting company?" he asked.

Sofia managed a shake of her head.

The car doors opened, and suited henchmen began spilling out. Sofia's stomach sank even further when Veneziano Santiori got out of the back seat.

Sofia could handle the mini-mobster. His father was a different story.

And…speaking of the devil.

Rick, looking inordinately pleased with himself, emerged from the SUV. He smoothed down his silk tie and checked his slicked-back hair in the side mirror.

Graham disappeared inside the cabin. He emerged a moment later holding a shotgun.

"This is private property," Graham said in a harsh voice Sofia had never heard before. There was nothing soft or friendly in his demeanor as he stalked down the porch steps.

"I don't believe we've had the pleasure," Veneziano said. "I'm Veneziano Santiori."

"And you're trespassing," Graham growled. He pumped the shotgun.

Three other guns were raised as Veneziano's men crowded around him.

"Now, now." Veneziano made a placating gesture with his hands. "There's no reason for anyone to get hurt."

"How did you find us?" Sofia asked, barely managing to keep a civil tone.

"My son put a GPS tracking device on your…vehicle." Veneziano gave Graham's truck a look of disdain.

Rick raised his chin at Sofia in a mocking acknowledgement.

"I'm sorry to say my son is a disappointment more often than not," Veneziano continued. "But every so often, he manages to follow simple instructions."

Rick's air of self-importance faltered.

Sofia didn't let her distress show. She remembered Rick and his bodyguard sniffing around their truck, but it hadn't occurred to her that they would—

One of the henchmen went over to Graham's truck, reached under, and emerged with the small device. He handed it to Veneziano.

With a flourish, Veneziano tossed the tracker to Graham, who caught it one-handed without lowering his shotgun.

Damnit, Sofia silently fumed. *Damnit, damnit, damnit.*

Their private refuge…the one place they'd been free from the Santioris…was no longer safe.

Veneziano parted his men and took a few steps closer to Sofia and Graham. "I'm just here for the magical ingredients." He gave Sofia a hard stare. "Where's your brother?"

And didn't that just figure? Only a man would assume that a burgeoning magical ingredient business could only be handled by another man. Or maybe it was her lack of magic that made her seem like less of a threat to this gangster. Either way, it was offensive.

"My brother isn't here right now," Sofia said.

"I must say, I'm very intrigued about how you got a hold of real magical ingredients." Veneziano slid his hands into his pockets and leaned elegantly against his car. "I confess I'm somewhat doubtful."

"It's true, Papà," Rick insisted.

Veneziano leveled a warning stare on his son. Rick shrank back and hunched his shoulders in submission. After his father's attention turned elsewhere, Rick raised his head. His mouth was contorted into an ugly grimace, but the emotion in his eyes was what caught Sofia's attention.

It wasn't fear or resentment. It was pure, unadulterated hatred.

"You need to leave," Graham ordered. "Now."

"Young man, I applaud your courage," Veneziano told Graham. "I could use more men like you on my payroll. But you'll want to step aside before anything unfortunate happens here."

Graham didn't move.

"We don't have any magical ingredients," Sofia said, feeling her nerves begin to fray. "And neither does Braxton. We can't help you."

"Mm." Veneziano pursed his lips and gave her a thoughtful nod. "Nevertheless, I have a few questions for your famous culinary magician of a brother. Where did you say he was, again?"

"Out," Sofia replied shortly. "He went grocery shopping."

"Is that so?" Veneziano cocked his head.

All three of his henchmen turned so their guns were no longer pointing at Graham. Instead, they were aimed directly at Sofia.

"No," Graham choked.

"Put down your weapon if you want her to live," Veneziano ordered.

There was a dull thump as the shotgun fell to the ground. Graham put his hands up.

One of the bodyguards strode forward. He came close enough for Sofia to smell heat and metal emanating from his gun. There was also body odor mixed with cologne, which was just gross enough to keep her from completely panicking.

"Leave her alone," Graham said, his voice sounding unhinged. "You can have me."

Veneziano didn't spare Graham a glance. His polished shoes crunched along the gravel as he took slow, purposeful strides to Sofia.

"Where," Veneziano said in a voice so quiet it was barely audible, "is your brother?"

Sofia lifted her chin and met his gaze. Her mouth was dry as a bone, which was the only reason she didn't spit in his face.

"I already told you. He's at the grocery store."

Sofia couldn't silence her little gasp when she felt the unyielding press of metal against her temple.

Graham made a strangled sound. "555 West 87th Street in Manhattan," he said, speaking so fast his words blurred into one. "That's where Braxton went."

"Graham," Sofia gasped.

"And what's he doing there?" Veneziano demanded.

"Let her go, and I'll tell you," Graham said.

"That's not how this works," Veneziano replied. "But I am a man of my word. Tell me what I want to know, and Ms. McKaid will be unharmed."

"Shut up," Sofia begged Graham.

Graham didn't. The whole story about the Gourmands spilled out. There was nothing Sofia could do to stop him.

The only detail he didn't divulge was that a new batch of ingredients would be arriving in half an hour. Sofia hadn't shared that piece of news with anyone except Braxton. She debated now whether she should.

Except now that Veneziano knew where Braxton was, there was nothing to stop him from going after Braxton *and* claiming the ingredients.

"Interesting," Veneziano murmured, when Graham had finished. "Very interesting." He gestured to his men to lower their guns. To Rick, he said, "Get our Manhattan contacts on the line."

Sofia felt a brush of cool air in the place where a gun had been pressed to her forehead. She didn't have a chance to properly freak out—or scream herself hoarse at Graham—before a faint whistling sound filled the air.

There was a sharp grunt, and then one of Veneziano's men collapsed. An arrow was sticking straight through his neck.

Rick dove behind one of the other men, just as another arrow flew right past him and stuck into the cabin's outer wall.

With a roar, Aralia threw herself out of the woods and released another arrow. A second bodyguard fell.

Aralia darted behind a tree as the third henchman opened fire.

Graham's shotgun cracked, and the third bodyguard crumpled.

Aralia made a whooping sound as she sprinted across the driveway.

"Bitch," Rick hissed.

Aralia's arm pulled back. She aimed her arrow right at Rick.

"Gimme a reason," Aralia said. "I fight even better than I fuck."

"Gross," Graham muttered.

"I told you once before, Aralia," Rick sneered. "You picked the wrong side."

"We'll see about that," she replied.

"Enough," Veneziano said, still in control even though all three of his bodyguards were dead. "Put down your weapons, and we'll leave."

"And then we'll come back with an army to turn this place into rubble," Rick muttered.

"Not if I kill you now," Aralia replied, bouncing on her feet and practically salivating.

"If you kill us," Veneziano said calmly, "then you really will bring an army down on your heads. My people have instructions to come here if I do not make a timely appearance at my next appointment."

Aralia made a fierce, animalistic sound.

"However," Veneziano continued. "I hope that any further violence will be unnecessary. I gave the McKaids my word they would be safe once they repaid their debt." He nodded to Sofia. "All I want is to have a conversation with your brother. As long as you stay out of my way, I'll have no need to return here." Veneziano's cold gaze met Sofia's.

"You can't be serious, Papà," Rick spluttered.

"Someday, I hope you discover the worth of integrity," Veneziano told his son. "Until then, hold your tongue."

Rick's sour expression transformed to pure rage. Apparently, someone had daddy issues.

Veneziano turned his back on Graham and Aralia, both of whom still had their weapons raised. With an ugly snarl in Aralia's direction, Rick followed.

The car engine turned over, and then the SUV was flying back down the drive.

Sofia's knees were a little wobbly, and her thoughts were scattered. *Braxton. She had to warn him.*

"You bitch!" Aralia shouted, stomping over to Sofia. She dug her nails into Sofia's shoulder and gave her a hard shake. "Do you have any idea what you've done?!"

"Stop it," Graham ordered, pulling Aralia away from Sofia. "This isn't her fault."

"They've seen your face!" Aralia screeched at him.

Sofia didn't give a damn about any of that. Braxton was about to be descended on by God-knew how many of Santiori's men.

She grabbed his phone with trembling hands and searched his contacts for Elyannah Levy. Nothing.

"Who has a way to get in touch with Chef Levy?" she demanded, raising her voice to be heard over Aralia and Graham's argument.

Graham gave a slow shake of his head.

Aralia spared her a glance. "Do you really think an ex-Mossad would go around giving out her phone number?"

"I'm sorry," Graham said. "I should have lied."

"You think?!"

Once Veneziano's men figured out that Braxton didn't have the ingredients, there was no telling what they'd do to him.

"I just saw them aiming their guns at you and panicked." Graham looked down at the ground.

"Now what are we supposed to do?" Aralia snatched the GPS tracker off the ground and threw it back down as hard as she could. The plastic exterior cracked, showing off its electrical innards. "What if they figure out who you are?" She started stomping on the tracker. "What if—"

Aralia continued punishing the tracker while Graham tried to calm her.

Sofia shoved down her panic long enough to cobble together a hasty plan.

"Get your keys," she ordered Graham. "We're going to go meet Clementine and get those ingredients. Then, we're going to save my brother."

CHAPTER 33

BRAXTON

Something doesn't feel right," Chef Levy said. "Drive around the block."

"I don't see anything," Braxton said, peering down the street filled with neat brownstones and expensive cars. It was dusk, though, and the darkening sky didn't help with visibility.

"If I want your opinion, I'll ask for it," Chef Levy snapped. "Drive around the block."

Braxton ground his teeth. He obeyed, even though it killed him to be driving away from the answers he needed.

"Here," Chef Levy commanded, pointing to a tiny parking spot. Unsurprisingly, she grumbled while Braxton maneuvered Aralia's giant truck into the space.

"Took you long enough," Chef Levy grumbled, grabbing her bag and hopping out.

"Happy to be at your service." Braxton tipped his imaginary hat before following her.

Chef Levy was already scaling some rickety scaffolding on a half-finished building. There was no part of it that seemed stable. This climb would be dangerous during the light of day, but at night—

At least no one would be able to witness his humiliation when he fell and broke his neck.

"If I die before I can rescue my girl," Braxton huffed as he hauled himself up into the metal lattice, "my ghost is going to come back and kick your arse."

Chef Levy was already on the roof of the building. She balanced on two toothpick-thin cables as she peered through a pair of binoculars.

"Hm," she said.

"Care to elaborate?" Braxton grunted as his foot slid off a narrow-as-fuck pole. He swung his legs like some kind of deranged acrobat while he used his arms to keep himself from plunging to his death. "Wait, where are you going?"

Chef Levy slipped between narrow gaps in the crisscrossed scaffolding as she sped past him on her way back down.

Braxton cursed. Then, he reversed course and followed the ninja chef back down.

"Come on," Chef Levy called as she sprinted down the block.

Braxton didn't bother asking what was up. He just followed. At least this time, she was heading in the right direction.

Chef Levy bolted up the steps to the Moriertys' house and threw open the unlocked door.

All of Braxton's questions died the second he stepped inside. The lights were on, illuminating the broken glass and splintered wood covering the floor. There were also streaks of blood.

Chef Levy knelt down and swiped a finger through the blood. "Still wet," she observed. "This didn't happen long ago."

Braxton darted past her, looking into every room despite already knowing they would be empty. Except for some fresh blood streaks and more signs of struggle in various rooms, there were no clues about where the Moriertys had gone.

"Shit!" Braxton buried his face in his hands.

"Either they're dead or on the run," Chef Levy said. "Let's go see what's happening next door."

Benedict Vandermeer's house was dark and empty. As far as Braxton could tell, there were no signs of a break-in. The door was closed and locked. After trying the knob, Chef Levy pulled a set of lockpicks out of her pocket. A second later, they were in.

"And I thought you were scary when you were just a food critic," Braxton muttered.

"Don't you forget it, McKaid," Chef Levy replied.

They stepped into a dark foyer. Braxton stayed still while his eyes adjusted to the gloom. Everything was quiet.

Chef Levy held up her hand in the universal *Wait here* signal before disappearing. Less than a minute passed before she reappeared.

"It's empty," she said. "You think you can handle things here on your own? I'm going to go check the street cameras to see if I can figure out what happened to the Moriertys."

"I've got this," Braxton said, reaching into his jacket for the baggie of breadcrumbs he'd made back at the cabin.

"Meet me back at the truck when you're finished," Chef Levy said. Then, she was gone.

Braxton opened the bag and stared down at the breadcrumbs. He took a deep breath, in and out.

He rolled the grainy crumbs between his fingers. He inhaled the pepper and Italian seasoning, and tasted the slightly bitter tang of the burnt pieces. Braxton focused on wrapping the crumbs in a net of magic. Then, he overturned the baggie.

The breadcrumbs flew straight up before pausing in mid-air. They moved slowly, the way they might if the room was zero-G.

Braxton tightened his magic.

The breadcrumbs began to congeal into a straight line. Then, they all zipped forward.

"Thank Christ," Braxton muttered. If there was nothing worth finding in the house, the breadcrumbs would have just fallen onto the floor.

Braxton hurried after the breadcrumb trail, which zoomed down the hallway and underneath a closed door.

Braxton turned the handle, relieved to find the room unlocked and empty.

Since there were no windows in the room, Braxton shut the door behind him and flipped on the light. He was standing in the Gourmand leader's home office.

Braxton's gaze passed over the massive, L-shaped desk and floor-to-ceiling bookshelves. His attention went straight to the breadcrumbs, which were clinging to a painting of a roasted pig with an apple in its mouth.

Bingo.

"What have we here?" Braxton muttered, carefully removing the painting from the wall.

The breadcrumbs leapt off the painting and stuck to the wall, right over a small hatch that camouflaged almost seamlessly with the wall. Braxton hooked his fingers into the grooves around the hatch and pulled it open.

He felt around in the alcove. There was only one object inside: a book.

It was a hand-written recipe book. There was no title, but as Braxton flipped through the pages, he found detailed ingredient lists and step-by-step instructions for integrating the magic.

The book was broken into two parts, and each half contained a single recipe. They were the two most complex dishes he'd ever encountered.

The breadcrumbs fell to the floor, inert. That meant Braxton had gotten what he'd come for.

He tucked the book under his arm, figuring he could puzzle over it with the others back at the cabin.

Braxton closed the latch on the wall and repositioned the painting exactly as he'd found it. He swept the breadcrumbs underneath a rug and made sure he hadn't left any other clues that would tie him to the robbery.

"I think we pulled this off, Aid," Braxton muttered. Hell, it was almost easy.

He switched off the office light. That was when he heard the front door open.

His hope that it was Chef Levy died as soon as he heard heavy footsteps and male voices. And they were heading straight for the office.

CHAPTER 34

KENZIE

Kenzie had no idea how much time had passed. Her head felt like it had gone through a few rounds of the industrial dishwasher they'd used in Ashner's. Her vision was blurry.

Every so often, she heard the soft squeak of Nurse Ratched's sneakers on the tile floor. Tasteless food was shoved down her throat, and then warm nothingness would follow.

Rinse, repeat.

"Do you think she'll be well enough for her match against Hammer?" a voice asked from somewhere nearby.

Polly.

Kenzie's vision might not be working, but sickly-sweet powdered sugar wafted through the room, which was basically Polly's signature scent.

"She'll be ready," Nurse Ratched replied. "Why do you care, anyway? I thought you wanted Hammer to win."

"Oh, I do," Polly said. "But I want it to be a good match. Cutthroat Cuisine is just so exciting, don't you think?"

Oh, hell no. Kenzie was never going to become the next Gourmand leader.

Benedict had made it sound like, if she won Cutthroat Cuisine, she'd be working for the good of all culinary magician-kind. She knew the reality wouldn't be that bright.

He'd use her. Anyone who went against the Gourmands would be in danger of losing their magic. She would be his weapon.

Kenzie was so screwed.

"Tell Benedict she'll be ready by morning," Nurse Ratched said.

There was a little prick on Kenzie's arm. Then, the voices slipped away. Kenzie fell into a hazy sea of nothingness.

CHAPTER 35

BRAXTON

Braxton pressed himself against the wall and clutched the stolen recipe book.

Walk on by, he silently pleaded the men who were standing in the entryway and talking in low voices. *Nothing to see here.*

"What can I do for you, Mr. Santiori?" an unfamiliar male voice asked.

Braxton's pulse stuttered. *Veneziano was here?*

"Henry and Tina Morierty told me you live here," Veneziano replied, his voice as calm and in-charge as always.

Christ. It sounded like they were standing right outside the office.

Braxton peered through the crack in the partly-open door. He could just make out Veneziano and another man who seemed to be a decade or two older. He had a graying goatee and was leaning on a cane, but he seemed the furthest thing from feeble. The man's whole demeanor screamed authority.

From Kenzie's description, Braxton knew at once that this man was Benedict Vandermeer.

Benedict and Veneziano were standing in the hallway outside the office. There was no way Braxton could slip out without being seen.

"I could have you killed for coming to my place of residence," Benedict said.

"Yes, the Gourmands do possess an inordinate amount of power in our community," Veneziano agreed. "That is precisely the reason for my unannounced visit this evening."

There were some shuffling noises. Braxton saw a few other figures crowd into the narrow entryway, but he couldn't make out faces. Probably Veneziano's goons.

"I cannot be bought, Mr. Santiori," Benedict said as the mobster offered him what looked like a hatbox.

"I am not trying to buy you, Benedict," Veneziano replied.

Benedict turned his body so Braxton had a clear view of the box as the top came off.

It was lucky that Benedict's surprised gasp was louder than Braxton's.

"Thomas Morierty, may he rest in peace," Veneziano said. He reached into the box and lifted the severed head by its greasy hair.

The head spun gently, giving Braxton a clear view of the dead man's petrified expression, along with a tangle of shredded flesh and other innards that were still dripping blood.

"Is this meant to intimidate me?" Benedict asked.

The conversation was so civil, they may as well have been talking about the weather.

"Not at all," Veneziano replied. "But I did have an illuminating conversation with this young man's parents. I was fascinated to hear about your search for a successor, and that you've been holding a secret culinary competition to identify the next chef in line for your position.

"Henry and Tina were kind enough to tell me where to find their son before they…expired."

"Tina Morierty was a Gourmand," Benedict snarled, dropping all pretenses of politeness. "You have impeded Gourmand business. Give me one good reason why I shouldn't kill you and all of your associates."

"Because," Veneziano said. "It would be poor form to murder your Cutthroat Cuisine finalist before he can cook for the championship title."

"What?" Benedict demanded in a whisper that made Braxton's nerves tingle in warning.

"Thomas—*Hammer*—Morierty was a Cutthroat Cuisine finalist," Veneziano said, speaking slowly and annunciating every word. "I killed him." He tapped the disembodied head on its nose. "Therefore, I'm your new finalist."

"You murdered three culinary magicians!" Benedict thundered. "There will be repercussions."

"There's only one problem with that," Veneziano said, raising a finger. "My men know where you live now." He turned so his back was to Braxton. "See that rooftop?"

Braxton couldn't see where they were looking, but he had a fairly good idea where this conversation was heading. It turned out Braxton wasn't the only one who got threatened by Veneziano Santiori.

"…very talented sniper…." Veneziano was saying. "…everywhere you go."

Braxton could see from the Gourmand leader's reddening face that Veneziano had him.

I know the feeling, mate.

"Very well," Benedict said, his tone frigid. "You will report to the Hex Kitchen dome, and my people will escort you down to the arena for the finale."

The men were still talking, but Braxton's brain had splintered. They were holding this secret competition below Hex Kitchen?

All this time, Kenzie had been right there. She'd been right fucking there.

He could *walk* to Kenzie from where he was right now.

"The finale will happen as soon as can be arranged," Benedict was saying. "I do hope you're well-prepared. Your competitor does not hold her punches."

Kenzie. He was talking about Kenzie. Braxton pressed his fist to his mouth to silence his harsh breathing.

"I'll be ready," Veneziano assured Benedict. "I may not be the culinary magician I once was, but I still have a few tricks up my sleeve."

"I'd be happy to help you prepare, Papà," a new voice said.

All of Braxton's churning thoughts ground to a halt as Rick, his sneering face on full display, stepped into Braxton's view.

"I told you to stay in the car, Ricardo," Veneziano told his son.

"Yeah, but I was thinking," Rick said. "I shouldn't be expected to keep my mouth shut about this Cutthroat Cuisine thing without compensation, should I? I mean, my father is getting something for his trouble. Seems only fair I should get a little recompense, too."

He flinched a little when Veneziano raised his hand to adjust his cuff, but he didn't back down.

So, the weasel had grown a spine.

Rick pulled his phone out of his pocket and held it up. "I recorded this conversation and have it set to upload to my social media in an hour."

"Ricardo—" his father warned.

For once, Rick didn't cower in the face of his father's fury. He continued, "I'll stop the upload and delete it, but you have to do one thing for me." His beady gaze was fixed on the Gourmand leader.

"What is that?" Benedict asked. His mouth was scrunched up like he'd just eaten a sour grape.

Rick lifted his leg and wiggled his ankle.

"I want to do magic without being monitored." His voice took on a whine that was much more familiar than the sound of him bargaining with almost as much finesse as Sofia.

"Impossible," Benedict said.

"Ricardo," Veneziano hissed. "You are treading on thin ice."

Benedict raised his cane, somehow conveying his desire for Veneziano to be silent. The mobster, his face turning the shade of an overripe plum, went quiet.

"Do you really want the whole culinary magic community to know your identity and what you really spend your time doing?" Rick pressed. "I know a hundred chefs who are mad as hell about sanctions the Gourmands have passed over the years. I'm sure they're just itching to come over here and give you a piece of their minds."

Damn. If Braxton didn't hate Rick with every molecule of his being, he'd be impressed. Braxton knew Rick had a cruel streak a kilometer wide, but he didn't know the arse had brains. It was something to consider later. If he ever made it out of here.

"Very well," Benedict capitulated. "Come with me."

Then, they were all on the move. Their footsteps drew closer.

Braxton's gaze bounced around the small room, but there was no escape. He was too big to fit under the desk. Behind the bookshelf, maybe?

"Strange," Benedict's voice said from much too close. "I don't recall leaving this door open."

The handle wiggled. Braxton tried to sink deeper into the shadows, but it was no use. As soon as Benedict flicked on the light, the game would be up. He'd be fucked.

The office door flew open.

CHAPTER 36

SOFIA

Sofia, wait," Graham said.

Not a chance. Her brother was in that house with the Gourmand leader and the Santioris. Sofia crunched over broken glass that was littered across the sidewalk. She ignored Elyannah Levy's much-less-polite echoes of Graham's command to wait.

Sofia already had everything she needed—she'd had the entire drive from upstate New York to catalog all of the magical ingredients. She was itching to use them.

Sofia tore open a packet of hickory leaves as she raced down the sidewalk. She bunched the leaves together and then twisted them in half as she ran. She got to the top of the porch steps, kicked open the door, and threw the leaves inside.

White smoke began to billow out of the open door. In seconds, the smoke was so thick she couldn't see her hand when she held it in front of her face.

Shouts and coughing came from near enough that Sofia could probably reach out and touch the people making the sounds. Someone tried to barrel past her on their way to the door. She listened to make sure his footsteps weren't Braxton's, and then she elbowed him. Hard.

The man grunted and lost his footing. Sofia heard the floorboards protest when he fell. Her lungs and throat were burning. Tears streamed out of her squinted eyes.

Sofia opened the next envelope she'd been waiting to use. She put half of the slightly-bitter Swiss chard leaf in her mouth and chewed.

It was obvious when the magic kicked in, because her breathing became easy. It felt like her lungs had expanded to double their usual size. A single breath felt like it would hold her for a week.

Thank you, Qiang Lee.

The Reaper would kill her if he knew she was using his ingredients for herself—again—but this was an extenuating circumstance. At least, that was what she told herself as she opened the next package.

It contained a tiny, shriveled carrot. She popped it in her mouth…dirt particles and all.

Her blurry vision immediately focused. Not only had the scratchy, burning feeling dissipated, but she could see through the smoke.

Aside from the few bodyguards she'd passed on her way into the house, everyone was congregated around an open doorway. Sofia beelined for it. If she knew her brother, he'd be right in the thick of trouble.

Sofia elbowed her way through the group of men who were stumbling around like blind mice. She stepped into a small office.

"Braxton," she whispered.

"Sofe?"

Braxton doubled over in a fit of coughing as he tried to get to her.

"No, not—"

Braxton walked right into a desk.

"Shit," he gasped, which only made him cough harder.

Sofia hurried over and grabbed his arm before he fell through a wall or knocked himself out.

"Eat this," she ordered, giving Braxton the other half of her Swiss chard leaf. He was too blind to find it, so she just crammed the leaf in his mouth.

"Don't you dare spit that out," she ordered.

Neither of her brothers had ever been fond of uncooked vegetables.

"Where—" Braxton heaved in another breath. "—did you come from?"

"Just keep your eyes closed," Sofia ordered as she steered him out of the office. "I'll explain everything later."

Sofia navigated them around a man who was crawling on his hands and knees, fumbling for a cane that was just out of reach.

Sofia kept her arm looped through her brother's until they made it to the front door. Sofia led her brother outside and then shut the door with a quiet click. The smoke wouldn't kill anyone—just disorient them long enough for Sofia and Braxton to disappear.

"Christ, Sofia," Braxton said, as soon as she'd guided him down the porch steps and onto the sidewalk. "Your timing's never been better." He rubbed at his red eyes with his free hand. That was when Sofia noticed the book tucked under his arm.

"What's that?" she asked.

"Recipe book, I think," Braxton said, his voice still hoarse from the smoke. "Tell you about it later."

"I think I have some ingredients in Graham's truck that'll help your eyes," Sofia offered.

"No time," Braxton replied. "I have to talk to Chef Levy. I know where Kenzie is."

Oh, right. Of course.

Sofia held back her bitter *You're welcome for rescuing you* and tagged along behind him. She would have been more aggravated, but magic was singing through her system. She felt electric.

Braxton took off in a jog as soon as Aralia's truck, with Chef Levy behind the wheel, came into view.

"I'll just wait here, then," Sofia said, even though there was no one to hear her. Braxton was already climbing into the car and talking animatedly with Chef Levy.

Sofia sighed. She was in no mood to stand around waiting for her brother, so she started walking. She was too energized to stay put, anyway. She caught the outline of Graham's truck parked under a street lamp halfway down the block and started for it.

Sofia slowed when she noticed Graham and Aralia standing on the sidewalk next to the truck. Their postures were both rigid, and Aralia's voice had that shrill note it carried whenever she was upset.

Sofia stopped where she was, not wanting to intrude.

"I've never asked you for anything, Aralia," Graham said. "But I'm asking you for this. Let Braxton out of your deal."

Sofia had been about to give them some privacy, but the sound of her brother's name halted her in her tracks.

"I'd give you the whole world on a silver platter," Aralia replied. "You know that. But this is different. I have a chance to give you your life back." Aralia's voice was uncharacteristically earnest.

Sofia knew she should walk away or make some noise so they knew she was there.

She did neither. She crept closer, letting the long shadows and parallel-parked cars hide her from view.

"I don't want it like this," Graham said. "Not at someone else's expense."

"Fuck that," Aralia said. "The Santioris know where we live now. Where the hell else are we gonna go? This is the only way to keep you safe."

"We can rebuild somewhere else," Graham argued.

"Let's be honest, here," Aralia said. The softness in her voice was replaced by barely-contained fury. "This has everything to do with the fact that you've gone mental over Sofia McKaid."

Sofia's heart gave two quick thumps. *Da-dum, da-dum.* Her whole body felt pleasantly warm.

"I won't deny I care about her," Graham said. His voice was so low, Sofia had to strain to hear it.

"You care about her enough to give up your only chance at freedom?" Aralia asked.

"Yes."

That one word jumbled Sofia's insides like she was in free-fall.

"But," Aralia stuttered, seeming at a loss for words. "It was always supposed to be us against the world."

Those words tugged on Sofia's heartstrings. It was a sentiment she could relate to, because she'd always thought of her family as a single force that was going to conquer the world. Until she began to lose them one by one.

"Aralia," Graham said. His voice lowered, and Sofia could only make out fragments of the conversation.

"…always be here for you…never going to change…tired of hiding…."

"You're as big a fool for Sofia as Braxton is for Number Eight," Aralia sneered. "And you know what? You saps are going to get the rest of us killed."

"I'd never let anything happen to you," Graham replied, sounding hurt.

"And what about you?" Aralia shot back. "Don't I get the right to protect you?"

Graham said something that was too quiet for Sofia to make out.

Aralia made a disgusted sound. She stalked away from Graham.

Sofia had to crouch behind a car to keep from being seen. She waited until Aralia had made it to her own truck and slammed the door before she stood back up.

Sofia didn't even think about what she was doing before she stepped out of her hiding place and into Graham's view.

"Sofia," he said, startled.

"I'm sorry," she said. "I wasn't out here to spy on you, but I heard you both talking, and—" She trailed off, not quite sure how to finish her sentence.

"It's alright." Graham sighed.

Even in the dim street lights, Sofia could see Graham's whiskey eyes had lost their usual fire. He looked as exhausted as she felt.

"What's Aralia trying to do to my brother?" Sofia asked.

She didn't want to put Graham in a position where he had to betray Aralia's confidence, but if Braxton was in danger, Sofia needed to know about it.

"It doesn't matter," Graham said, his tired expression giving way to something fierce. "I'm not going to let her do it. You have nothing to worry about."

Sofia didn't miss the way he skirted around the truth.

What aren't you telling me, Graham?

"You're shivering," Graham murmured. He shrugged out of his jacket and wrapped it over her shoulders. Then, he wound his arms around her.

Sofia should pull away out of principle, but her body had other ideas. She leaned against his hard chest, letting him surround her like a comforting blanket.

"You smell nice," he murmured.

Ditto, she thought.

He drew back. There was something about the way he looked at her that made Sofia feel like nothing else in the world existed except for the two of them. It was heady and unfamiliar and…nice. Really nice.

"I'm sorry we didn't get a chance to go kayaking the other night," he said, his smoky voice heating her blood. "Maybe—"

Sofia tilted her face up. Graham took the hint and leaned down until their lips touched.

She immediately tried to deepen the kiss, wanting more, but Graham had other ideas.

"Sofia," he said, his voice uneven. "I have to tell you something."

Sofia's heart stuttered. This was it…the secret he'd been holding back.

Guilt flooded her as she remembered her recent conversation with Peter, her PI acquaintance. She shouldn't have asked him to find out whatever Graham was hiding. She should have taken a chance and trusted him—

Graham cleared his throat. "Obviously you've put together that I'm not…normal. I can't take you on regular dates or live in the open. It would make it difficult to be together, but if you're willing—"

"Wait." Sofia held up her hand. "Dates? *Together*?"

Graham's dark eyebrows pulled down. "I didn't mean to be presumptuous. I just thought this was what you wanted…what we both wanted."

Sofia felt a knot of tension in her chest that was making it difficult to breathe.

She knew how this story ended. She'd seen it play out with Braxton and Kenzie.

"How about we start with you telling me *why* you can't go out in public," Sofia said when she managed to find her voice.

Graham shook his head. "I can't tell you that."

Right. He could touch her and kiss her, but he couldn't trust her. And here she'd almost convinced herself that he was different.

"Got it," Sofia said, letting her resentment build until it hardened the bruised places inside her. "And yet, you want to date me? Sorry—you want to hide out with me? I'll be honest with you, Graham. You're extremely hot. If you're looking for a little fun, then I'm your girl. But you can save your empty promises and sappy shit for someone else. Because I'm not buying what you're selling."

She held his penetrating gaze with a fierce glare of her own.

Any second now, Graham's features would relax. He'd admit this was for the best…that a no-strings attachment was what he'd really wanted all along.

For every other man she'd ever been with, it had been enough. More than enough, for a couple of them.

Graham shook his head and stepped away from her. Like actually stepped away.

"I know we haven't spent much time together," he said, "but I think there's something between us. Don't you feel it, too?"

"Yes, Graham. It's called lust." She waved her hand between them. "Attraction. Pheromones. Call it whatever you want, but that's all this is. And in case you haven't noticed, we've both got our hands full at the moment. I don't think it's the right time for either of us to be going on dates or throwing around words like *being together*. Especially when you can't trust me enough to tell me about your past."

Graham was silent for a moment. "So, you'd be happy with just…sex?"

The darkness made it difficult to tell, but it seemed like he might be blushing.

It was kind of adorable.

"Provided you're good at it," she replied, trying to lighten the mood.

Graham's expression only grew more serious. "I'm sorry, but that doesn't work for me."

Come again?

Most men took one look at her blonde hair and long legs and lost their heads.

Except this one, apparently.

"I'm not just talking about our physical connection," Graham said. "I think if you're honest with yourself, it's more than that for you, too. If you let down your shield, you'll see how much more we have to offer each other."

"I don't have a shield," she said, her voice rising.

"I've seen you be fearless when you were fighting for your life," Graham said, reaching for her hand. "But you're not willing to take this risk with me. Why? What are you so afraid of?"

Sofia huffed and tore her hand free from his. "I'm not afraid. I'm busy."

Graham moved so his body was in front of hers. "You want to know what I think?"

"Not really."

"I think you don't want to admit how much you're starting to care about me, because that would make you vulnerable," Graham said. "And I also think that, if you let me, I could make you happy."

"I am happy," she retorted, wondering why she was engaging in this pointless argument in the first place. *Oh, right.* Because Graham was her ride home.

"You're delusional if you think the only thing missing in my life is you," she sneered.

"I didn't say—"

"Furthermore. Why the hell should I trust someone who can't even bring himself to tell me why he can never go out in public?"

Graham flinched. Sofia saw her advantage and pressed forward.

"Why should I trust someone who starts shaking and sweating every time he hears a siren? What are you hiding, Graham?"

He didn't say anything. Disappointment mingled with her sense of victory.

"That's what I thought." She ducked around him and stomped back in the direction they'd come. Graham didn't follow her.

And that was just fine.

Soon enough, Peter would find out exactly what Graham was hiding. Then, Sofia would have her curiosity sated, and she could walk away from this infuriating man without a backward glance.

CHAPTER 37

BRAXTON

It was more than a little creepy to be cooking in a dead family's kitchen. Yet, as Chef Levy and Aralia had pointed out, it wasn't like the Moriertys had any use for it anymore. The place was well-stocked. More importantly, it was empty.

Benedict Vandermeer and the Santioris had cleared out hours ago. Braxton had watched from the rooftop of a nearby building as Gourmands came to clean up all evidence of magic and murder. Sofia had offered up various magical ingredients that had protected their movements from any watchful eyes.

Now, there was no one to stop them as they prepared themselves to infiltrate the Gourmands' stronghold.

Braxton couldn't fucking wait.

He pulled the last pan of paella off the stove. The magic was cooked through, and the whole house smelled like fragrant rice and Spanish paprika. A dusting of saffron threads littered the counter.

Aralia took the pan and spooned the piping hot mixture into a blender. Chef Levy, who was sitting at the table and cleaning a disassembled rifle, reviewed their plan like the drill sergeant she was. Her voice was a little muted from the scarf that was tied around her nose and mouth.

All three of them had their faces covered to keep them from breathing in more of the paella steam than was absolutely necessary. The magic was strong—it would have to be in order to work the way it was intended—but that also meant it could affect them just as easily as their intended targets.

Aralia was already touching him far more than necessary, and after cooking six batches of his food-gasm paella, Braxton was having trouble keeping his body in check. Although, the sight of Chef Levy with that rifle was doing a decent job of combatting the magic wafting through the air.

Braxton had wanted to make something deadlier to take down the people holding Kenzie captive. Unfortunately, Aralia was busy cooking a *magical surprise* that she refused to explain, and Braxton was too magically wrung-out to manage anything complicated. He'd made this recipe before, which meant the magic came more easily and required less effort to hold. As a bonus, all of the necessary ingredients had already been stocked in the Moriertys' fridge.

Some people shot their enemies. He was going to pleasure his.

Ugh.

"What is that smell?" Sofia asked, coming in from outside and sniffing the air.

"Cover your nose and mouth," Braxton ordered. "Now."

Christ. The last thing he needed was—

"Don't even think about it," he warned Graham, who appeared as though he'd been summoned by Sofia's presence. The man was looking at Braxton's sister like she was dessert. And she was looking back at him with the same hungry expression.

Sofia shook her head like she was trying to clear it. "I need to get going. I've got a feeling Qiang won't give me any more ingredients unless I answer for myself in person." She made an impatient sound.

"What's he going to say when he finds out you used all the ingredients he already gave you to help me?" Braxton asked.

He didn't know anything about the Reaper aside from what his sister had told him. The man didn't sound violent, but anyone who had the ability to grow magical ingredients as powerful as his—and went by the title *the Reaper*—wasn't someone to be trifled with. Braxton wasn't keen on Sofia going there by herself.

"It's fine," Sofia said breezily. "You just worry about not turning yourself into Gourmand mincemeat. I'll take care of Qiang."

"I'll go with you," Graham said. He accompanied the offer with a hesitant smile that hid none of his feelings.

Braxton ground his teeth.

"No, you won't," Aralia told Graham. "And if you continue taking stupid risks for that girl, I'll just have to kill her to solve the problem."

"Aralia," Graham warned.

"You're welcome to try," Sofia told her loftily.

Aralia opened her mouth to speak, but Braxton didn't let her get the words out.

"Be very careful," Braxton said, dropping his spoon and turning the full weight of the McKaid stare on Aralia. "That's my sister you're threatening."

Aralia reached for the knife on her belt.

"Everyone calm down!" Chef Levy ordered without looking up from her rifle. "Your yammering is giving me a migraine."

"Are you sure it isn't the vodka?" Sofia retorted, motioning to the half-empty bottle resting on the table next to the rifle.

Chef Levy chuckled. "I like you better than your brother."

Thanks a lot, Chef.

"That makes two of us," Aralia chimed in.

"It's unanimous," Braxton grumbled. "Can we please get back to work now? I'd like to rescue Kenzie sometime this century."

"That's the spirit," Chef Levy said with a roll of her eyes.

Braxton turned to Sofia. "You sure you don't want to wait for me to come with you?"

Sofia scoffed at him. "Just do me a favor and don't get killed," she ordered. "If you do, I swear I'll bring you back to life just so I can kill you again."

Her words were flippant, but Braxton understood what she wasn't saying. Because it was the same anxiety that flooded him every time Sofia did something dangerous.

"I'll be careful if you will," he said. He went to the table and picked up the recipe book he'd stolen from Benedict's house. He handed it to Sofia, but stopped shy of saying something that started with *If I don't make it back…*.

"Deal." Sofia tucked the recipe book under her arm before pinching his cheek. He ruffled her hair. They shared a grin, and then his sister was heading for the door. Graham, who was studiously ignoring Aralia's death-glares, followed.

Braxton forced himself to put his worries about Sofia aside so he could focus on his own impossible task.

"I'm ready," Aralia announced. She held up a bowl full of dark bread dough that smelled intensely of stout and yeast.

"What's this for?" he asked.

The smile Aralia offered him was all teeth. "To make things explode."

✳ ✳ ✳

"Don't forget," Chef Levy whispered as the elevator descended from the garage to the Hex Kitchen tournament venue. "You can save your girlfriend, but we're not leaving until I have the answers I came for. I'm getting to the bottom of how Hanna died."

Chef Levy raised her rifle. Aralia whipped an arrow from the quiver on her back and nocked her bow. Braxton wielded a spray bottle full of liquid paella in each hand.

He could only imagine how absurd and unthreatening he looked. It was fortunate he didn't have insecurities about his masculinity.

The elevator dinged, and the doors slid open. They were standing in the audience seating area surrounding the Hex Kitchen dome. The glass enclosure itself was dark.

"Hey! Who's there?" an authoritative voice called out.

"No one you need to worry about," Chef Levy said, raising her rifle and aiming it at the man. "As long as you get down on the ground and keep your mouth shut."

The man pressed his lips together before flattening himself on the floor.

Chef Levy produced zip ties from her pocket, which she efficiently used to secure the man's wrists and ankles.

More footsteps were heading their way.

"Oh, goody," Aralia squealed.

"Stop right there!" a voice commanded. "You're trespassing on Gourmand property. Take another step, and we'll take you down."

The man's hand went to the weapon holstered at his belt. Aralia was faster.

She had her arrow pointed at the guard's neck before he could raise his weapon. Knowing he was beat, the man raised his hands.

"You gonna be a good boy and stay here quietly?" Aralia asked.

"Y-yes, madam."

Aralia tapped her arrow against the man's cheek. "Next time, fight a little," she purred. "I like that."

Movement flashed in the rows of audience seats. Braxton gripped his spray bottles and went out to meet his enemies.

Security guards were swarming up the carpeted aisles like ants. The good news was that they were wearing red, which made it easy to pick them out in the dim lighting, and they seemed to only be armed with Tasers.

"I'll take left, you go right," Braxton told Aralia, who had just finished tying up the guard she had face-down on the floor.

With a whoop, Aralia leapt on top of a row of audience seats and started firing her arrows at the guards. Braxton went in the opposite direction.

Everyone was shouting. Guards were yelling into walkie-talkies for backup. Electricity sizzled through the air from the Tasers. Aralia's maniacal laughter floated up from the other side of the room.

Braxton sighted the nearest guard and squeezed the handle of his spray bottle.

The gentle hiss was far less satisfying than the crack of Chef Levy's rifle or twang of Aralia's bowstring, but it did its job. The man coming at Braxton stopped in his tracks.

"Oh wow," the guard said, licking the fine spray of mist from his lips. He didn't even notice he'd dropped his Taser.

Braxton had infused enough magic into the paella that, with a single taste, a person wouldn't be able to focus on anything else for at least a few minutes.

The guard contorted his tongue, trying to get every drop of paella. "Amazing. Fucking incredible." He wiped the remnants of paella from his cheek and then licked his palm. He moaned and shuddered as his hand dropped to the button of his pants.

"Why did I think this was a good idea?" Braxton muttered to himself as he caught another guard's fist with his forearm before spraying him in the face with his liquid paella.

Giving all these guards food-gasms was way more awkward than he'd anticipated.

Unfortunately, he didn't have either the time or the ingredients to reevaluate his plan. Guards were coming at him from all sides.

Braxton ran down the aisle, spritzing everyone who came near him. Within moments, the lofty ceiling was filled with moans and cries of pleasure.

See what I get up to without you, Aid? he silently asked his twin.

If Aidan was here to witness this, he'd be rolling on the floor in hysterics.

Braxton and Aralia met in the middle. They were both breathing hard. Aralia's quiver was empty, and Braxton's spray bottles were down to the dregs.

"You two, get over here!" Chef Levy commanded. She was inside the dome, which was now illuminated by a few floor lights. "Wherever the entrance to this underground bunker is, I can't find it. We're going down the old-fashioned way."

Braxton and Aralia joined Chef Levy, who had marked off a circle on the floor with chunks of Aralia's bread.

"On the count of three," Chef Levy told Aralia.

Aralia knelt down and hovered her hands above the bread.

"Wait," Braxton ordered. "How can you be sure the explosion won't hurt Kenzie?"

"This isn't my first rodeo," Chef Levy grumbled. She turned to Aralia. "One—two—three."

Aralia's lips moved as she whispered something to herself. Her cheeks turned red, and her fingers twitched.

A tremendous blast rocketed them off their feet.

It took several seconds for Braxton's ears to stop ringing and the explosive vibrations to quiet down.

"Holy shit," Braxton said. "Why didn't you warn us?"

"I guess the magic was a little more powerful than anticipated," Aralia said unapologetically.

Braxton would have been angrier about his—hopefully—temporary deafness, except for the fact that the bread had worked. There was now a hole in the ground that was large enough for all of them to fit through.

Chef Levy got to her feet and dusted off her shirt. Her clothes were covered in dark soot.

"I'm coming for you!" she shouted down the hole. Then, she pulled a length of rope and grappling hook out of her backpack.

"I'll go first," Braxton said after Chef Levy had secured the rope to a metal beam.

Braxton slid down the rope with absolutely no finesse. He huffed out a curse as the rope chafed his inner legs. A warm sting spread across his palms.

Braxton landed hard at the bottom, feeling his ankles give way before he thudded down on his arse.

Chef Levy and Aralia soon followed, although both of them landed lightly on their feet.

The three of them stood back-to-back as they took in their surroundings.

They were standing in the middle of a…well, he didn't know what the hell this place was. It was an arena, like the ones used for animal shows that he'd seen a few times when his family went to the fair. The only difference was that there were two full kitchens in the center of the hard-packed dirt floor.

Rotten tomatoes and squashed pieces of popcorn littered the ground. And was that a—

"Christ," he whispered.

A detached human thumb was on the ground, partially obscured by loose dirt. A jagged bone dangled from the appendage.

Braxton looked at the arena with new eyes. What he'd assumed to be streaks of tomato innards now looked very much like bloodstains.

What the hell were the Gourmands doing here? More importantly, what were they doing to Kenzie?

A vision of her delicate fingers being yanked off had him swaying on his feet.

"Oh my," a familiar voice boomed through some kind of speaker system. "How did you get down here? Guards!"

Polly Berrywhite was standing next to an open door on the far end of the arena. She was dressed in a poofy blue gown and dripping in diamonds.

Polly was flanked by two men in red uniforms.

As the men beelined for him, all Braxton could think was how these men were involved in keeping Kenzie down here. With a roar, Braxton threw down his spray bottles and ran for the closer guard. The other man didn't even get a chance to use his Taser. Braxton tackled him, using his superior size to pin the guard down and knock him unconscious.

Aralia got the second guard. She held her knife so it just grazed the folds of his neck.

Braxton saw her flick her tongue over the shell of the man's ear.

"Move an inch, and you'll lose it," she told him. "And by *it*, I mean your dick."

Aralia moved her blade down to the relevant area. Tears sprang to the guard's eyes.

"Polly Berrywhite!" Chef Levy shouted. "I'm coming for you, bitch!"

Polly yelped and ducked back into the doorway.

"No," Chef Levy said, stopping Braxton before he went after her. "She's mine. You go that way." She pointed to another closed door behind him.

Braxton wasn't about to waste time arguing. Kenzie was here. Somewhere.

"Just a minute, Romeo," Chef Levy said, grabbing his sleeve and hauling him back. She pointed to Aralia. "You stay here and make sure our way out stays clear."

"With pleasure," Aralia said.

The guard she held against her whimpered when her knife hand twitched.

To Braxton, Chef Levy said, "Meet back here in half an hour." She passed him a small egg timer that buzzed faintly in his hand. The minutes were already ticking down.

"Get up the rope before the timer goes off," Chef Levy said. She shoved her backpack into Braxton's arms. "If I'm not back in time, light this place up with the rest of Aralia's bread."

"What?" he replied.

"Just do it, McKaid!" she ordered, already jogging in the opposite direction. "That's an order."

Chef Levy didn't give Braxton a chance to respond. She was already sprinting after Polly. With a nod to Aralia, who was cooing to the guard she still held against her, Braxton collected his spray bottles from the ground. There was still a small amount of liquid paella in each.

Something told him he'd need every last drop before all this was over.

He tried to keep his footsteps quiet, but it didn't matter. There was no one to stop him as he wound through a matrix of narrow tunnels. The dirt floor eventually gave way to a hallway with linoleum floors.

Breathing hard, Braxton scanned the closed doorways on either side of the hall. There were no windows to see into the rooms, but whiteboards next to each door displayed names printed in friendly bubble letters.

And there, at the very end of the hallway….

Kenzie Ashner.

Braxton didn't even remember reaching the door. He grasped the handle, but it was locked.

"Kenzie?" Braxton called.

No answer.

Panic tightened into a painful knot inside him.

"Kenzie? It's me," he called. "Get away from the door, baby."

He kicked the hinges with enough force that a satisfying *snap* announced they'd broken right off. Braxton wrestled the door aside before peering into the room.

His breath caught. There she was.

CHAPTER 38

KENZIE

Kenzie launched herself out of the bed, where she'd been pretending to sleep.

One of her eyes was swollen shut and the other wasn't much better, so she couldn't get a good look at her intruder. Her hearing was also a little muffled from a punch she'd taken to the side of her head, so she couldn't make out the words coming through the door.

None of that mattered. She just had to—

With a ferocious roar, she threw herself at the man.

Just before she collided with his broad chest, Kenzie looked up. Through her slitted vision, she caught a glimpse of brilliant green eyes.

"B—Braxton?"

She pried her eyes open enough to make sure it was really him, and not just a figment of her imagination.

"Kenzie!"

She found herself engulfed in familiar arms. Her legs gave out on her, but she didn't fall. Braxton was holding her.

"I'm here," he said in a ragged voice.

Tears burned her tender skin and made her already-precarious eyesight even worse. She didn't care.

"You came," she said, pressing her face to his chest and breathing him in.

"Always," he murmured into her hair, holding her tighter.

Kenzie clung hard enough to Braxton that she was in danger of cracking his ribs.

"I'm here," Braxton said again.

Kenzie started to cry in earnest. It wasn't the appropriate response, but she couldn't help herself.

Braxton had come for her. Even after all the pain she'd caused him and everything he'd lost because of her. He'd still come.

"Let's get out of here," Braxton said, releasing her so he could interlock their fingers.

Sweeter words had never been spoken.

Braxton picked up a spray bottle from the floor that was coated in a rust-colored residue. Kenzie didn't waste time asking what it was for. She just gripped Braxton's hand as they left her room behind.

They'd barely made it a few steps before a door opened beside them. Nurse Ratched, along with two security guards, were right there. Kenzie screamed.

Braxton flicked his spray bottle. A few drops splattered onto Nurse Ratched and the guards.

Kenzie tasted magic on the air. Hopefully, whatever was in Braxton's bottle would melt these people into puddles of goo.

Disappointment surged through Kenzie when the trio didn't immediately dissolve on the spot. But they had stopped in their tracks. They weren't reaching for weapons or shouting promises of death. In fact, they weren't even paying attention to Kenzie and Braxton. All of their focus was on each other.

Nurse Ratched grabbed each man by the collar and hauled them to her. Their mouths met in the sloppiest three-way kiss Kenzie had ever seen. Okay, it was the only three-way kiss she'd ever seen, but still.

"Kenz, come on," Braxton urged.

Kenzie stayed where she was. She was frozen in horror as she watched Nurse Ratched grind her voluminous butt into one guard's crotch while she worked her hand into the other one's pants.

"Am I hallucinating?" she asked.

"Food-gasm," Braxton said, his lips curving into the hint of a smile. "Guess who gave me the inspiration for this dish?"

He winked at her.

Kenzie was too dumbfounded to reply. When Nurse Ratched started shimmying out of her scrub bottoms, Kenzie's feet unfroze. She fumbled for Braxton's hand and pulled him away.

Nurse Ratched getting it on was one image she didn't need plaguing her nightmares, thank you very much.

They ran on. Kenzie kept expecting Benedict or Polly to pop out of some hidden doorway and grab them, but no one appeared.

Kenzie's adrenaline was wearing off, and she could feel herself flagging. Her feet, which she'd just realized were covered in nothing except socks, refused to cooperate. They had reached the tunnel that led to the arena—*the holding pen*, she'd heard the guards call it. She was exhausted and bruised and sick from the sedatives Nurse Ratched had forced into her. Her body felt like it had been turned into stone.

She didn't want to set foot in the arena again. Kenzie didn't didn't think she could bear to see the place where she'd killed Brute and her other competitors.

"Kenz, come on," Braxton said.

When she still didn't move, he backtracked and swept her into his arms.

"Don't make me go in there," she babbled, clawing at Braxton's shirt like it would stop him. "Please."

Some logical part of her knew Braxton wasn't going to force her to cook to the death, but her emotions were a wild riot inside her.

Crack.

Brute's neck snapped, and his body sank to the dirt.

Scarlet screamed as Kenzie plunged the bread dagger into her chest. Warm blood oozed over Kenzie's hands.

"I'm sorry," Kenzie mumbled. "I'm sorry. I'm sorry. I'm sorry."

"We're getting out of here," Braxton promised. "I've got you."

"Polly and Benedict are out there," she said, trying and failing to squirm out of Braxton's arms. "We can't go that way."

Kenzie's pulse felt like a hummingbird's wings.

Braxton, carrying a very unwilling Kenzie, burst into the brightly-lit arena. Instead of finding themselves in the midst of a Cutthroat Cuisine match, the place was strangely empty. And there was a giant hole in the ceiling. Weirdly enough, the sight of that gaping hole calmed her.

"Did you do this?" she asked, craning her neck to see up.

"Yep," Braxton replied. "Well, technically, Elyannah Levy and Aralia did it."

As if on cue, Crazy Aralia appeared from the shadows, her hunting knife in hand.

"Hiya, Number Eight," she said. "You look like shit."

Kenzie wheezed out a laugh. "Hi to you, too."

Braxton put Kenzie down and grasped a rope that was dangling from the hole in the ceiling.

"Is that safe?" Kenzie asked.

Braxton shrugged in a way that wasn't at all reassuring. "I'll make sure it is." He gave Aralia a look that clearly told her to protect Kenzie without saying the words out loud. He seemed to be under the mistaken impression that she still had any pride.

"Your ass looks great from this angle," Aralia called up as Braxton began to climb the rope.

It really did.

"That ass is already spoken for," Kenzie informed Aralia. "I suggest you stop staring unless you want to be walking funny."

Somewhere above them, Braxton snickered.

Kenzie shielded her eyes against the painfully-bright light and watched Braxton work his way up the rope. His progress wasn't fast or pretty, but he managed to get to the hole in the ceiling and haul himself up onto the ledge.

"Grab the rope," Braxton called down a few seconds later. "I'll pull you up."

And thank God for that. Indiana Jones, she wasn't.

Braxton hauled up Kenzie's dead weight, since it was taking all of her concentration to stay semi-vertical. As soon as Kenzie was on solid ground again, Braxton dropped the rope back down for Aralia.

Aralia scampered up the rope like it was something she did on a regular basis. Kenzie promised herself that, as soon as her life wasn't in danger, she'd start working out. Well, maybe after a short vacation. And nothing that involved lifting weights. Or sit-ups.

Aralia ignored the hand Kenzie offered and pulled herself up into the ravished Hex Kitchen dome.

"Now what," Kenzie began, but was interrupted by a dinging sound. It was coming from Braxton's pocket.

He reached in and pulled out a plastic egg timer.

"What's that for?" Kenzie asked.

Braxton and Aralia exchanged a look that was full of apprehension. Neither of them responded.

"What is it?" Kenzie asked, her own anxiety growing with every passing moment.

"Chef Levy," Braxton said heavily. He ran a hand through his hair. "She told us—"

Kenzie jumped when a door slammed. Security guards shouted to each other as they emerged from the audience wings. They were approaching the glass dome from all sides. Kenzie thought she heard the clack of a cane against the floor, but that could just be her subconscious freaking out.

"Get down!" Aralia shouted.

They hit the floor, just as gunfire erupted.

"Kill the other two," a voice commanded, somehow cutting through the other sounds. "Bring Kenzie to me."

Benedict.

"We're surrounded," Aralia panted. "We've gotta do it."

Do what?

Kenzie's vision was going spotty. Their escape attempt had failed. Not only was she going right back to the lion's den, but she was the reason why Braxton and Aralia were here…the reason they were about to be….

"Fuck," Braxton said.

That about summed things up.

"I'll lead them away," Kenzie said, trying to scrounge up the last reserves of her strength.

Braxton shook his head. He pulled off his backpack and rummaged through it.

"There's no time," Kenzie said, her voice high and panicky.

The Gourmands' guards were closing in around them.

Kenzie kept trying to move her body so it would be harder for anyone with a gun to get a clear shot at Braxton or Aralia. It wasn't an especially effective strategy, since she was the smallest person in their group.

Braxton's hand emerged from the backpack holding—of all things—a half-loaf of beer bread. He tossed the loaf to Aralia, who started tearing off pieces and throwing them at the guards.

Bread versus bullets. Super.

Kenzie fluttered around, trying to help but not knowing what to do. Whatever magic was in the bread was making her head spin.

The guards were close enough for Kenzie to see triumph on their faces.

Kenzie turned to Braxton. "What are we waiting for—"

BOOM!

They all flew off their feet. Plaster and chunks of ceiling rained down, but the destruction was confined to the areas where Aralia had tossed her bread. Guards cried out as they were buried alive.

Kenzie yelped as shattered glass rained down on them.

"Finish it," Aralia ordered Braxton, who was busy trying to shield Kenzie from the worst of the falling glass.

Aralia yanked up their rope and fought with the guard who was clinging to it. The man lashed out with a pocket knife, which Aralia dodged. She kicked the man hard enough to send him falling back down the hole. His cry echoed twice before abruptly cutting off.

Kenzie fell backward as a spray of bullets erupted from the Cutthroat Cuisine arena below them. More glass rained down on their heads.

"Finish it, Braxton!" Aralia shouted. "She's probably already dead."

That's when Kenzie's sluggish brain caught up. They were talking about Chef Levy.

Chef Levy, who had come here with them but wasn't here now.

When Kenzie turned to Braxton, she saw that he was holding the remaining beer bread loaf.

"No." She clutched his arm. "You can't. There are prisoners down there."

She thought about Rosemary. Kenzie hadn't seen her since their failed escape attempt, but she'd heard her screams. And there had to be other people down there just like them.

More shots rang out.

"Braxton, please," Kenzie begged. "There has to be another way."

When he didn't answer, she forced her swollen eyes open. For the first time since he'd rescued her, Kenzie really looked at him. His green eyes were bloodshot, but that wasn't what caught her attention. There was something else in his gaze that was unfamiliar. His expression was eerily empty.

"Get Kenzie out of here," Braxton said quietly.

Aralia didn't hesitate. She grabbed Kenzie's arm and started to drag her away.

"No," Kenzie said, tugging against Aralia's iron grip. "Braxton!"

"Come on, Number Eight. Quit struggling."

Aralia half-carried her all the way to the elevator, ignoring Kenzie's babbled commentary about how they couldn't kill the guards without also killing the defenseless prisoners who were still locked down below.

The elevator door slid open.

Aralia's grip tightened as she began muttering to herself. Kenzie saw wispy strands of magic begin to encircle the bread in Braxton's hands.

"Braxton!" Aralia called.

Braxton dropped the bread down the hole.

"No!" Kenzie shrieked.

Braxton sprinted up the hallway toward the elevator. Kenzie flinched as gunfire sprayed the walls, missing Braxton by inches.

A tremendous boom made the walls shudder. A puff of smoke came up from the hole in the dome's floor.

Then, the tiled floor began to give way.

"Braxton!" Kenzie screamed.

He raced toward the elevator. Steps behind him, the floor was collapsing. He was so close, but the ground was crumbling feet away from him…and then inches….

Braxton dove into the elevator. The door slid shut.

Then, they were rising to the surface. To freedom.

CHAPTER 39

BRAXTON

Braxton had blown up the whole underground arena beneath the dome. He'd killed security guards, Gourmands, prisoners….

He'd killed Elyannah Levy.

It was cold comfort that the explosion hadn't been enough to cause any shockwaves in the street above. So, at least they wouldn't have to deal with exposing a veritable underground city full of cooking equipment.

"You came for me," Kenzie murmured. Braxton had one arm around her as they ran, since Kenzie wasn't seeming especially stable on her feet. He turned to look at her.

Kenzie's hip bone seemed ready to poke through the baggy hospital scrubs she was wearing. And she was covered in bruises.

"I told you I would," he told her.

And that was the point of all of this. He might have done things today he could never forgive himself for, but he'd done what he came here to do. He had Kenzie.

Aralia opened the truck's passenger door, and Braxton practically threw Kenzie inside. He climbed in after her. Aralia ran around to the other side and got in. Then, they were screeching out of the underground garage.

"Careful," Braxton warned Aralia. "The last thing we need is to get pulled over."

Braxton didn't know how many Gourmands had been down there during the explosion, or how long it would take for the rest of them to find out what had happened. All Braxton knew was that he wanted to be long gone before then.

Kenzie fell asleep with her head against his shoulder as soon as the skyline disappeared from their rearview mirror. Braxton's adrenaline melted away, making room for a searing headache. His limbs were shaky and weak, and his skin felt like he was burning with a fever.

"Sleep it off," Aralia advised him, somehow sensing his discomfort.

Braxton nodded, but he didn't close his eyes. He was afraid if he fell asleep, his brain would conjure up phantoms of all the people he'd killed.

He leaned against Kenzie and tried not to think about anything else.

His eyes were just beginning to fall closed when Aralia announced, "We've got trouble, stud."

Braxton sat up and glanced out the rear window. A limo was barreling down the road and quickly gaining on them.

Traffic choked the roadway in front of them, and there were no turn-offs. They had nowhere to go.

He and Aralia cursed loudly, waking Kenzie.

"What do we do?" Kenzie asked, squinting at the limo through her swollen eyes.

"We fight," Aralia replied.

She pulled a fresh quiver of arrows out of the truck's cab with one hand, while she used the other to jerk the truck onto the narrow shoulder. Aralia tossed her hunting knife to Braxton. He managed to catch it without slicing his own hand off.

The limo came to a screeching halt. It was parked at an angle, blocking off their little group from traffic.

Good thinking. Now, the Gourmands could kill the three of them without getting hit by oncoming traffic.

A few passing cars honked, but most just swerved around, giving them a wide berth. Any hope Braxton had of the police coming along and saving them quickly evaporated.

The limo's windows were too tinted for Braxton to count how many people were inside. He wasn't left with much time to wonder, anyway. The driver's door opened.

A hoarse laugh erupted out of Braxton as Elyannah Levy emerged. Her usually-spiky hair lay flat and scorched against her head. There was a nasty gash on her cheek. Otherwise, she looked unhurt.

Braxton unlocked his door, and he and Kenzie stumbled onto the pavement.

"Chef Levy," Braxton said, dizzy with relief.

"Don't even think about trying to hug me, McKaid," she warned him.

Braxton laughed. "You're alright. We thought—"

Chef Levy waved a hand, dismissing him. She wrenched open the limo's passenger door and reached in.

There was some grunting and huffing, followed by a high-pitched squeal. Then, a figure emerged.

Polly Berrywhite barely looked like herself. Her hair had fallen out of its elaborate coiffe and hung limply around her wrinkled face. Her glasses were askew, and one of her chandelier earrings was missing. And the sleeve of her gown was torn.

"P-please," Polly stammered. Her wild eyes moved from Chef Levy to Braxton. "Braxton, dearest. Help me!"

Chef Levy punched Polly in her rotund stomach.

A wretched wheezing sound tore out of the old woman. Braxton felt ill.

Chef Levy put her hands on Polly shoulders and kneed the older woman. Polly doubled over.

"Chef Levy, stop," Braxton said.

"Stay out of this, McKaid," she snarled. "I've been waiting twenty years for this. Get in my way, and I'll kill you, too."

When he took another step forward, Kenzie grabbed his arm and held him back. Her beautiful, bruised face was contorted in rage.

"She's the reason I got kidnapped in the first place," Kenzie said.

Braxton turned back to Polly. Blood was leaking from her nose and staining her collar. She was sobbing.

Braxton's brain couldn't reconcile what Kenzie and Chef Levy had revealed about this sweet old woman, who was known as the darling of the culinary magic community. She was a philanthropist...an icon.

Chef Levy slammed Polly back against the limo, making Braxton's own head ache in sympathy.

"What did you do with her?!" Chef Levy shrieked. "What happened to Hanna?"

"Who?" Polly's chin wobbled.

"Hanna!" Chef Levy gave Polly's lapels a vicious shake, making the older woman's neck flop around like a bobblehead. "The girl I loved. The one *you* helped disappear twenty years ago."

Polly's split lip quivered.

"Don't say you don't remember," Chef Levy warned. There was something manic and unfocused in her gaze. She pulled a switchblade out of her pocket and dug it under Polly's double-chin.

"Okay," Polly gasped. "I'll tell you."

Chef Levy pulled back her knife, just a little.

Polly dabbed at the blood on her lips. "That girl was flaunting culinary magic in front of Vanillas, and the Gourmands couldn't risk—"

"I know that part," Chef Levy growled. "Tell me what I want to know."

Polly let out a wavering breath. "She was killed while she was out swimming alone. I have it on good authority her passing was entirely painless."

Kenzie made a small noise. When Braxton turned to her, she was shaking like a leaf. He wrapped one arm around her while he clutched Aralia's dagger with his free hand.

When Braxton turned his focus back to Chef Levy, he saw that she'd let go of Polly and was sagging against the limo. Grief was etched into every line of Chef Levy's face. Her ramrod-straight posture had collapsed in on itself.

A small squeak from Kenzie alerted Braxton to the fact that he was holding her too tightly. He loosened his grip while simultaneously promising himself that no one would ever separate them again.

Polly, sensing an opportunity at Chef Levy's momentary distraction, glanced around. She must have realized there was a better chance of Armageddon than getting past Chef Levy, because she didn't try to run.

"I had nothing to do with your… Hanna's…death," Polly said hurriedly, pressing her advantage during the slight reprieve. "I promise you, Elyannah. I was so busy getting my magical food bank up and running that I hardly noticed who the Gourmands were going after."

Pure hatred flashed in Chef Levy's eyes.

"What did they do with Hanna's body?" Chef Levy asked, her voice a deadly quiet.

Polly's hopeful smile wobbled. "Our associate, the Bonecruncher, has been taking care of all that for the last fifty years or so." She licked her cracked lips. "He's been very helpful more recently with disposing of the culinary magicians from Cutthroat Cuisine. But don't worry," she quickly added. "Those poor chefs' magical essence was used to create new, artificial magic ingredients, so their deaths weren't in vain. Benedict and the other Gourmands have been working quite diligently…." She trailed off, finally noticing Chef Levy's savage expression.

A shudder went through Braxton as he remembered those husklike bodies from the Bonecruncher's memory. Now, it made more sense. Those corpses looked all shriveled because their magic force had been drained out of them.

Christ.

"You have to understand," Polly pleaded. "It's all part of the Gourmands' greater plan. Benedict has been working on it for his entire tenure. He's been stockpiling magic ingredients while he waited for his crowning achievement to be ready."

"And what might that be?" Chef Levy asked in a flat voice.

"It's—"

Polly's head snapped back. Blood trickled from a hole in the center of her forehead.

Braxton didn't understand. Chef Levy's knife hadn't moved.

"Sniper!" Aralia shouted.

No, no, no. Not again.

Images of Mum falling to the ground crowded into Braxton's mind. Blood gushing from her chest. Sofia's screams….

Braxton didn't think. He yanked Kenzie down to the ground and rolled over her, covering her body with his own. The sound of gunshots filled the air.

CHAPTER 40

SOFIA

Sofia woke to the smell of cinnamon and strawberry syrup. She was in her bed in the cabin's spare room, although she had no memory of leaving the truck. She must have fallen asleep on the drive back and been carried up here. By Graham.

Her laptop was closed and resting on the nightstand next to a plate of French toast that was the source of the incredible smell tickling her nostrils.

Even if he hadn't been the only other person in the house with her, she would have known this was Graham's doing. Quiet kindnesses seemed to be his MO.

Ravenous in a way she couldn't remember ever being, she dug in. The French toast was still warm. There was no magic in the food, which was oddly refreshing. As she ate, her brain insisted on conjuring images of Graham's earnest face and the sound of his smoky voice.

She replayed their—well, not really fight, but disagreement—while syrup and golden bread melted on her tongue.

Was it possible she'd been wrong? Would it be so horrible to give him a chance…to give *them* a chance?

Good God, she was a cliché, refusing to trust anyone because she was afraid of getting hurt.

How could she expect Graham to turn out his secrets for her when she couldn't even be honest about her own feelings?

Sofia threw on one of Aralia's awful dresses and went to find Graham.

She didn't have to go far. He was sitting at the kitchen table, across from Clementine, who was wearing a pink miniskirt and sparkly sweater. The outfit looked wrong amid the cabin's rustic decor. She was also leaning way closer to Graham than was strictly necessary. Or acceptable.

"What's going on here?" Sofia asked, trying to keep a neutral tone.

"You left your phone down here," Graham said, a note of apology in his voice. "I saw Clementine was calling, so I answered."

"So sweet of you to give me directions here," Clementine gushed. She stroked her delicate fingers over Graham's forearm. His bare, sinewy forearm. "I would have been completely lost without you." She batted her eyelashes.

Sofia made a concerted effort to laser the girl with her mind.

Graham slid his arm out from under Clementine's, which saved Sofia from having to explain to the Reaper why his assistant was missing some limbs.

"What are you doing here?" Sofia asked. "And where's Qiang?"

Clementine nibbled on her bottom lip. "Reaper Lee doesn't know I'm here. He's…quite upset with you." She gave Sofia puppy-dog eyes.

"This is ridiculous," Sofia muttered. "If he'd just talk to me, I could explain."

"I'm not sure that would help," Clementine said, worrying at a loose thread on her sweater. "Reaper Lee is very stubborn. But if you want to talk to him, I left my cell phone with him. I can't promise he'll answer—Reaper Lee doesn't approve of technology—but—"

Sofia swiped her cell off the table and was calling Clementine's phone before the other girl even finished her sentence.

"You shouldn't be driving without a phone," Graham told Clementine.

"Ohmygosh, you're totally right," Clementine agreed. "That's so sweet of you to worry about me. You're, like, a knight in shining armor."

Sofia threw up a little bit. She turned her back on the two of them as she waited for Qiang to answer.

"Master Lee doesn't really understand how to talk into a phone unless I put it on speaker for him," Clementine said apologetically. "You might want—"

"Hel-lo?" Qiang shouted when he picked up.

Sofia winced and held the phone away from her ear. "It's Sofia," she said. "Sofia McKaid."

Several seconds of silence passed.

"You did not keep your word!" Qiang yelled.

Sofia heard something slam on the other side of the line—probably Qiang's fist against his table.

"Qiang, er, Reaper Lee—"

"You used my ingredients for yourself," Qiang thundered. "I never should have trusted you."

Sofia bristled. She'd built her professional reputation on being tough but straightforward. There was plenty people could say about her, but no one could call her dishonest.

"The only reason I used the ingredients was because lives were in danger," Sofia began.

Liar, her pesky conscience hissed. *You liked being powerful. You'd do it again if given half a chance.*

"This is how it always begins." Qiang punctuated the words with what sounded like another smack to his table.

"Relax, Reaper Lee," Clementine whispered under her breath. "Your blood pressure…."

Sofia realized that Graham and Clementine could hear every word of this conversation, which made the whole situation exponentially more humiliating. She was about to take her phone somewhere more private, when Qiang spoke again.

"My ancestors' ingredients have been used and abused by some of the strongest culinary magicians throughout the ages," he said. "Every one of them was ruined by their own greed and ambition."

Sofia dug her nails into her palm. "In that case, it's fortunate I'm not a culinary magician."

"The problem is you want to be one," Qiang hollered, loud enough that the entire east coast probably heard him. "I see you, Sofia McKaid. You are so focused on what you are lacking, that it blinds you."

Ouch.

"I'm going to ask you to trust me with your ingredients once more," Sofia said. It was an effort to keep her voice even as her pulse raged in her ears.

The truth was, she wasn't entirely sure why she needed this so badly. Her family's debt to the Santioris was repaid. More money was always useful, but at the moment, it wasn't necessary. So, why did it feel like she would die if Qiang took this opportunity away from her?

"You are shrouded in ambition," Qiang said. "It hangs over you like smoke. You are poisoned."

"Enough."

The quiet command came from Graham. He looked enormous as he loomed over Sofia and plucked the phone out of her hand.

"Don't tell Reaper Lee I'm here!" Clementine whisper-begged.

"Do not try to contact me," Qiang hollered, unaware of the fact that Sofia no longer had possession of her phone. "You will never touch my ingredients again!"

"Wait," Sofia began, but it was too late. Graham had already ended the call.

"What the hell?" she demanded, grabbing her phone back.

"I'm sorry," Graham said, even though he didn't look sorry at all. "But I didn't like the way he was speaking to you."

Clementine made a distressed sound and fluttered her eyelashes at Graham. "Reaper Lee doesn't mean any harm." To Sofia, she said, "I told you he wouldn't change his mind."

"Is that why you drove all the way here?" Sofia snapped. "To rub my face in it?"

Genuine hurt crossed Clementine's doll-like face.

"Of course not," Clementine said. She took Sofia's hand in her tiny ones.

Sofia was about to wrench her hand back and give this impertinent girl a lecture about personal space, when she felt cool metal on her palm. It was a key.

"In the trunk," Clementine said in a furtive whisper, even though there was no one in hearing distance besides the three of them. "I brought the rest of this year's harvest. I was supposed to destroy it, so Reaper Lee won't find out I brought the ingredients here unless someone tells him."

"Why?" Sofia croaked. Admittedly, she hadn't been the nicest to Clementine.

"Because." Clementine shrugged her slender shoulders. "I know what it's like to be underestimated. People take one look at us and make assumptions. It gets old after a while, you know?"

Sofia felt her face heat, because she did know. She was also guilty of making the exact kind of assumptions about Clementine that were so irksome when they were directed at her.

"But," Sofia faltered. "You could get in trouble if Qiang finds out."

Clementine offered a delicate shrug. "That is why you need to do good things with the ingredients. So even if Reaper Lee finds out, he will know I made the right decision."

Clementine adjusted her skirt and stood from the table. She gave Graham a coy look over her shoulder as she headed for the door.

Stunned speechless, Sofia followed her into the sunlit morning.

Sofia was a little wobbly, so she let Clementine unlock the back of the U-Haul. When Sofia peered inside, she barely managed to hold back a Clementine-like squeal.

There were five large crates packed all the way to the top. Sofia smelled cool mint and peppery eucalyptus and sharp magic.

Bloody hell, there was so much magic. Sofia's heart soared. Her mouth watered. Her mind shuffled through a thousand different uses for all of the magic contained inside these crates.

"Want me to help you get them inside?" Graham asked.

Sofia realized she'd just been standing there, gaping at the crates like an ingredient-voyeur.

"That'd be great," she managed.

They each helped carry the ingredients into the house. The crates were deliciously heavy.

"I've got this," Graham said when only one crate remained. He hefted it out of the truck and started for the house, leaving Sofia and Clementine alone.

"I," Sofia began, not even knowing how to go about thanking Clementine. Or apologizing.

"Make sure you use them well," Clementine said. "There won't be any more until the next harvest."

"I will," Sofia assured her.

Clementine gave her a bright smile. "Good." She hopped into the U-Haul and buckled her seatbelt. "Call me," she said, like they were two girlfriends parting at a slumber party. "Reaper Lee gets so boring sometimes."

Sofia thought she said something like *I will,* but her head was still buzzing from everything that had just happened. She stood and watched without seeing as Clementine drove away.

When her phone started to ring, she answered without even bothering to look at the caller ID.

"Yeah?" she said.

"Sofia?" a male voice asked. It was familiar, but she was too distracted to immediately place it. "Aw, don't break my heart and tell me you didn't save my number. It's Peter. The sexiest PI on the planet."

Sofia tossed her head, trying to clear her brain. "Right. Hi."

"Graham Malyung," Peter said.

"Huh?"

"That guy you asked me to check into," Peter said. "I found out who he is."

Sofia blinked. She turned, looking for the man in question. She saw his silhouette through the partly-open window before he disappeared from view.

Sofia focused all of her attention on the voice in her ear.

"—murdered his own parents," Peter was saying. "Sofia. If this man is anywhere near you, then you need to get the fuck away from him. Now."

CHAPTER 41

KENZIE

N o!"

The word came out of Kenzie as a whisper, because all of Braxton's weight was crushing her into the asphalt. Polly was dead. That meant Kenzie's best chance at getting answers about whatever the Gourmands were working on in that kitchen was lying in a pool of her own blood.

"Get in the limo!" Chef Levy shouted from somewhere nearby.

Braxton rolled off Kenzie and helped her up. He kept his body curved around hers to shield her.

Kenzie would have argued, but there wasn't time. She let Braxton herd her toward the limo, which was so close and so far. She kept waiting for a sniper bullet to punch straight through both of them.

Chef Levy was crouching behind Aralia's truck, which was peppered with bullet holes. She clicked off shot after shot from her rifle.

Braxton pulled Kenzie between the two vehicles, but that didn't stop her from flinching as more bullets streaked across the truck's far side. There was a dull hiss as one of the tires began deflating.

Braxton was fumbling with the limo door and trying to push Kenzie in, but something had caught her eye. She planted her feet.

"Kenz—"

There he was, standing on a patch of grass on the opposite side of the four-lane road.

Benedict.

He was next to a man whose body was partially-obstructed by a row of skinny trees. The man lay on his belly as he aimed a sniper rifle at them.

The same rifle he'd used to kill Polly Berrywhite. The rifle he'd probably use to kill the rest of them.

The man aimed his rifle, and—

"Braxton!"

Kenzie shoved him with all of her strength, causing both of them to fall into the limo's half-open door. Braxton cried out and let go of her. Blood spurted from his forearm.

"Get in the limo!" Chef Levy roared. She clicked her gun, but nothing happened. She was out of bullets.

Before Kenzie could take stock of where the sniper was aiming next, two more limos skidded to a halt on the road. Gourmand security poured out.

"How did they survive?" Braxton demanded.

This time, Kenzie didn't try to resist when Braxton motioned for her to get into the limo. Aralia squashed in on Kenzie's other side, while Chef Levy threw herself into the driver's seat and started the engine. Except, there was nowhere to go. The two other vehicles had boxed them in.

They were screwed.

The limos belched out men with guns and…Nurse Ratched.

Her face was burned terribly, but Kenzie still recognized the evil twist to her features.

"Get her!" Nurse Ratched bellowed.

Kenzie turned to Braxton, who was cradling his arm. It was still bleeding.

Kenzie shouted something about a tourniquet. When she looked up again, a scream lodged in her throat. Nurse Ratched and Benedict were standing right outside her window. Even though the glass was tinted, Benedict was staring straight at Kenzie. He gestured for her to lower her window.

Kenzie opened it a crack.

"Leave them alone and I'll come quietly," Kenzie called out.

"Not a chance," Braxton growled, letting go of his bleeding arm to grip her wrist.

"Hey asshole," Aralia said, leaning over Kenzie to address Benedict. "How's your leg feeling? Want me to even them out?"

Benedict snarled something back, but Kenzie's attention snagged on one of the security guards. He wasn't behaving like the others, who had their weapons drawn and were surrounding the limo. This guard was shuffling around and keeping his head down. He was also wearing a Yankees cap that definitely wasn't part of the Gourmand security uniform.

As Kenzie watched, the guard unzipped his jacket. Or *her* jacket, as Kenzie was quickly realizing. As the woman moved, Kenzie saw a flash of the green scrubs she was wearing underneath her security uniform.

Everyone else was focusing elsewhere, so Kenzie was pretty sure she was the only one who saw the woman pull a small flask out of her pocket.

The woman tipped the contents in her mouth and chewed. She blew a translucent black bubble out of her mouth.

The bubble grew and grew. Kenzie waited for it to pop, but it didn't.

Two things happened at once. Everyone else caught on to the guard who wasn't a guard. And Kenzie noticed a gleam around the woman's throat. It was a charm necklace.

There was only one person Kenzie knew who wore a necklace like that. Rosemary.

"Stop her!" Nurse Ratched and Benedict shouted at the same time.

All the guns turned on Rosemary. Shots rang out.

Kenzie turned her face into Braxton's shirt, unable to watch Rosemary be riddled full of bullets.

At Braxton's whispered, "What the fuck?" Kenzie dared to look.

The sight that met her made no sense. The bubble that had emerged from Rosemary's mouth had gotten big enough to enclose her entire body. Bullets struck the bubble and stuck to the translucent shield, looking like little peppercorns. And the bubble was still expanding.

The security guards were shoved back, away from the growing bubble. Kenzie heard a little *thwup* as the bubble swallowed the limo they were in. The bubble was no longer connected to Rosemary's mouth, but it continued to encircle both her and the limo. When the guards tried to reach Rosemary, they bounced back. The bubble's sides wiggled and rippled, but neither bullets nor people could penetrate it.

As the bubble continued to grow, it shoved away the vehicles as though they weighed nothing. There was honking and the sound of crumpling metal as cars began to pile up on the roadway behind them.

The path in front of them was finally clear.

"Hurry," Rosemary said, sliding into the seat next to Chef Levy. "Won't last long."

When Rosemary lifted her hand, Kenzie saw the flask she was holding was see-through. It looked like it contained milk tea with black tapioca pearls.

Chef Levy floored the gas.

Rosemary turned back and gave Kenzie a lopsided little grin.

"You saved us," Kenzie managed.

"Rosemary and thyme and basil and coriander and caraway and dill," Rosemary sang in her off-key voice.

"Friend of yours?" Braxton murmured. His face was white as a ghost and his arm was still leaking blood, but his green eyes were bright with amusement.

"The Thief saved me," Rosemary said.

Kenzie cringed at the use of her Cutthroat Cuisine name. She didn't have the energy to explain right now, and it seemed like Braxton didn't have the energy to ask. No one spoke as Chef Levy put as much distance between them and their enemies as possible.

As they sped away, Kenzie caught a glimpse of Benedict through the rear window. He was pointing with his cane, his mouth moving as he barked out orders.

As though sensing her attention, Benedict turned his head to look at her. They were already too far away for Kenzie to read the expression on his face, but it didn't matter. She knew Benedict would come after her. And he wouldn't stop until he had her back in his clutches.

CHAPTER 42

KENZIE

The drive back to wherever they were going passed in a blur. Aralia looked at Braxton's arm and determined that a bullet had only grazed it.

The diagnosis did little to calm Kenzie.

Braxton and Kenzie's shirts were donated to the tourniquet cause, and he bled through both of them before they finally got the wound to stop leaking.

All the while, Rosemary sang to fill the tense silence. She'd added verses, moving from herbs to other ingredients. Kenzie had never been more desperate for a pair of earplugs. Aralia and Chef Levy were both threatening to kill Rosemary, but she didn't let up. She petted her charm necklace and sang her heart out.

Off tune.

"Rosemary and thyme and basil and coriander and caraway and dill," Rosemary chanted.

"Shut up," Chef Levy ordered.

"Flour power," Rosemary sang. "Feel the cornmeal."

"How about we all try and get some sleep?" Braxton suggested.

"It's my fault if I forget the salt. Too much pepper, and I'll become a leperrrrrrr."

"Can I cut out her tongue?" Aralia asked, covering her ears with her hands.

"Cranberries. Nice and red, or you'll be dead. All hale the holy kale. Nev—er forget the jalapeño pepp—er!"

Chef Levy and Aralia moved at the same time, drawing a handgun and hunting knife…respectively.

"Singing time's over," Chef Levy said. "Shut up, or we'll shut you up."

Rosemary stopped singing.

Almost as soon as Rosemary went quiet, Kenzie sort of wished she'd start up again. An argument that had been brewing between Aralia, Chef Levy, and Braxton was quickly gaining steam. From what Kenzie gathered, their safe house was no longer safe since the Santioris had discovered it.

"Where else are we going to go?" Braxton asked. "Besides, it's in Veneziano's best interest not to tell anyone our location. He'll keep that in his back pocket to hold over us."

"Until he doesn't," Chef Levy shot back. "If you idiots had used your pea-brains and swept your vehicle before driving off into the sunset, we wouldn't be in this position."

"We're not going anywhere," Aralia said decisively. "Graham and I will booby-trap the cabin. Veneziano might know where we are, but I know those woods like the back of my hand. At least if we stay there, we'll be able to defend ourselves."

That seemed to settle the matter for the time being…which meant the three of them continued to mutter angrily under their breath for the remainder of the drive.

It was dark out by the time they made it to Aralia's remote upstate cabin, where Braxton and Sofia had apparently been hiding out since Hex Kitchen. Golden light streamed out of the tall bay windows, welcoming them home.

Who knew Crazy Aralia had good taste.

The sorry group of them trudged into the cabin, which was warm and smelled faintly like fresh bread.

"Ohmygod!"

Sofia, looking as gorgeous and put-together as ever, jumped up from where she'd been sitting on the couch. Her laptop would have crashed to the floor, if it hadn't been for the man sitting next to her. He calmly caught the computer out of the air and placed it on a table.

Sofia raced over to Braxton and inspected his arm.

"What did you do to him?" Sofia demanded.

The harsh accusation was aimed at Kenzie.

"I'm fine, Sofe," Braxton said in a thin voice. "Believe it or not, Kenzie wasn't the one shooting at me."

Sofia grumbled something under her breath. It sounded like *Not.*

Kenzie should probably try to defend herself, but she was too exhausted. And Sofia's anger was more than justifiable. Braxton wouldn't have come anywhere near Cutthroat Cuisine if it hadn't been for Kenzie. He wouldn't have gotten shot.

The unfamiliar man got up from the couch and came up behind Sofia. Kenzie thought she saw him brush his hand down Sofia's back, but since she didn't bite his head off, Kenzie assumed she was imagining things.

The guy went to Aralia, and the two exchanged a very G-rated hug. It was a shock to discover that Aralia knew how to do G-rated anything.

"We've got another couple of stragglers to join the party," Aralia told him, motioning to Kenzie and Rosemary.

"I'm Graham," the guy said, holding his hand out to Kenzie. "Nice to meet you."

Kenzie was standing next to Braxton, so she could feel the way his muscles tensed, as though Graham had said something deeply offensive.

She gave him a strange look before shaking Graham's hand. "Nice to meet you, too. I'm Kenzie."

"Kind of figured that." Graham offered her a warm smile. "You've been a pretty big conversation topic around here lately."

I'll bet.

Kenzie smiled back. Beside her, Braxton seemed to be growing more agitated by the second. He was also glaring at Graham.

Graham either didn't notice the way Braxton was staring daggers at him or didn't care.

Kenzie took a second to observe him, trying to figure out how he fit into this motley group. He was an extremely handsome man with dark skin and eyes such a deep brown they looked almost black, except for the shocking ring of gold around his irises. His hair was cut close to his scalp, while his eyelashes seemed to go on for miles. He was as tall as Braxton and even more muscular, but his stance was relaxed and his expression friendly. Kenzie liked him immediately.

Then again, she'd liked Polly, too…right up until the whole kidnapping fiasco. Clearly, Kenzie didn't have stellar instincts when it came to character assessments.

"The cuckoo's name is Rosemary," Aralia informed Graham, pointing to the woman who was still humming and petting her charm necklace.

"Nice to meet you, Rosemary," Graham said, offering her the same polite welcome he'd given Kenzie.

Graham didn't seem at all put out when Rosemary completely ignored his outstretched hand.

"Rosemary and thyme and basil and coriander and caraway and dill." Rosemary giggled.

Graham raised an eyebrow.

Sofia said, "Just what this place needed: more wackos."

The others were still talking, but Kenzie wasn't listening.

"Kiwi!"

There he was, in his habitat, looking completely at ease.

Kenzie ran over to the wooden table where her chameleon's habitat was perched. Kiwi was his normal resting color of green with yellow stripes and orange dots. He turned his head to regard her, his bulbous eyes rotating around in his skull. He yawned.

"Hello to you too, little guy," Kenzie said, unable to suppress a relieved chuckle.

Kenzie studied the habitat with a critical eye. Kiwi's water was clean, his heat lamp was at the right temperature, and the mister was set to the correct time to keep the air sufficiently moist.

Kenzie turned to Braxton.

"I can't believe you did this," she said, her voice catching. "How did you—"

"I didn't," he said, giving her a sheepish look. "I mean, I rescued Kiwi from Hex Kitchen, but Sofia is the one who's been taking care of him."

Come again?

Kenzie must have misheard him. Because it sounded like Braxton had said that the woman who poisoned her had also taken care of her pet.

"Why?" Kenzie asked Sofia, who was bent over Braxton's arm. Sofia was cleaning away the blood with a white hand towel that was quickly turning red. Kenzie cleared her throat. "I mean, thank you."

Sofia didn't acknowledge her words. She didn't even glance at Kenzie.

"I wanted to fry him up for a light snack," Aralia said, breaking the tension. "I've heard they taste like chicken." She licked her lips.

"Don't even think about it," Kenzie growled, positioning herself between Crazy Aralia and Kiwi's habitat. No way was anyone eating her pet.

"Aralia, cut it out," Braxton said.

"I'd be doing everyone a favor." Aralia sniffed. "Animals are not meant to be domesticated. This little reptile could bring down an entire ecosystem, for fuck's sake. Have I ever told you about how…."

"Uh-huh," Sofia said loudly. "Yeah. Really interesting, Aralia."

"Whatever you say, Aralia," Braxton echoed, sharing a knowing grin with his sister.

Graham gave Aralia a sympathetic pat on her shoulder.

Aralia was still spouting anti-pet propaganda as the rest of the group dispersed. Kenzie kissed two fingers and pressed them to the glass of Kiwi's habitat. Her chameleon didn't return the show of affection, but Kenzie didn't mind. Kiwi might not be the most effusive guy in the world, but he'd been her companion ever since she moved out of New York. The two of them had history.

Kenzie turned to Sofia, who was still focused on Braxton's arm.

"I really can't tell you how much I appreciate this," Kenzie said, gesturing to Kiwi's habitat.

The words came out stilted and awkward. What Kenzie really wanted was to give the other girl a hug. Although, if she tried it, she'd probably end up with her head on a spike.

"I have some emails to deal with," Sofia announced, clearly overwhelmed by this dizzying display of emotion. She narrowed her eyes at Kenzie. "Try not to get my brother killed before I finish."

Braxton sighed and slung his good arm around Kenzie. Once Sofia was out of earshot, he said, "Taking care of Kiwi was her way of apologizing for trying to kill you."

He gave her a small smile that didn't reach his eyes. Kenzie noticed the unfamiliar flatness in his gaze was still there.

What had happened to him during the time they'd been apart? If it was anything half as messed up as Kenzie's experience….

"Alright everyone," Chef Levy said, needlessly clapping her hands to get their attention. "Go get cleaned up. You're all soft and unused to any kind of discomfort, which is why I'm allotting you two hours for showering and sleeping. We'll meet back down here after, so don't be late. Lots to discuss."

"Aralia and I can get dinner ready," Graham offered.

"I have a moose cooling on ice out back," Aralia said in confirmation. "I'll just butcher him up and be back in a jiffy."

Alrighty, then.

"Rosemary can cook," Rosemary said. "Rosemary can help."

It said something about Kenzie's recent goings on that an adult woman talking in the third person didn't seem remotely strange.

"Come on," Braxton said, leading Kenzie up an elegant wooden staircase.

He brought her to a spacious bathroom that was all wood and stone and soft lighting. The walk-in shower had a pebbled floor and glass partition that separated it from the rest of the bathroom. Two stone sinks were perched on wooden pedestals on opposite sides of the room. It looked like something one would find in a high-end nature retreat.

Not that Kenzie had ever been to one of those, but still.

Braxton turned the shower onto full blast. Seconds later, steam began to fill the room.

Kenzie didn't remember moving. She must have though, because a second later, she was colliding with Braxton. They fell back against the wall, just kind of clinging to each other.

Braxton let out a small gasp, and Kenzie realized she was gripping his bad arm.

"Sorry!" she yelped, trying to disentangle herself.

Braxton just wrapped her more tightly against him. He leaned down to kiss her.

"Hey!"

Sofia's voice, along with a sharp rap at the door, brought Kenzie back to Earth.

"You're not the only ones who need to use the bathroom," Sofia called.

Kenzie could hear the impatient *tap tap tap* of her shoe on the floor.

"Buzzkill," Braxton muttered.

Kenzie peered up at him. The steam from the shower had darkened his golden hair. Somehow, the mist swirling through the room made his green eyes even brighter. They bore into her and seemed to see right into the heart of her.

Could he see the guilt that was rotting her from the inside out?

Kenzie pulled back so quickly they both stumbled a little.

"Let's get your arm cleaned up," she said, her voice unsteady.

Would Braxton still want her when he learned what she'd done? That she'd murdered…again. And this time, it hadn't been an accident. She'd looked into her opponents' eyes and decided their lives were worth less than her own.

Kenzie bit back a groan. Forget about Braxton still wanting her. How was she ever going to be able to look herself in the mirror again?

She realized Braxton was studying her, his mouth pressed into a frown.

"What did they do to you?" he whispered.

Kenzie bit her lip. She wondered if the haunted expression she saw on Braxton's face was also on hers.

"Hey." Braxton curled his finger under her chin and gently raised her face. "We can talk about it later, okay? Or never. Whatever you want. I'm just glad you're alright."

Braxton pressed a gentle kiss to her forehead. They helped each other out of their bloody, filthy clothes before stepping into the shower. There was definite heat in Braxton's eyes as they cleaned each other's various cuts and scrapes, but his touches were more tender than sexual. He let her fuss over his arm, which didn't look quite so bad after all the blood was cleaned away. He gently dabbed soap onto the cuts surrounding her stinging, swollen eyes.

The tears Kenzie had been holding back finally spilled over.

As if that wasn't bad enough, her knees gave way without warning and she sank to the floor.

Braxton followed her, gathering her into his lap.

He didn't say anything. He just held her until their skin turned pruney and the rest of the house was threatening to break down the door.

CHAPTER 43

BRAXTON

Everyone gathered around the kitchen table, where a veritable feast had been laid out.

Moose meat stew and a giant bowl of golden egg noodles sat in the center of the table. There was also a warm farro salad with arugula and blood orange wedges. Small clay pots of baked beans were scattered across the table, along with jars of homemade pickles. A large bowl of mulled wine sat on the sideboard. Cinnamon sticks and sliced fruit floated along the top of the dark liquid.

Braxton rustled up some sparkling juice for Kenzie, since she didn't drink alcohol. She gave him a grateful smile and took the juice before sagging in her chair.

Everyone else was busy passing around bowls and platters, but Braxton couldn't take his eyes off Kenzie. She looked exhausted and…sad.

They were together now, he reminded himself. That was all that mattered. He could fix the rest in time. Christ, though, what he would give to get a real smile out of her.

Braxton wasn't the only one lost in his thoughts. In fact, the only person who seemed to be in a chatty mood was Aralia. She regaled the table with the story of how she'd single-handedly rescued Kenzie. At least, that was the gist of Aralia's version of the tale.

Sofia was unusually quiet. She and Graham kept sneaking looks at each other when they thought the other wasn't paying attention. Braxton noticed, though. Their looks weren't sexual, which should have been a relief, except Braxton wasn't sure how to interpret his sister's body language. Her expression was too shuttered for him to guess what she was thinking.

Kenzie elbowed him.

"Mind your business," she whispered, making a subtle gesture toward Sofia and Graham.

Braxton grumbled and shoved a bite of food in his mouth.

After dinner, while the others sipped mulled wine and Kenzie nursed a mug of hot chocolate, Rosemary hopped up from the table. Braxton thought she was going to start cleaning up, but instead, she went to the fridge and started taking out ingredients.

"You still hungry?" Braxton asked, eyeing the bounty of leftovers scattered all over the kitchen.

Rosemary didn't respond as she buried her head in the fridge. She pulled out a few quarts of fresh berries, a preserving jar full of kimchi, and bundles of fresh herbs.

It was fortunate this kitchen was so well-stocked. Although, if Rosemary kept up like this, it wouldn't be for long.

"Whatcha doing, psycho pants?" Aralia asked.

Rosemary didn't answer. She was petting her charm necklace and humming to a fennel bulb.

"We can make you something else if you want," Graham offered, before turning to Aralia and mouthing *Be nice*.

That was one thing about Graham—he was good at playing the part of a perfect gentleman. It only made him more dangerous as far as Braxton was concerned.

"Gotta remember," Rosemary said. She stared at Kenzie when she said it, her eyes round and pleading.

"Remember what?" Kenzie asked.

Rosemary didn't answer. She just went back to rearranging her ingredients and singing her food song.

"Rosemary and thyme and basil and coriander and caraway and dill," Rosemary sang, adding the relevant herbs to a bowl. "Flour power." A poof of white dusted the front of her shirt as she measured out a cup and dumped it into a different bowl. "Feel the cornmeal."

Cornmeal went in with the flour.

"It's my fault if I forget the salt. Too much pepper, and I'll become a leperrrrrr." She held the word until her voice warbled.

Rosemary added two tablespoons of kosher salt and a quarter-teaspoon of pepper.

"What are you making?" Sofia asked.

"Doesn't matter," Rosemary replied without looking up. "Can't remember. Can't remember. Can't remember."

Stroking her charm necklace, Rosemary frowned at a saucepan that was giving off an acrid odor.

"Juniper berries?" she muttered. "No. Cranberries. Nice and red, or you'll be dead."

"She's been through a lot," Kenzie explained.

Braxton was dying to ask exactly what that entailed. It was obvious she'd been through hell, but he couldn't begin to guess at the gritty details. He didn't want to inadvertently do or say the wrong thing.

"It's time you told us everything about what went on in that kitchen," Chef Levy said, as though she could read Braxton's mind.

Kenzie made a choked sound. Her pale cheeks turned slightly green.

"Maybe we should sleep first," Braxton suggested, wrapping a protective arm behind Kenzie's chair.

"How many times do I need to tell you, McKaid?" Chef Levy slammed her mug down on the table. "I don't give a flying fuck about your girlfriend's sensitive psyche. I want to know what the Gourmands are planning. And we need to get our shit together and find somewhere else to hunker down before the Santioris decide to turn this place into matchsticks."

"Wow, Chef," Kenzie muttered under her breath. "Tell us how you really feel."

"No one's turning my goddamn house to matchsticks," Aralia snarled.

A high-pitched wailing filled the kitchen.

Rosemary, her hands covered in flour and berry stains, plopped down on the floor. She was sobbing.

Kenzie leapt up and hurried over to comfort the mad chef. Sofia went over to Kiwi's cage, took the sleeping chameleon out, and brought him over.

"Here," Sofia said, offering a less-than-enthusiastic Kiwi to Rosemary.

"Um," Kenzie said, her gaze darting between Kiwi and Rosemary.

"He can be her emotional support animal," Sofia said, placing the chameleon on Rosemary's shoulder. "It's a thing."

Sure enough, Rosemary calmed down.

"Can't remember," Rosemary snuffled.

"What can't you remember?" Kenzie asked in a gentle voice.

Rosemary stroked her necklace with one hand while holding the other steady so Kiwi could climb up to her head.

"The r-recipe," she blubbered.

Something nagged at Braxton's brain, but whatever it was stayed just out of reach.

"Recipe for what?" Kenzie asked.

"S-super food," Rosemary said. She scrubbed away her tears with the back of her hand.

At the blank looks everyone gave her, Rosemary huffed and said, "The Gourmands' solution."

"Solution to what?" Braxton asked. The hairs on his arms were standing on end. That knowing sense of…something was firing up.

"Solution to *magic*," Rosemary said impatiently. "To giving culinary magic. Or taking it away."

For several seconds, no one spoke.

"Braxton," Kenzie said, clutching his sleeve. "When I was down there, Benedict made us eat this stuff." She gestured between herself and Rosemary. "It made Rosemary's magic erratic and way too powerful. Then, he gave her something else that made her magic disappear altogether."

Braxton shook his head, trying to process what Kenzie was telling him.

"What happened when you ate it?" Chef Levy asked Kenzie.

"Nothing." Kenzie lifted a shoulder. "Benedict said it was proof that I'm a Culinarian. It means—"

"*You're* a Culinarian?" Chef Levy demanded.

Holy shit.

As far as Braxton knew…as far as his culinary magic textbooks had taught him…there hadn't been a Culinarian in the population in hundreds of years. Fragments of their magic had been passed on through the generations, which was how chefs like Braxton had their magic. It was like green eyes or twins. Some people got the gene, while others were passed over.

Then again, he'd never been able to reconcile his understanding about the rules of culinary magic with Kenzie's performance in the kitchen.

"Are you certain?" Chef Levy asked.

Kenzie hesitated for only a moment before nodding. "I…." She stared down at her hands, which were clasped in her lap. "I took away someone's magic in the Cutthroat Cuisine arena."

Someone gasped. Braxton made an effort not to let his shock show on his face, since Kenzie seemed plenty freaked out, already.

"That's why Benedict wants me to be his successor," Kenzie said with a little shudder. "He's been working on these two super food recipes to…replicate what I can do. But I guess it isn't as good as, well, me…."

"Recipes are very long," Rosemary lamented. "Complicated. Rosemary made them many times, but Rosemary's memory isn't so good."

Two secret, complicated recipes….

"Holy shit!" Braxton jumped up so fast that Kiwi shifted from his regular green color to the rust-orange of Rosemary's hair.

"Sofe," Braxton said. "Where's that recipe book I gave you?"

Sofia's forehead crinkled in confusion before understanding dawned. She got up and went into the living room. She returned a second later carrying the recipe book Braxton had stolen from Benedict Vandermeer's home office.

Rosemary squealed…like actually squealed.

"I found this in Benedict Vandermeer's house," Braxton explained to Kenzie. "It was hidden in a secret wall compartment behind a painting."

Kenzie took a few seconds to scrape her jaw off the floor. "You went into Benedict's house?"

"Well, yeah. I was looking for you."

Kenzie didn't say anything, but the expression in her slate-gray eyes made Braxton desperate to get her alone somewhere. He was torn between wrapping her in a protective hug and ripping her clothes off.

Unfortunately, there wasn't time for either.

"Hey," Sofia grumbled as Rosemary pulled the recipe book out of her hands.

Rosemary started flipping through the pages so vigorously that Kiwi grumpily (and slowly) started climbing down from his human perch. He shifted his color from the orange of Rosemary's hair to a dark gray that matched Kenzie's tattoo sleeves as she held out an arm to rescue him. Kenzie placed a quick kiss on the top of Kiwi's scaled head before depositing him back in his habitat.

Rosemary hummed as she continued to examine the recipe book. The rest of them leaned over her shoulder to get a closer look.

Braxton hadn't given the book more than a cursory glance before. Now that he was really looking, he realized it was even more complicated than he'd thought. Even Aidan's recipe books, which Braxton had cooked his way through so many times he'd memorized them, weren't like this.

"You ever seen recipes this complicated, McKaid?" Chef Levy asked.

"Never," Braxton replied. "There's a million ways it'll go wrong if any of the steps are done out of order."

Rosemary began to sing as she flipped through the book.

"Oh," Kenzie said, coming to the same realization as Braxton.

Oh.

"What?" Aralia asked.

"Listen," Kenzie ordered.

They all went quiet, except for Rosemary, who was singing her food song in an off-key, squeaky voice that was only slightly less irritating than nails on a chalkboard.

"Rosemary and thyme and basil and coriander and caraway and dill," Rosemary chanted.

Braxton flipped back a few pages and pointed. Those exact herbs were listed in a flowing script at the top of the page.

"Flour power," Rosemary sang. "Feel the cornmeal."

He turned the page. Sure enough, the two ingredients were listed.

"It's my fault if I forget the salt. Too much pepper, and I'll become a leperrrrrrr."

Salt and pepper were listed below the other ingredients, along with notations about the precise amounts and corresponding magic.

"Cranberries. Nice and red, or you'll be dead. All hale the holy kale. Nev—er forget the jalapeño pepp—er."

Cranberries, kale, and jalapeños were written out, along with measurements and magic.

"Hot damn," Aralia said into the silence that followed. "I think I might owe psycho-pants an apology."

Rosemary wasn't paying attention to any of them. All of her focus was on the recipe book.

"I forgot the wheatgrass," she said, shaking her head in amazement. "And acai berries. And papaya! And, ooh!" She tapped a page and let out another hoot of delight. "Only two parts seaweed, not three. And there are seven goji berries, not six."

"Rosemary," Chef Levy said with enough force to make the other woman stop singing and look up from the recipe book. "Is this the super food recipe?"

"Yes, yes," Rosemary said, stroking her necklace. "And anti-super food."

"Anti-super food?" Chef Levy prompted.

"Makes the magic go away," Rosemary said. "Yucky."

"So, this is it, then," Chef Levy said. Her voice was hoarse and strangely devoid of its usual rancor.

It unsettled Braxton more than when Chef Levy was shouting and cursing.

"It isn't enough for the Gourmands to have full authority over us," Chef Levy said. "They want to play God, too."

They were all quiet while they tried to process everything.

"Well, we have the book," Braxton pointed out. "Benedict can't control magic without these two recipes."

"Unless he has copies," Sofia said. "If it were me, I'd have a copy on the Cloud, another on a hard drive, and a few dozen printouts in various safes."

"No," Rosemary said. "Only one. Benedict doesn't share."

"Benedict isn't the type who would put this recipe somewhere the other Gourmands could see it," Kenzie translated. The hollowness that took over her features had Braxton clenching his hands into fists.

Rosemary made a little sound of protest as Chef Levy wrenched the recipe book out of her hands.

"Chef, what are you—"

Rosemary screamed and lunged forward. Graham reacted first, grabbing Rosemary's shoulders to keep her from diving head-first into the fire. Where the recipe book was burning.

"What the hell, Chef?" Braxton demanded.

"The super food and anti-super food," Chef Levy said to Rosemary. "Who else knows how to make these recipes?"

When Rosemary didn't immediately answer, Chef Levy grasped the front of her shirt and shook her like a ragdoll.

"N-no one," Rosemary stuttered. "Just me. There were other chefs, but they only did one part and then left the kitchen. I was the only one who stayed for the whole recipe. Benedict didn't want—" She screamed when Chef Levy pulled a gun and pressed it to Rosemary's head.

"No!" Kenzie cried.

"Chef, stop!" Braxton ordered.

"She's a weapon," Chef Levy snarled. "Benedict will come for her."

"Then we'll stop him," Kenzie said in a pleading voice.

"Like you did while you were his prisoner?" Chef Levy demanded. "Not so easy to defy our highest authority, is it?"

"You're not killing her in here," Aralia said, wiping some crumbs off the table. "Take her out back so I won't have to deal with bloodstains on our floor. Graham sanded and stained every board himself."

"No one's killing anyone," Braxton said, even though the whole situation was far beyond his control.

Rosemary was wailing.

"Maybe there's another way," Sofia said hurriedly.

Braxton gave his sister a grateful look. He was down for any plan that got Chef Levy to put her gun away.

"I'm listening," Chef Levy growled.

"We need to take control of the Gourmands," Sofia said.

Braxton's hopes sank. Rosemary was a dead woman.

"You don't go after the Gourmands!" Chef Levy shouted. She looked and sounded half-mad. Maybe all the way mad. "They come for you. Even if we could track them down a second time—which would likely take another two decades at the least—we don't have the manpower to challenge them. They'd kill us all."

"You're forgetting one thing," Sofia said. She crossed her arms and leaned back against the wall.

Braxton knew that expression on her face. It was her scheming look. And it was directed at Kenzie.

"Sofe," Braxton warned. He knew he wasn't going to like whatever was about to come out of his sister's mouth.

He really should have tried harder to keep her from speaking.

"There is one way for us to get control of the Gourmands, and soon." Sofia waited until the kitchen was absolutely silent before she dropped the bombshell. "Kenzie needs to go back to Cutthroat Cuisine. And she needs to win."

CHAPTER 44

SOFIA

Sofia got away from the rest of the group as soon as she could. She ignored Graham, who had been trying to catch her eye all night. She couldn't talk to him…not until she figured out what to do. No matter how many times she mentally replayed her conversation with Peter, she couldn't make sense of what he'd told her.

Sofia closed herself in the room she was supposed to be sharing with Chef Levy. Since she could still hear the woman shouting at everyone downstairs, Sofia figured she still had some time before her roommate came to bed.

Sofia turned the lock and then called Peter, who had left her a dozen texts and voicemails since he told her what Graham had done.

Peter answered after the first ring.

"Sofia, Jesus. Are you alright?"

"I'm fine," she replied in her perfect robot-imitation.

How was one supposed to feel when they found out the person they were falling for was a murderer?

Maybe she should ask her brother….

"*Sofia.* Did you hear a word I just said?"

"Sorry." Sofia blinked a few times. "What?"

Peter sighed. "Sweetheart, you have to tell me where Graham Malyung's hiding."

Sofia's response got stuck in her throat. "I—I just—" she stammered.

"Look," Peter said. "I didn't have a chance to tell you earlier, but it's worse than you can imagine. Graham Malyung didn't just kill his own parents. His father was an NYC cop, and his mother was a detective. Also, Graham killed them when he was *sixteen* years old."

Graham. The man who tucked her in and made her French toast. Who accompanied her on bizarre errands without question and set her whole body on fire with just a kiss.

"The police have been searching for him ever since," Peter continued. "He just disappeared off the face of the Earth. You have to tell me where he is, Sofia. The police—"

"Just shut up for a second, will you?"

Sofia massaged the back of her neck while she tried to gather her thoughts.

What could she say? What should she do?

You should have known, her inner voice whispered. If something seemed too good to be true, it was. She knew that. And yet, she'd let herself succumb to Graham's gentle touches and what had seemed like a limitless supply of generosity.

All at once, Braxton's hatred made sense. He knew what Graham had done.

God. What was it with her and her brother…was there something in their DNA that made them predisposed to falling in love with murderers?

Sofia clutched at the hollow feeling in her chest.

"Check your email, love," Peter said.

She'd forgotten he was even still on the phone.

Sofia's phone binged. She tapped on the images Peter had just emailed her.

The first photo was of an attractive couple in police uniform. They were both smiling as they leaned their heads together.

The woman had skin a few shades darker than Graham's. Her eyes were the same—almost black, with that gorgeous amber rim. The man beside her was Caucasian, but Sofia still noted the resemblance to his son. There was a scattering of freckles over his nose and cheeks, just like Graham. He also had Graham's broad shoulders, thick biceps, and sturdy presence. Their smiles were the same, too.

Sofia scrolled down to the next set of images. A strange sound came out of her mouth.

"I know," Peter said grimly.

Sofia covered her mouth. She'd thought she was immune to gore and death, but…no.

She couldn't tear her gaze away from the photos filling up her phone screen. Blood, bone and something pink was smeared across a beige carpet. There was most of a corpse, except the head was missing. The man was still wearing his cop uniform. His bloated hand was stretched out on the carpet toward the second body.

Graham's mother.

Her body was as brutalized as her husband's. Her skull looked like it had been crushed with a giant meat mallet.

Graham hadn't just killed these people. He'd pulverized them.

"You still there, love?" Peter asked.

"Still here," Sofia managed.

"Can you tell me where to find this monster?"

Sofia shook her head, even though Peter couldn't see her. She couldn't bring the cops here. Sofia was new to the life of an outlaw, but she was pretty sure it was ill-advised to invite law enforcement to a place that was teeming with lawbreakers.

"I—I'll bring him to you," Sofia scraped out.

"Tell me when and where," Peter said. "NYPD is going to want to make the arrest, but if you can get him to anywhere in the United States, we'll take care of the rest."

"I'll text you the details," she managed.

It was getting more and more difficult to breathe.

"Don't let him get any hint of what you're doing," Peter warned her. "And Sofia. Please be careful."

Sofia mechanically got ready for bed and shut off the light. She huddled under the covers, since there was no way on Earth she was going to fall asleep with those images swirling through her head.

When a knock came at her door, Sofia had to muffle her little scream with the blanket.

"Sofia?" Graham's low voice said from the other side. "Are you awake?"

She forced herself to go perfectly still. She didn't even breathe until his footsteps retreated and she heard his door click shut.

CHAPTER 45

KENZIE

Kenzie left the others arguing at the table and slipped upstairs. So far, the conversation basically consisted of Braxton refusing to let Kenzie have anything to do with the Gourmands, while everyone else was on team *Throw Kenzie to the Wolves.*

Tough crowd.

"This will solve our problem with the Santioris, too," Sofia was arguing. "If Kenzie wins Cutthroat Cuisine, no one will be able to attack us. And then we'll finally have enough power to take them down for what they did to Mum."

Rick had done something to Braxton and Sofia's mother? That was news to Kenzie, although it wasn't like there'd been much time for catching up.

Braxton said something in a voice that was too low for Kenzie to make out. She didn't want to hear any more of the conversation, anyway.

Logically, it made sense for her to win Cutthroat Cuisine and become the next Gourmand leader. If only that thought didn't make her want to puke and cry and hide in a closet.

Since her phone was long gone, Kenzie grabbed Braxton's off the bathroom counter where he'd abandoned it earlier. Guilt sliced through her as she unlocked it with the numbers of his birthday…and Aidan's. Then, she pulled up the phone number for Riker's Island.

She paced around Aralia's bedroom, which was where Tyrant Levy—sorry, *Chef* Levy—had ordered her to sleep. It took close to half an hour to jump through the administrative hoops necessary to get her father on the phone.

She sank down on the pile of animal pelts next to Aralia's bed that was Kenzie's designated sleeping area. The furs were a lot more comfortable and less scratchy than they appeared, and Kenzie felt her eyelids grow heavy. At least until she looked up and realized a bear head was nailed to the wall directly across from her sleeping area. Its teeth were bared, and its glassy eyes stared down at her in an *I will eat you, human* kind of expression.

Kenzie would have preferred to spend the night cuddling with Braxton, but Chef Levy had made it clear there would be no *hanky panky-ing*. Her words. Thus, Braxton would be sleeping on the living room couch. And Kenzie was bunking with her nemesis-turned-savior. Who happened to have a crazy streak a mile wide. Yay.

"Kenzie? Hon, is that you?"

"Dad!"

"Are you alright?" he asked, when it was really she who should be asking him.

"Um, yeah," she managed.

It was so good to hear his voice. She wished she could see his kind face and let herself be engulfed in one of his hugs. She wished she was calling to tell him that she'd figured out a way to rescue him from a sentence he didn't deserve.

"Why don't you tell me what's bothering you, honey," her dad encouraged.

Kenzie let her head fall back against the mound of furs. "Everything's so messed up," she whispered.

"Start at the beginning," her dad suggested.

Hah. They'd be here all night.

"Okay, so, hypothetically…."

She spent the next several minutes outlining her dilemma in the broadest possible terms. Her voice was cracking by the time she got to the end.

"If I do nothing," she said, "then someone really bad will become in charge of this incredibly powerful group."

Really bad didn't begin to cover the nightmare that was Veneziano Santiori, but she left it at that. She also didn't mention that Chef Levy was planning to blow Rosemary's brains out so the Gourmands wouldn't be able to make the super food or its counter-recipe.

"I have the chance to be in charge of this organization," Kenzie continued. "But to get the position, I'll have to kill this bad man. And I'll have to work closely with horrible people who just want to control me."

Her dad sighed. "That's quite a dilemma."

"Tell me about it."

"It sounds to me like you've already made your decision," he said gently.

Yeah. Yeah, she had. Damnit.

Why did being noble have to suck so hard?

Crack. She heard the snap of Brute's neck. She felt Scarlet's hot blood seeping between her fingers. She saw Toxic's horrified expression when he realized his magic was gone.

"Hey, Dad?" Kenzie forced herself to loosen her grip on the phone. "I'm going to get you out of prison. I promise."

Her dad sighed, seeming to understand all the things she couldn't bring herself to say.

"I can't begin to imagine what these last five years have been like for you," he said.

Once again, those were words she should have said to him. Guilt rose up inside Kenzie until it threatened to eat her alive.

"I wish I could have been there for you," he continued.

"Dad," Kenzie choked.

He'd tried to be, but Kenzie had been so angry with him for ruining everything…for abandoning her…that she'd ignored him when he needed her most.

"But I want you to know that I trust you to make the right choices, regardless of the situation you're in," her dad continued. "Don't worry about me."

Before Kenzie could respond, an automated voice came on the line and told them their time was ending.

"Just remember I'm proud of you," her dad said. "Love you, hon."

"Love you too, Dad."

Kenzie had to stare very hard at the weird antlers hanging from Aralia's ceiling after the call ended. Once she'd mostly composed herself, she scrolled through Braxton's contacts. She didn't find the one she wanted, but his son would have to do.

Throwing herself back on her pile of furs, she called Rick Santiori.

"Let me guess," Rick drawled. "You need money? No, wait. You want to thank me for getting rid of your hag of a mother?"

Every obnoxious greeting she'd had on the tip of her tongue vanished.

Was Rick saying he'd killed Braxton's mom? That would explain Sofia's eagerness for revenge, but holy…. Braxton had already lost his brother and father. Could fate really be that cruel?

Stupid question, she mentally chastised herself.

"McKaid? You there?"

Game face, Kenzie.

"Hey, Dick," she said with enough false brightness to interrupt Rick's newest slew of insults.

"Number Eight." Rick chuckled. "You finally decide McKaid isn't doing it for you? You do seem rather preoccupied with my—"

"Why don't you be a good boy and put your father on the phone?" she interrupted. "I want to talk to the person who's actually in charge."

She knew she'd riled him up by the silence that followed.

"Dick?" Kenzie asked sweetly. "You need me to repeat that? I. Need. To. Talk. To. Your. Dad."

Rick might be an asshole, but Kenzie was at the top of her immature game.

"Fuck you," Rick spat.

"Not on the menu, unfortunately," Kenzie said. "Now, don't keep me waiting. Otherwise, I'll have to tell Chef Levy on you. Do you know that woman has an Uzi? It's *awesome.*"

There was some grumbling on the other end of the line. An obnoxious amount of time passed.

"Ms. Ashner," came the smooth mobster voice that sent a chill through Kenzie. "You wished to speak with me?"

Not especially.

"Yeah. I'm your opponent for the Cutthroat Cuisine finale, but the only problem is, my friends destroyed the arena. I need to know when and where to meet."

Kenzie wasn't sure how to interpret the long silence that followed.

"I'm glad you came to your senses," Veneziano said. "If you'd stayed hidden, I would have needed to pay your upstate cabin a little visit."

Kenzie gripped the phone harder. "You actually want to compete against me? I didn't realize you were suicidal."

Veneziano's laugh was dry as a bone. "The only way for me to claim Benedict's job is for the Gourmands to witness me defeating you."

"Sorry to break it to you," Kenzie said, "but you're not going to win."

Veneziano gave another of those soul-crushing chuckles.

"Don't count me out just yet, Ms. Ashner," he said. "I still have a trick up my sleeve."

"So, in other words…you're going to cheat?"

"Let's call it more of a handicap," Veneziano replied. "After all, as you already pointed out, we both know you're the stronger chef. I'm sure you won't begrudge me for leveling the playing field."

Kenzie pffed. "I'm sure your prospective underlings will be thrilled to find out you killed and cheated your way to the top."

"I haven't broken any of the competition rules," Veneziano replied primly. "I only need to beat you in the finale for my victory to be legitimized."

"Then I guess it wouldn't be against the rules for me to do something vindictive, too," Kenzie said. "Like blowing up all of your bakeries with magic, for instance."

Not that she would. Probably.

Veneziano's indulgent sigh huffed across the line. "Keep your phone on, and I will let you know where to meet," he said. "Within the week, one of us will be the next Gourmand leader."

Kenzie repressed a shudder. "May the best culinary magician win," she said, then disconnected before Veneziano could get the last word.

After the phone screen went dark and her brave mask fell away, the reality of what she was about to do hit her at full force. She'd just escaped Cutthroat Cuisine, and soon, she'd willingly return.

Kenzie needed her head examined.

How fortunate there would be a nurse present….

✳ ✳ ✳

Kenzie tossed and turned on her pile of furs. Aralia was breathing peacefully, which was somehow more annoying than when she snored.

Of course Aralia wasn't having trouble sleeping. She didn't have to cook for her life…freaking *again*. She wasn't the Eve of all culinary magicians.

Kenzie stopped squirming when the door opened an inch. Light spilled in from the hallway.

"Kenz?" Braxton whispered.

"I'm awake," she whispered back. She started to disentangle herself from the blankets so she could go out to the hall to talk to Braxton, but he was already inside the room. He shut the door behind him with a resounding *click*. His footsteps were silent, and he made it to her without smacking his leg into the dresser the way she had earlier…despite the fact that the lights had been on at the time.

Braxton slid under the covers and pulled her against him.

"Are you okay?" he asked, nuzzling against her neck. "With all this Cutthroat Cuisine stuff, I mean."

The whole group of them had talked about Kenzie's decision to go back into the arena…or whichever kitchen served as their battleground…until three in the morning. There had been arguments about whether she should plan her final dish out ahead of time, or wait until she saw the mystery ingredient. They'd discussed whether she should practice using her

Culinarian magic-stealing ability or not. Eventually, they'd come to the consensus that it was better for her to save her strength.

Kenzie's brain hurt, and her stomach was tied up in knots. She didn't want to think about anything right then.

She rested her cheek against Braxton's chest and listened to his steady heartbeat.

"It's a lot to process," she whispered, reaching up to let her fingers slide through his soft hair.

Translation: I'm scared shitless.

"Figured you might need a little help relaxing," he replied. His green eyes gleamed as he smiled in the dark.

"What—"

Braxton pressed his lips to hers. Hard.

It felt so good, Kenzie had to hold back a moan. She'd been craving him with every fiber of her being. Who knew what would happen the next day, but for now, at least, she had this. She had him.

Kenzie managed a startled breath as Braxton rolled her onto her back. He slid one hand under her shirt while the other gripped the back of her neck, angling her mouth up to meet his.

Kenzie's body wanted nothing more than to let him have his way with her. Her brain had other ideas. Aralia was ten feet away from them, but that wasn't what was stopping her.

Braxton wasn't just trying to take her mind off things. Something was wrong with him.

This wasn't passion so much as desperation.

"Braxton." She drew back, their harsh breaths filling the space between them. "What's the matter?"

"Kenz, I—" He pulled his hand away from her so he could rake it through his hair. "Everything's such a mess."

I know what Rick did to your mom, she almost said, but held herself back.

Kenzie pressed a finger to his lips to stop him. Her eyes were stinging as she whispered, "I have things to tell you, too." *Like how I used my magic to murder. Again.* "It might change the way you feel about me."

Braxton chuckled quietly. "There's nothing that could change how I feel about you, baby."

"Braxton." She spoke against his lips. "I love you."

It was the first time she'd said those words to him out loud. It wasn't scary, though. A thrill went through her. The words felt right.

Instead of saying anything, Braxton kissed her.

This time, it was slow and sweet rather than frantic. His fingers traced the shape of her dragon tattoo, even though there was no way he could see it in the dark.

"Later," he murmured against her lips. "Later, we'll talk about all of it. Tonight, I just need you."

"Aralia's here," Kenzie whispered, thinking maybe Braxton had forgotten their sleeping arrangements.

And there was no way they could get down and dirty on the living room couch where Braxton was supposed to be sleeping. With a house full of chefs, there was always someone in the kitchen no matter the hour.

Braxton smiled. There was a hint of mischief in his voice when he whispered, "Aralia's asleep." He nibbled on the shell of her ear, making her shudder. "I can be quiet if you can."

"Braxton." She let out a little laugh that turned into a gasp when his fingers slid beneath the waistband of her leggings.

Kenzie couldn't believe Braxton was doing this. She couldn't believe she was letting him.

She should stop this before it went any further.

The thought floated away as Braxton's hand moved lower. There was only one word in her head now. *More.*

She needed this—she needed *him*—more than she needed her next breath…which at the moment was lodged in her chest. If she let it out, she was going to moan.

Braxton, seeming to enjoy this new brand of torture, was in absolutely no hurry. He chuckled softly against her neck when she tried to make him go faster. His touches became even more maddeningly slow and gentle.

The jerk.

Braxton pushed her to the edge over and over again until she was writhing and threatening him in breathless whispers.

Braxton fused his mouth to hers and swallowed her cry when she finally came apart in his arms. Then, he held her like he hadn't just shattered her world before putting it back together again.

They lay there for long minutes, tangled in the blankets and each other, while Kenzie's heart rate came down.

"My turn," she whispered. "And if you think I'm going to go easy on you, you've got another think coming, buddy."

"Bring it, baby," Braxton growled, rolling his hips against hers.

Kenzie reached her hand between them, but before she made contact with anything, she was blinded by light.

"Ah!" Braxton shielded his eyes. "What the fuck?"

"You know," Aralia said, sitting up in her bed and giving them an amused look. "It's very rude to crash in someone's room and not invite them to join in the fun."

Kenzie choked on air. Braxton recovered first.

"Sorry, Aralia, but we're not into that sort of thing," Braxton said. He turned to Kenzie and raised an eyebrow. "Are we?"

"Ohmygod. No." Kenzie buried her face in her hands to hide her flaming cheeks. When she peeked up and found Braxton and Aralia still looking at her, she added an extra, emphatic, "*No.*"

Braxton grinned at her with absolutely no remorse. Aralia flopped back on her bed and grumbled about prudish Number Eights. And for the life of her, Kenzie couldn't stop smiling.

CHAPTER 46

BRAXTON

The next morning was tense. Everyone's gazes kept straying to Braxton. Well, not so much him, but his phone. Which was how they would soon learn when and where Kenzie would be cooking against Veneziano Santiori to become the new Gourmand leader.

Just for something to do with his hands, Braxton busied himself with cooking breakfast. While he was crisping bacon and frying eggs, he wouldn't have to contemplate what it would mean for him and Kenzie once she was initiated into an organization that was more powerful and secretive than the KGB.

"I don't think anyone's up for eating, Brax," Sofia noted as he pulled a basket of fresh blueberries out of the fridge.

"I am," Aralia said. "I haven't lost my appetite just because Number Eight is going to her death. Or her doom."

"And here I thought we were finally getting along," Kenzie grumbled. She had just come down the stairs, her hair still wet from the shower.

Braxton's eyes followed a drop of water that trickled down her chest and got lost in her cleavage. If they'd been alone, he would have licked it off.

"Meanwhile, you look good in my clothes," Aralia told Kenzie.

Yeah, she did.

"Your boobs are so small, though," Aralia continued with a devilish smile. She popped a blueberry in her mouth. "They look like they're going to fall right out of that dress."

"If they do, I'll catch them," Braxton assured Kenzie, giving her a wink.

Chef Levy and Sofia groaned.

Kenzie joined Braxton at the stove, knowing how to help without any words being spoken. For several minutes, they cooked in relative silence. A sense of unease grew in Braxton until it occurred to him what was wrong.

"You're not humming," Braxton said in a low voice.

"Huh?" Kenzie stopped flipping pancakes and turned to him.

"You used to hum when you cook," he said. "You're not doing it anymore."

"Oh. Well. Cutthroat Cuisine might have soured me on the whole magical cooking thing."

Fury burned bright-hot in Braxton. Kenzie's love of cooking was one of the purest things he'd ever encountered. And the Gourmands had taken it away from her.

"Yeah," he scraped out. "Fuck culinary magic."

His vehemence might have made his voice a few decibels louder than he'd intended. Everyone else in the kitchen stopped what they were doing to look at him.

"Seriously, Brax?" Sofia frowned. "Maybe try being a little more grateful for your magic, huh? I mean, I know you've always had it, so it's easy to take for granted. But give me a break. You have *magic*."

"I—" Braxton looked at his sister, bewildered.

Rosemary, who had been sitting cross-legged on the floor and watching Kiwi sleep, started to sing her super food song.

Braxton was grateful for the distraction when his phone dinged…until he saw who the text was from.

He felt everyone's eyes on him as he stared down at the new message.

Braxton cursed.

"What?" several voices asked at once.

Braxton turned to Kenzie. "I don't want you to panic," he began.

"Jeez, Brax," Sofia cut in. "You only say that if you actually want people to panic."

Kenzie laughed a little, although it sounded forced. "True story. My feet are starting to tingle from all of my not-panicking."

Braxton moved behind Kenzie so he could rub her shoulders. Ignoring his sister's tortured groans, he leaned down and kissed Kenzie's neck.

"McKaid," Chef Levy barked. She banged her hand on the table for emphasis. "You were saying?"

Oh. Right.

"Rick texted me the location for the final Cutthroat Cuisine match."

Braxton trailed his fingers down Kenzie's arms in a way that always raised goosebumps on her skin.

More than anything, he wished he could fight this battle for her. He didn't want her anywhere near these people. And he really didn't want to drag her back to where she'd come from just because Benedict Vandermeer had a twisted sense of humor.

"Just say it, Braxton," Kenzie said. "Please."

"The Gourmands are giving us twenty-four hours to get to the venue."

"Okayyy," Kenzie drew out the word. "Where will that be?"

Braxton grimaced. This was where the *not panicking* part would come in to play.

"*Good Ol' Apple Pie.*"

Kenzie's brows scrunched. She tilted her head to the side to peer up at him.

Christ, she was so damn adorable.

"My old diner?" Kenzie asked. "What about it?"

"That's where Benedict is holding the finale."

The little color there was in Kenzie's face drained away.

"I'm sorry," he told her.

Kenzie let out a shuddering breath. "I think I need some coffee," she said, her voice higher-pitched than usual.

Braxton poured it for her, because he was worried she would burn herself with her unsteady hands.

"You're not going to walk in there alone," he said as he passed her the mug. "I'll be there with you every step of the way. And if Veneziano tries anything dirty, I'll make sure to end him."

Braxton had never seen Veneziano Santiori cook, but the man had been a Hex Kitchen champion before he became an infamous gangster. He was older now and past his prime, but that only made him more dangerous. If there was anything Braxton knew about Veneziano, it was that he didn't play games unless he already knew he was going to win.

"Veneziano will be planning to cheat," Sofia said in her pragmatic way. "That means we need to be ready to do the same. Kenzie has to win."

"Aww, sweet," Kenzie said.

"Maybe I should have said that Veneziano needs to lose," Sofia amended, making a show of turning to exclude Kenzie from the conversation. "In any case," she continued. "I have plenty of real magical ingredients we can bring. Just in case Kenzie can't hold her own in there."

"Your faith in me is overwhelming," Kenzie said, wiping away a fake tear.

Sofia said something under her breath.

Braxton took his attention off the two of them to frown at Graham, who was hovering around Sofia like an oversized insect.

"Are you sure that's a good idea?" Graham asked Sofia. "Don't you need to give those ingredients to people who would be most benefitted by them? You know, so you can convince Qiang that he was wrong about you?"

Uh-oh.

Sofia rounded on Graham. "Oh, and you're the expert on what I need, now?"

Braxton couldn't quite hide his smirk. Sofia had clearly come to her senses and was over her little crush on the lying sack of shit.

Good.

"No," Graham said. "I just don't want you to do something you'll regret."

"Too late," she muttered.

If Braxton didn't know better, he'd feel sorry for Graham. The bloke looked like he'd just taken one of Aralia's arrows to his chest.

"It's settled, then," Chef Levy said. "Aralia, you stay here with Rosemary. If Kenzie loses this match, you'll have to kill Rosemary before the Gourmands can get to her."

Rosemary let out a little cry and clutched at her necklace.

"No one's killing you," Kenzie told the woman in a kind voice. "I'll make sure of it."

Braxton's chest ached at the courage and determination glittering in Kenzie's gorgeous gray eyes.

"And if you start to lose," Sofia told Kenzie, "I've got five crates of magical ingredients that'll get the job done for you. We can't let Veneziano become the next Gourmand leader."

A collective shudder went through the room at that bleak image.

"What Sofia is trying to say," Braxton told Kenzie, "is that we all believe in you. But we'll also have your back if anything goes wrong."

Kenzie nodded. Her hands were steady on her coffee mug, but all of the color had drained from her face.

"Just a minute there, stud," Aralia said.

She prowled across the kitchen toward him. Her smile was all menace, and Braxton knew what was coming next. All at once, he was grateful he hadn't eaten anything yet. He couldn't look at Kenzie or his sister.

"Have you forgotten something?" Aralia made a pointed gesture at Kenzie. "You got Number Eight back. Now, your time is officially up."

Braxton didn't answer her. He couldn't. His mouth was dry as a desert.

"Brax," Sofia said, her irritation transforming to alarm at whatever expression he was wearing.

"Tell me your word isn't worthless, McKaid," Aralia pressed. Her usual flirty routine was gone.

Braxton swallowed. "It's not worthless." He forced himself to meet Sofia and Kenzie's questioning stares. "I have to tell you both something."

"No."

The adamant word came from Graham. He stood from the table.

"Don't start," Aralia warned.

"This is not happening," Graham told her. "Do you hear me, Aralia? Not today. Not ever."

What the hell?

Graham was the last person who should be objecting this bargain. It was for his benefit, after all.

Why would Graham want to throw away his one chance at a normal life just to save Braxton?

The answer came a second later, when Graham leaned closer to Sofia. His voice softened when he told her, "Don't worry. I won't let anything happen to your brother."

Aralia made a tortured-animal sound.

"That's not good enough," Sofia said. "I want to know what's going on." She pushed aside Graham's hulking body and glared at Braxton. "Tell me what the hell's going on."

"I second that," Kenzie said. "You—"

"It doesn't matter!" Chef Levy smacked the table hard enough to make all of them jump. "I don't give a pig's ass about your petty little drama."

"But—" Kenzie protested, proving that she was, in fact, the bravest of them all.

"Shut it, Ashner," Chef Levy warned. "We're hours away from a culinary battle that will change the future for all of us. I don't want to hear a single word out of you morons unless it's about Cutthroat Cuisine. Is that clear?"

"Yes, Chef," they all mumbled.

"Good." Chef Levy somehow managed to look down on all of them, even though she was the shortest person in the room. "Now, put everything else out of your tiny-brained heads, and get in the game!"

After that, there was a flurry of activity as five crates of magical ingredients were packed in the limo, which was the only vehicle that was big enough to accommodate their group. Aralia and Graham had a short, hushed argument, which ended with Aralia stomping back into the house and threatening to shoot anyone who so much as looked at her funny.

Graham got into the limo, where Chef Levy and Sofia were already waiting.

"You ready for this?" Braxton asked Kenzie.

She let out a shuddering breath. "As ready as I'll ever be."

"McKaid!" Chef Levy laid on the horn. "I'm getting old waiting for you two."

Braxton ignored her and pulled Kenzie a few feet away from the limo.

"Look," he said, loosening his grip on her hand when he realized how hard he'd been squeezing. "I'm going to be watching you the whole time. If Veneziano tries anything, or you need me, I'll be there."

Kenzie's lip wobbled for just a second before she locked down her emotions.

"Thanks," she whispered.

"I mean it, Kenz. Either we leave that diner together or not at all. Okay?"

"McKaid! Ashner! Get your bony asses in the car, or I'll tie you to the bumper and drag you."

Chef Levy didn't seem like she was joking.

"Let's do this," Kenzie said, lifting her chin and giving him a fierce smile. "By the time I'm done, Veneziano Santiori won't know what hit him."

"That's my girl." He gave her butt a little smack as she got into the limo.

A second later, they were on their way. It was time for some real cutthroat cuisine.

CHAPTER 47

SOFIA

It had been a long-arse drive down to Tennessee, and yet, Sofia wished it could have gone on forever. Now that they were here, she had to follow through on the arrangement she'd made with Peter.

Nausea churned in her stomach.

"Aren't you coming?" Braxton leaned into the limo's open window and gave Sofia a quizzical look.

"I have some ingredients to deliver," she lied. "May as well make myself useful, right?"

"Why don't you just wait until after?" Braxton asked. His gaze flickered to the horrible bubble gum-pink diner, where Kenzie and Chef Levy were already heading.

In typical Graham fashion, he'd somehow convinced Aralia to stay at the cabin with Rosemary, while he came to Tennessee to help in any way he could. Now, Graham sat still and calm beside Sofia in the limo's back seat.

"I'll be back before the finale starts," Sofia told her brother. Turning to Graham, she asked, "Can you drive?"

"Of course."

His easy response made her feel even worse about what she was about to do.

Braxton chewed on his lip, and Sofia was sure he was about to say something patronizing and overprotective.

"Alright," he said.

Sofia gaped at her brother. "You mean you're not going to insist on coming with me?"

Braxton gave her a rueful grin. "Nah. I trust you, little sis."

Warmth spread through Sofia's chest, helping to ease some of her anxiety. She reached through the open window and pinched Braxton's cheek.

"Yeah, yeah," he swatted at her hand. With a last frown in Graham's direction, Braxton strode over to the diner. There was a hand-written *Closed for business* notice taped under the peeling *Good Ol' Apple Pie* sign.

"Take a left out of here," Sofia directed Graham, once they were re-situated in the limo's front seat.

They had to wait as three black SUVs pulled into the lot. The last car in the convoy stopped when it was right next to the limo. One of the rear windows lowered, and Rick Santiori's sleezy face appeared.

"Where are you goin', beautiful?" Rick asked.

"Wouldn't you like to know," she snapped. She rolled up her window, because she was already on edge enough. She didn't need to get in a pissing contest with the mini-mobster.

Graham pulled out of the lot as soon as the SUVs made way.

They drove down a sad, potholed street lined with sad, dilapidated houses. The few people who were out and about stared at the limo like they'd never seen anything so fancy. Or maybe they were staring at the bullet holes.

It had been a bloody miracle they hadn't gotten pulled over on their twelve-hour drive down here.

"Right at the light," Sofia said.

She texted a quick update without looking down at her phone.

Be there in ten.

For the next few minutes, the only time either of them spoke was when Sofia was giving directions to Graham. A weighted silence hung between them.

Graham kept glancing in his rearview mirror and frowning.

"What?" Sofia asked.

"I thought…never mind. They turned off."

Sofia was too preoccupied to ask for more of an explanation.

"Are we going to talk about this?" Graham asked. "Us, I mean."

Sofia's inner turmoil rose to a fever pitch.

Stop this, she told herself. She was going to make herself sick for no reason. There was nothing to feel guilty about. She was doing the right thing.

Wasn't she?

"We have nothing to talk about," Sofia said. She tried to ignore the pained look that flashed across Graham's face.

He gave her a solemn nod and returned his focus to the road.

It was starting to rain, which made this bleak little town even more depressing. Why Kenzie would have chosen to live here was beyond comprehension.

"You ready to tell me where we're really going?" Graham asked. He offered her a hesitant smile. "Anything I should know in advance? Angry gangsters…killer bees…whatever?"

"I said we were delivering ingredients," Sofia managed.

Sofia was usually more proficient at stretching the truth.

"You're nervous," Graham reached over and put a warm hand over hers. It was only then that she realized she'd been drumming her nails on the dashboard.

Her phone screen lit up with a text. She angled it away so Graham wouldn't be able to see it.

We're here.

As they pulled up at the next intersection, Sofia was overwhelmed by a sense of wrongness. This was wrong.

"Stop," she ordered. "Go back."

"Sofia?"

Graham stopped at the red light before turning to her. He curled his index finger under her chin, seeking her eyes.

She couldn't look at him.

Graham was a murderer, but that didn't change what he'd been to her. What he was to her.

"Tell me what's wrong." He was close enough that Sofia could see his freckles.

Rain sluiced down the windows. The loud drumbeat on the windshield matched her stuttering pulse.

"Just turn around," she told him. "Please."

Graham hesitated, then switched the limo's blinker and started easing into the left lane.

"I need to tell you something," Sofia said before she lost her nerve.

"Me too." Graham sighed. "I should have told you days ago."

Sofia waited. Was Graham about to tell her what she already knew…that he was a cop killer? That he'd murdered his own parents?

Would he tell her something that would explain those horrible pictures Peter had sent her?

Graham rubbed the back of his neck. "I was unfair to you the other day when I said I wanted more than just sex." His gaze skittered away from hers. "I know there's something between us, and I want us to have the space to figure out what that is. So, I guess what I'm trying to say is that I want you to take the lead. I won't try to push you for more than you're ready to give."

Sofia had to hold herself back from reaching for his hand. She had to stop herself from leaning in and kissing him.

When Sofia still didn't speak, Graham said, "All I'm asking is that you stay open to the possibility of more."

Sofia tried to find her voice. That wasn't what she'd expected Graham to say. She couldn't stop a small laugh from escaping.

Confusion washed across Graham's face, which turned into hurt.

Sofia composed herself and was about to explain, when—

Sirens.

Graham whipped around. There was a police cruiser less than a block behind them. Another appeared from a side street and swerved to cut off the road in front of them. Two more appeared beside the limo, preventing them from turning.

Even with the rain beating on the windshield, the slight squeak of the windshield wipers, and the deafening sirens, Sofia could hear Graham's teeth chattering. He hit the brakes with enough force to send Sofia lurching against her seatbelt.

Graham's breaths were coming in short pants. His eyes were wild as he silently pleaded with her to do something…to get them out of this.

She had no idea what expression crossed her face, but she saw the exact moment when Graham put the pieces together. She saw his realization dawn.

"You?"

He barely whispered the word, but it reverberated in her head like a gunshot.

Whatever response she might have given was lost when Graham opened his door and stumbled out. He didn't make it more than a few steps before the cops were on him.

There were guns and Tasers and truncheons, even though Graham was unarmed.

"No!" Sofia yelled, fumbling with the door and hurrying out. "Wait!"

She tried to get to Graham but was pulled away by strong hands and harsh voices. *Five* police officers surrounded Graham. When he turned around to look at her, a policewoman cracked her truncheon across Graham's back.

Sofia bit the inside of her cheek hard enough to taste blood.

Peter, his stupid hair plastered to his stupid face, got out of one of the police cruisers. He was wearing a bulletproof vest and holding an umbrella. He smiled at her.

"Well done, love," Peter said, loud enough for the whole goddamn town to hear. "You're safe now."

There was a dull thud as the cops shoved Graham against the nearest car, even though he was making no move to get away.

This is right, she told herself.

Sofia knew what it meant for a murderer to go unpunished. For the last five years, she'd been dealing with the fallout that Kenzie Ashner had left in her wake. Sofia had lost her family because of Kenzie.

Murderers needed to be brought to justice.

She'd seen the crime scene photos from Graham's parents' double-murder. She'd read the police report Peter sent her, which broke down irrefutable DNA evidence that tied Graham to the crime scene.

And yet, all Sofia could think about as she watched his arrest was the way Graham had kissed her in Qiang Lee's garden. How he'd given her everything and asked for nothing in return.

"Graham Malyung," one of the cops said. He wrenched Graham's arms behind his back with far more force than was needed. "You are under arrest for the murder of Carla and Matthew Malyung."

The cop continued to read Graham his rights, but he wasn't listening. He was staring at Sofia. His eyes were full of betrayal.

Peter was talking in her ear. Sofia heard the words *prison for life* as the cop restraining Graham hit him again.

"I'll be right back," Sofia said, pulling away from Peter and blindly racing for the limo. She opened the door, hardly noticing the rain that was dripping down her hair and into her eyes.

She yanked off the cover of the nearest crate and plunged her hand in. She scanned the labels, looking for one that would be useful.

"What you got there?" Peter asked, hovering over her with the umbrella when she emerged from the back seat.

Sofia didn't bother responding. She tore open the envelope with her teeth. She had spent long enough cataloging each ingredient and their uses that she immediately knew what to do with the little yellow seeds this one contained. She poured the seeds out of the envelope and onto her palm.

From Clementine's neatly-written note on the packet, Sofia knew one seed would be more than enough for what she was planning. So, she stuffed all of the seeds into her pocket except one. Then, she looked up, sighting the distance to Graham.

The policewoman restraining Graham let go of him to unhook the handcuffs from her belt.

Graham moved so fast, he was a blur.

He thrust his elbow into the nearest cop. He punched another in the face.

Three cops piled on top of him, shouting and reaching for their weapons as they forced him to the ground.

"No," Sofia cried. "No!"

She hurled the seed right at them.

There was a sharp *bang*. The air around the pile of cops filled with a putrid yellow smoke.

Gunfire erupted. Sofia's heart stopped beating.

The smoke cleared slowly, its sulfur residue hanging in the air even as the rain continued to beat down. Sofia saw the outline of the cops first. They were shouting and waving their weapons.

Her frantic gaze swept the ground, searching for a body. The smoke hovering over the ground was thick. Sofia couldn't tell for sure whether there was a corpse there or if it was just her eyes playing tricks on her.

The cops were scuffling through the smoke. The crack of their guns matched the frantic thrum of Sofia's pulse.

The smoke finally cleared, revealing the street. Sofia counted five cops, all of whom were racing for their cruisers. There was no dead body on the ground...no prisoner to fill the empty handcuffs.

Graham was gone.

* * *

Sofia was grateful for the rain as she drove back to the diner. It was coming down so hard, it took every bit of her concentration to keep from going off the road.

Between the rain, and a big car that had pulled in behind her, no one had noticed her drive away. Peter and the cops were probably still running around like headless chickens.

Sofia turned the wipers onto full speed and squinted out the windshield. God, the visibility was horrible. Maybe she should pull over—

She didn't even see the black car driving straight at her until it was too late.

"Shit!"

She jerked the wheel and slammed on the brakes. There was a crunch of metal, and Sofia felt a sickening thud as she was thrust forward. The airbag hit her chest with enough force to knock the wind out of her.

Shit, shit, shit.

The limo was stolen property of the Gourmands. Sofia doubted her car insurance would cover that.

Argh! Braxton was going to kill her.

All she could do now was hope the other driver was in a charitable mood. Maybe the damage had been worse to her car than theirs….

Sofia managed to disentangle herself from the airbag and stumbled out of the limo.

"I'm so sorry," she began, shielding her face from the rain and trying to make out the people getting out of the other car. There were three of them…maybe four.

"Aww, don't sweat it, beautiful," a man's voice said.

Sofia knew that voice. She goddamn hated it more than any other sound on Earth.

Rick Santiori.

He appeared out of the rain like an apparition. Cold dread slithered through Sofia. She couldn't even feel the rain anymore.

Too late, it occurred to her that the big car that had fortuitously showed up and blocked her from the cops' view hadn't been random at all. Rick had been following her.

"What are you doing here?" she asked. She couldn't completely hide the tremor in her voice.

"Don't worry," Rick said. One of his goons hovered next to him, holding an umbrella over his head. "I don't want your insurance information. I don't even want your money." His cheeks flushed as he craned his neck to see past her. "But I'd sure like to get a better look at those ingredients in your back seat."

CHAPTER 48

KENZIE

Being back inside *Good Ol' Apple Pie* was weird. Standing in the middle of the tarnished kitchen, surrounded by twenty Gourmands wearing red robes, was even weirder. Their hoods obscured their faces and muffled their voices. Because this whole setup didn't scream *creepy AF* enough.

Benedict's hood was thrown back, probably since there was no point in hiding his identity. They all knew who he was.

Nurse Ratched stood a little off to the side, dressed in her usual scrubs and white sneakers. Kenzie would be more intimidated by the woman's presence, but her blistered face and singed hair took away from her evil villain routine. A little.

Veneziano stood next to Kenzie, facing Benedict.

Kenzie's stomach was churning. Maybe she shouldn't have had that second cup of coffee. Or third. Or—

Focus, Kenzie….

"Let's get one thing straight right now," she said, trying to sound like she had some modicum of control over this shitshow. "I'm only going to compete if you allow my friends to live." She jutted her chin toward the dining room, where Braxton and Chef Levy had been told to wait with Veneziano's bodyguards.

There were a few unintelligible murmurs from the cloaked Gourmands. Benedict scrutinized her.

"I will guarantee their safety during the finale," he said. "Afterward, however, I can make no promises about their fate. Once a winner is declared, your friends' lives will be at the mercy of the new Gourmand leader."

Swell. Like Kenzie wasn't already under enough pressure to make sure she won.

"Don't worry," Veneziano interjected, using what had to be the world's most patronizing tone. "I don't kill for sport. So unless your friends do anything…untoward…you needn't be concerned."

"Don't expect me to take your word on that," Kenzie shot back.

"Silence," one of the hooded Gourmands hissed.

The man was close enough that his hot breath fanned across the back of Kenzie's neck. The other Gourmands murmured their agreement.

Kenzie's skin crawled. There were so many eyes on her. She thought she recognized some of their voices as ones that had jeered at her from behind the one-way glass inside the arena.

Before she started hyperventilating, she sought out Braxton. He and Chef Levy were standing on the other side of the swinging door that separated the kitchen from the dining room. They were both watching through the smudged window.

Chef Levy was scowling at the Gourmands. Braxton's green eyes were fixed on her and seemed to be trying to tell her a thousand things at once.

I've got your back. I love you.

Or maybe that was just Kenzie's subconscious filling in the blanks.

"There will be no outside involvement," Benedict said, bringing Kenzie's attention back to the circle of Gourmands. "This battle is between the two finalists and no other."

Kenzie nodded.

"I understand," Veneziano said. He smoothed a hand down his silk tie.

"You will use culinary magic to fight to the death," Benedict said. "This match is binding, which means that no matter what happens, only one chef will walk out of this kitchen alive. The winner will become the next Gourmand leader. Do you understand?"

Again, they both agreed.

"Very well," Benedict said. "In that case, we will give you both a few minutes to change into your Cutthroat Cuisine uniforms." He gave a disdainful glare at Kenzie's immodest animal-hide dress.

Oh, I'm sorry. Am I offending your delicate sensibilities, Mr. I Let Chefs Cook to the Death for Fun?

Two Gourmands gestured for Kenzie to follow them, while two more escorted Veneziano Santiori in the opposite direction. This whole thing felt a little like a religious cult initiation.

"If we have to do a virgin sacrifice," she told the mute and stoic Gourmands, "you can count me out."

No response.

They led Kenzie past the freezer. Even though the door was shut and all evidence had been cleared away, Kenzie could still see Loretta and Max's mangled bodies. She could still hear Polly's voice, explaining that their murders were a necessary evil of keeping culinary magic secret from the rest of the world.

And that was why Kenzie was doing this. Even though she wanted to be part of the Gourmands the same way she wanted to poke her own eyeballs out with a shrimp fork, she had to win this. As the new Gourmand leader, she'd be able to stop all the killing.

The two Gourmands left her alone in the storage room, which really amounted to an oversized closet that still held a mountain of industrial-sized rolls of the cheapest toilet paper ever made. Kenzie breathed in the familiar scents of old grease and watered-down cleaner. She could swear she caught a hint of Loretta's drugstore perfume.

She changed out of Aralia's dress, which she was beginning to like a lot more now that she knew Benedict hated it, and donned the shapeless white outfit she'd been given. She tied on her Cutthroat Cuisine red apron for the last time.

She'd do this for Loretta and Max, and for Chef Levy's girlfriend, and for every person who had been killed by the Gourmands.

Kenzie pulled her hair back into a high ponytail and studied herself in the tiny, fogged mirror that Loretta had used to reapply her lipstick between customers.

"You can do this," she told herself.

She heard a slight squeak from the door hinges. Kenzie readied herself for the Gourmands, or maybe Nurse Ratched.

"Do you always talk to yourself, Number Eight?"

Rick, of all people, slipped into the room and shut the door behind him.

Kenzie hadn't noticed him in the dining room with the rest of his father's bodyguards, but it wasn't like she'd been looking for him.

"Where'd you come from?" she demanded.

"Climbed in through a window in the pantry." Rick scrunched up his nose. "Assuming you call that filthy old broom closet a pantry."

"Buzz off, Dick," Kenzie said, just because she knew messing up his name would piss him off.

Rick's lip curled in distaste.

"You're never going to be the Gourmand leader, you know," he said. "You don't have the stomach for it. Or the brains. You should leave governing to people who know what the fuck they're doing."

"Gee." Kenzie blinked at him. "Do you have a pen? I feel like I should be writing these nuggets of wisdom down."

"You're not half as good a culinary magician as you think you are," Rick sneered.

Kenzie was ready to fire back, but she noticed that Rick had a red handprint on one of his cheeks. It was starting to swell. He was also moving stiffly.

Rick might be one of the most loathsome creatures on the planet, but that didn't stop the rush of pity Kenzie felt on his behalf. It had to be his father who had done this to him, since no one else would dare.

Well, Braxton would, but he wouldn't have slapped Rick. He would have broken his nose.

"What do you want, Dick?" Kenzie asked.

"I was out of commission for a while," Rick said. He lifted his leg and tapped on his ankle. As far as Kenzie could tell, it looked like an ordinary ankle. "You can't imagine how fucking annoying it is to not be able to cook magic without the Gourmands tracking your every move."

"Um…sure," Kenzie said. She really had no idea what Rick was talking about and didn't much care.

"Anyway, it wasn't a total loss," Rick said. "I used my cooking hiatus to…reevaluate stuff. It was very productive." He took a few steps forward. His hands were shoved deep in his pockets.

For the first time since he came into the room, Kenzie wondered if she should be afraid. Was Rick here to kill her so his dad could win by default?

Should she scream? Braxton was in the dining room and would come before Rick could do any real damage. On the other hand….

Kenzie lunged for a crowbar that was leaning against a stack of toilet paper. She had used it during her waitressing days to open delivery crates that came boarded up like Fort Knox.

"Go ahead, Dick," Kenzie goaded, brandishing the weapon. "Try me."

"I'm not gonna kill you," Rick said. "For what I have planned, I need you alive."

"Wha—"

Rick pulled something out of his pocket. It looked like some kind of dried flower. He rested it on the palm of his hand, brought it to his mouth, and blew on it.

Tiny particles of pollen floated through the air toward Kenzie. A sweet aroma tickled her nostrils.

The crowbar slipped out of her hand and clunked onto the floor. Kenzie tried to reach for it, but her arm refused to obey the simple command. She opened her mouth to say something, but no sound came out.

Everything around her began to grow fuzzy. She blinked, but it only made the effect worse. Rick blurred out of focus.

What the hell was happening to her?

She hadn't been poisoned. Kenzie knew that for a fact, since she'd experienced that unpleasantness firsthand.

Kenzie just felt odd. Then, she felt nothing at all.

CHAPTER 49

BRAXTON

Even though Braxton was the one standing outside the kitchen and looking in, he felt like a caged animal. Kenzie and Veneziano were about to cook to the death, and there was nothing Braxton could do to help her.

Where the hell was Sofia?

She should have been back by now. She was supposed to have ingredients to help Kenzie if she got into trouble.

Damnit, Sofe.

All of the Gourmands were inside that dingy kitchen. Veneziano's thugs had gone back out to the parking lot to smoke and steal sips from metal flasks. That left Braxton and Chef Levy peering through a dusty windowpane.

Christ, he wanted Kenzie out of there. Braxton didn't like the smug expression on Veneziano's face.

Kenzie was standing perfectly still on her side of the counter. Benedict was reminding them that the contest was to the death, and the survivor would be the next Gourmand leader…as though anyone could forget. They were each presented with a few grocery bags of fresh ingredients, as well as a closed wicker basket.

"Contestants," Benedict said. "Reveal your magical ingredient."

Kenzie attacked her basket, while Veneziano stood there, pompous and relaxed. The bastard clearly already knew what was inside.

Braxton craned his neck to see into Kenzie's open basket.

"Magical acorn squash," Benedict said in a droll tone. The man had none of Polly Berrywhite's stage presence; that was for sure.

"It needs to be cooked through before the magic will activate," Benedict added.

Braxton winced. Acorn squash took an age to roast.

Benedict made his final remarks, and then the finale was underway.

In less than a minute, Veneziano had his squash halved, de-seeded, and in the oven. Meanwhile, Kenzie was just…standing at her prep station. She wore a strange little smirk, like she knew something her opponent didn't.

"Come on, Kenz," Braxton muttered. "You've got this."

As though she could hear him, Kenzie sprang into action. She went to the fridge and took out fresh thyme, garlic, butter, and several brown-paper packages of meat. The packages' labels were too small for Braxton to read, so he had no idea what dish she was planning to make.

Kenzie returned to her station and began cleaning, chopping, and mixing. The one thing she didn't do was touch her acorn squash. Braxton was beginning to think she'd somehow forgotten about her magical ingredient when she went over, picked it up, and—

An audible, collective gasp came from the Gourmands. Braxton blinked, wanting to make sure he wasn't seeing things.

Had Kenzie seriously just…thrown away her magical ingredient?

"What the hell are you doing, Ashner?" Chef Levy snarled under her breath.

Good question, Chef….

The green squash sat forlornly on the top of her rubbish bin.

Kenzie dusted her hands off on her apron and went back to work. There was no sense of hesitation as she began to cook. She said something to Veneziano, but Braxton couldn't hear it above the clanging of pans.

The smell of sizzling garlic and fresh herbs wafted into the dining room.

"Maybe your girl isn't completely useless," Chef Levy observed. "At least she's going to have something on the plate."

Braxton didn't spare Chef Levy the attention it would take to reply. He was too busy watching Kenzie cook.

There was no doubt that she seemed to have everything under control, and yet, something didn't seem quite right. Kenzie usually moved around the kitchen as joyful and nimble as if she were walking on air…the exact opposite of her endearing clumsiness in every other part of her life. Now, though, she was moving…differently. She wasn't slow or acting like she was in pain. She just wasn't….

Braxton shook his head. Of course Kenzie wasn't cooking with her usual enthusiasm. She'd barely gotten away from her kidnappers, and now she was right back here with them again. If it had been anyone else, they would probably be having a panic attack instead of calmly making a roux.

Veneziano was working on a wild rice concoction to go with his acorn squash. He kept glancing at the timer above his oven and frowning. It was clear his acorn squash was going to be the limiting factor in his dish. The squash needed at least another ten minutes to cook through.

Meanwhile, Kenzie seemed to be plating her final dish. Her back was turned and she was hunched over her plate, hiding her creation from everyone else.

"What are you up to?" Chef Levy whispered.

Again, it was a fair question. Braxton's apprehension was growing with each passing moment.

Kenzie was making swirling motions with her hand as she drizzled something on top of her plate. She was all confidence and focus.

And yet, that acorn squash sat abandoned in her trash can, now buried under a heap of bloodied butcher paper. The sight of it bothered Braxton. In all the times he'd seen her cook, Kenzie had always gravitated to the fresh ingredients. But she'd thrown away the squash and hadn't so much as touched the ripe plums Braxton could see poking out of one of her grocery bags.

"Something's wrong with Kenzie," Braxton said in an urgent whisper to Chef Levy.

"Stop being an overprotective chauvinist," Chef Levy replied.

Kenzie, who seemed to have finished her dish, looked over at Veneziano and grinned. It wasn't a friendly smile, and for reasons Braxton couldn't work out, it seemed unfamiliar. Wrong.

Veneziano was still fretting over his acorn squash, which had five minutes left on the timer. Even after he removed it from the oven, he would need to combine its inherent magic with whatever power he'd cooked into his rice medley.

Kenzie said something to Veneziano, but again, the sound didn't carry enough for Braxton to catch her words.

"Move your ass, Ashner," Chef Levy muttered.

Come on, Kenz.

Braxton resisted the urge to pace as Kenzie put a metal cover over her dish. She carried it over to Veneziano's side of the kitchen. Braxton tensed, ready to go barreling through the door if anything went wrong.

"The Gourmands will kill you before you can lift a finger," Chef Levy warned, gripping his arm tight enough to cut off his blood flow. "Don't interfere."

Kenzie whipped the covering off her dish to reveal a single, center-cut bone marrow. Braxton could smell the fatty, umami minced-meat filling she'd cooked into the marrow.

No fucking way.

Braxton knew this recipe. It had infamously been created by a culinary magician who gave new meaning to the word *spiteful.* The man had made the dish for his wife on their anniversary after discovering she'd cheated on him.

The recipe hadn't been cooked in fifty years, but it was still brought up in every Culinary Magic Ethics class Braxton had ever taken.

The dish was brutal. Horrible. And it wasn't one that Kenzie would even know about, let alone make.

Veneziano, who was frantically stuffing his acorn squash halves, looked up. His gaze went to the plate Kenzie had balanced on her palm. His eyes bulged.

"No!" Veneziano shouted.

He tried to get away, but the oven was at his back and Gourmands surrounded them on all sides. With an inhuman roar, Kenzie picked up the marrow bone and jabbed it against Veneziano's chest as though it were a knife.

The bone marrow didn't pierce the mobster's skin, but as soon as it came into contact with his chest, the magic fused the bone to his body.

Veneziano tried to pry the bone marrow off him. It was useless. The bone stuck fast.

"You bitch," Veneziano began. Whatever else he was going to say was cut off by his blood-curdling screech. The mobster moved a few steps, giving Braxton a clear view of the recipe taking effect.

Braxton heard a muted splinter, like the sound of a chicken bone snapping. Then, one of Veneziano's finger bones burst out of his skin. Little white bits emerged from his knuckles as he howled.

Braxton's stomach churned as, one by one, his finger bones poked right out of his skin. The mobster writhed against the counter.

Veneziano's ribs were next. He screamed as they protruded from his sides in an inverted U-shape. The white dress shirt he was wearing under his apron was soaked through with blood.

A particular cruelty of this recipe was how it slowly and methodically worked its way through the human body, beginning with the bones that wouldn't kill its victim.

Veneziano's cries turned to wheezy gurgles from what was probably a collapsed lung. Little bones and big bones wriggled out of Veneziano's body. Tears and blood streamed out of him.

It took forever.

Braxton wanted to smash his own eardrums, just so he wouldn't need to hear that wheezing sound for another second. It was impossible to look away.

Finally, Veneziano passed out. Braxton felt himself wavering on the verge of madness just from observing this recipe work its magic. Beside him, Chef Levy was speechless.

Veneziano's spine peeled out of his ruined back. His body sagged to the kitchen floor, his bones making a clattering sound as they struck the tiles. Veneziano's wheezing cut off.

Finally, it was over. Veneziano Santiori was dead.

Braxton jerked when laughter broke the shocked silence. It was Kenzie. She was laughing.

"Yes!" She threw her hands in the air as she leapt on top of Veneziano's shattered body. "YES!"

Then, Kenzie began to crumble. No. She began to grow. Her slender body filled out. She gained a few inches in height while her black hair seemed to retract into her head. Her gray eyes became brown. Her tattoos faded, along with her breasts.

"It can't be," Chef Levy whispered.

It was.

Braxton stood there, glued to the window and unable to unlock his frozen limbs, as Rick Santiori strode across the kitchen. His shoes left faint rust-colored prints from the blood still leaking out of Veneziano. His father.

"I'm Rick Santiori," Rick said, stretching out his hand to Benedict Vandermeer. "And I'm now the leader of the Gourmands."

CHAPTER 50

KENZIE

Even if Kenzie wasn't bound in a thick length of rope, she'd still be screwed. Rick had used some magical pollen to completely paralyze her before he'd tied her up. Like *completely* paralyze. She couldn't talk, wiggle her pinky finger, or even blink.

She lay there, silently cursing Rick's existence and plotting evil revenge, while her body remained as inert and useless as unmolded gelatin.

As soon as the magic began to wear off, Kenzie lost no time in struggling. And swearing up a blue streak. Not that it did her much good…the swearing part, anyway. Rick had stuffed a rag into her mouth since, as he'd smugly explained, he needed her to stay quiet longer than the magical ingredient would hold. Hence the gag. And the ropes.

He'd also made it clear that he needed her to stay alive until he was finished with whatever he was doing. Lucky her.

Unlike her attempts to shout the place down, her struggling was getting her somewhere. She somehow managed to wriggle her way to her abandoned crowbar, feeling all the while like a cocooned butterfly. A very determined butterfly. She managed to get hold of the crossbar in her left hand and shove it under the ropes binding her ankles. She squirmed and grunted against her gag, and finally managed to loosen the ropes. A little.

Winning.

She didn't know how much time passed before she got her hands free. All she knew was that she didn't want to waste any more. She had no clue what Rick was up to, but she'd bet the farm it wasn't anything pleasant.

Kenzie hurriedly untied the rest of her body and tore the gag out of her mouth. She raced out of the storage room on wobbling legs.

Kenzie made a beeline for the kitchen, but stopped short when she saw the Gourmands crowded against the wall. They were blocking the kitchen's back entrance. Kenzie stretched on her toes to see between the Gourmands' red robes.

She blinked, wondering if a mirror had been installed in the kitchen after she left. Why else would she be staring across the kitchen and seeing…herself?

The only problem with the mirror theory was that she was standing still, and her reflection was shouting in victory as she lifted what appeared to be a beef marrow bone over her head.

And what the hell was that…thing…on the floor? It bore a slight resemblance to a human, except it had bones poking out of it like porcupine quills.

Kenzie stopped trying to identify the human-ish lump when her doppelganger began to transform.

"Umm, what the…" she said out loud.

Her identical twin mutated into…Rick.

Freaking Rick.

"I'm Rick Santiori," Rick said. He faced off against Benedict who, for once, looked as shocked as Kenzie felt. He didn't react as Rick offered his hand—which was no longer covered with tattoos like Kenzie's—and said, "And I'm now the leader of the Gourmands."

The world seemed to tilt on its axis.

"I don't understand," Benedict spluttered.

Nurse Ratched and the rest of the Gourmands made noises of agreement.

"Well," Rick drawled, clearly basking in the attention. "I recently inherited some extremely powerful magical ingredients. They enabled me to…subdue Kenzie Ashner and take on her appearance. Temporarily." He smirked.

"Then you have broken the sacred rules of this tournament," Benedict said, anger emerging through his shock. His cheeks were turning red and splotchy.

"Nah," Rick said. "I might have looked like a fine-ass girl, but this magic was all mine." He picked up a loose bone and let it fall, clattering, back onto the floor. "You said before that this match was to the death, and the winning chef would be your successor. It was my dish, my magic." He gave Benedict a self-satisfied smile. "I killed my opponent. Thus, this is my victory."

No, Kenzie internally shouted. *No no no!*

Benedict turned to the other Gourmands.

In other circumstances, Kenzie would have relished his helpless shrug. Right now, though, she was trying to process the calamity that Rick had brought about.

Kenzie hadn't wanted to be the Gourmand leader, but it was the only way to wrest control from the worst person imaginable: Veneziano Santiori. At least, he'd seemed like the worst possible option. Until….

"I suppose you're right," Benedict relented. "Congratulations, Mr. Santiori."

Kenzie had heard enough. She needed to find Braxton and get the hell out of here.

She eased out of the restaurant through the employees' entrance out back. She stayed under the eaves and mostly avoided the rain as she made her way around the side of the building. She let herself into the dining room, which was empty except for two figures standing next to the swinging door.

Chef Levy and Braxton turned.

"Kenzie!" Braxton closed the distance between them in two long strides and caught her up in a hug. "What—"

The door behind Kenzie flew open, letting in a burst of warm rain and a very wet and wild-eyed Sofia.

"Sofe, where the hell have you been?" Braxton exclaimed, still holding onto Kenzie.

"No…time," Sofia panted. "Rick…got the ingredients. All of them. Gotta go."

"Where's Graham?" Chef Levy asked.

Sofia's expression shuttered. "He's not coming."

Chef Levy said something in Hebrew. "Alright," she began. "Here is what's going to happen."

She didn't have a chance to finish.

"My first decree as the new Gourmand leader," Rick said, loudly enough to be heard over the rain that was blowing in through the open door and splattering against the plastic booths, "is to order the execution of that little group there."

Everyone turned to look at Kenzie & co.

That was when it truly hit Kenzie that she had lost Cutthroat Cuisine…and Rick had won. That meant—

"There are more important issues to discuss at the present," Benedict told Rick. "You may chase your personal vendettas later."

Rick pointed at Kenzie and Braxton. "Go on and get a head start, then." He smirked. "I'll be coming for you soon enough."

Kenzie's group didn't need to be told twice. They started hustling out of the diner.

Kenzie turned back just before she reached the door. She met Benedict's gaze, and he gave her a subtle nod.

In that simple gesture, Kenzie somehow understood the gift Benedict had given her and her friends. The man might be a kidnapper and a first-rate douche, but he was also giving them time to escape.

Not willing to question Benedict's temporary benevolence, Kenzie hurried outside after the others.

The diner's sagging porch was crawling with Rick's thugs, who hadn't yet gotten the memo that Kenzie's group was off limits…for a little while, anyway. The bodyguards tossed down their flasks, picked up their guns, and swarmed.

"Get to the limo!" Chef Levy yelled.

"Yeah, that might be a problem," Sofia said, as the four of them sprinted to the parking lot.

Kenzie was instantly soaked. She shielded her face against the rain as she searched for their getaway vehicle, but all she could see were the Santioris' black SUVs.

Gourmands shouted as they filled up the doorway. Kenzie heard the metallic click of guns being readied.

"Grab hands," Sofia ordered.

Kenzie found one of her palms enclosed in Braxton's firm grip, and the other in Chef Levy's. Sofia plunged the hand she wasn't using to hold onto Braxton's into her pocket. She pulled out a handful of yellow seeds and threw them in the air.

There was a loud *bang*. Yellow smoke began to billow all around them.

"Come on!" Sofia yelled.

Kenzie clasped Braxton's hand. Together, they ran away from Rick, the Gourmands, and *Good Ol' Apple Pie*.

CHAPTER 51

SOFIA

In between hotwiring cars, Chef Levy passed the time by shouting at the rest of them for their various fuck-ups.

Since no one let Sofia get behind the wheel during the fifteen, traffic-ridden hours it took to drive back to upstate New York, Sofia had nothing to do besides contemplate the failures that had brought her to this moment.

Rick had stolen all of her magical ingredients, except for the seeds she'd still had in her pocket. Now, those were gone too.

Just like Graham.

Sofia had no idea where he'd gone and had no way to contact him. Even if she did, what would she say?

"We'll need to get Aralia and deal with Rosemary, and then find somewhere to hole up as soon as possible," Chef Levy was saying. "The cabin will be the first place Rick comes, so we need to be long gone before he shows up."

"You're not killing Rosemary," Kenzie said. "I won't let you."

Chef Levy *hmmed*. "Maybe it would be best to keep her alive. For now."

Sofia tuned out the conversation. She pretended to sleep so no one would try to talk to her. It wasn't until their tires were crunching up the gravel driveway and the cabin came into view that anyone addressed her directly.

"What happened with the ingredients, Sofe?" Braxton asked as they all got out of the car. "I thought you were going to be there. You said—"

She held up a hand to stop him before turning to Chef Levy and Kenzie.

"Can my brother and I have some privacy?"

"Of course," Kenzie said, throwing Braxton a worried look before going into the house.

"You have five minutes," Chef Levy said.

Sofia waited until the door closed and the two of them were alone on the porch.

"Why didn't you tell me?" she demanded. "Why didn't you tell me Graham murdered his parents?"

Braxton gaped at her. "Those were his *parents*?!"

Sofia faltered. "Wait…what?"

Braxton shook his head in disbelief.

"I wanted to tell you, but Aralia made me eat her promise granola," he said. Regret twisted his features. "Every time I tried to warn you about him, the recipe stopped me." Braxton scrubbed a hand across his jaw. "The only reason I can talk about it now is because I'm not endangering him by revealing his secret…since you already know."

Sofia didn't give a damn about the magic's intricacies.

"How did you find out?" she asked, not even sure why it mattered anymore.

Braxton's gaze darted to the side, like he was looking for an escape.

"A bunch of years back, Aidan told me he helped someone…a murderer…escape arrest."

"*What?*"

"That was my reaction, too," Braxton said, chuckling darkly. "Aidan met Aralia at a culinary magic competition they both went to, and I guess they got to talking, and she said her foster brother was in trouble. And, well, you know how Aid is." Braxton pressed his fingertips into his temple and shook his head. "Was."

Sofia's heart squeezed, but she didn't say anything.

"Anyway," Braxton continued. "Aidan couldn't say no to helping anyone, especially when it involved creating a new recipe. All he told me was that Aralia needed his help to hide her brother, who had murdered someone. Aid wouldn't tell me any of the details because he said he didn't want me to get in trouble if anyone ever found out about his involvement." Braxton gave her a helpless shrug. "So, I dropped it. I actually kind of forgot about the whole thing until I needed Aralia to help us make that poison for Kenzie, and I wanted something to hold over her head. I told her if she didn't help us, I'd tell the police she knew where Graham was hiding."

"And you never thought to tell me any of this?" Sofia asked, trying and failing to disguise her hurt.

Of course Braxton had kept it from her. He and Aidan had always been that way. They'd never meant to exclude her, but it was like the two of them operated on a different plane of existence from the rest of the world.

"I didn't want Aid to get in trouble," Braxton said. He held up a hand. "Not that I didn't trust you. Just—"

Sofia waved his stilted apology away. It didn't matter now.

"I knew Graham was a murderer," Braxton said. "It's why I wanted you to stay the hell away from him." Braxton leaned in and grasped her shoulder. "Did that bastard hurt you?"

"No, he didn't." *I hurt him.*

"Sofia," Braxton said, his voice full of new urgency. "What happened? Where is he now?"

I think I did something awful.

"I think I made a mistake," she whispered.

She'd known it from the moment she heard those sirens, even if she hadn't understood.

Aralia emerged from a footpath in the trees and waved to them. She had a dead rabbit slung over one shoulder and her bow over the other. She was whistling.

"Where's Graham?" Aralia asked, as soon as she was close enough for them to hear.

Sofia exchanged a look with her brother.

"Where is Graham?" Aralia asked again. There was a shrillness to her voice that hadn't been there before.

Sofia lifted her chin and faced her. "I don't know. The police tried to arrest him, but he got away."

"What?"

Sofia never knew that one word could carry so much emotion.

Aralia stalked forward.

Even though she didn't take her eyes off Aralia, Sofia saw the less-than-subtle way her brother shifted into a protective stance.

"My friend who's a PI told me who Graham is," Sofia said, feeling the need to defend herself. "He showed me the pictures of what Graham did to his mother and father. I know they were both in the NYPD, and that the authorities have been looking for him ever since."

Aralia's face went from ghost-white, to red, to eggplant. She lunged.

Before Sofia could react, Braxton grabbed Aralia around her waist and hauled her back.

"Calm down," he ordered.

Aralia screamed and twisted in his arms. Braxton, even with his height and weight advantage, could barely contain her.

"What have you done?!" Aralia shrieked.

She clawed at Braxton's neck. Blood beaded up along his throat before he pinned Aralia's arms at her sides.

"I did the right thing," Sofia said. She was sure everyone could hear the uncertainty in her voice.

"You stupid bitch!" Aralia screamed.

She writhed against Braxton, even snapping her teeth. If there was ever any question of how she'd come by the nickname *Crazy Aralia*....

"How could you protect him?" Sofia asked. She hated how her voice warbled. "How could you sleep in the same house as someone who murdered his own parents?"

Aralia stilled in Braxton's arms.

"Let me tell you about this *murderer*," Aralia seethed. "Graham's *cop* father used to beat the hell out of him because he was a weak culinary magician."

Sofia inhaled noisily, but Aralia didn't give her a chance to say anything.

"Graham was a scrawny little kid, if you can believe it. His dad whaled on him bad enough that he was hospitalized a few times. But because Daddy was a cop and Mommy was a detective, no one ever did shit about it."

Sofia tried to reconcile the picture Aralia was painting with the stoic, strong-as-an-ox man she'd come to deeply care for.

"When those shit-for-brains realized beating their son wasn't going to make him a better culinary magician, they started looking for foster kids who fit the mold of what they wanted in their child." Aralia tapped her own chest, indicating that she was their solution.

"After that," Aralia continued, "our parents trained me and mostly ignored him. Especially once Graham started getting big enough to defend himself."

"That's awful," Sofia said. She tried to clear the hoarseness and regret from her voice. "But why didn't he go to the Gourmands? Social services? Something?"

As soon as the words were out of her mouth, Sofia knew they were the wrong ones. She felt her cheeks heat. When her gaze darted to her brother, Sofia could tell he recognized the irony of her words.

The two of them hadn't been content to let the authorities deal with Aidan's murderer. They'd taken the law into their own hands. They'd thought they could make their own justice.

And they'd seen how well that turned out.

"Who the fuck would have believed a couple of kids?" Aralia shot back. "It was our word against our parents. Did I mention they were *cops*?"

"But…you said your dad stopped beating him," Sofia said weakly. "So, did Graham do that to them when he got older to punish them?"

"That wasn't the reason," Aralia snapped. "Graham doesn't have a vindictive bone in his body. At least, not on his own behalf."

Aralia glanced out at the lake. Something like vulnerability creased her features.

It was as strange and off-putting as Sofia's own uncertainty. Her emotions were a tumultuous mess.

"I was thirteen, and I'd just won my first culinary magic competition," Aralia said.

Sofia remembered her brothers' first major culinary magic tournament. Braxton and Aidan had ended up as finalists against each other. Aidan had ultimately won, and afterward, their parents had taken the whole family to the best restaurant in Sydney. Then, they'd driven to a campsite where they'd cooked kettle corn and stargazed.

It had been a really good night.

"And?" Sofia pressed, impatience taking over.

Aralia still stared determinedly into the distance.

"Dad wanted to…celebrate. He'd always been a hugger and I'd never thought much about it before, but that day, he'd gone out drinking with his buddies."

A sick feeling unfurled in Sofia's stomach as she guessed where this story was going. She just prayed she was wrong.

"I was so surprised, I didn't try to fight him," Aralia said quietly. "And then, by the time I tried to fight, I couldn't. I was small and he was big, and well—" She picked at a scab on her thumb. "I must have been screaming, because my foster mom came. I thought she was there to rescue me, but she just—" Aralia squeezed her eyes shut. "Told me to be quiet. And then she closed the door."

"Oh God," Sofia whispered.

A vise was squeezing her chest, making it hard to breathe. She thought she'd seen all the ugliness life had to offer. This was something else entirely.

"Graham got home from baseball practice sometime in the middle of it all," Aralia said. "I don't really remember much, except that he had his bat. And, yeah. Let's just say he didn't tell me to be quiet and shut the door on me."

A weighted silence fell over the room.

Braxton spoke first.

"I didn't know, Aralia," he said, sounding as wrecked as Sofia felt. "Aidan never told me why he helped Graham…and I just assumed…." He groaned and buried his face in his hands.

Sofia felt like all of her blood had turned to ice water.

Flashes of Graham's earnest face flew through her mind, followed by his look of betrayal when Sofia delivered him to the cops.

A low, urgent thrum began in the back of her throat. It probably sounded like she was keening. It felt like being torn apart.

"We have to find him," Sofia choked out.

It was almost impossible to speak around the guilt, which was crashing over her in wave after endless wave.

Braxton nodded wordlessly.

"No," Aralia snarled. "I saved your lives at Hex Kitchen and gave you a place to hide when you had nowhere else to go. I kept up my end of our bargain, but then Graham refused to let me call in my payment." She gave Sofia a look that sliced right through her. "Thanks to you, Graham isn't here to stop me."

Aralia turned and jabbed her finger into Braxton's chest. "You know what you have to do. I'm calling in my bargain."

CHAPTER 52

BRAXTON

No," Sofia said, grabbing Braxton's arm. "You can't. I won't let you."

Braxton had thought it would be terrible when Sofia found out the deal he'd made with Aralia. Instead, he just felt relieved. He'd been carrying around this secret, and now, it was finally out there. He didn't need to hide it anymore.

Aralia had just told Sofia that, in exchange for a way out of Hex Kitchen, Braxton had agreed to take Graham's place in jail for his parents' murder.

Braxton already had a recipe that would transform his appearance. It wasn't perfect, and he'd have to find a way into the prison kitchen so he could re-up the illusion once a week or so, but it could be done. It *would* be done. Because Braxton had given Aralia his word.

"Sofe." He put his hands on her shoulders and spun her around to look at him. "It's okay. I'm a lot happier to give up my life for Graham's now that I know he had a good reason for what he did."

Understatement of the century.

Aidan had known the truth all along. He'd helped Graham evade the cops and had probably saved his life in the process.

Meanwhile, Braxton had been using his twin's good deed as leverage.

It should have been me instead of Aidan.

"You can't," Sofia argued.

"Of course he can," Aralia said. "Once he turns himself in, the police will stop searching for the real Graham. The case will be closed, and Graham will be free."

It tugged on Braxton's heart when tears sprang into his fearless sister's eyes.

Christ. He wasn't looking forward to having this whole conversation again with Kenzie. He'd just gotten her back, and now—

"The minimum sentence for murder in New York State is twenty years," Sofia said, her composure unraveling. "And it'll be worse for Graham…or you pretending to be Graham. You'll get life without parole. I'll never see you again!"

"I know."

He'd be abandoning Sofia when she needed him most. And Kenzie—

He couldn't let himself think about it.

"It's done," Aralia said. To Braxton, she ordered, "Tell me how you're going to make it happen. And it better be damn convincing."

Braxton spent the next several minutes describing the recipe that would transform his appearance into Graham's. It was similar to the magical ingredient Rick had stolen from Sofia and used on Kenzie…except this recipe would last longer. And it was stronger.

The recipe was one of Aidan's, which he and Braxton had used on Halloween and whenever they wanted to switch places to mess with someone. The recipe was slow to digest, which meant it could last for up to a week. The only problem was that, if he made any other magical recipes, the transformation would immediately disappear. That meant he wouldn't be able to cook anything else that might allow him to protect himself from the other inmates. And with his magical reserves already on the brink of collapse….

"I need some air," Sofia muttered.

Braxton let her go, since there was nothing he could say to make this easier for her. He wondered if it was too much to hope for that Sofia and Kenzie would become friends.

Braxton was still working up the nerve to go inside and repeat this conversation with Kenzie, when Sofia reappeared.

"Let's go for a drive," Sofia said. "If you're really going to do this, I have some magical ingredients that'll help you."

"Really?" Hope began to take root amid his despair.

"Yep," Sofia said, sounding much calmer than she had a few minutes ago. "I kept a few for emergencies and put them somewhere safe, in case we needed them."

"We'll have to be quick," Braxton pointed out. "Otherwise Chef Levy might leave us here as a live offering to Rick."

"Just a short drive," Sofia assured him. "But I'll need your help to dig the ingredients up."

A few minutes later, the two of them were driving down the unmarked road that led away from the cabin. It felt wrong to be using Graham's truck after everything that had gone down, but it wasn't like they had a lot of options for available vehicles. The stolen van that had gotten them from Tennessee back to New York was their only other ride, and Chef Levy was busy packing it full of necessary supplies before they fled.

"Where are we going?" Braxton asked…not for the first time.

"Just keep driving," his bossy sister informed him. "I'll tell you when we get there. And give me your phone. The radiofrequency radiation could mess with the ingredients."

Braxton knew better than to question her when she got in one of these moods. So, he slid the device out of his pocket and passed it over.

They were both quiet, lost in their own thoughts, as the truck ate up the roadway.

"Are you sure you know where we're going?" Braxton ventured.

They'd passed a single, abandoned gas station in the last ten minutes. Everything else was green hills and cows. So many cows.

"Yes," Sofia replied without offering any further explanation.

They drove for fifteen more minutes before Sofia told him to pull over.

"Here?" Braxton looked around. "There's nothing." Not even cows.

Sofia just waited.

With a huff, Braxton eased the truck onto the shoulder and killed the engine.

"Give me the keys," Sofia ordered. "The steel in them could mess with the ingredients, too."

"I've gotta ask," Braxton said. "If these ingredients are this sensitive, then how are they going to help me?"

"It'll be easier to show you than explain," Sofia said, holding out her hand. "Now give me the bloody keys!"

With no other choice, Braxton did as he was told. His sister snatched the keys out of his outstretched hand.

"See that tree?" Sofia asked, pointing about a hundred paces away.

"Um, yeah…."

"I have the ingredients buried on the far side," Sofia said. "You'll see a marker showing you where to dig. There's a shovel in the back."

"Aren't you coming?" Braxton asked.

"We don't both need to get wet, do we?" was her snippy response.

It was barely drizzling, but whatever.

Braxton grunted his annoyance and then got out of the truck. He grabbed the shovel from the truck bed and started off toward the tree. He scanned the ground for some sign of where to dig, but there was nothing.

"Sofe, I don't see shit," he called back. "Why don't you just show me—"

Braxton whipped around at the sound of an engine. Sofia was sitting in the driver's seat. There was a click as the doors locked.

Sofia rolled down her window.

"What the hell are you doing?" Braxton demanded, stomping back through a tangle of weeds to the road.

"Sorry, Brax, but it's for your own good."

Braxton's mouth fell open. He dropped the shovel and started to run.

Sofia put the truck in Reverse.

"Sofia!"

"Love you, big brother. And I'm going to keep you safe if it's the last thing I do."

She hit the gas and sped away. Braxton was left standing in the middle of the road. Alone.

CHAPTER 53

SOFIA

Hang on," Kenzie said, holding out a placating hand to Sofia. "Why are you going to jail, exactly?"

None of your concern and *This is above your paygrade* almost flew out of Sofia's mouth. She was asking Kenzie for a favor, though. She had to play nice.

Sofia surprised herself by telling the truth. Well, at least part of it.

Her brother's wellbeing was probably the only thing she and Kenzie could agree on. Well, that, and Kiwi. Sofia was growing rather fond of that reptilian troublemaker.

"I don't think your brother would be very happy with me if I helped you get yourself arrested," Kenzie pointed out, when Sofia had finished. "Wait." Her gray eyes filled with suspicion. "Is this just some ploy to get your brother to break up with me?"

Sofia huffed. "As appealing as that sounds, getting rid of you isn't my number one priority at the moment."

"Um…thanks?" Kenzie said, quirking an eyebrow.

Sofia wanted to scream in frustration. This would all have been so easy if Rick hadn't stolen all of her magical ingredients. Then, she could have just done what needed doing without anyone else's help.

Sofia gave Kenzie her best glare…the one that had been known to make grown men weep.

Kenzie just chuckled. "I've dealt with people way scarier than you in the last week," she informed Sofia. "And I'm still here."

Huh. It turned out Kenzie had more spine than Sofia gave her credit for. She wasn't sure if that improved her opinion of the other girl or made Kenzie more of a nuisance. Probably both.

"Listen," Sofia said, taking a deep breath. "If you don't help me, Braxton's going to die in jail. He's been pushing himself to the breaking point for weeks, and he isn't thinking clearly."

Kenzie made a distressed sound.

Sofia would never admit as much to Kenzie, but her determination to take Braxton's place in jail wasn't one-hundred-percent altruistic. She had no idea how Graham could ever forgive her for what she'd done, but this was one thing she could do to make amends.

"Where is Braxton?" Kenzie asked, peering out the window.

"He'll be back later," Sofia said vaguely. "That's why we need to do this fast, before he can try to stop me."

Her brother's hero complex was like a tsunami…endlessly bashing itself against any obstacle in its path.

"Fine," Kenzie surrendered. "What do you need from me?"

Triumph rushed through Sofia.

"You can give culinary magic as well as take it away," Sofia said. She stated it as a fact rather than a question, since she wasn't letting Kenzie back down now that she'd agreed to help.

Kenzie nodded and shrugged at the same time. "So I'm told. But I've only taken away someone's magic. I've never given it."

"Well, I'm going to need you to do that," Sofia said. She clucked her tongue in annoyance when Kenzie didn't start doing…whatever it was she needed to do.

"Sofia, I don't—"

"Just trust me," Sofia said. "I don't have a death wish, and I've got a plan."

"Okay," Kenzie conceded. "But fair warning. I've never done this before. It's possible that I'll wind up making you grow hairy warts all over your face, or something."

"It's a risk I'm willing to take," Sofia replied dryly.

"Aye aye, Captain."

They went into the kitchen, where Kenzie began assembling ingredients and muttering to herself. At one point, Aralia, Chef Levy, and Rosemary appeared to watch Kenzie work.

Chef Levy made noises about leaving the cabin *immediately if not sooner*, while Rosemary hummed her super food song. Sofia paced around the kitchen, checking out the window and periodically ordering Kenzie to hurry up.

"Looks like super food, yes," Rosemary said, when Kenzie was finished.

They stared into the blender, which held a strawberry-colored puree.

"Kind of," Kenzie said, fanning her face, which was almost as red as the puree. "Except my version requires…well, me. Not to sound egocentric, or anything." She held up a spoonful of the red gloop and assessed it. "Now that I've made this, I can also see where the Gourmands' recipe is flawed."

Rosemary made a dejected sound before slinking into the other room to stare at a sleeping Kiwi.

"Is it done?" Sofia asked.

In answer, Kenzie handed her a clean spoon.

Sofia's nose wrinkled as she dipped the spoon into the ruby-red puree. She might not be a chef, but she knew all about good food. And she could tell without even tasting it that there were way too may ingredients in this dish. It was overwhelming.

Still, she didn't utter a sound of protest. She slurped down the spoonful, which managed to be sour, sweet, and spicy all at the same time. She dipped her spoon in again. And again.

She kept going until she'd eaten every last drop. She even scraped the crusty bits off the bottom.

"Well?" Kenzie asked.

Everyone in the kitchen was staring at Sofia like they were waiting for her to grow fangs.

"Whoa." Sofia put a hand on her stomach. It was starting to gurgle.

"Is that—" Chef Levy began.

"Magic," Aralia finished.

Sure enough, almost-invisible sparks had begun to flutter around Sofia.

She'd heard her brothers describe it before, but without her own magic, Sofia had never been able to see those threads. Suddenly, she could.

Her stomach settled as tendrils of power began to snake out of her. They wrapped around her, cocooning her.

It should have felt confining, but it didn't. It felt right. Powerful.

After a few seconds, the magic stopped swirling. It was still there—an invisible but steady presence around her.

"How do you feel?" Kenzie asked, chewing her lip and watching Sofia like she was still waiting for her to sprout those hairy warts.

"Never better." Sofia couldn't help but laugh. There was a pressure all around her from the magic, but it was a good pressure.

She felt light as a feather and completely grounded all at the same time. It was the same euphoria she felt whenever she'd used Qiang's magical ingredients, except stronger. The magic was inside her now.

It felt bloody terrific.

Sofia had to stop herself from whooping and jumping up and down.

"Put your money where your mouth is," Chef Levy said. "Cook something magical."

Of all of them, Chef Levy was the only one who didn't seem awed by what Kenzie had just done.

"Here," Aralia said, sliding a hand-written recipe across the counter. "It's the magical pea soup your brother was going to use to turn himself into Graham."

"Right." Sofia's stomach was fluttering again, but this time, it had nothing to do with the magic that had settled and congealed around her.

Sofia wasn't exactly known for her cooking prowess. Now, some of the best culinary magicians in the world were going to watch her cook her first magical dish.

The last time she'd cooked anything, it had been back in university when she heated a premade toastie in the microwave. And she'd almost burned down the dorm.

"We can help," Kenzie offered, taking pity on her. "You'll have to do the actual cooking and magic, but we can give you a hand with the mise en place."

The next several minutes were a whirlwind of chopping, sautéing, and Chef Levy complaining about having better things to do than be a sous chef.

Sofia could feel censure filling the room as she threw onion pieces into a too-hot pan.

"Your flame's too high," Chef Levy barked. "I thought you were supposed to be the McKaid who had some brains."

"You've got this," Kenzie said, giving Sofia an encouraging smile.

It might not have been pretty or easy, but Sofia finally managed to finish the dish. She ladled out a bowlful of the soup, which Chef Levy accurately noted looked more like mud than soup.

Sofia was about to ask what she was supposed to do now, but she was distracted by a strange tugging sensation at the back of her mind. She gave into the urge and let a few strands of magic loose from herself. Using nothing but her mind, she sent the magic spiraling into the soup. She didn't know how she did it, exactly, and she figured it was probably best if she didn't overthink the process.

"That's good," Kenzie said from beside her. "I can see the magic you're putting in. You just have to make a few adjustments, and then you'll be set."

The encouragement gave Sofia what she needed to finish the job. Her bowl of pea soup gurgled once before settling back down.

"I think it's ready," Sofia said.

The group of them stared dubiously into the bowl.

"Go on," Aralia said, nudging the bowl toward her. "Bottoms up."

Sofia might have hesitated longer, but she knew from the timer she'd set on her phone that Braxton would be back in fourteen to sixteen minutes. Fourteen, assuming Braxton's rage would give him an extra burst of speed.

Sofia lifted the bowl and drank.

Kenzie hovered over her like some kind of spotter. Although it was unclear what Kenzie would do if Sofia accidentally blew herself and everyone else up.

"Now you have to initiate the magic," Aralia said.

Sofia didn't dare utter her *Huh?* out loud, lest Chef Levy take another jab at her intelligence.

Instead, Sofia took a page out of her brother's book and closed her eyes. For reasons she couldn't explain, she could see the strands of magic more clearly that way. She saw them weaving between the pea soup and herself.

She mentally plucked a few of the magic strings, just to see what would happen. She found the whole process less daunting when she thought about it like a giant spreadsheet, where she inwardly organized the cells and adjusted her formulas.

Incredibly, it worked.

Just like she would when building a financial model, she began making little tweaks once she had the foundation in place. Inside her, the magic twisted and rearranged itself.

An image of Graham's face appeared in her mind. She saw his freckles and the way that amber ring around his irises lit up when he looked at her. She remembered the sheer wonder on his face the night they'd kissed in Qiang's garden.

She heard Graham's smoky voice and felt the warm pressure of his muscular arms around her. She remembered the way he focused on her, like nothing and no one else existed.

Sofia knew the magic was working, even before exclamations began to fill the kitchen.

Sofia's eyes flew open. She rushed over to a mirror that hung behind the couch.

"Wicked," Aralia said.

"Whoa," Kenzie exclaimed.

Sofia's skin was darkening while her slim form bulked up. Her long, blonde hair pulled back into her skull. Her eyebrows thickened, her torso elongated, and a dusting of freckles appeared across her nose. In less than a minute, Sofia's appearance had fully transformed.

Graham stared back at her in the mirror.

"Say something," Chef Levy ordered.

"This is weird," Sofia said, except she didn't sound like herself. Her voice had deepened. It sounded masculine.

She sounded like Graham.

"Now that you've made the soup once," Kenzie said. "Do you think you'll be able to do it again?"

"I'll have to," was Sofia's succinct answer.

At least the ingredients were simple enough that she could find them in any kitchen…even in a prison.

Kenzie chewed on her nail, her brow furrowed in worry. Chef Levy was tapping her foot and muttering in Hebrew.

"I better get moving," Sofia said in Graham's voice. She needed to be long gone before her brother got back and blew a gasket.

"Hold on," Kenzie replied. "There's just one more thing I need to make."

Five minutes later, the kitchen was full of the scents of butter and vanilla.

"Almost done?" Sofia asked, looking out the window for the umpteenth time.

Braxton would be back any minute.

Her anxiety was heightened by the fact that it was supremely unsettling to have her crush's voice coming out of her mouth. She'd stopped looking in the mirror because it caused a veritable hurricane of unwelcome emotions that she wasn't inclined to deal with. Also, because it wasn't normal to want to make out with your own reflection.

The oven binged, and Kenzie waltzed over. She removed a pan that held a single sugar cookie. It was perfectly shaped, with the slightest hint of golden-brown around the edges. A layer of sugar crystals glistened on top.

"What's this for?" Sofia asked.

It'd better be worth the wait….

"Convince the cop who arrests you to eat this," Kenzie explained as she wrapped the cookie in a sheet of wax paper. "The magic will let you make subtle suggestions to them."

"Subtle suggestions?" Sofia gave her a dubious look. "Like what?"

Kenzie hesitated before answering. "Like suggesting you get taken to Rikers Island."

Sofia tilted her head. "And why would I want to do that?"

She already knew the answer, of course, but she wanted to buy herself another few seconds to decide whether it was a good or terrible idea.

"My dad is at Rikers, which you probably already know," Kenzie said. "He might be able to help you. And, maybe…you could help him."

Sofia was struck by an unexpected wave of sympathy. It made no sense, because Kenzie was the reason why her father was in prison. And yet, Sofia couldn't stop herself from thinking about how she would feel in Kenzie's position.

"I can do that," Sofia said as she pocketed the cookie. "At least, I'll try."

Sofia jerked in surprise when Kenzie grasped both of her—or Graham's—hands and gave them a squeeze.

"Thank you," Kenzie whispered. There was a telltale gleam in her eyes.

Before the waterworks started, Sofia said, "Take care of my brother. Also, I've noticed Kiwi prefers his mealworms in the morning and crickets in the afternoon. Keep that in mind."

"I will," Kenzie promised, sniffling a little.

"I don't hate you anymore," Sofia informed her.

Kenzie choked back a laugh. "I like you too, Sofia." She held on for a beat longer. "Be careful, okay?"

Sofia smiled at her. Then, she took the keys Aralia offered her and hurried out of the cabin.

She tore out of the driveway at a speed that would have given her brother heartburn if he was here to see it. Then again, she wasn't worried about breaking any laws. Afterall, Sofia was about to get arrested.

THE END

✳ ✳ ✳

Because reviews are so important for a book to be successful, please consider leaving a brief review on your favorite retailer if you enjoyed *Cutthroat Cuisine*. Many thanks!

* * *

Sign up for Stephanie Fazio's e-Newsletter to learn about upcoming books at:
https://StephanieFazio.com/subscribe/

Acknowledgements

Thank you to all of the amazing people on my team who helped bring this story together.

To my editor, Ellen Schaeffer. Thank you for your attention to detail and wonderful suggestions!

To Keith Tarrier, for making such incredibly beautiful covers. Thank you also to my terrific ARC team. Your advice, support, and encouragement are invaluable.

To Mom and Dad, for your endless support and advice. Thanks for always believing in me.

To my incredible readers. Thanks for making what I do matter!

And to Andrew for being the most amazing person ever.

About the Author:

Stephanie Fazio is a fantasy author. She grew up in Syracuse, New York, and prior to writing full time, she worked in the fields of journalism, secondary education, and higher education. She has an undergraduate degree in English from Colgate University and a Master's degree in Reading, Writing, and Literacy from the University of Pennsylvania. Stephanie lives in Austin with her husband and crazy rescue dog. When she isn't writing, she's getting lost in parks, hosting taco nights, or ironically and miserably losing at word games, but having fun while she does it.

Connect with Stephanie Fazio:

Visit her Website: https://www.StephanieFazio.com
Sign up for her newsletter: https://StephanieFazio.com/subscribe/

Discover other books by Stephanie Fazio

The Fount Series

The Prince's Chosen

The Forsaken's Choice

The Chosen Union

Opal Contagion Series

Opal Smoke

Opal Slayer

Opal Storm

Bisecter Series

Bisecter

Halve Human

Dusker Dark

Captain Harkibel

Mags & Nats Series

The Nat Makes 7

Mag Subject 6

Steel for 5

Hex Kitchen Series

Hex Kitchen

Cutthroat Cuisine

Bloody Delicious